BETTER
WHEN
HE'S BOLD

BY JAY CROWNOVER

BETTER WHEN HE'S BOLD

A Welcome to the Point Novel

JAY CROWNOVER

WILLIAM MORROW
An Imprint of HarperCollins*Publishers*

BETTER WHEN HE'S BOLD. Copyright © 2015 by Jennifer M. Voorhees. Excerpt from *Better When He's Bad* copyright © 2014 by Jennifer M. Voorhees. All rights reserved. Printed in the United States of America. No part of this book may be used or reproduced in any manner whatsoever without written permission except in the case of brief quotations embodied in critical articles and reviews. For information address HarperCollins Publishers, 195 Broadway, New York, NY 10007.

HarperCollins books may be purchased for educational, business, or sales promotional use. For information please e-mail the Special Markets Department at SPsales@harpercollins.com.

FIRST EDITION

Library of Congress Cataloging-in-Publication Data has been applied for.

ISBN 978-0-06-235191-3

15 16 17 18 19   OV/RRD   10 9 8 7 6 5 4 3 2 1

Dedicated to anyone that has had to spend time down in the gutter.
It's not where you are that matters, it's what you make of where you are
that does.

~We're all in the gutter, but some of us are looking at the stars.
Oscar Wilde

INTRODUCTION

THERE IS SOMETHING ABOUT writing this series and spending time with these characters that makes me so happy. I love a challenge. I love a mess. I love something different and something that stretches me to do more and think harder.

I want to personally thank every single one of you who continues on this wild ride with me. It matters so much to me that you let me stretch my wings and do more than just one kind of book. I have so many ideas, so many stories to tell, I almost think I can't get them all out and I know I would suffocate on my own creativity if all I had to do was the same thing over and over again. I love you and I love that we get to keep traveling this crazy journey together.

I know the Point and the boys that run it aren't for everyone. I even understand that Race won't be for everyone since he is very different from my typical rough-and-tumble boys. So it makes it extra special when I hear from those of you who like the change, in scenery and in men, because you have been there, have lived the hard life, or know someone who has, and appreciate the gutter getting as much love as the slick and polished big city. The dark side is fun . . . the boys who walk on it are something else.

I'm always going to write what interests me, what speaks to

me, what moves me, and what I find fascinating and intriguing. Along the way I've met so many cool book people who appreciate that.

So enjoy the next dangerous installment of the Point series . . . here's to chaos, here's to blood, here's to family, here's to risk, here's to chance, and most of all here's to change because without it our view would never ever evolve and grow, no matter where we're looking from.

~ Jay

Welcome to the Point . . . where this time, fortune favors the bold!

Chapter 1

Brysen

S OME MEN ARE IMPOSSIBLE to ignore. It's like everyone else around them is moving in slow motion, like everyone else is painted in black and white and he's the only spot of color; the only thing moving in the room. Race Hartman was that kind of man. Even though an entire room full of loud, drunk, and excited party people separated us, even though I doubted he knew I was at the same house party as he was, all I could see was him. Tall and blond with a face and body designed to make the fairer sex stupid with lust, he was undeniably beautiful and delicious, like everything that was bad for you tended to be. I didn't want to keep staring, but I couldn't stop myself. He was just that dynamic—just that bold—and in my world, where things were gray and lifeless, he was a sensory feast and I was happy to gorge.

I missed the days when I just went to school, partied, had a good time, and acted like I didn't have a care in the world. Those days were long gone, so I needed to stop gaping at Race like an idiot and get on with trying to enjoy the one night I had off from work and wasn't needed at home. My little sister was at a sleepover, and my dad had agreed to stay home with my mom. It was a rare occurrence when I got to behave like a normal twenty-one-year-old, and I was squandering it by lusting after my best friend's older brother, and probably the worst, most inappropriate guy in the entire world to have a crush on.

"Do you know him?"

My friend Adria was the one who had convinced me to come out tonight. I remembered parties like this being more fun. I took a sip of lukewarm beer out of a red plastic cup and fought the way my eyes wanted to magnetically drift to Race.

"He's Dovie's older brother."

"Really?"

Her disbelief was justified. Where Race looked regal, like some kind of golden god sent down to rule over us mere mortals, Dovie Pryce was a rumpled redhead covered in freckles and about as unobvious as one person could be. She was cute at best, not impressive and heart-stopping like her brother. She was also the nicest person in the world. I was pretty sure Race didn't have a nice bone anywhere in his impressive body.

My fingers curled around the cup tighter when his head turned and those mossy-green eyes met mine.

"Really." My voice was huskier than normal even to my own ears.

"How can that be?"

I liked Adria. We had Business Finance together and she was one of the few people who hadn't ditched me when I was forced to move back home after everything with my mom went down. I didn't have much fun anymore, which meant I didn't have many friends anymore either. Trying to explain to her the complicated dynamics in the Hartman family, though, was not something I planned on spending the evening doing. Race and Dovie's lineage wasn't a story that was particularly good times, and that's what I was after tonight—a good time.

I gulped because Race was making his way through the crowd of dancing and grinding college students toward where we were standing. People just instinctively moved out of his way. It was like there was a force field of badass that surrounded him that only those who liked to live dangerously dared to test. I wasn't one of those people. At least that's what I told myself every time I was around him.

Sure, I was dangerously attracted, had been ever since the first time I saw him when he dropped Dovie off at work, but he would never know. Race wasn't a good guy and my life was hard enough without adding in the kind of complication he was bound to be.

To keep Race and those traitorous feelings at bay, I was awful to him . . . I mean really, really awful. I was cold. I was disinterested. I was rude, and sometimes I was flat-out mean. I acted like he was annoying, treated him like he was a vile, nasty human being, and when that didn't work, I ignored him and acted like he wasn't worth my time. It was getting harder and harder to do, and the more disdain I tossed in his direction, the more charm and liquid sex appeal he leveled at me. We were involved in a tantalizing back-and-forth game that I was terrified I would eventually lose. Race wanted me, and he didn't make it a secret. I didn't know how much longer my wayward lust was going to be held at bay under the assault of those evergreen-colored eyes and that gorgeous head of spun-gold hair.

He flashed a million-watt smile in my direction and stopped

so he was looming over me. Even with me wearing five-inch heels, he towered over me.

"Well, hello, Brysen."

I rolled my eyes and raised the cup to hide my involuntary gulp as his gruff voice slid over my skin.

"Race."

Adria nudged me in the side with the sharp edge of her elbow. I cleared my throat and inclined my head in her direction.

"This is my friend Adria."

He stuck out a big hand and clasped her much smaller one. I practically saw her panties melt and her vagina throw out a welcome mat.

"What are you doing here?"

I should be asking him that. This was a college party, filled with drunk coeds and undergrads. I actually attended the university around the corner, but Race had long since given up the academic life for one that involved crime and lots and lots of illegal activity. He was the one who shouldn't be here.

"Just out having some fun." I tried to keep my tone flat and uninterested, but if he could hear the way my heart pounded, the jig would be up for certain.

He lifted a blond eyebrow at me and flashed a half grin. Gah . . . he even had a killer dimple in his left cheek. I wanted to lick it so bad. I dug the tips of my fingernails into my palms and took a deep breath.

"I'm surprised you know how to do that, Bry . . . have fun."

He was right, so all I could do was narrow my eyes at him and put on the ice-queen mask I perpetually wore in his presence.

"What are you doing here, Race? Shaking down poor college kids for their student loan checks?"

His other eyebrow shot up to join the first one, and when he unleashed a full smile on us, it practically knocked both Adria and me over. Something darker flashed in his green eyes and I wanted to take a step back. Race was dangerous in more ways than one, and I needed to remember that.

"Most college kids have zero sense and like a challenge. That's a breeding ground for a guy like me. Plus football season starts next weekend and I just needed to check in on a few early clients." His eyes slid over the top of my sleek bob to the toes of my pointed black heels. "I stayed longer for the scenery."

Adria cleared her throat and looked back and forth between the two of us.

"Clients? At a house party? What exactly do you do?" If she only knew the kinds of illicit things Race did.

He cocked his head to the side and the blinding smile he wielded like a weapon fell off of his face. There were a lot of facets to Race Hartman, and this darker, harder side of him had only made an appearance when he decided he was going to take over the reins of a major crime syndicate after he had played a big role in bringing down the kingpin, Novak. Race wasn't just a bad guy, a criminal, he was *the* bad guy. He was running numbers, loan-sharking, operating illegal gambling houses, helping his best friend chop and move stolen cars, and making sure every man, woman, and child in the Point knew he was the guy calling the shots on the streets now. He was too pretty to be that awful, but because of Dovie I knew exactly how filthy Race's hands had become since taking over Novak's empire. Not to mention his new business partner was a pimp, a money launderer, and absolutely ruthless and cold. Nassir had to be shady and enigmatic considering he ran every underground operation that existed in the inner city and it seemed a lot of those qualities had rubbed off on Race.

"I make money, sweetheart."

And he did. I shifted uneasily on my too-tall shoes and tried not to let him see how my pulse fluttered under his unwavering gaze. There was something about being desired by a man that you knew could destroy anyone in the room. It shouldn't feel good, shouldn't make my thighs clench and my insides pulse, but it did . . . he did.

I smirked at him and tossed the longer part of my razor-straight bob over my shoulder.

"Race is an entrepreneur of sorts." The kind you would only find in a place that was as dark and as broken as the Point.

Adria obviously wanted to ask more questions. I saw her open her mouth, but before she could get a word out, a loud *BANG* rang out and the typical college party I had been using to try and escape the aching reality of my every day turned into a chaotic riot.

There was no mistaking the smell of gunpowder as pandemonium erupted and more shots rang out. I went to grab Adria, but because we were so close to the door, a flood of panicked bodies separated us in a split second. I felt hard hands grab me and pull me out of the way of the stampede. My face was pressed into a rock-hard chest and a big hand held my head down as I was roughly moved through the press of running and flailing bodies.

My heart was in my throat and I heard the gun go off one more time, followed by the shriek of a female voice. Race let out a litany of swearwords from somewhere above my head, and he let me go for just a second. I heard glass breaking, felt him shift, pull me along behind him, and then the cool night air was around us. He set me away from him a little bit, but grabbed my hand and proceeded to pull me along behind him. Our feet crunched over the broken glass of the back door he had obviously shattered in order for us to escape.

I was panting and running in stilettos and skinny jeans after a guy with legs twice as long as mine, which was practically impossible to do, but I did it. He didn't stop until we had rounded the yard on the other side of the house and made our way across the street. Most of the other partygoers had dispersed, and the wail of sirens could already be heard in the distance. I put my hands on his chest and pleaded with him:

"We have to find Adria."

His eyes were practically black, full of emotions I was scared to name.

"I can't be here when the cops show up, Brysen. I have to go."

I gasped at him and balled my hands into fists so I could thump him on the chest—hard.

"Help me find her, Race!"

He just shook that perfect blond head and gazed down at me.

"You're the only one I was worried about."

My heart tripped, but the sirens were getting closer and he was moving away from me. I grabbed on to his wrist and realized I was shaking so hard I could barely hold on to him.

"Don't leave me." My voice sounded scared and lost. I didn't know what to do in a situation that involved guns and violence. It unnerved me how nonchalant he was with it all.

The shadows in his eyes moved and his mouth turned down at the corners. Before I could react, his hands slid around the back of my neck, under the edge of my hair, and he yanked me up onto the tips of my toes. I clasped both hands around his wrists, tried not to freak out when my chest flattened against his. I pretty much just dangled there while he proceeded to kiss the shit out of me.

It was dark, people were stumbling about drunk and bewildered, I was worried about my friend, and I was angry at him . . . always angry, but for the first time since I had laid eyes on him, all that want, all that tangling, greedy lust, was let loose, and I kissed him back.

It wasn't romantic, it wasn't sweet and filled with tangible longing or loving care. It was brutal, violent, hard and hot, and nothing in my entire life had ever felt better. His tongue invaded. His teeth scraped. His hands bruised, and I could feel his erection through the front of his jeans where we were pushed together. I should've protested, said something to make him stop, but all I could do was moan and rub against him like some kind of wanton cat in heat.

And just when I was contemplating curling around him, coiling into that big body and making myself at home, he dropped me, stepped back, left me blinking up at him like an idiot, shook that golden head, and disappeared into darkness without another word. I stared at the spot where he had been, wrapped my arms around my chest, and tried to keep from falling apart on the spot.

"Brysen!"

I jerked my head up as Adria came barreling into me. She almost took both of us to the ground.

"Oh my God, I was freaking out! Where did you go?"

I hugged her back, mostly to see if it would stop the shaking. It didn't.

"Race took me out the back, for some reason."

Her eyes were huge in her face.

"Why would he do that? No one knew where the gunman was."

I just shook my head. "I don't know, I just followed him. He didn't really give me a choice."

"Some guy caught his girlfriend with another guy. Can you believe that? All that for something so stupid."

I didn't get to ask her how she knew what the ruckus was all about because the police were finally on the scene and they were giving those of us left lingering about the third degree.

The university and the house where the party was at were both located on the Hill. Things like random gunfire, jealous boyfriends, and cheating girlfriends belonged in the Point; at least that's what most people from the Hill tried to fool themselves into believing. By the time it was all said and done, I was exhausted, and could still taste Race on my lips. My night out in order to forget had turned into one that I would remember forever, even if I knew how bad an idea it was to hold on to any memory of him. Maybe gray wasn't such a bad shade to be surrounded in after all. It was boring and bland, but it was safe.

I drove Adria back to her apartment, fielding questions about Race the entire way. She was fascinated by him, could feel that magnetic pull he just naturally had. I tried to tell her that he was bad news, that the world he operated in was as far away from her almost M.B.A. as she could imagine, but of course that only added to his mystique and appeal. What nice girl from the Hill didn't lust after a naughty boy from the Point? It couldn't have been any more clichéd if it tried. By the time I was headed home, I had a headache and my stomach was in knots.

When I parked in front of the cookie-cutter trilevel my parents had built before everything fell apart, I had to really think about whether or not I wanted to keep the engine running and just continue driving until I was somewhere else, until I hit a different life. Two years ago, everything in my world had been cheery and full of color and light. I was living in an apartment with girlfriends, attending college, fending off boys with only one thing on their mind. I was silly. I was carefree, and I never thought about any of it going away.

Now I was living back at home, taking care of one parent suffering from a crippling bout of depression and with a tendency to self-medicate, and another who was a workaholic and obviously burying himself in his job to avoid the troubling things going on at home. Mostly I came back to keep my little sister, Karsen, from being affected by the sadness and the darkness of it all. She was sixteen, a straight-A student, and bound for college in just a couple more years. I could tough it out until then. After all, my parents had always worked hard to keep our family on the fine line between the Hill and the Point, and I felt like it was the least I could do to repay them. We had never been obnoxiously wealthy, but we had never been forced to try and survive on the battleground that was life on the streets of the Point either. I really felt like I owed them for that at the very least.

Sighing, I made my way inside. There were no lights on because Karsen wasn't home and my mom was undoubtedly passed out in bed. I swung by the kitchen to grab a beer that was actually cold and puttered by my dad's office on the way up to the floor where my room was. He was seated behind the computer, like always. His balding head bent down and his eyes locked on whatever was on the screen. I frowned a little and twisted the cap off the neck of the bottle.

"Hey."

I saw him start and his gaze jerked away from the monitor. "Brysen Carter, you scared the piss out of me."

"How was she?"

He cleared his throat and returned his attention to the computer. "Fine. Everything was fine."

That was highly unlikely.

"Did you even check on her tonight, Dad?"

"Brysen, this is very important. Can it wait?"

Not really, but everything came second to his job. I didn't say anything, just pulled off my shoes and wandered around the corner to where the master bedroom was located. The door was cracked and the TV was on. I pushed the door open with the flat of my hand and hissed out a swearword.

My mom was sprawled sideways across the bed. Her head was hanging over the edge and the same whitish-blond hair that I had on my head was in a tangled mess, touching the floor. An empty bottle of vodka was resting on the pillow and light snores were coming from her. I put the bottle of beer down on the dresser and went in to set her to rights. Clearly Dad hadn't bothered to pull himself away long enough to make sure she was all right. He had just left her to her own devices, and this was always the end result.

She peeled one watery eye open to look at me and mumbled my name as I wrestled her under the covers. I snatched up the empty bottle and resisted the urge to smash it on the floor. Just barely. She hadn't always been this way. She was always a little off, struggled with emotional ups and downs, but then a car accident, a horrible back injury and endless amounts of pain, plus the inability for her to go back to work, and my mother had become this drunken, sad shell of a woman. It always made my heart twist and my guts tug because it didn't have to be this way. She could get help, my dad could support her, and maybe my life could go back to some kind of normal, but that wasn't happening, and for now I just had to make do until Karsen was old enough to get out on her own.

I flipped off the TV and shut the door behind me with a thud. It would take a tornado to rouse my mom from that kind of drunken slumber anyway. I sighed heavily and finally found my way to my own room.

Living back at home as an adult was so weird. It wasn't like I had a curfew, or the same rules and regulations to follow as I had when I was a teenager, but everything about this childhood room felt wrong. I felt like I left some part of myself outside the door every time I resigned myself to another night, another day, spent here.

I pulled my phone out of my back pocket and pulled up the last message I had sent to Dovie asking her to go to the party with me tonight. Now that she had a full-time job at a group home for all the kids lost in the system, I hardly saw her anymore. Add in the fact that she was living with and involved with the only guy in the Point I considered scarier than Race meant I rarely went by her house or saw her outside of school anymore. Tonight she had declined the invite because she had homework to do, but I secretly wondered if Bax had told her not to go.

He hated everything that had to do with the Hill. He was from the streets, an ex-con, a thief, and there was no doubt he was up to his eyeballs in Race's criminal enterprise. Shane Baxter had a reputation in these parts that was as legendary as the man who sired him. The man he and Race had taken down. They were not the kind of guys you wanted to mess with, but I really liked Dovie, so I braved the shark-filled waters she swam in to keep her in my life and call her my bestie.

I twisted my phone around and sent her a message:

Saw Race at the party tonight.

It took a few minutes for her to answer back.

What was he doing there?

He said working.

I bet.

I rolled my eyes a little at what was construed as "work" for him and typed out:

Someone had a gun and fired off shots inside. Race got me out but took off because of the police.

I was still pretty steamed about it, and still heated from the inside out by that kiss. Why did he have to taste so good, feel so right, yet be so wrong?

She answered back in a matter-of-fact way only someone firmly immersed in the Point could do:

He can't risk messing around with the police. No one from here really can. I'm not surprised he took off. Is everyone okay?

Fine. Everyone was fine.

I wasn't fine. Having an idea that someone was a criminal, that they might not be on the up-and-up, was something entirely different from having the proof right in front of your face. I didn't understand that world, didn't want to understand it, therefore, no matter how hot he was, how much he pulled me out of the monotony of my day-to-day life, Race Hartman would never be the guy for me, and that made things deep inside me burn.

Dovie and I chitchatted some more. Me about nothing in

particular, and her about the guys. Bax scared me so much I was nervous and anxious around him, and I think Dovie tried to make him more human, more likable in my eyes, to offset that. And Race . . . well, he spun me around and it took every effort I could make to pretend disinterest instead of rabid curiosity every time she mentioned something about him. It was getting harder and harder to do.

I told her good night and sent a message to my sister to tell her good night as well. Karsen was a good egg, a kid who deserved to make it out of this house unscathed and unscarred from the state the Carters were currently in. She was a small little thing, with the same pale hair I had, but our mom's brown eyes instead of Dad's blue like I had. She was as sweet as could be, and when she shot back a smiley face, I finally settled into my routine for the night.

It was while I washed my face and climbed into the shower that I could finally admit that I was lonely, that I was sad, that I was overwhelmed with all the things I was feeling and the battle of always keeping the things churning inside me in check. In the shower I could cry and no one could tell. This wasn't the life I wanted. This wasn't where I thought I would be at twenty-one, but I had to adapt, had to change in order to do what was best for everyone, and that was just the way it was going to be. I didn't have any choice in the matter.

I toweled off, ran a brush through my hair, and climbed into a pair of yoga pants and a tank to sleep in. The adrenaline from everything started to leach out of my system and I finally got to fall onto the mattress face-first. I was letting my eyes drift shut, trying really hard not to relive every flick of Race's tongue, every scrape of teeth, when my phone lit up with a new message. It was late, and the only person I thought it could be was Karsen, so I bolted upright and swiped a finger over the screen.

It wasn't from Karsen. It wasn't from a number I recognized at all. It was five words, no big deal, but the rock that settled in my stomach when I read them told me something was off.

You looked so pretty tonight.

I just stared for a second before answering back.

Who is this?

So sorry I missed you.

What in the hell was that supposed to mean? I asked who it was again, and when I didn't get a response, I just switched off my phone and tossed it back on the nightstand. I sat there in the dark for a long moment with my pulse thrumming hard and a creepy sense of unease making the hair on the back of my neck stand on end. I shivered before lying back down on the bed and pulling the covers all the way up over the top of my head.

Talking about "missing" someone when gunshots had been going off wasn't funny, and I was raw enough not to like it one little bit. I closed my eyes and my brain started to question why exactly Race had pulled me out the back of the house when everyone else had been stampeding toward the front door.

This is why I didn't have time for a guy like Race. If he had been anyone else, his motivations would have never even been in question. And what had he meant by "you're the only one I'm worried about"? It was just because he wanted me, liked to play games with me because I was a challenge. But that was it . . . right?

Ugh. I didn't have the time or the space for any of it. And yet when I finally drifted off, it was his pretty face and his perfect mouth that followed me into dreamland and not the anxiety and apprehension that was gnawing on me after that weird text.

Chapter 2

Race

I PULLED MY FULLY restored and totally tricked out '66, cherry-red Mustang through the security gates that surrounded the garage that looked like nothing more than a crumbling pile of concrete and rusted metal. If only the outside world knew the treasure trove of monster mechanics that were housed behind the ugly façade. Millions of dollars' worth of restored muscle cars and sleek foreign imports lined the walls. Some were there to be revitalized and repaired, but most were being housed because I was waiting for their owners to come through on this debt or that loan that they owed me. If the owner didn't pay up, I kept the car and then let my best friend chop it and turn it over for a tidy little profit.

It was a system that had proven profitable and played to both my and Bax's strengths. People didn't like it when you took their ride. It was hard to explain the missing family car to your wife and kids, so my payoff rate was higher than the average number runner and loan shark. Bax had connections upon connections in the world of stolen cars, and when a debtor didn't come through, it was an easy way to recoup the loss. Besides, I think Bax still needed the thrill of jacking a car now that he was mostly on the straight and living pretty clean. We had a hard-and-fast rule that we never discussed this part of the garage business around my sister.

Dovie was a doll. She was sweet, full of love and kindness, and had somehow gotten through all the barbed wire and chain link that surrounded Bax's heart and taken up permanent residence. She was from the streets, had grown up very differently from me, and she knew inherently that life wasn't always easy, that the things we did in the Point changed us. I knew Bax had clued her in on what was going on in the highly secured compound he had started to build shortly after the death of his dad—Novak—the man who had ruled the underbelly of the city with his brutal iron fists. But she loved us both enough not to ask questions or get between us and what we had to do. So far it was a system that was working out for everyone and my business keeps growing and growing.

Dovie was awesome, and as much as I had initially hated the idea of her and Bax as a couple, I understood now that she needed someone like my best friend to keep her safe; protect her from this place and this life. And Bax . . . well, he needed Dovie to keep him human, to give him something real and tangible to keep on living for. I needed both of them to make the takeover of the underground of the Point complete. Bax was my right-hand man. He had the connections both inside and outside of prison walls, the reputation, the presence to make shit happen, and Dovie was the conscience, the light that reminded me why someone like me needed to take over where Novak had left off.

In a place like the Point, there were always going to be bad things that fueled the day-to-day grind. When people live in a place covered in filth and grime, they have to have vices to make it through. Sex, drugs, money, gambling, murder, and all sorts of general mayhem were commonplace on this particular battle-field, and when a tyrant—an evil, horrible man—was in charge of the flow of all of those things . . . he could hold the city in a choke hold. I had no desire to do that.

I understood that those things were never going to go any-where in the Point, and as long as I was the guy in charge of how they were running, how they were being doled out to the pitiful masses, then I could make a place that was pretty much uncivi-lized at least mostly tolerable to live in. It was tricky and risky, but I had always thrived on a good challenge, which was how I had ended up tangled up in the criminal underground with Bax all those years ago. It was also why I couldn't get enough of Brysen Carter.

Everything about her was cool and pale. The disdain she felt for me practically rolled off of her elegant shoulders whenever we were within breathing distance of each other. Her denim-colored gaze tried to freeze me in place every time she looked at me, and the way she stiffened and tensed that gorgeous body whenever I got close made my dick hard . . . every single time. She was polished and perfect. She reminded me of another life I had kicked to the curb, and I wanted her like I wanted my next breath. The fact that she couldn't stand me—obviously thought I was scum—made her allure even more potent. All I wanted to do was get her naked and rumple her up, but because Dovie was so fond of her, I maintained some sense of control. Well, control I had up until tonight.

As I pulled the car into the garage, closing the bulletproof, metal bay door shut behind me, I had to shift behind the steering wheel at the thought of her mouth on mine. Brysen Carter was a good girl. A pretty blonde from the right side of town, but, man, could she kiss like a dirty girl, like a girl from my side of town. It made all the blood-heating, spine-tingling hunger she had eating at my insides get even more insistent.

I slammed the car door and rounded the fender just as Bax came wandering out of his office. I never questioned it when he was here late. These cars, the old muscle cars, the classics in disrepair, meant something to him. He was bringing them all back to life piece by piece, which meant that since I lived upstairs in a converted loft, I had to listen to the sounds of revving engines and clattering tools well into the early hours of the morning sometimes. We shared a fist bump, and Bax ran his hands over the shaved surface of his head.

Physically, we were on opposite sides of the fence. Bax had dark hair, dark eyes, a black star tattooed next to his eye, a hard, unsmiling mouth, and a big, bulky build that was used as a weapon more often than not. He looked like a thug and a criminal but it worked well for him. We were both tall, a few generous inches over six feet, but I was a lot leaner, lankier, and had been born with all the characteristics that made for a perfect fit with my country-club background. I could hold my own, if things ever became physical, but I preferred to talk my way out of a tight spot, figured my brain was always my best weapon, not that this was reflected on the surface. I had wavy blond hair, shot through with gold and honey, that was a little long and shaggy and, more often than not, hanging in my green eyes. I looked like a trust-fund kid on vacation. I knew it, and even though I called the Point home now, I refused to change it. The way I looked made people underestimate me all the time, and since both Bax and I were still in our early twenties, trying to run a city built on the souls of those broken years before we had even been born, I needed every advantage I could get.

Bax shoved the end of a cigarette in his mouth and lifted a black eyebrow up at me.

"You get the cash from the frat dude?"

I nodded and rolled my head around on my shoulders.

"He wasn't happy about it." One of the first lessons I had learned was people didn't gamble because they thought they would win. They gambled because they were compelled to do it. It was an addiction like anything else.

"How not happy?"

I squinted at him through the smoke floating between us.

"He pulled a gun and popped off a few rounds." In a house full of drunk college kids. What an idiot, and what a total waste of a threat. Getting hardware pulled on me was just a hazard of my job. Unless the gun was pointed at my face, I tended to just ignore it.

"Shit. Glad I asked Dovie not to go."

I shook my head at him and crossed my arms over my chest. "You asked her not to go because you're freaked out that she's going to meet some charming undergrad that can promise her a better life and she'll drop you on your ass."

He grunted and flicked his cigarette butt into one of the drains on the floor and rolled his massive shoulders.

"She can always do better."

I snorted. "Not according to her." She loved him, scars, his shitty attitude, his rough past, and the fact he hovered really close to the line of being tamed and being wild—she loved every last bit of it. Bax was her perfect, and I was still surprised he didn't seem to grasp it.

"What happened at the party?"

"I don't know. I saw Brysen and got distracted. I already had the money, so I thought it was all good, then the idiot starts flashing a piece around and a clusterfuck broke loose."

I had grabbed Brysen, headed for the back of the house because I couldn't see the shooter, and everyone else was trying to shove through the front door. I wasn't going to let anything happen to her, and I got the added bonus of getting to put my hands on her. I felt like a dick for having to bail on her, but the life I had now didn't line up with sticking around to chat with the cops. I was more of a slink-into-the-shadows kind of guy nowadays.

"You roll into the party packing?"

Ever since I had made the decision to try and pick up where Novak had left off, Bax was on me to be more careful. He might be comfortable carrying a gun around, might be used to blood and gunfire, to fists breaking faces and people quaking in fear when he entered a room, but I was still adjusting to this new life and wasn't really ready to give that much of myself over to the Point yet.

"No. It was just a bunch of kids. It was fine. He'll just have to find a new way to pay for his books and beer this semester. He wasn't really a threat." People shouldn't risk what they couldn't afford to lose. I'd learned that lesson the hard way.

"Everyone is a threat when you have what they want or when they owe you something they don't want to give. You need to take each and every situation you go into seriously. Kids have killed for less, Race."

"Duly noted."

"You still have a hard-on for the icy blonde?"

I barked out a laugh and lifted an eyebrow at him. He wasn't a huge fan of Brysen, but I think it had more to do with the fact she lived closer to the Hill than the Point and Bax just didn't trust anyone who didn't know what life down here in the gutter was like. I was an exception to that rule, but I had had to earn my stripes through blood, sweat, and tears. I was still working my way back into the inner sanctum because I had made some hard choices a few years ago that resulted in Bax going to jail. We were tight, ran a business together, he was in love with my sister, but I don't think all the open wounds I had left with my betrayal had fully healed over yet.

"Big-time. There is just something about her that gets to me. I want to do dirty, nasty things to her."

He grunted and reached up to pull the hood of his black sweatshirt up over his shaved head. Like he needed anything to make him look any more menacing.

"She doesn't look like the type. She almost cries whenever I walk into the room. I bet a broken fingernail would result in hysterics."

I might have agreed with him if I hadn't kissed her. There was more to her than the perfect, flawless exterior she presented to the world. There was desperation on the tip of her tongue, there was passion in her breath, and there was want in the way her hands had pulled at me. At least there had been until I had bailed on her, because while we might have once been on the same playing field, we were now from two totally different worlds. I couldn't stay with her, couldn't wait around until she found her friend, and a girl like Brysen wouldn't stand for a guy who had his priorities all fucked up like that.

"Doesn't matter. She's hot and I like the way she looks at me like I'm something she scraped off her shoe. It makes chasing after her so much more fun."

He laughed and pulled the keys to his Hemi 'Cuda that he had just finished the restoration on out of his pocket.

"You are so screwed up."

After everything that had happened to us in the last five years, I don't know how we could be anything but screwed up.

"Tell Dovie I said 'hey.'"

He nodded and made his way to his car. When he pulled out of the garage it was with a roar that shook all the metal that filled the place against the concrete. That motor was something else. The car wasn't street legal; it could outrun anything else on the road and was big, loud, and nasty, and was a perfect chrome and steel representation of the man who drove it.

I made sure to reset all the security alarms, walked up the metal stairs to the loft, and took a minute to shove the frat dude's money into the safe I'd built into the wall. The safe was nicer than all the furniture in the entire loft. It was also full of ill-gotten gains that I was waiting on Nassir to filter through his clubs and turn into usable money.

I didn't love being in business with Nassir Gates. I didn't trust him, hated the way he manipulated and used people to his own ends, but he was the only person who could take the money I was earning from running numbers and make it clean. Nassir ran every club, every bed of sin and debauchery, that existed in the Point. He set up illegal fights, had a legion of girls he ran out the back door of his businesses, and as much as I didn't like him, I needed him. I wouldn't mess with girls—with selling sex—but someone had to, and Nassir had no morals and zero qualms about getting his hands dirty. We had an uneasy alliance going, and so far, it was working. Dealing with Nassir was like walking through a minefield every day—dangerous, deadly, and filled with hidden threats I would never see coming. I was always waiting for him to turn on me.

I went to the freezer, took out a bottle of Oban I had stashed in there, poured a healthy amount into the bottom of a rocks glass, and threw myself onto the couch that doubled as my bed. Sure, I could move, find a place that was cleaner, farther out of the heart of the city, but I liked it here. I felt safe here. No one was coming into the garage, breaching the compound without me knowing about it, and after the beating, the way my body had broken when Novak and his goons had found me, I needed that sense of security to sleep at night.

This was so far from the life I was born into, so different from where most people who knew my parents and knew my past ever thought I would be. I hadn't been born with a silver spoon shoved in my face, but an entire goddamn platinum service set choking me from the get-go. My parents were rich. Disgustingly, filthy, unholy rich. They lived a life a luxury, untouched by need and struggle, uncaring of what was happening to those not so well-to-do.

Until I was sixteen, I was numb. Entitled, spoiled rotten, stuffed full of self-importance and overindulgence. I didn't feel anything. I existed in a bubble where anything I wanted, anything I needed, was handed directly to me and I never questioned the greater world, things beyond my mommy and daddy's fat wallet.

One night I had been on a date. The girl I chose not to remember, but everything else was crystal clear. My dad had given me a Roush Mustang for my birthday. I was showing off, thought I was the shit, untouchable and unbeatable, until I took a wrong turn and somehow ended up lost on a road that trailed between the Hill and the Point. I was at a stoplight, trying to find directions on my phone, when the window on the driver's side shattered and hard hands had reached in to pull me out of the car. I remembered the girl screaming, remembered smelling my own blood as I scrambled against flying fists, but more than anything, I remembered feeling alive.

I was nervous, I was scared, but I wasn't going to give up the Mustang without a fight. It was the most "real" my life had ever been. All the numbness melted away. I got a lucky punch, saw the big, dark guy go down at a weird angle with all of his weight falling onto his hands. Bone crunched in an ugly way, and I collapsed in the middle of the street across from a kid who was no older than me, but looked like he had lived a hundred more lifetimes.

Bax was holding his wrist, blood oozing across his face and out of his nose, and he was just staring at me. The girl got out of the car and screamed she was calling the police and all I could do was marvel at how fast my heart was beating, thrill at the adrenaline that was coursing through my body.

"I never thought a pretty boy like you could throw a punch like that. Even if it was just lucky."

It was the best compliment I had ever received. I flicked blood and hair out of my eyes and asked him if he needed a ride to the hospital. It was strange, he had just tried to carjack me, had beat the crap out of me, but it was a defining moment in my life. Bax, his life, his world, woke me up and I couldn't go back to my fluffy dreamland.

I wasn't as immersed in the underground as he was. I didn't have the street cred, the attitude to pull it off. But I was smart and I was an asset, and before too long, we were a team. I didn't steal cars, didn't break the law, but when he needed help, I had his back, and I liked to think that long before he fell in love with my sister, I was his voice of reason. It was exciting; living hard like that opened up a whole new world to me. There were girls, women really, who showed me things no teenage boy should know. There were drugs, there was excitement and challenge around every corner, and it was a blast until things got too deep.

Bax was taking more risks, Novak was using him more and more. We were getting lost in the mire and poison that was the lifeblood of the Point, and I wanted out, wanted to save us both before we went under. Only Novak was far smarter than I ever gave him credit for and far more twisted. He wanted Bax and had no qualms about using me to get to him.

My father, like most rich men, couldn't keep his junk in his very expensively tailored pants. Dovie was my half sister, born to a junkie who got paid off after agreeing to abort her. No one should trust a junkie; the next fix matters more than anything else. Dovie was lost in the system until she wasn't.

Novak used her, used my dad's need to keep his secrets, to play me. My dad paid Novak to have her killed, only Novak double-crossed him, recorded the entire conversation, and pulled me into his dark and twisted game. There was no way I was going to let anything happen to my blood, my sister, even if I didn't know her, so I blackmailed my dad, pulled Dovie out of the system, and agreed to Novak's twisted scheme that had been designed to tie Bax to him forever.

The mobster was smart, but I was smarter. I set Bax up. No two ways about it. I betrayed my only friend, sold him up the river so I could save Dovie, so my dad would be forced to be Novak's puppet. I led Bax into a trap, knew it was going to end badly, but because Bax was Bax, he had made everything ten times worse by running from the cops. An arrest that should've resulted in six months at the most turned into a total shit show that had him getting locked up for a solid five years and had me taking Dovie and disappearing until he got out and I could exact my revenge. I lived with the guilt and the threat of Novak hanging over me for five fucking endless years.

As soon as Bax got out of jail, I set things in motion, took over the chessboard, and started moving pieces around that would free all of us from Novak's hold. Only once again, Bax had thrown a wrench in the plan by falling in love with my sister and giving a really bad man a vulnerable place to attack him from. Bax was ready to sacrifice himself, to burn the entire Point to the ground if it meant Dovie made it out alive. Luckily, things hadn't had to come to that, and everyone made it out, beaten, broken, and slightly worse off than before. But Novak was no more, and now we were rebuilding the underground, the foundation of this horrible place, brick by oily, soiled brick, because if we didn't then somebody else would.

My dad had cast me out, watched me with wide, panicked eyes, waiting to see if I was going to sell him out. He cut me off financially, disowned me, pretended like he never even knew me, all while knowing I could bring his lux and ostentatious world down around him at any minute. I steered clear, wanting to make

sure Dovie was insulated from him and his desperate machinations. My father knew that Bax was in Dovie's life, knew that no
one was getting to her unless they went through him first, and for
now that was enough. Keeping her safe was top priority, always.
It was one of the main reasons, besides not having any other legitimate way to make money, why I was doing what I was doing.

In all honesty, I was born to run numbers. I had a mind
custom made to be a bookie and a loan shark. I had a photographic
memory. I remembered every name, every face, and every dollar
amount owed and borrowed of the people I dealt with. I didn't
need a spreadsheet, didn't need to write anything down. The
feds would never find a little black book, never find incriminat-
ing evidence on my computer. It was all up in my noggin, safe
and sound. It made figuring the lines and the spreads easier as
well. I had endless scores, miles of stats, all the schedules of every
game, team rosters for days all lost up there, just waiting to be recalled when needed. It was pretty sweet for me, but not so much
for those that were risking what they didn't have to lose. I didn't
forget, so there was absolutely no wiggling out of a debt, no tying
to argue what was owed, which is why the garage was full of
boosted cars waiting on their owners to be accountable.

I poured another Scotch and was stripping down to hop in
a shower before bed when my phone rang. It always went off.
People wanted to place bets, wanted to ask for money at all hours
of the day and night, but the ring tone trilling throughout the
loft belonged to Dovie, so I dropped my jeans and tucked the
phone to my ear while messing with the shower. There was
no middle temperature in the loft, it was either burning hot or
freezing cold.

"Bax just left. He should be there shortly." It was a twenty-minute drive from the heart of the city to the burbs where Bax and Dovie lived, which meant he could make it in ten.

She laughed a little. It always made my heart swell to hear the unfiltered joy she had inside of her now.

"He's home already. I just wanted to check on you. Brysen mentioned there was a shootout at the party, and Bax told me you went to collect money unarmed . . . again."

There was censure there. I never would've thought I would be in a place where my little sister was encouraging me to carry a gun.

"They were just kids. It was fine."

"Whenever someone is shooting at you, it isn't fine. Someone could have gotten hurt."

By "someone," I assumed she meant Brysen. They were close and Dovie didn't have many friends, so I understood her subtle warning. I needed to be more careful when and where I conducted the nitty-gritty tied to my business dealings.

"I made sure she got out safe."

Dovie sighed. "Thank you, but I was talking about you too, Race. I can't have anything happen to you."

We all had wounds that were still trying to mend back together in the aftermath of Novak's fall.

"I know, girly. I know."

She made a noise and called something to Bax in the background.

"Brysen doesn't get out much since she moved home. It sucks her one night off from work had to end that way."

I shoved a hand into the water and yanked it right back out.

Ice cubes couldn't be any colder. I shivered and twisted the knob the opposite direction.

"Why does she work so hard? I thought her family was pretty well off. I know she lives in a nice area, has a nice house."

Dovie sighed again. "I don't really know the entire story. When I stayed with her while things with Bax were all over the place, I got the vibe that she's running the house. She takes care of her little sister. I didn't even see the parents while I was there. You should know better than anyone not to judge people based on the zip code they grew up in."

Fair enough.

"I'm getting ready to take a shower. Are we good?"

"I love you, Race. Please keep that in mind."

"I know, Dovie. Believe me, I know."

"And I think Brysen has a crush on you."

That had me howling with laughter. "You wish. She loathes me."

But there was that kiss. The kiss that was just the tip of the iceberg to the sexual fantasies I had where she was concerned.

"Seriously. I talk about you all the time. When I bring Bax up, she changes the subject, gets nervous and weird, but when I bring you up, she just lets me talk and talk. You would look beautiful together."

We would, and I would give up every dollar I had stashed in that safe just to get a peek at Brysen Carter naked.

"It's nice you haven't lost your ability to dream."

She laughed in her lighthearted way and told me good night. I tossed my phone next to the sink and stripped down so I could climb under the scalding-hot water. I hissed at the discomfort between my teeth and let the steam and burn work out some of the sexual frustration that was coiled in my gut.

I could feel her. Full breasts, soft skin, silky hair, and a mouth that was equal parts greedy and sweet. She kissed me like she knew just how naughty and raunchy I wanted her to get for me. I winced as the blazing-hot water cascaded over my rising erection. Maybe I should have picked the cold water if X-rated images of her were going to follow me into the shower.

Chapter 3

Brysen

I DON'T KNOW WHAT that guy's problem is."

I shoved my latest test adorned with a big fat *D* on the top of it into my bag and shook my head. I was walking out of my Math Theory class and looking at my friend Drew out of the corner of my eye. I only had one semester left before I graduated with my B.S. in math, at least I did if I managed to get past this class. The professor was fine, but for some reason, the TA he had working under him hated me, and I could see my GPA taking a nosedive after every single exam. I had tried to talk to the teacher about it, but he just assured me that all tests were graded fairly and suggested I looked into finding a tutor.

I sighed and shoved some of my hair out of my face. I wanted to be an accountant. Numbers I understood, had a quick mind for them, and there was no reason I should be failing this class. Drew laughed at me and wrapped an arm around my shoulders.

"Maybe you shouldn't have laughed in his face when he asked you out. I think he might've taken it personally."

I winced involuntarily because he had a point. I hadn't been laughing at the TA, I had been laughing at the idea of finding time in my life to work in something as frivolous as a date. And if by some miracle I did get a break in my schedule, I wasn't inclined to spend it with a guy who had greasy hair, acne, and a weird twitch he couldn't seem to control when he looked at me. I also didn't think dating him was appropriate, since he was involved in the class and had a say in my grade. Unfortunately, since he was also a student, there were no hard-and-fast rules in place to prevent him from leering at me or seeming to be messing with my educational future. Not without undeniable proof on my end, which I hadn't been able to produce.

"The idea of a date with anyone is a joke."

Drew gave me a little squeeze and let me go. I had two more classes and then I was supposed to touch base with Dovie before her night classes started. I worked tonight and then had to get back to the house to make sure my sister's homework was done and that Mom wasn't drinking herself into oblivion. It was all getting so tiring and there wasn't a break anywhere on the horizon.

"Adria told me there was some guy at the party that had you all googly-eyed. What's up with that?"

Adria had a big mouth and didn't understand why lusting after Race was my own personal hell and temptation.

I shifted uneasily and narrowed my gaze a little bit. Drew was a nice guy, and he was cute in a very all-American, wavy-brown-hair-and-bright-blue-eyed way. He had mentioned on more than one occasion that if I was interested in taking our friendship to another level, he would have no arguments with it. But again, I didn't have the time or the space for a guy in my life, and when it came right down to it, even if I did make the space or found the time, Drew wasn't the guy I wanted.

"Nothing is up with anything. Race is just someone I know through a mutual friend. Why?"

He shrugged, obviously going for nonchalant and failing miserably. He lifted a hand and rubbed the back of his neck while looking at the ground between his feet.

"She just mentioned that you seemed pretty entranced by him, and last I heard, you weren't interested in anybody."

It wasn't any of his business, and this line of questioning didn't seem nearly as harmless as he wanted it to come across.

"I'm not, and if I was, it wouldn't be any concern of yours, Drew."

He put a hand on my shoulder and pulled me to a stop. I looked up at him, ready to tell him to step off and mind his own business, when he gave me a sad smile.

"Look, I know you and I aren't going to be a thing, you've made that pretty clear. But I like you and I care about you, so you need to know that Race Hartman is nothing but bad news."

I already knew that, but it bothered me to hear a guy like Drew, a guy who had no idea what the world looked like outside of the Hill, say it about him.

"Race is Race. I have no illusions about what kind of guy he is."

Drew sighed and let his hand fall off my shoulder. "He's a criminal, a gangster. He has people beaten up that owe him money and takes their cars for collateral if they can't pay. People say he was the one that set Novak up and that he did it so he could take over the black market Novak ran."

I knew all of that and more because I was friends with Dovie and couldn't ignore it when she had been right in the thick of it.

"People have to do what they need to in order to survive, Drew. Not everyone has a full-ride scholarship or comes equipped with rich parents able to fund a college education."

He reared back and narrowed his eyes at me.

"Well, since you're so tight with him, then you know that's not the case with Race. His parents have more money than God, and he had a trust fund that could buy and sell this university a hundred times over. He picked that life. He chose to be a criminal. He had all the same opportunities as the rest of us, he just squandered them and sank into the black hole of the Point."

I doubted it was as easy as that, but this wasn't a conversation I felt like I needed to be having anymore. I spent too much time having to force Race out of my mind as it was; I didn't need to be arguing about him with anyone else in my life.

"I think the way things look on the surface is always misleading. Passing judgment based on rumor and speculation isn't a smart thing to do, and like I said, none of it matters, Race and I are just acquaintances." I shifted my bag on my shoulder and took a step back. "I have to go to my next class."

He gave me a concerned look that I turned my back on and walked away from. I knew all about things on the outside hiding the real, ugly truth of the way things were once you got past the front door. I didn't know Race well enough to try and judge the choices he made or the life he was living, but I was smart enough and intuitive enough to know that there was more to the story, deeper circumstances at work, than what people gossiped and speculated about.

My next two classes, both of which I had high A's in, flew by and I was rushing across the sprawling campus to meet Dovie for a quick cup of coffee. Now that she no longer worked at the restaurant where we had met waitressing, it was hard to sneak in time to hang out. I spotted her bright, orange-ish-red hair with no problem and threw myself into the chair across from her. She already had a drink waiting for me because it was just in her nature to be that generous and sweet.

She smiled at me, the freckles on her nose wrinkling up, and her eyes, the exact same forest green as Race's, twinkling at me. Being in love with an unholy terror looked good on her, there was no denying it.

"Hey."

I had to grin back. "Hey. You look happy."

She blushed a little; there was no hiding it with that fair red-head complexion.

"I am. What about you? How are things going?"

Ugh. Like they had been for the last year. I shrugged a shoulder and let it fall. "Okay, I guess. I have an evil teacher's assistant out to ruin my GPA, I almost got shot this weekend, and I got a weird text message on Saturday night after that party. Things at the restaurant are about the same . . . and things at home . . ." All I could do was shake my head. "I just have to wait until Karsen is out of the house."

She cocked her head and concern colored her mossy-toned gaze. "Jeez, Brysen, that's a load of stuff."

I laughed drily and fished out my laptop so I could take a look at what I had due tomorrow and what I needed to work on after my shift tonight. "Yeah."

"What kind of weird text did you get?"

That was the part she was going to pick out of the shit storm that was my current circumstances?

"Just some creeper telling me I looked pretty and that they were sorry they missed me."

She frowned, her coppery eyebrows dipping low over her eyes. "That's freaky. You didn't recognize the number?"

"Nope, and I have turned down plenty of weirdos that ask me out either here on campus or at the restaurant that would love nothing more than to mess with me. It's pretty easy nowadays to find someone's number on the Internet if you're determined enough."

"I don't like that at all, Bry."

Considering she had been kidnapped, cut up, and used as a pawn by Novak to get Bax to behave, I bet she didn't, but those kinds of things didn't happen in my world.

"It was probably just a prank, or meant for someone else. It just annoyed me because of the way the party ended. Gunshots are terrifying when you experience them in person."

She bit her lip and didn't agree or disagree with me. I entered my password and then froze. The screen was blue . . . not good. I looked up at Dovie over the monitor and tried to keep from screaming.

"My laptop has a blue screen."

She blinked and got up to walk around the side of the table so she could look at it.

"Uh-oh."

I gulped and turned it off and started it back up. Still ugly, glaring blue.

"Shit."

She squeezed my shoulder. "That's bad."

"You have no idea. My entire college life is in there. My paper due tomorrow, all my notes, and if I want any kind of shot at passing Math Theory, I need everything that the blue screen just swallowed. This can't be happening."

I barely resisted throwing the entire thing on the floor and tap-dancing all over the pieces.

"You can probably recover the stuff on the hard drive." She was trying to sound optimistic, but it wasn't helping.

"Well, that's one problem that might be solved, but I can't afford a new computer." I didn't mean to say it, it just slipped out.

Dovie had been to the house; she knew that at one point in time my parents had been pretty well off. It sounded dumb, not having money for a new computer when I lived in a nice suburb and drove a BMW, but the truth was I HAD to keep my job at the restaurant if I wanted to keep my car, if I wanted to finish my degree. There was no more money. Between Mom's medical bills and whatever Dad was doing in the stock market, we were lucky to still have lights on in the house.

"And I don't have the time or the energy to try and fit in a second job to pay for one. This sucks."

I shoved my fingers through my hair and rubbed the heels of my palms into my temples. All that stuff I shoved down on a day-to-day basis rose up in the back of my throat, threatening to choke me. Really, how much more could one person be expected to endure? Why was the universe trying to break me?

"Can I offer a suggestion?"

I looked up at her and she was twisting one of her curls around her fingers, a telltale sign she was nervous. I knew I wasn't going to like whatever she had to say.

"Sure, as long as it doesn't involve me working a corner in the District."

The District was the part of the Point where girls a lot

younger than me practiced the oldest job in the world. It was where men went to have a good time and spend money on women who would forget them as soon as they had that same money in hand. I had never actually been to that part of town, but it was legendary and really the last resort for too many.

She smacked the back of one of my hands when I put them back on the table, and scowled at me. "Stop being ridiculous. Look, I know you and Race aren't exactly buddies." She paused and I rolled my eyes. Of course we weren't buddies. I couldn't be buddies with someone I wanted to strip naked and crawl all over. "But he is good, like scary good, with computers. You could ask him to look at it for you. I bet he could fix it, no problem."

Great. A solution that would be financially helpful, but would test my already-frayed resistance where her golden god of a brother was concerned. Like I stood a chance after that kiss. I grumbled under my breath and threw my hands up in surrender.

"Give me his number and I'll call him."

She made a face. "It's not exactly that easy to get ahold of him anymore. He has a bunch of different numbers for the different things he's into, and he doesn't check his personal phone that much because, really, I'm the only one that calls him on it. I'll just tell him to swing by the restaurant and have a look at it for you."

Again, irrefutable proof that I had no business crushing on Race Hartman. I had no clue what to do with a guy who had to have multiple cell phones to run his different criminal ventures out the back door.

"All right. If you think he wouldn't mind."

She smiled again. "He won't mind. He'll do it because I'm asking him to, but he likes you. He always has."

"How is that possible? I've never encouraged him in any way." In fact, I went out of my way to discourage him at every turn.

She smirked at me and grabbed her bag and her phone. "Race is a difficult guy to explain. The choices he's made, the things he's decided to take on . . ." She trailed off and shrugged helplessly. "He isn't scared of a challenge, scared of working his way around obstacles. Look at his best friend. Bax never trusted anyone, never let anyone matter, except for Race. He's just the kind of guy who works his way into where he wants to be."

Well, shit. That didn't bode well for me being able to keep his charm and allure at arm's length, but I didn't have a choice. I really couldn't afford a new computer.

"Shoot me a text after you hear from him to let me know when to expect him."

She nodded and gave me a hug. She smelled like sunshine and something bright. I don't know how someone who had been continually beaten down, handed the worst life had to offer over and over again, could be so delightful. She was a marvel and I felt really lucky that she liked me enough to let me into her closely guarded inner circle.

"Thanks, Doyie."

She snorted. "Don't thank me until you know if he can actually fix it or not. Blue screens usually mean death when it comes to computers."

I wished she hadn't reminded me. I put my stuff away as well and climbed to my feet. I had to head over to the restaurant and get ready for my shift.

"Well, still, thanks for thinking of a solution I can actually afford."

We walked toward the center of the campus and she stopped

me with a hand on my forearm right before we had to split and go our separate ways.

"Look, Brysen." Her dark green eyes were serious and steady. "You took me in without asking questions when my life was a mess. You've always been nice, never pried or asked questions I couldn't or wouldn't answer. If you need some help, let me know." Her gaze shifted to the ground then back up to me. "I don't have a lot, but Bax does, and he'll hand it over without question if I want it."

She was going to make me cry. I reached out and gave her one last squeeze. "No, I'm fine. I just have to bide my time. We all have to make sacrifices, I guess."

She was willing to risk life and limb and even her freedom in order to stay with her man. I was willing to sacrifice my independence—my vision of what I thought my life would be—for my sister.

I made my way to the car and drove to the restaurant I had worked at for almost two years. It hovered right on the edge of the Point and the Hill, so there was an odd mix of customers we served. I made decent money, and I liked that it was close to school and offered me a break from the stress at home and the opportunity to meet people I probably never would've otherwise.

I went into the back bathroom and switched into the tiny black skirt and too-tight black T-shirt that constituted as my uniform. Really, as long as we wore all black, the owner didn't care how we dressed, but I had learned real quick that the sexier the outfit, the redder the lipstick, the shinier my hair looked, the more money I brought home from the shift. It was so "unevolved," so sexist, that it galled, but I needed every single penny

I could put my hands on, and looking hot was a surefire way to get it.

I mean, I wasn't anything that special. I had nice skin and big blue eyes, but a pretty blonde was a dime a dozen, and there was nothing I had going on that made me stand out in a crowd. I think the fact that I was naturally curvy, not too tall, not too short, but endowed in all the right places and then some, really was what most of my recent admirers had been after. I had a rocking body and had no trouble exploiting that fact if it meant I kept my head above water financially and didn't have to resort to grinding on a pole or paying the bills on my back.

I fluffed up my asymmetrical bob, spritzed on some perfume, and hit the floor running. It was "Thirsty Thursday," so that meant the place would be packed with a lot of kids from the university headed in different directions to drink the night away. The clubs on the Hill offered expensive martini bars and high-end dance clubs. The places kids went in the Point were all underground. You had to know someone that knew someone to even find out where they were. I heard the stories of the drugs, the bloody fights, the thumping music, and "anything goes" atmosphere. I had even been to one once with Dovie when she had been tricked into going just so she would have to watch Bax get the crap pounded out of him by a drugged-up monster. I didn't fit in either place, so it was no skin off my nose that I could work the crowd and make money off either taste while they pre-gamed. Really, it was the story of my life. Too poor to belong up on the Hill, and too rich to fit in with the hard-knock life of the Point. I just existed somewhere in the middle of everything.

I was running like crazy for the first few hours. Ramon, the bartender, was taking forever with the drinks, and the kitchen crashed more than once while the tickets piled up. I was pretty organized and had impeccable time-management skills, so it all went pretty smooth. By the time I got to take a breather and find a second to shove a taco in my face before the next wave, I was surprised when Ramon wandered over to the service area, where I was hiding with a bemused expression on his face.

"Hey."

I wiped sour cream off my chin and lifted an eyebrow at him.

"What's up?"

"Were you planning on meeting someone here tonight?"

I frowned and pulled my phone out of my bra, where I stashed it looking to see if Dovie had sent me a message about Race. There was nothing, just a message from Karsen asking me to bring her home some ice cream.

"No. Why?"

He lifted his elegantly groomed eyebrows and clicked his tongue at me. "There was this guy at the bar. He kept looking around and looking around. I asked him like five hundred times if I could help him with anything but he just ordered a soda and sat at the bar. I saw you come out of the kitchen with an order and so did he. I watched him watch you for a minute then he got up and left. I thought maybe it was a friend or something."

I felt my jaw drop and I blinked at him like an idiot. "What did he look like?"

Considering Ramon liked the fellas way more than I did right now, I figured he would have a spot-on description for me, but he shrugged.

"Nothing special. In fact, it was weird, like he was trying to blend in. He had on glasses and a hat, like he was trying to look different. He didn't say anything to anyone either."

I felt a chill race up my spine and suddenly my taco tasted like dirt in my mouth. Sure, there were creepy guys that came in and tried to hit on me and gave me the lurking looks, but a weirdo who didn't say anything, combined with that strange text message, had me totally freaked out.

"That's weird."

Ramon nodded. "It was very odd."

"If you see him again can you let me know?"

"Sure thing. Maybe you need to wait and have someone walk out with you."

I shivered again and numbly agreed. My phone went off and I groaned when I saw Dovie's message.

He'll be there at close. Wait for him.

Could life hand me anything else difficult and covered in thorns to work my way through? I was starting to doubt it.

I texted back that that was fine and went to work the later crowd that filtered in right before we closed the kitchen down every night. I was hypervigilant, my eyes shifting all across the restaurant. I didn't like the idea of some lurker hanging around watching me, liked it even less with the weird text messages still floating around in the back of my mind. I tended to think I could take care of myself, I was smart and considered myself savvy, but I had never actually had to put that theory to the test. It was a frightening thought.

By the time my last table finished and I was done doing the side work and my cash out for the night, I was tired and stressed out. I was ready to change back into my normal clothes, get my sister some ice cream, and go home . . . well, not so much the last part, but still.

I twisted my hair up out of my face in the front, changed back into my jeans, and shoved my uniform into my purse to take it home to wash. Ramon still had a straggler at the bar and all the guys in the kitchen were busy cleaning or just ignoring me, so it looked like I was walking out to the car to grab my computer by myself. I really wished the idea didn't have the hair on the back of my neck standing on end, and I was secretly disappointed that Race wasn't already here to accompany me on the trek.

I pushed out into the night and let my gaze skim across the parking lot. Things were generally mellow here, but we had encountered more than one rowdy drunk on occasion. The last time it happened, Bax had shown up just in the nick of time, and ever since then things had been quiet. Dovie's boyfriend had a reputation that reached far and wide, but she didn't work here anymore, so now the degenerates were popping back up.

I always parked under the single flickering light that sat in parking lot and almost groaned out loud when I saw that tonight was the night it had decided to give up the ghost and burn out. The parking lot was dark and the walk to my car looked like it was a thousand miles instead of a few steps. My tummy started to churn and goose bumps broke out over my exposed skin. Taking a deep breath, I shored up the reserves and practically sprinted to where the BMW was parked. I put a hand on the door handle with a sigh and shrieked bloody murder when a heavy hand fell on my shoulder from behind.

Without stopping to think, I screamed at the top of my

lungs, threw my head back until I felt it connect with something hard, and whirled around with my knee already rising into position to do the most damage. My assailant slapped a heavy hand across my mouth, clamped a rock-hard arm across my chest as I turned, and shoved me into the side of the car. I was still screaming behind the hand and my chest was heaving, but when familiar green eyes glared down at me, some of my panic started to subside. I wrapped my hands around the wrist of the arm that was covering my mouth and slumped against the car.

"What in the holy fuck was that?" Race pushed off of me and lifted a hand to rub the edge of his chin where the back of my skull had connected.

I put both of my shaking hands to my mouth and shook my head back and forth. I wanted to apologize, but the words were lodged in my throat.

"Didn't Dovie tell you I was gonna swing by after your shift?" He sounded irritated, and I couldn't blame him.

"Sorry. I'm jumpy in the parking lot this late."

He looked up at the broken light and then back at me and scowled. "Why are you out here this late alone in the first place?"

"Everyone was busy trying to close for the night. You know how it goes, everyone is in a rush to head home after closing time."

The look that crossed his handsome face said he didn't like that very much at all. Race always looked regal, like a king, all golden and elegant. Tonight, in the harsh shadow of the broken light and with the cracked asphalt under his feet, he looked more like a Nordic warrior, both fierce and unhappy. It wasn't a look I would have ever figured he could pull off, but intimidation was right at home on those too-pretty features. When he didn't like something, he was going to do something about it, and I could see it brewing in his eyes.

I reached out a hand and clamped it on his thick wrist.

"Don't worry about it, Race. I really just need you to help me with the computer, or else I'm totally screwed."

He considered me silently, obviously trying to decide which matter he found more pressing, my safety or my current electronic crisis. Thank God the computer won out, but his voice was gruff and scratchy when he told me, "Not the end of this conversation, Bry."

I nodded stiffly and bent over to get my laptop out from under the seat where I'd stashed it. When I turned back around, I felt heat rush into my face because bent over like that, I had clearly given Race the opportunity to check my ass out at its best. The green in his eyes had turned to something much darker, and I gulped nervously.

"What's wrong with the computer?"

I held it protectively against my chest while his eyes rolled over me. It was unnerving to be the sole focus of a guy like Race. I felt like he was trying to get a look inside me, like he was systematically trying to figure out all the bits and pieces that made me tick.

"I don't know. I turned it on and the screen was just blue. I know it's bad, but everything I need for school is in there, so I have to do something."

He lifted a sandy brow and reached for the laptop. "You don't back anything up on an external drive or on an outside database, like Google Drive?"

I groaned and shoved my palms into my eye sockets. "Really, Race? If I was smart enough to do that, do you think I would be praying that you can fix it? Nothing is ever that easy in my life."

He just watched me, his mouth turning down in a little frown. I much preferred that look on his exquisite face to the one he wore when he was flashing that sexy dimple at me. It was easier to resist.

"When do you need it back by?"

"I have a paper on there that is due tomorrow, but the teacher is pretty cool and will let me slide until Monday if I explain the situation. What I really need are my Math Theory notes. I have an evil TA who's got it in for me because I turned him down when he asked me out. I'm barely passing the class, and without the notes, I'm beyond screwed."

His eyes sank even further into midnight and his frown got even tighter. His broad chest rose and fell as he took a deep breath and let it out slowly.

His eyebrows dipped low over those dark eyes, and his voice was even rougher than normal when he asked me, "What is going on with you, Brysen? Why does every single thing you've said to me tonight make me want to hurt things and various people?"

I gulped a little and shivered as we just watched each other silently.

"Life isn't always fun and games, Race. You have to know that better than most people."

He shook his blond head and took a step back from me. I really, really wanted to reach out and snatch him back. He was so bad for my self-control.

"No, it's not, but you're a good girl and too pretty for words. Things shouldn't be that hard for you."

Well, they were that hard, and I was just going to have to live with it.

"Do you think you can save it?"

He took another step back and grinned. I swear everything that made me female melted and turned liquid when that dimple indented his cheek.

"I'm pretty skilled at whatever I put my mind to, Brysen."

The sexy undercurrent made me want to whimper.

"When do you think I can have it back?"

"Give me your number. I have a bunch of shit to take care of tomorrow, but after that's all handled, I'll look at it. Give me until the weekend."

That was only three days. Aside from Math Theory, I should be able to make do until then. I rattled off my number and scowled when he didn't pull out his phone to enter it in.

"You're going to remember that?" I hated that I sounded like I was pouting about it.

"I won't forget it, Bry. Everything about you is very memorable."

Ugh . . . that kiss. It was going to haunt me forever. I shifted uneasily and pushed off the car.

"I have to take my little sister some ice cream and make sure she has her homework done."

He gave me a considering look and tilted his head to the side a little bit. I didn't want to be the object of Race Hartman's attention; it made hiding the way I reacted to him too hard.

"You're gonna have someone walk you to your car from here on out." It wasn't a question, just a blanket statement.

"I'll try." I would prefer it but life didn't seem so inclined to give me anything I preferred right now.

"Do it, Brysen." His tone suggested I listen or I might not like what followed.

"Yes, Race. I'll make it happen from here on out."

He grunted and turned to walk to where his bright red Mustang was parked. It was a supersexy car for a totally dead-sexy guy. Completely not fair.

"I'll be in touch."

He left without another word and I felt like I was going to fold in on myself. Every single person had limits to what they could endure. Adding Race into the mix of the mess I was already in the center of felt like there simply wasn't any more room inside of me for things to stay stuffed down. Everything was coming to the surface, all the feelings and emotions I refused to acknowledge, refused to fret over, were popping the seams and threatening to spill out. That wasn't a spill anyone was going to want a hand in cleaning up when I finally ruptured.

I sighed and called Karsen to see what kind of ice cream she wanted me to get for her.

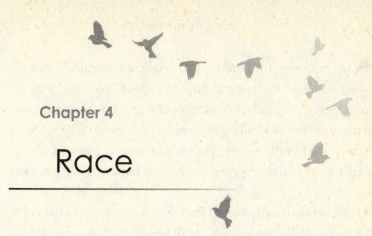

Chapter 4

Race

THERE WAS A TIME in my life where the thud of heavy fists smacking into flesh, the smell of blood, and the agonizing sounds of human suffering moved me. It used to make my skin crawl and my guts go tight. Now it was a necessary evil, and as bad as it appeared it was just part of the job.

I was in the back room of Spanky's, the strip club to end all strip clubs in the District. The girls who danced here were no run-of-the-mill strippers. They were gorgeous, professional, and served dual roles as dancers and hostesses when the stage lights were off and the club turned into an illegal casino. Spanky's had been a cash cow for Novak. Now Nassir and I both had our hands in the pot and we were currently watching Chuck, the giant African American man who was the head of security for the joint, beat the living hell out of a client who didn't know how to keep his hands to himself.

I had my arms crossed and was leaning against the wall while the guy, who could very easily be anyone's dad, got the shit kicked out of him. He had already spit out teeth, and his face looked like hamburger, but Chuck didn't seem like he was in a hurry to stop the beating, and Nassir wasn't calling him off. Nassir had eyes the color of burned caramel and they were focused intently on the scene in front of him. He took the security of the girls who worked for him seriously, regardless if they were turning tricks or not—and Honor, not her real name of course, wasn't a girl you were going to put your hands on and get away with it.

She was as much a part of the District as Bax was of the Point. We had a sordid history, and in all honesty, I was surprised she wasn't back here kicking the shit out of Grabby Hands McGee because that's the kind of chick she was. The victim grunted, his puffy and swollen eyes rolled back in his head as he listed over onto his side in an unconscious heap. Chuck gave him one more kick with the toe of his shoe and leaned down to wipe his bloody hands on the guy's torn and ripped shirt.

Nassir lifted a black eyebrow. "Feel better?"

Chuck grunted and looked back and forth between the two of us. "Something in the air. Don't know what it is, but people keep showing up and pushing limits. Had to make a point and make it clear."

Nassir and I shared a look and he shrugged his shoulders. He always looked like he was off to some kind of high-powered business meeting. His suits cost more than my car, and his exotic looks and lethal way of carrying himself made him intimidating and domineering without any effort. I already treated him like he was going to shove a knife in my back at any second, but just being in his dark presence made me keen to make sure I was always on my toes.

"What's going on?"

He rubbed his thumb along the edge of his jaw and considered me thoughtfully. "Some of the girls have come back complaining that clients aren't wanting to pay. They said that the word going around is that you and I, we're too new. The city is in flux, no one is in charge, and no one is in line to answer to, so people are getting ballsy and pushing their luck."

I gritted my back teeth and frowned. "What are you doing about it?"

"*We,* Race. What are *we* doing about it?"

He seriously was the last person on the planet I wanted to be in business with, but it wasn't like I had much of a choice.

"What are we doing about it, Nassir?"

"Putting a fucking stop to it right fucking now." He motioned to the guy on the floor. "I got names, I got addresses, and a whole world of hurt is coming anyone's way who wants to question who is or isn't in charge. I suggest you do the exact same if someone doesn't come through on what they owe you."

I hadn't run into that problem yet, but my time as a bookie was still pretty new.

"Yeah. I guess there can't be any perceived weakness."

Nassir's eyes flashed. "There won't be any weakness period. I waited far too long for someone else to handle Novak and all his madness. I should've done something about him long ago, but I waited, and his poison spread. You and I might not see eye to eye, Race, but we both agree that someone has to feed the monster, and that as long as honorable men are doing it, the city doesn't have to be sacrificed to keep it fed."

Honorable wasn't a word I would equate with Nassir, but that wasn't a point I wanted to push right now.

"Is Honor all right?"

Something crossed his face that was beyond frightening. I

didn't know much about his past, or where he came from, but I
never mistook Nassir for just some guy in a suit afraid of getting
his hands in the dirt and muck. He was a man who could kill if
he felt it necessary, the kind of man who would take on an entire
army if he thought the battle needed to be fought.

"She's pissed."

I sighed heavily. "I have a deposit I want to hand over. College football started."

He nodded and we left Chuck alone to clean up the mess
on the floor. It was cold, it was inhumane, and a tiny piece of
me knew it was wrong, but it was just the way it had to be. We
went into the office that the guy who used to run the club used,
and I handed over the bundled-up stacks of cash. When I was
younger, throwing around hundreds of thousands of dollars had
meant nothing to me. Now I watched Nassir take it and put it in
the safe behind the desk with all kinds of trepidation. One thing
about being a criminal that really sucked was that you had to
rely on other criminals to make a living. As a whole, we weren't
really a trustworthy lot, and we were all inherently looking out
for number one.

My apprehension must have shown on my face, because
Nassir lifted a dark eyebrow and gave me a grin that was anything but reassuring.

"I need you, Race. I'm not going to rip you off."

I snorted. "What happens when you decide you don't need
me?"

"You're a smart man. You can figure out the answer to that
on your own. By the way, I heard one of those punk college kids
pulled a gun on you while you were collecting. You need to take
a stand when shit like that goes down."

I sighed. "He was just some kid."

Nassir pointed a finger at me and his voice was all seriousness when he told me, "So are you, only you're just some kid running an entire city from the outside. Anyone fucks with you, Race, and you put them in their place. Bax has a reputation to stand on, it's in his blood. He was born as bad as they come. You're just some rich kid playing at being a crime boss. You need to prove that you are serious, that you are in this to the end. Be that by your blood or theirs. There is only one way to do things . . . our way."

I wasn't ruthless like that. I don't think I would ever be the kind of man who just took and took without a thought as to whom I was taking from. It was too close to the coldness; the black and empty way my father operated. I never wanted to be the kind of man who could consider killing his own flesh and blood just because it was a messy story he didn't want to try and explain.

"I handle my business, Nassir. Don't worry about what I'm doing or what I'm not doing."

He grunted and took a seat at the desk and steepled his fingers under his chin. "I'm more worried about Bax coming unglued if you get your dumb ass killed and ruining everything we've managed to patchwork together. Plus, the cop would start poking around, and that would be unpleasant for both of us."

The cop was Bax's half brother, Titus King. He had played a big part in helping take Novak down, and was now a constant pain in my ass. I liked Titus. He was a good man, a dedicated cop, but if he really knew what I was into, the kinds of things Bax and I had working on the side, he would flip his shit and have no qualms about shutting my operation down cold. He was always watching us with an eagle eye, and I think he knew more than he let on, but Nassir was a ruthless bastard, and if Titus did indeed get too close, I didn't doubt he would try and take him out of the game.

I didn't have anything else to say to him and my patience at having to deal with the slick bastard had reached its limits. I wasn't playing at anything. I knew how serious this shit I was deep into was, and treated it as such. I just didn't have any intention of turning into a Novak while doing it.

As I rounded the corner I almost slammed into Honor. Her real name was Keelyn Foster and she was probably the most beautiful girl in the entire world. Granted, she paid a lot of money to keep that appearance up, but in the dark, there was no difference between man-made and heaven-sent in my book. She had on a silky black robe, her long, auburn hair was a tangled mess, and her heavy makeup was smeared all over her face. Even in the dim light of the strip club, I could see the nasty split in her bottom lip and the bruise flowering across her high and elegant cheekbone.

I let out a whistle. "Are you all right?"

She winced a little and lifted her fingers to her cheek. "Been better. Did Nassir bring that idiot back here?"

I nodded and warned, "If Nassir gets a good look at your face, that idiot is leaving the club in a body bag."

"Good. Asshole deserves it. No touching means no touching. He's lucky I didn't castrate him with one of my heels."

It was impossible to live this life and not develop that edge. Beautiful girls shouldn't have to live this hard. It was a shame.

"He had Chuck work him over pretty good, but I'm serious about him killing the guy if he catches sight of the damage. I think the devil has a soft spot for you."

She rolled her dark gray eyes at me and crossed her arms over her silk-covered breasts. I was very familiar with her naked body, knew she made the money she did for a reason, but there was a hardness about her now that hadn't been there when I left five years ago.

"Nassir is like a wild animal that escaped from the zoo. He's amazing to look at, fascinating to watch, but I would prefer that bars and glass separated us. There is nothing soft about that man."

I lifted an eyebrow. "You don't like him having control of the club?"

She blinked obscenely long lashes at me and her perfectly bowed mouth crooked up in a half grin. Only Honor could look that good with a split open lip.

"Ernie was a slob and easy to manipulate. He liked to pretend he was in charge, but we really ran the show. Back in the day this was a fun job that the girls could do hungover and with zero effort. Flash some tit and the tentpole rises. Nassir is all business, and now the dancers have to work for every dollar. There is no playing around, and with Novak gone, every Tom, Dick, and Harry is grappling to prove they're the next badass. Things are more dangerous, more desperate. Everyone is trying to carve out their own piece of the city, and it shows." She gestured at her battered face. "Case in point."

I hated what she said, but it was true. "Why don't you quit? Go find something less in the line of fire to do?"

She reached out a hand and tapped my cheek lightly. "You always were too pretty and too smart for your own good, Race." She flipped her hair out to the side. "What do you think I'm qualified to do? I've taken my clothes off for a living since I was seven-

teen. I didn't finish high school. I don't have rich parents waiting
in the wings. Where else can I make a grand a night and the only
risk is an overly zealous soccer dad? This is what I know."

I was a firm believer in the principle that knowledge was
something that continued to grow, continued to develop, as long
as you had the desire to chase after it. For me there was always
more to know, but I couldn't fault her for doing what she felt like
she had to do in order to survive. I bent down so I could kiss her
bruised cheek.

"Take care of yourself."

She returned the kiss on my dimple. "For what it's worth,
I'm glad you're back. I just hope you know what you're doing
getting into business with a shark like Nassir."

"Me too, but it usually only takes one mistake for me to
learn my lesson."

She gave me a sad little smile. "One mistake is too many in
this world, Race. This isn't the Hill. Remember that."

I watched her disappear into the office where I had left
Nassir. I wished everyone would stop bringing up where I was
from. I knew that Spanky's wasn't the Hill. Nothing here even
looked the same as there, including me. I guess only time would
tell if I had what it took to make the rest of the city see that.

I walked to the Mustang and pulled my phone out of my
pocket. I called Brysen to see when she was going to get off
work. Her laptop was a paperweight. There was no salvaging it.
I pulled as much limited data as I could off the burned-up hard
drive and transferred it to a new MacBook I bought for her. I
knew she wasn't going to want to take it, but I didn't plan on
giving her a choice in the matter. She needed it for school and
Dovie mentioned she couldn't afford a new one, so she was leav-

ing with the Mac whether she liked it or not. Plus, I managed to dig most of her Math Theory junk out of the wasteland, so I was hoping that would smooth the way into getting her to accept it.

She answered in a rush and told me she would be off a little after midnight. That was only half an hour away, so I told her I would just wait for her in the parking lot. It would've been easier to go inside and have the showdown with her in front of witnesses, but I wanted to see if she had actually listened to me and was going to get an escort out of the restaurant to her car. I didn't like the idea of her alone in this part of town after dark. Sure, my sister walked the same path, had even taken the bus to and from work, but Dovie had street smarts and could pick out a threat from a mile away. Brysen looked like an ice princess from a fairy tale. I didn't think she was stupid, but I also didn't think she had any kind of clue what really lurked in the shadows and the dark.

The front door of the restaurant opened and Brysen's superblond hair glinted off the glass doors. She had on a tight T-shirt and a short skirt, and obviously hadn't bothered to change after her shift. A tall Latin guy was walking next to her. She was laughing at something he said and tossed her head back. She really was the prettiest girl I had ever seen. There was just something so easy about her, so effortless, that it made my heart thud heavy in my ears. She put her hand on her escort's arm and pointed to where the Mustang was sitting. The guy nodded at her, bent down to kiss her on the cheek, and turned around to walk back inside.

Brysen started walking toward me, so I kicked open the car door and rose to my feet. I don't know where the headlights came from, don't know how I missed another car idling in the parking lot, but the next thing I knew, there was a squeal of tires, the smell of rubber burning, and a sedan barreling right at her. I saw her go still as I broke into a run. There was too much space between where she was and where I was and the car was headed right toward her. I saw her throw her hands up as the engine revved up even higher. She didn't scream, didn't make any kind of noise, so I called her name. Her head snapped around to look at me and I hollered, "Move!" at the top of my lungs.

Right before the impact, right before I had to watch her end up splattered all over the windshield, the guy who had walked her out suddenly hit her from the side in a flying tackle that had both of them careening hard to the asphalt. I heard her shriek when she hit and turned to try and grab the license plate off of the fleeing sedan. I frowned as I reached the huddled pair on the ground because the plates on the car were missing, making this feel very deliberate and not like an accident at all. I nudged the Spanish guy on the shoulder and he looked up at me.

"Move."

He huffed at me and rolled off of Brysen. She peeked up at me from between the fingers she had clamped over her eyes like that was somehow going to prevent her from getting run over by a speeding car. I reached down to pull her to her feet and felt my back teeth click together when I saw the bloody mess her arm and legs were from where she had hit the ground.

"Oh my God, Ramon!" She broke away from me and threw herself at the other guy. He wrapped her up in a hug and shook his head.

"That was crazy. A drunk driver maybe?"

Ramon muttered the words while he looked right at me as I just stared at him. I wanted him to let Brysen go—like yesterday.

She took a step away from him and cradled her injured arm to her chest with her other hand. "Thank you so much. You just saved my life."

"Weird things are in your orbit, chica. You need to keep your head up." He gave her shoulder a squeeze and looked at me pointedly. "Find someone to watch your back."

We watched him walk away in silence, and she finally turned and looked at me. I frowned down at her and she lifted up her pale eyebrows to almost her hairline.

"Why are you looking at me like I did something wrong? It's not my fault that guy was wasted and out of control." She sounded huffy, but under it her voice was shaking. She was scared out of her mind.

I inclined my chin and let out the breath I hadn't been aware I was holding.

"That wasn't a drunk driver. The car had no plates, didn't have any lights on until you came out of the building, and it was aiming right for you. If your buddy hadn't taken you to the ground it would have run you over very purposefully. What in the hell is going on with you?"

She blinked up at me and bit down hard on her bottom lip. I wanted to replace her teeth with my own.

"My arm really hurts." It should. She had a pretty nasty case of road rash and it was bleeding steadily, and half the parking lot was embedded in it.

"Want me to follow you home so you can clean up?"

She shook her head vehemently "no" and asked in a whisper, "Can you just take me somewhere so I can wash it out? I don't want my sister or my mom to see me like this."

One of these days I was going to have to get the entire story of what was going on with this girl. I liked a challenge, but she had passed "challenging" a month ago. Right now she was hovering pretty close to "impossible."

"I can run you by my place."

She nodded vigorously then looked at her little BMW. "I can't leave the car. It won't be here by the time we get back."

She made a valid point. I sighed and gave her a once-over. She was a mess and there was no way she could drive a stick shift with one working arm. I put a hand on her uninjured arm and guided her to the Mustang. I opened the door for her and pulled my phone out of my pocket. I waited until the nervous voice on the other end answered before telling Brysen to give me her keys.

"Aldo?"

"Yeah?"

I was probably the last person he wanted to hear from. "You want a break on the two Gs you still owe me on the Alabama game from last weekend?"

There was a long silence and I saw Brysen look up at me curiously. I just shut the door on her and walked around to the other side of the car. I tried not to be too sad about the fact she was probably bleeding all over my vintage interior.

"What do I gotta do?" Aldo asked. It was a fair question. No good deed was without a return favor in this world.

"Black BMW in the parking lot on the corner of Paradise and Loft. I want it at the garage within the next twenty minutes. I'm leaving the keys in it, so if it gets stolen in the next five minutes, I'm adding the car to the total of what you already owe me." Nothing like a little motivation to get the ball rolling in the direction I wanted it to roll.

"I'm across town, dude."

"I suggest you get unacross town in a big hurry."

I hung up on him and walked over to her little car and stashed the keys under the floor mat. It was a risky move, but I knew Aldo didn't have the cash on hand to pay his debt, so he would make it happen one way or another just to be clear of the debt and my wrath.

I got back in the Mustang and looked at my passenger in the dark. Her eyes were wide and the pupils were huge in the center. I wondered if I needed to worry about her having a concussion.

"You okay?"

She rolled her head from side to side on the leather seat. "No. Nothing's been okay for a long time."

I started the car and pulled out of the parking lot. The rumble of the engine was oddly comforting and I saw her shift a little as the blood on her legs started to drip toward the floor mat. I wanted to tell her not to worry about it, but her words were buzzing around in my head like a bunch of angry bees.

"Why did someone try to run you over in the parking lot tonight?"

She shot me a sideways look and pushed her hair out of her face to tuck it behind her ear.

"I don't know. I also don't know why I'm getting strange text messages, or getting shot at during parties, or why I'm failing a class that should be a piece of cake, or why I keep making excuses for my parents. I don't have any clue how it became my responsibility to make sure my sister makes it to adulthood as minimally affected by the nonsense at home as possible. None of it makes sense to me, but it just keeps happening and happening and I don't have any kind of control of my own life anymore."

She sighed and I saw her eyes gleam with shiny, unshed tears. It was probably the most personal, most open, she had ever been in my presence, and I wanted to react, but all I could focus on was the fact she had gotten weird text messages and that she thought the gunshots at the party were somehow related to her. That didn't line up in any kind of okay direction for me at all.

"You have someone threatening you, Brysen?"

Her teeth dug harder into her lip. "I don't know. I got a weird text after the party from a number I didn't know, and then Ramon, the bartender who just saved my life, said there was some guy lurking around the restaurant during my shift. I mean I have been known to rub a guy the wrong way when I've turned down a date or two, but generally only when they don't get the hint. It could all be coincidental, but after tonight, I just don't know what to think."

We got to the garage and I used the keypad to get the gates to swing open. As soon as the big metal barriers clanged shut behind us, she finally relaxed. I pulled the car into the bay and shut the door. It was insulating, like being in the heart of a big iron-and-steel box, and when I walked around the car to help her to her feet, I had to make a seriously concentrated effort to keep all the anger and confusion her words had churned up in me in check. I didn't like women being threatened or feeling fear in general, but considering it was *her,* and something about *her* was firmly entrenched under my skin, all of it made me see red.

She gave me her good hand and I pulled her to her feet. We were chest to chest, her eyes glimmered so enticingly, and it was all I could do not to bend down and pull that gnawed-on lower lip into my own mouth. She was hurt, she was scared, and she was pretending really hard that she didn't like me at all. None of that stopped my dick from going hard and my nostrils from flaring at her alluring scent.

"Let's go get the rocks out of your knee and arm before they cause you more problems than you already have."

She nodded jerkily and took my hand so I could guide her up to the loft. I could feel her palm quiver against my own.

"By the way, did you save my laptop?"

With all the drama of almost watching her get run over, I had forgotten all about the reason I was waiting for her in the parking lot in the first place.

"No. It was DOA, but I did get most of your Math Theory shit onto a new hard drive. You're right; it's an easy class and you shouldn't be failing it."

She made a light noise behind me and I didn't bother trying to give her a tour of the place since everything was really in one room and she could see everything I owned in one glance. I took her right to the tiny bathroom and pushed open the door.

"Great. And the good news keeps on coming." She sounded so sad, so defeated, it twisted something hard at the center of my chest.

"I got you a new one." I gave her a little nudge so I could reach around her to crank on the water in the shower. "I think you should try and rinse out as much of the gravel as you can in the shower first. The water is either the temperature of the sun or of the Antarctic, so you'll have to pick whichever one hurts less."

I leaned back and paused because she was staring up at me with huge blue eyes the color of the summer sky. I could float away and get lost in them with very little effort.

"You bought me a new computer?" Her voice was barely a whisper.

"Yeah, and you're gonna take it and tell me why someone really might have it in for you, and then I'm going to find whoever it is and make them think twice about their current life decisions."

She opened her mouth to argue, or to say thank you, but she didn't get the chance to do either because I got a text from Aldo saying he was out front and needed a way to get the BMW inside the gates. I also decided he had much more to do for me before his debt was going to be wiped clean.

"Take a shower, Bry. Clean up, and when I get back I'll help you get the rest of the grit out, wrap you up, and send you home."

I was halfway out the bathroom door when she put a hand on my arm and drew me to a stop. I looked down at her tiny, shaking hand and then into her lovely, sad eyes. I was going to strangle whoever was responsible for putting that look there.

"Race . . ." She trailed off and all I wanted to do was scoop her up and put her somewhere flat and climb all over her. She was hurt, and it was totally inappropriate, but my libido didn't care. "Why are you doing this? I'm friends with your sister, not you. I've never even been very nice to you. Why are you being so helpful?"

My motivations seemed to be in question to anyone and everyone. It was starting to get old. I reached out a finger and moved the longer, front part of her hair off of her face so I could hook it around the delicate shell of her ear. The action made her shiver.

"I take care of my own, Brysen. Like it or not, that includes you."

I stepped away from her as her pretty mouth fell into a little O of surprise. I was getting to the bottom of what was going on with Brysen Carter, and while I was at it, I was kicking down that stupid wall she had erected between us. Like Nassir had said earlier—there was only one way to do things, and that was my way. Whatever she was dealing with, whatever control she was missing in her life, she was about to have all kinds of the worst sort of help getting it back. I just hoped she was ready to give a little so I didn't destroy both of us in the process of pounding ruthlessly against those shields she was constantly throwing up.

Chapter 5

Brysen

THE WATER BURNED EVERY place on my body where the skin had ripped off. The runoff swirled pink and dingy with leftover parking-lot goo, blood, and grime as it ran over my feet. Race hadn't been lying, the shower was inferno hot, but it felt nice because I was ice cold on the inside.

I had no clue what was going on, why anyone would want to hurt me, but there was no trying to explain away the fact that I had almost been run down tonight. Along the way of giving up my life, of trying to take care of my family, it appeared I had managed to upset someone enough that they wanted to hurt me. I never went anywhere, kept my nose clean, and never wandered out of the basic suburban box my life had always existed in, so it didn't make any sense. It was scary, and I didn't even know where to start with trying to figure it out. For right now I was going to let the superhot water wash away as much of the blood and aching in my bones as it could, and try not to jump on Race in all his protective and glowering hotness. No one had claimed me as their own in a very long time. Add in the fact he was even more sexy and alluring when he was being threatening and up in arms on my behalf, and my resolve was flickering out like a low-burning wick on a candle.

He left me a T-shirt and a pair of sweatpants Dovie had left behind when she was staying here with him, but I left both of them sitting on the counter next to the cracked sink and just wrapped myself up in a threadbare towel he had tossed haphazardly on the closed toilet. I still needed his help fishing a nice-size rock out of my elbow, and the outside of my knee looked like someone had attacked it with a cheese grater. Cleaning it was going to hurt like a bitch and I was going to be bummed out if I ended up with a gnarly scar. Right now I didn't feel like I had very much going for me, and it would suck if the one thing I had always been able to fall back on—my looks—was suddenly compromised as well. I stuck my tongue out at my reflection in the mirror and twisted my hands through my hair to wring out some of the water. I looked like hell, but it fit since I felt like hell.

I pulled open the door a fraction and called Race's name. There wasn't a response, and I was about to go explore the tiny space he'd brought me to, when he suddenly appeared in front of me, green eyes flashing and that dimple indenting his cheek. No boy who was as bad as he was should be that beautiful. It wasn't fair. Somewhere along the way he had ditched his button-down shirt and was now only wearing a white wife-beater, and his hair was sticking up in a sexy mess all over his head. He had a bottle of peroxide in his hand, along with a clean white towel.

"Let's fix you up."

I nodded and took a step back into the bathroom. It was too small a place to be in with him considering my lack of clothes and how much I wanted to be all over him. I felt my heart dip and his mossy gaze scanned over me from head to toe, turning darker and blacker the more naked skin his eyes took in.

"Sit down."

I propped myself on the closed toilet lid and gazed at him with big eyes. "Be gentle."

The dark center of his eyes flared and the corners of his sexy mouth turned down.

"What's going on, Brysen? Why is someone fucking with you?"

I could only shake my head and shrug. It was a bad idea because the towel already didn't offer much coverage, and with each move I made it dipped lower across the swell of my breasts. Neither one of us mentioned it, but both of our breathing changed. Mine rapid, his shallow and raspy.

"I don't know. Honestly. For the most part, I'm a pretty nice person, I mind my own business . . . I don't know." My voice was barely a whisper that quickly turned into a yelp of pain when the white cloth soaked in peroxide hit the raw surface of my knee. I jolted so hard, the towel almost fell all the way down.

Race closed his eyes briefly and sank to his knees in front of me so he could grab my arm. He straightened it out with light fingers and looked me dead in the eye.

"The gunshots at the party were about me, not you. I was there to collect money, and the kid who owed it wasn't happy about it. Why did you think someone was shooting at you?"

His long fingers softly manipulated the cut. I felt him stroke over the rock that was embedded in there still, and then heard him swear under his breath.

"I need to find something to get that out with."

As he rose effortlessly to his feet and loomed over me I gulped and blinked back tears that suddenly filled my eyes.

"I got home from the party and someone sent me a text from a strange number telling me that I looked pretty and that they were sorry they missed me. It felt really threatening, like they missed me with a bullet, ya know?"

It sounded so crazy, so far-fetched, but the way his teeth clenched and his jaw went hard made me glad to share it with someone who wasn't going to just dismiss my concern.

"You have no idea who it could be?"

All I could do was shake my head. He just stared at me for a second before disappearing and coming back with a pair of tweezers. I wasn't looking forward to this part, but having his hands on me was distracting, and being this close to him, breathing him in, was a sensual treat I wouldn't ever typically be awarded.

"Keep your arm straight." He took my hand and put it on his shoulder before sinking down on his knees in front of me again. He was so pretty. I just wanted to touch him, to pet him and stroke him all over. I vaguely wondered if he got away with all he did just because it was impossible to fight against the pull of all that magnetism.

I curled the edge of my fingernails into the cords of his neck when the tip of the tweezers started poking around the wound. I swore, clamped my teeth down hard on my bottom lip, and tried to stop from screaming. It hurt, really hurt, even though he was moving slowly and trying his best to do as minimal damage as possible. I tasted blood, heard him say my name, felt the burn of peroxide, and then his mouth was on top of mine.

His hands were in my hair. His tongue was twisted and turned all around my own. I was pulled off the toilet and onto his lap as he fell back with a dull thud against the wall. Race wasn't a small guy, and the bathroom wasn't exactly roomy, which meant

I was all over him and the towel I had been using for minimal coverage was a thing of the past. I was very naked, very on top of him. His rock hardness and the sharp sting of the tile against my injured knee barely registered because all the parts of me touching all the parts of him were hot and tingly and things like cuts and scrapes didn't matter. His chest under the thin material of his white wife-beater was strong and warm. I wanted to curl into him, fall into him, and put everything else I was always holding on to down. As dangerous as he was for me to get tangled up with, feeling him, pressing into him, made me feel safe, and had security floating around my head in such a heady way that I practically mauled him trying to get closer.

I tunneled my fingers through his hair and heard him groan into my mouth. If he was going to adopt the habit of kissing me senseless every single time he felt I needed a distraction, I was going to have to make a point of getting out of sorts around him more often. I felt his body react underneath mine. Felt him get even harder through the layer of denim separating us, and his hands got tighter in my hair. There was always an edge to Race, a razor-fine line that lurked behind all that Midas glow he possessed that hinted at a stronger core, a wilder side to him that I think he kept out of sight from the rest of the world. He was so much more than a disinherited rich kid, had so much more going on than being Bax's partner in crime, but it was so easy to be blinded by his sheer beauty and suave manner that I think all the facets to him were easily overlooked. Right now, with his hands getting a little rough, his breath rasping in and out, and his eyes glinting all hot and dark, there was no mistaking that he was capable of doing really bad things to me . . . God, how I wanted him to do all of them.

He pulled back a little and slicked his tongue over the full curve of his bottom lip. That gesture alone could have made me spontaneously orgasm, but he trailed his thumbs along the edge of my jaw, used the edges of his palms to tilt my head back a little, and leaned forward to kiss me softly behind the ear. His mouth was indulgent, sucking, tickling, and knew every single secret spot I seemed to have. I was shivering so hard and whimpering in such a needy way, I had to do something to stop myself from coming apart in his hands like a cheaply made toy. He was handling me like he owned me. Like he had been doing it forever. Like he wanted to give me back everything I had given away in the last year, and I was going to start crying again if I didn't do something with my hands or with my mouth.

I pressed forward, bent down so I could seal my mouth back over his, and kissed him with all the desperation, all the fearless anticipation, I could feel swirling around in the tiny space with us. I had never been locked in such a passionate embrace, been so turned on and worked up in such an unromantic setting, but none of it mattered because Race's touch was electric and everything about him and me just seemed to HAVE to happen.

I used my teeth to nip at his lip, swirled my tongue across his, and breathed him in and out. I clutched at his silky hair and tried to refrain from grinding on the erection that was becoming more and more persistent where my legs were spread wantonly across his lap. I wasn't a sexual dynamo or a shrinking violet. I was just a normal girl with normal needs, but something about this guy made my head go crazy, made my blood go hot and fiery, and I wanted to do things, say things that I had never even thought of before. That was the danger of Race, always making me want what I couldn't and shouldn't have.

He pulled back from my ravenous kiss and we looked at each other with lust-filled eyes. We were both breathing like long-distance runners and there was no missing the reaction from either of our bodies to the other. I was all liquid and needy, he was all hard and ready. I think all we were waiting for was the other to give a solid green light. I was naked and sprawled all over him, and I didn't know how much more welcoming I could be when he suddenly used the edge of one of his knuckles and guided it across my collarbone and down the center of my chest. It made my heart skip a beat and both of my nipples pucker into painful points of readiness, knowing they were undoubtedly his destination.

I exhaled his name, curled my fingers tighter into his hair, and prepared myself for what was going to come next. His mouth on me . . . anywhere on me . . . yes, please. Only all the excitement, all the arousal and pulsating need that was throbbing between my legs and in my blood, went still, froze when I heard my phone go off from somewhere in the midst of the pile of torn and bloody clothes I had left on the floor. Race was good, really good, and I was turned on, more so than I think I had ever been in my life, but the ring tone was the one I had assigned specifically to Karsen, and it struck me in a blinding rush that I should've been home hours ago. I hadn't told anyone what was going on or where I was. A call this late from her when she had school the next morning couldn't mean anything good.

I scrambled up off Race's rock-hard form so fast his head actually thunked back against the wall with an echoing sound. I pawed through the pile of clothes until I found my cell and sprang to my feet. I pulled on the long-abandoned T-shirt resting on the sink and wandered out of the tiny bathroom.

"Karsen?"

"Brysen, will you be home soon?" My sister's voice was shaky and unsure. I wanted to kick myself. I looked over my shoulder as Race followed me out into the minuscule living space.

"I will. Something came up after work and I just lost track of time. I'll be there in twenty. Why are you still up?"

I heard her sigh and then sniffle like she was crying and I swore at myself silently.

"Mom came out of her room a little while ago and got mad at Dad for something. He shut the door to the office and she went into the kitchen and started throwing things all around. She was screaming and yelling that no one in this family appreciates her and that she could just disappear and we would never notice. She broke all the dishes. I went in to tell her I would clean it up and she screamed at me that I was a worthless pain in the ass."

Now I swore out loud and tugged hard enough on my hair that it hurt.

"Just go to your room and stay there. Ignore her, Karsen. She's just in one of her moods." I was sure it was fueled by vodka or something else, but that was still no excuse. My little sister didn't deserve to be the target of that kind of unjustified anger.

I heard her whimper a little and then take a deep breath. "I'm sorry. You shouldn't have to rush home to deal with this."

I just shook my head. There was no one else who could do it. I tried my best to keep the house dry, to keep what was basically a loaded weapon out of my mother's hands, but every time I turned around it was like I was being circumvented and another bottle of vodka appeared. "I'll see you in a minute."

I ended the call and turned to find Race watching me with curious eyes. All the dark and lusty black had retreated back into

the color of fresh pine and there was no running from the probing quality of his gaze. I took the sweatpants he held out to me,
even though Dovie was way shorter than me. I needed to cover
up the damage to my skin as much as possible. I didn't need to
give Karsen any more reason to freak out for the night.

"I need to get home."

He tilted his head a little and ran his hands over his messy
hair. I wanted to sigh and rub up against him like a cat.

"I'll follow you."

I bit down on my lip and fought back an automatic rejection.
Having him follow me home made this feel like something more
than an almost hookup. He lifted one blond brow and walked
over to the couch, where his abandoned shirt was lying.

"Someone tried to run you over a couple hours ago, Bry. You
really think I'm letting you out of here on your own right now?"

I wanted to tell him that I appreciated it, that no one had
kept an eye on me for way longer than I wanted to admit to.

"Thanks, Race."

He didn't say anything else, just waited for me to get myself
situated, and then guided me out of the loft part of the garage
into the part that actually had all the cars. I wasn't a mechani-
cal girl but even I could tell there was way more than basic car
repair happening under the place Race was calling home. We
walked outside and I had to admit I was surprised and pleased
that the BMW was there in one piece and unscathed.

"It must be nice to have minions."

He pulled the driver's door open for me and flashed that
dimple at me. That dimple was going to be my utter downfall, I
just knew it, and so did my vagina.

"I can give or take a minion. It's having the authority and the power to make shit happen that's nice."

I looked at Race over the frame of the door and blinked at him. "Is that why you're doing what you're doing? The power?"

I wanted to ask how he could be so comfortable in a role that had people pulling guns on him and putting him in danger. He didn't seem like a cavalier person. There was too much working behind those forest-colored eyes and under all of that glorious hair on the top of his head.

The dimple got a little deeper and he pushed off the car, making the muscles in his shoulders ripple and my tummy dip.

"In a place like this, there aren't very many good people running around. That means there are a lot of bad things happening under the surface and a lot of bad people doing those things. I'm not a bad guy, Brysen, but I'm not a good guy either. I'm just enough of both to keep a handle on those bad things to stop them from spilling over and infecting the few good ones left in this godforsaken place. That's why I do what I do."

I gulped and tried to tell myself that this didn't make a difference, but it really did. He smirked at me and turned to walk to his flashy car.

"Besides, someone needs to get paid to do it, might as well be me. I don't have a trust fund anymore."

There it was. The two sides of him that made him unpredictable and hard to really get my head around. Altruistic and selfless while, in turn, being arrogant and flippant about his current circumstances.

I got in my car and waited for him to get the big, metal gate open so I could exit the compound. It was an odd place for him to be living. It was industrial, more a fortress than any kind of home, and it was right in the center of the Point, which automatically lent itself to a sort of filthy, postapocalyptic feel. For all his posturing about not being part of this place, Race oozed an essence of wealth and refinement that was just part of his genetic makeup. Living in a place that didn't even really have furniture or anything to make it welcoming or comforting spoke to something greater going on with him. If my own living circumstances weren't so all over the place, there was a really solid chance I would spend an inordinate amount of time trying to unearth the deeper subtext behind his choices.

The drive out of the city was fast, mostly because I was in a rush and worried about what was happening at my house, and partly because I was subconsciously trying to outrun the man and the red sports car behind me. I knew that scene in the bathroom wasn't leaving my mind anytime soon, and I also knew if Karsen hadn't called and interrupted, I would've taken a step with Race that would fundamentally alter the relationship we had.

All the lights were off in the front of the house when I pulled into the driveway. I took a long second to collect myself, found a long-sleeved sweater in the backseat of the car to cover my arm, and climbed out of the car. I was just going to wave Race on, hope he just kept driving, but he stopped and got out of the car, the new Mac clasped in one hand. Crap. I had forgotten all about the computer.

He didn't give me a chance to say anything, just shoved the lightweight laptop in my hands, bent down, and pressed a hard, marking kiss to my parted lips and told me, "Keep your eyes peeled for anything weird until I can get a handle on who might be screwing with you. Forward me any more shitty text messages, and look over the notes I saved for you. I rearranged them in a different order. I don't know who is teaching that class, but they are clearly an idiot and should never have gotten tenure."

All I could do was gape at him as he turned on his heel and went back to the Mustang.

"Race . . ." I called his name and he looked at me over his broad shoulder. I didn't know what else to say to him, so he grinned at me and I just shook my head.

"This"—he pointed a finger between him and me as he pulled open the car door—"is happening. Maybe not now because it isn't a good time for you, and maybe not later because I might not be around all that long, but at some point in between, sooner or later, it's going down. Be ready for it, Brysen."

How could anyone ever be ready for that? I practically ran inside when I heard the motor on his car rev up. I slammed the front door behind me and marched toward the kitchen, full of so many different emotions that I could taste all the different sweet and sour flavors of them on my tongue.

My mom didn't just break every dish we had; she had also pulled everything out of the fridge and splattered the contents along the floors and counters. All of the cabinets were empty. The water in the sink was running, and it looked like she had taken the entire jug of dishwashing liquid and poured it all along the floor. It was a mess, a nightmare that was totally preventable and unnecessary, just like the current state of my life. I wanted to kick something, namely both my parents, but that wouldn't get me anywhere, so I ground my teeth together and went upstairs to set the expensive gift from Race down on my bed and check on my sister. It was going to take hours to clean the kitchen up, and that was after I checked on my mom and ripped my dad a new one. Not that either of those things would do any good. Nothing ever seemed to change.

I knocked on Karsen's door lightly and waited to see if she would respond. I kind of hoped she had gone to bed and forgotten about the scene from downstairs, but no such luck. I actually heard the lock on the door snick open. She was so scared that she had locked herself in her room.

"Hey. You all right in there?"

Her big brown eyes were so wide in her face it made her look like a cartoon character.

"I'm glad you're home. Did you see the kitchen?"

I nodded and reached out to fluff her soft hair.

"Yeah. Don't worry about it, sprite. I'll get it cleaned up."

She shook her head slowly from side to side and I saw her bottom lip quiver.

"Dad just ignored the whole thing, Brysen. He just shut the door to his office and let her rant and rave like nothing was going on. I screamed at him to help, but he just wouldn't."

Of course he wouldn't. He was too busy locked away behind his door pretending like he didn't have a solid hand in the steady decline that was going on inside the walls of this house. And we all knew the booze had to come in through the front door somehow. He was a master at turning a blind eye to his part in the devastation of this family.

"I think it's hard for him. It just takes some time to adjust to a new way of living with each other."

That was bullshit but I hoped Karsen loved me enough to let it slide.

"How much time? It feels like it has been forever." She was preaching to the choir. It still felt like forever to her and she had me acting as a buffer between her and how bad things really were. She had no clue how long this year felt like to me.

"It'll be fine, Karsen. Just finish your homework. Stay on top of your schoolwork so you can be valedictorian and get a full ride to college. Once you're out there in the real world, everything that happens here is just secondary and you get to focus on building your own life the way you want it."

I took a step back and gave her a sad smile. She reached out a hand and grabbed my wrist. Some of the sadness left her coffee-colored eyes and she grinned at me.

"So who was the guy?"

Ugh . . . she would have had to be looking out the window when Race kissed me.

"Just a guy."

"Is he what came up after work?"

Oh, he had definitely been up, all right. I was going to need another shower, this one cold, if I had any hope of getting to sleep tonight.

"My laptop crashed and he tried to fix it for me. Remember Dovie? That's her brother."

Karsen made the "no way" face everyone made when I mentioned the relationship between Dovie and Race.

"He's pretty."

"Very pretty." I couldn't argue the fact. "He's also really complicated, bossy, and I have zero time to try and figure him out. I'm gonna go stick my head in Mom's room, so take care of business and go to bed."

She let my arm go and muttered so softly I almost didn't hear her, "Thank you for coming home."

I knew she didn't just mean today.

I felt my shoulders droop a little and yet another sigh rattle in my chest. It wasn't like I had a choice. It was always one more mess to clean up and they didn't seem like they were going to come to an end anytime soon.

Chapter 6

Race

I HADN'T BEEN ABLE to sleep for shit. Not with the taste of Brysen still on my tongue and the image of that car heading right for her playing in slow motion behind my closed eyelids. I was a numbers guy by nature and I hated it when things didn't add up. Why would an innocent girl, a college student with no ties to anything scandalous or dangerous, suddenly be caught up in a threatening and scary situation? It didn't make any sense to me, and there was nothing I hated more than not understanding the way things worked.

The wafting smell of strong coffee hit my nose and made it twitch. I had an arm raised up over my eyes and was sprawled uncomfortably on the couch, which is how I typically crashed out. I hadn't heard anyone come up the stairs and figured the only two people who would venture into my sanctuary were my sister or Bax. I groaned and sat up to stretch out the kink that had formed a solid ball between my shoulder blades and blinked in surprise when I saw that my visitor was neither of the people I would've expected. I rubbed hard hands over my hair, which was sticking up everywhere, and yawned so hard my jaw popped.

"What are you doing here, Titus?"

The detective looked enough like my best friend that there was no mistaking they were brothers. Titus was bigger and his eyes were blue instead of midnight black, but he had the same hard, hewn face, the same constantly frowning mouth, and the same black hair. Titus was in his late twenties but he looked a little bit older and he always looked tired. He even had a small white spot of hair growing at his temple that had just appeared after the fateful showdown with Novak. Being a cop in this place was a thankless job, and it was starting to look like it was wearing on those already overburdened shoulders.

"What are you doing here, Race?" he asked.

He walked over from the tiny kitchenette and handed me a mug of steaming coffee. I looked up at him from under my eyebrows and didn't answer the question.

"Didn't I just ask you that? How did you get in?"

He snorted and took a seat on the only other piece of furniture that existed in the barren space.

"Bax is good at breaking and entering, but I'm better. Want to tell me that you have papers for every single one of those cars sitting in the garage and on the lot down there?"

I flashed him a grin and slumped back on the couch so I could rest my neck on the cushions.

"Do I need to? Have any of them been reported stolen?"

We stared at each other for a long, tense minute because he knew none of them were. That was the thing about taking a gambler's ride, my clients were so far in it was easier to just let me have the car than it was to try and get it back. The vice would always win, and I would always break even.

Titus grunted and his eyes narrowed at me a fraction.

"Do you have any idea what you're doing, Race? How deep in this are you willing to go? If things go bad, do you think you can do what Bax did? Serve a nickel behind bars, let Dovie be out here on her own? Have you thought about an end game in all of this?"

I took a sip of coffee and shrugged. "Dovie won't be alone as long as Bax is around, and I learned the hard way that even if I might have a perfect end planned out, the Point always has a different idea. I'm willing to go in as deep as I have to in order to keep someone like Novak from ending back up on top."

"Doesn't that mean you run the risk of becoming that man, Race?"

That was something I struggled with every day. How to get elbow-deep in the filth, get my hands dirty, and not let it change the man I was.

"Yes, but it's a risk I have to take."

"You know the trial for the rest of Novak's crew is eventually going to start. What kind of witnesses are you going to make? Bax is still boosting cars, you're running an entire criminal enterprise, and Nassir is so goddamn slippery that only an idiot would trust him. What happens when Benny and the rest of them get off and want the city back?"

The dig was not lost on me.

"Then they'll have to take it from us, brick by brick."

We stared at each other some more and his big chest rose and fell in a heavy sigh.

"Putting Bax in jail fucking sucked, Race, but I did it. I hope you know that if you step wrong—make one mistake—I'll do the same to you and I won't feel bad about it."

I knew it. I counted on it. Knowing that a moral, righteous man had his eyes on me constantly was one of the safeguards I had in place to keep my soul from being tainted by the things I was doing.

"Fair enough. Why are you really here?"

He set the coffee down on the floor by his feet because I wasn't even civilized enough to have something as basic as an end table or a coffee table in the loft. He rose to his full and impressive height and meandered back into the kitchen area to grab a manila folder that I hadn't seen before. He tossed it on my lap and pointed at it.

"Recognize either of those guys?"

I looked at him blankly, set my own mug of coffee down between my bare feet, and flipped open the file. A hard shudder racked my body and bile burned up the back of my throat at the first image that was on top of the papers in the folder. A body was broken and twisted. The neck wrenched around at an unnatural angle, the skin mottled blue with bruises and death. I had to blink a couple times to get my head to stop reeling and it took more than one deep breath before I could flip to the second image. Again, the body was abused, treated to a brutal beating, and this time there was a gory and gaping hole right between the sightless, staring eyes. I stared at the photos and tried to decide if it was better to lie or tell the truth. Considering this was Titus, the odds were he already knew the answer to the question he was asking me.

"The guy with the broken neck is a kid who lost his ass on a Texas A&M game a week ago. When I went to collect, he lost his shit and pulled a gun at a party full of people near the university. I took off before the cops showed up. The second guy got handsy with Honor over at Spanky's, and the last I saw of him, Chuck had given him a very clear lesson on why that was a bad idea. He was still breathing when I left. Bleeding and missing some teeth, but most definitely breathing."

I moved the gruesome images to the side and looked at the file underneath. Both men had been found within hours of each other, both behind different clubs that Nassir ran out of warehouses. I whistled out through my teeth and shut the top of the folder. Titus's blue gaze was steady and focused on me.

"You don't think I had anything to do with this?"

I asked it, but really it was a statement of fact. If he thought I was involved, then this conversation would have involved handcuffs not coffee.

"No, but I knew about the gun and the party, and the guy from the club tried to come in and press charges, but we took one look at the dancer's face and sent him on his way. Plus Nassir is a lot of things, but a dumb-ass isn't one of them. Leaving not one, but two bodies behind your own club isn't something he would ever do. What it tells me is someone is trying to send you guys a message . . . one you'd best pay attention to. A few cars go missing, some money changes hands, all that is easy to overlook. Bodies start falling, people start dying, and that gets a lot harder for the law to ignore."

I nodded numbly in agreement and rubbed the back of my neck with my hand.

"Any word on who might be trying to communicate this particular message?"

He shrugged. "Who knows? Someone trying to test the limits of whatever kind of agreement you've worked out with Nassir? Someone angling to get you both out of the way? Someone with a grudge who thinks they can set you up? In this place, the suspects are always too numerous to name, so you better be playing the game to win."

Well, losing wasn't an option, and I only ever played to win. I got to my feet and stretched my arms up over my head. I groaned out loud when I heard my spine crack all the way down. Titus rolled his eyes at me.

"Why are you still living in this place?"

"Because I feel comfortable here."

I was never going back to the palatial mansion my parents owned on the Hill. I wasn't going to pretend like what I did had a place in the quiet burb like Bax and Dovie, and living in a run-down apartment was no different from crashing at the loft. Plus the security was better here.

"How can you be comfortable? You don't even have any furniture. What do you do when you bring a girl over? Tell her to give you five minutes to get a rubber on and pull the bed out of the couch? Not even you have that much game, pretty boy."

He was wrong. I had more than enough game to sell that and anything else I wanted to pretty much any chick who came along. The problem was there hadn't been anyone in longer than I wanted to admit that I was interested in trying to sell anything to. Except for Brysen, and with her, man, I didn't need a bed, didn't need much of anything to get the mood going. Just the flutter of her eyelashes and the way her pretty mouth pouted and curled and I was ready to make things happen on the drop of a dime. If her phone hadn't rung yesterday, there was a good chance I would have christened my bathroom floor in the most spectacular manner.

I snorted at him and reached for the pair of jeans I had discarded the night before.

"Why do you care where I'm crashing? Bax is playing domestic house cat, he has a good life and a good girl. Are you trying to turn me into your pet project now that your little brother has his life all figured out?"

He swore at me and stalked to the opening that led to the hallway over the garage. He looked at me over his shoulder with a scowl.

"I know you aren't a bad dude, Race. Your life got fucked, but that's not anything different than happened to the rest of us. Yeah, it had to do with the choices you made, but I respect that you were doing what you felt like you had to do in order to keep your sister safe. I just wonder how long you can be a guy with dirty hands who still claims to want to live a clean life."

I didn't know the answer to that, didn't really know that it was possible either, but I was going to give it my best shot to make it happen.

"I wash my hands when I get home, Titus."

He barked out a bitter-sounding laugh. "I wish it was that easy."

I followed him to the top of the stairs and asked as an afterthought, "What would you do if you had a friend you thought might be being stalked?"

He stopped and turned on the stairs to gaze up at me.

"Why do you think that?"

"She's been getting weird text messages, and last night someone took aim at her with a car. She's just a normal chick. Goes to school, lives out in the burbs, kinda by Dovie and Bax. She even lives at home. This is not a girl who should be feeling threatened and scared. It doesn't have a place in the kind of life she's got going on."

Concern flashed across his face. "She got a wound-up ex or something you can look into?"

I shrugged because I didn't know if the pissed off TA or legion of spurned suitors really counted as being wound up enough to be dangerous.

"I don't know. I have a guy who owes me a favor or six keeping an eye on her for a minute, but I don't like it. It doesn't add up to me, and that means it's going to bug me until I get it all figured out."

"You need to be looking out for yourself. Add a pretty girl in the mix and you end up with a weak spot anyone from a million miles away can see. Just ask my brother."

"I dunno, Titus. Bax got wrapped up in Dovie and suddenly cared enough to take on the entire world for her. Seems to me that when you add a pretty girl into the mix, that's when you give a dangerous man something to really be dangerous for."

He tilted his head to the side. "Maybe. If you get any solid info—a name, a number, a license plate on the car—give me a holler and I'll see if I can run anything down for you."

I told him thank you and watched him disappear into the bowels of the garage. I was sure he was making a mental note of all the plates on the cars so he could run them against any that were reported as stolen. Titus was a good man, but he was a cop first. He might let Bax and me slide without any hard proof, but if we ever gave him a reason to, he would have no issue putting both Bax and me behind bars, and I knew that in his mind he would be doing it for our own good.

I trudged to the shower of doom and decided after a restless
night full of sexual frustration that it was going to be ice cubes
and not fire today. The way my neck creaked and cracked really
did give testimony to the fact that maybe I should look into getting a bed for the place. And the truth of the matter was, I knew,
just knew, things with Brysen and me were far from over and I
didn't want to be the schmuck trying to put the moves on her in
a place that had one chair, a foldout couch, and only a bottle of
Scotch in the freezer. She deserved better than that. I could offer
her better than that, but then what? She would leave and I would
have to pretend like I wasn't living this life where I was constantly on the alert, constantly thinking twenty moves ahead.

Really, one of the reasons I was living so sparsely, so unfettered, was because I knew what it was like to lose everything.
I had had all the opulence, all the material things that any one
person could want in order to live a materialistic and wasteful
life. Losing that hadn't hurt nearly as much as realizing that the
family, the illusion that provided it all, was just made of smoke
and mirrors. My dad was an attempted murderer and his hands
were just as filthy as my own. My mom . . . well, I didn't know
how complacent she was about everything, and I made a con-
scious effort not to really find out. I still had one parent I could
stand to be in the same room with, not that my father allowed
it. Ever since he had disowned me, my contact with either one of
them had been limited to a few one-word text messages.

When you didn't have much, losing it didn't seem that bad.

I got dressed for the day, shoved a stale bagel in my face
for some energy, and made my way down to the garage floor. I
wanted to swing by Nassir's and see what his take on the bodies
was. If we had a common enemy, we needed to put our heads

together and figure out who it might be. Plus it was fight night this weekend and I wanted to know what the odds on his fighters were. Nassir never did anything as simple as let two equally matched men go at each other; he always had a trick up his sleeve to make things more interesting, and now that we were in business together, I had to know just what those tricks were so I could make sure the lines and the odds on each fighter paid out to the highest potential.

Bax was talking to one of the legitimate mechanics that he had working for him. The actual garage operation since he took over had become a viable moneymaking venture. No one knew old muscle cars like Bax, and the product he was cranking out was unparalleled in quality. He didn't need to be helping me out on the side like he was, but I was grateful he did.

He tilted his chin at me and his dark eyes flashed. "You see Titus?"

"Yeah, and now I'm going to go and talk to Nassir."

"You don't think he coulda put a bullet in the guy who roughed up Honor?"

"I know he could have put a bullet in him, only I was there and the guy was alive when I left. Nassir wouldn't kill a guy and just toss him out the back door. He's fucked, but not that fucked. And the kid . . ." I shook my head sadly. "That was unnecessary. He was just a dumb jock who lost a bet; there is no reason he should be in an alley with his neck broken."

"Whoever is behind it means business, and I think this is probably just the start of it."

"I know."

"You going to be able to handle it?"

"Everyone keeps asking me that. I'm not sure what other

options I have. I let go and someone else takes over the city, runs it right back to where Novak had it. Not to mention, if I do that, I prove to everyone that I really am nothing more than a bored rich kid playing at being a criminal. My ego alone won't stand for that."

He chuckled.

"I saw the BMW on the video from last night. You and the icy blonde, huh?"

I lifted an eyebrow and knocked him on the edge of the shoulder with my fist.

"If it was me and the blonde, I would be in a far better mood than I am now and I wouldn't have let Titus stick around for nearly as long as he did. She's got some trouble brewing, and I just want to help her out. Did Dovie ever mention if she noticed anyone giving Brysen a hard time?"

He lifted an eyebrow at me and rubbed his thumb along the edge of his jaw. The star that was tattooed by his eye crinkled a little as he squinted in thought.

"I don't think so, but I don't listen to all the girly crap. I think she lives with her folks or something, though. Kinda hard to have a man if you can't give him anything to look forward to coming home to."

I agreed, but after that phone call last night, I was starting to think her reasons for living at home were as complex and as deep as my reasons for wanting to keep my finger firmly on the pulse of the Point.

"True. I don't know what's going on, but I'm going to find out. Maybe mention to my sister that her friend has an unwanted admirer and let her know to keep her eyes open when they are together."

The corners of his mouth turned down and his eyes went a scary, flat black. "Dovie gets hurt because someone has it in for her little friend and I will destroy anyone and anything involved."

Good. That's exactly what I wanted to hear.

"None of us live in a bubble, my friend. We all gotta look out for one another because no one else gives a shit if we make it out alive."

He grunted in agreement and turned back to the Jaguar he was in the middle of pulling the engine out of. Bax was always a man of few words.

I went to the Mustang and cruised through the city until I got to the old dog-food factory that was Nassir's main base of operations. It was the big club, the big draw for kids from all over the city. It was hidden, hard to find, impossible to get into if you didn't know someone, and totally different on the outside than it was on the inside. In the harsh light of day it looked like any dilapidated building that had been foreclosed on. But at night, when the sun went down and the miscreants came out to play, it was a hive of activity and on trend with any fancy nightclub in any major metropolitan city in the world.

Some nights it was a rave. Some nights it was a disco. Some nights it was a dirty, brutal fight club. Some nights it was den of sex and debauchery. Whatever the masses wanted, whatever the people clamored for, Nassir gave it to them—and then some. He really was a brilliant businessman on top of being a stone-cold killer and a soulless monster.

I walked down a set of rickety stairs that barely felt like they would hold my weight. At the end was a giant metal door that had a keypad entry similar to the ones installed at the garage. I punched in the code and waited for the approval from whoever was monitoring the security on the inside to open the door all the way. The hallways were empty and smelled like sweat and sex. Like every bad thing that had ever been done inside these walls had sunk into the concrete and just permeated the entire place. I went through another secure door, made my way across the vacant floor of the factory, which just looked industrial and run-down in the daytime, went behind the bar, and climbed a wrought-iron set of stairs that led to the VIP section, which was really just the old catwalks of the factory, and to the back office where I knew Nassir spent most of the day.

His office was as different from the run-down, desolate vibe of the rest of the warehouse as it could be. The entire place was enclosed in smoky, one-way glass that I knew was bulletproof and soundproof. He had monitors that covered the entire wall behind his desk that almost gave the security at the garage a run for its money. His desk was a black lacquer behemoth that sat on a polished marble floor. Nassir was a flashy guy, but he was also a lethal predator. No one that walked into this office would ever be fooled into thinking they were just there for a simple business meeting.

I plopped down in one of the wingbacks across from him and just stared at him while he talked on his cell phone. His dark eyebrows were pitched low on his forehead and his hair was standing up in the front like he had been shoving his hands through it, instead of lying flat in its usual ruthless style. I crossed my ankle on my knee and tapped out a random beat with my fingers while he glowered at me. Nassir didn't play well with others, and now that there was an unknown quantity in the mix, our uneasy truce might prove to be too much for him to handle.

He barked out something in a language I didn't understand

and threw the phone on the desk in front of him with way more force than the action required. He leaned back in his chair and glared at me with glowing eyes.

"If you ask me if I shot that guy, I very well may punch you in the face."

That made me grin.

"You have any idea who might be behind it?"

"Someone clumsy and obvious. It was foolish and gratuitous."

"The kid was overkill."

"The kid was to make a very clear point."

I uncrossed my legs and leaned forward with my forearms resting on my legs.

"What do you want to do about it?"

He grumbled something I didn't quite make out and raked his fingers through his dark hair.

"I'm having one of my guys go through the security footage outside both of the clubs to see if we can see anything. We need to know who to look for before we can decide what we want to do about it."

"All right."

I didn't think we were going to be in agreement about it, but so far, so good. Granted, I didn't trust Nassir, but until he gave me a reason to doubt his judgment, I was okay with handling this one step at a time. It was just logical.

"Now let's talk about the fights this Friday night."

His candy-colored gaze went sharp, and the edges of his mouth dug in at the sides.

"What's there to talk about? I've been doing fight nights as long as you've been running the streets. This isn't anything new."

"Right, but now I'm running the odds and I want to know what magic you're going to pull so that you have a guaranteed winner. If you're gonna play dirty, I want the odds to reflect it."

"That isn't how you make money, Race."

"No, but it is how you make the bet clean."

"Who cares about a clean bet?"

I hooked a thumb at my chest. "I do."

His frown dug in deeper, and we had a tense moment where we just stared at each other without speaking.

"That is naive and foolish. It isn't what this partnership is about."

"Look, I watched you set my best friend up against guys who were doped up, guys with knives stashed on them, guys who were fighting for their lives because you threatened to kill them or their loved ones if they lost, and I never did a goddamn thing about it. You want to weigh the fight in a certain fighter's favor, then that's on you, and we know the crowd loves that shit. But when it comes to the money, it's going to be a clean bet based on real odds. The payouts will be larger, but so will the stakes. Trust me on this."

He didn't want to concede. I could see it all over his face and in his posture, but for whatever reason, he had decided that it was easier to work with me than constantly against me, so he dipped his head in a single nod.

"Kenmore is going in with a healing ACL tear. He thinks he's okay to fight, but the other side knows about the injury and will do their best to take full advantage of it. You can't rule a guy like Kenmore out, though; he fights because he loves it, not for the money."

That meant the odds had to be skewed in the other guy's

favor, but if Kenmore managed to pull out a win, the payout would be enormous for those who were brave enough to bet on the underdog.

"Got it. I'll see you on Saturday."

I pushed up out of the chair and looked back at him when he called my name as I reached the door.

"I know you're in this with me, Race, but if blood gets spilled, are you honestly ready for that?"

Like I said before, I didn't really know much about Nassir's past, just that he had come on the scene about the same time that Bax and I got tangled up with Novak. For the most part he kept the Point alive with entertainment, oiled hands that needed oiling, and made things happen when no one else seemed able to. I had never actually seen him use his hands on anybody—never seen him lift a finger to hurt another person—but there was something about him, some innate quality that swirled under the surface of those unusual eyes that hinted at an untapped wealth of violence and mayhem just waiting to be unleashed.

"I'm more of a take-it-as-it-comes kind of guy, Nassir. I'll do what I have to do in order to make things right and keep things running in a way I think is appropriate. I can't tell you what I am or am not ready for because this place, the way it twists and turns on itself, is always a surprise. You just need to believe me when I say I'll do what I think has to be done."

"You think that's going to be enough?"

"It'll have to be."

I shut the office door behind me and let out the breath I hadn't really been aware I was holding.

I wasn't immune to violence, to the fight it took to make

it in the Point. I just had lofty hopes that when you put a man who prided his brain over his brawn in the driver's seat, some of that day in and day out battle would fade away. I hadn't counted on the very nature of the city, the very heartbeat of the Point, calling for everyone's blood despite my best efforts to calm the beast.

Chapter 7

Brysen

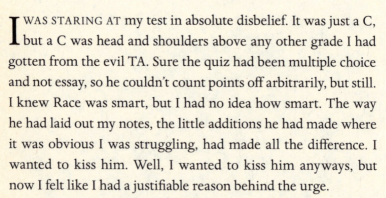

I WAS STARING AT my test in absolute disbelief. It was just a C, but a C was head and shoulders above any other grade I had gotten from the evil TA. Sure the quiz had been multiple choice and not essay, so he couldn't count points off arbitrarily, but still. I knew Race was smart, but I had no idea how smart. The way he had laid out my notes, the little additions he had made where it was obvious I was struggling, had made all the difference. I wanted to kiss him. Well, I wanted to kiss him anyways, but now I felt like I had a justifiable reason behind the urge.

I jolted a little when Drew draped an arm across my shoulders and let out a whistle when he saw the Scantron I was holding on to like it would suddenly fly away.

"How did you pull that off?"

Irritated, I shook him off and put the quiz away in my bag. "I studied."

"I guess your theory about the TA having it in for you was wrong after all."

I pushed some of my hair out of my face and huffed out a breath. "Well, it's not like he can flunk me when we all took the same quiz and I could check my answers against yours or whatever. Eventually he's going to do something obviously malicious and I'll be able to turn him in to the dean of academics." He just hadn't gone that far yet.

Drew bumped into me in a playful gesture and I let out a hiss between my teeth as he inadvertently brushed against my still-healing arm. I was a mess of scabs and ugly bruises and I couldn't shake the feeling that everywhere I went, every time I left my house, someone was watching me. I hadn't received any more texts, there were no more near misses with a runaway car, but my skin was tight and I felt eyes all over me. I hated it, and it was making me jumpy and suspicious of everything and everyone.

"What's wrong?"

Drew's voice was sharp and he grabbed my wrist and pulled me to a stop. Ever since he had given me the third degree about Race, he had been more intrusive, more forceful in the way he was with me. I didn't care for it at all. I pulled my hand back and narrowed my eyes at him.

"I fell leaving work the other night. I got a little banged up and that side took the brunt of it."

He lifted his eyebrows at me and made a face.

"You fell?" The accusation and disbelief in his tone were clear.

I didn't feel like I needed to explain myself to him, and I was about to tell him just that when Adria suddenly bounded over and grabbed me by both of my shoulders. She was bouncing up and down on her toes and babbling so fast I could barely understand her. I reached out both hands and clasped her on her shoulders to keep her still.

"What on earth are you talking about?"

Her eyes were all bright and shiny with excitement. "I got invited to fight night!"

A chill slid down my spine. I had been to fight night. It was gory and brutal. It was uncivilized and inhumane. It was definitely not something to get bouncy and excited about.

"Don't go." My voice was barely a whisper, but she heard it and stopped hopping around to frown at me.

"Why? You know how hard it is to get invited to any of that underground stuff in the Point? You have to know someone who knows someone who knows someone. I've never been. It sounds dangerous and exciting."

To me it sounded like a bored rich girl looking for a thrill. God, I didn't ever want to be like that.

"It's awful. They fight in a circle with people cheering for blood. The fights aren't fair, and real, live people end up getting hurt. Seriously, Adria, it's awful. There are a million better ways to spend a Friday night."

She flipped her hair over her shoulder and took a step away from me. I didn't notice Drew watching the exchange with curious eyes, but I could feel him shift next to me.

"I think you're just jealous."

I blinked because I didn't even have a clue what to say to that. "What?"

"You started working at that crappy restaurant and met Dovie. All of a sudden you have an in with people in the Point, you get in places like fight night and meet guys like Race Hartman. I don't think you want anyone else intruding, like it's your own private club or something."

I was so flabbergasted, all I could do was roll my eyes at her.

"That's nonsense and you know it. I go to work and I go

home. I don't run around the Point after dark leading some double life."

"I don't know, Brysen. You've been acting weirder and weirder lately."

Of course Drew picked that moment to chime in, "You have been more tense and high-strung over the last few months."

Of course I had. My home life was in a shambles, I was failing a class, I more than likely had a homicidal stalker following me around, I was trying to protect my sister, and I was in major lust with a guy who was absolutely the worst person in the world for me to be obsessing over. I didn't need either of them manufacturing reasons for my behavior however I happened to be acting.

I took a step away from both of them and pulled the layer of frost I had perfected over the years around my shoulders like a superhero cape.

"Fight night is terrible, but go if you really feel like it's something you have to witness. I don't have to justify my behavior to either of you, and frankly it pisses me off that you think you can speculate about what my life is like. You don't know; no one does."

I turned on my heel and flounced away with both of them calling after me. I had a good flounce. I chalked it up to the blond hair and long-legged gait, plus all the recent practice I got at home pretending like things that really bothered me were ignorable. I was getting pretty good at brushing off things that really pricked at me. Pretty soon I was going to be numb to all emotion and that equally thrilled me and terrified me. While I would love to shut down the sting of my mom's addiction and instability, would embrace with open arms my heart not hurting every time Karsen looked at me with tears in her eyes, I knew instinctively that missing out on the burn, the tingling anticipa-tion I felt whenever I was around Race, would suck. He made me feel alive, made me feel like I wasn't tied down to the grind of my reality by familial chains and my own weighty sense of responsibility. That would be hard to freeze out, even if I knew it was for the best. We weren't good for each other, had different troubles and problems hounding us, and it made no sense to try and add each other into that mix.

I went to the rest of my classes. Fell in love with my new computer and went to work at the restaurant. Friday nights were always pretty steady, so I was running at a good clip all the way until close. I made some pretty decent tips and was counting out the cash while waiting on Ramon to walk me to my car, when my phone started ringing. Karsen was at another sleepover, so I doubted it was her, and when I saw Adria's name on the display, I promptly ignored it. Ramon waved me to the front door and I scowled as my phone went off once more. Adria again.

I hooked an arm through Ramon's and waited while he scanned the parking lot. I still felt like someone was watching me, and the little hairs on my arms stood straight up. I peered into the darkened lot and looked up at Ramon as my phone went off a third time. I sighed and swiped a finger across the screen.

"What?" I barked the word out and Ramon snorted at me as we cautiously navigated the parking lot.

"Brysen, I need you to come get me." She was crying and sounded hysterical.

"What? Why?"

She made a little hiccuping noise and I could hear all the screaming and cheering from the bloodthirsty crowd in the background. I shivered in response.

"You were right. It's awful. The people here are scary and there is no security or anything. I was drinking with these guys and now I feel weird and I'm scared. Please come and get me. No one else will come down to this part of town this late."

That was because most people were smart enough to know the Point was no place for amateurs after dark. I looked up at Ramon and he shook his head in the negative.

I sighed heavily and pulled open the door to the BMW.

"Fine. I'll come and get you, but maybe next time you might want to listen to me."

She hiccuped again and the line went dead. Ramon clicked his tongue at me and shook his dark head. "You are looking for trouble, pretty girl."

"Someone has to go get her, and I know exactly where the club is."

"Someone who doesn't have a lunatic trying to run them over can go get her. Why don't you call the blond Adonis and ask him to grab her? I bet he's already floating around that part of town on fight night anyway."

I bit my lip. "That's not exactly in the scope of our relationship."

"Bry . . . the guy bought you a new computer and he stares at you like he wants to eat you up. Ask him to collect your sloppy friend and then go give him a proper thank-you."

It sounded so appealing, so easy. Handing something off to someone else to take care of was a pipe dream in my world, though, and I didn't know what I would do if Race actually stepped up to the plate and took care of Adria for me. I would probably fall in love with him. Like I wasn't already halfway there as it was.

"It's fine. I'll go pick her up and drop her at home. She would do it for me."

He lifted a perfectly groomed eyebrow at me and I rolled my eyes.

"Okay, she wouldn't, but I know how bad that place can be, and I can't, in good conscience, just leave her there."

Ramon bent down and pressed a kiss to my forehead as I slid behind the wheel of the car.

"You be careful, Bry. Lotta bad things seem to have it out for you right now."

They sure did. Which sucked, because really, at the heart of who I was, there was a good person there. Maybe at one point I had been spoiled, a little self-absorbed and unaware, but when it came time to put up or shut up, I had done what needed to be done. Where was my good karma for all of that?

As I drove into the Point I noticed that there was this weird line, I could almost see it, where things went from kind of run-down to absolutely decimated. It was like everything, the buildings, the roads, the lights, the very ground the place sat on, and the few brave souls daring enough to stake claim to the wildness of the Point, had just become what this area was all about. There was darkness that had nothing to do with nighttime. There was an oppression that hung in the air that had nothing to do with pollution or smog. There was a film of grime and dirt that had nothing to do with it being the inner city. It was all like the fabric, the threads that wove the Point together were made up of all the worst things that could be found in one place. And the deeper into the heart of the city I drove, the tighter and more obvious those knots and patterns became.

I didn't want to park the BMW and get out and expose

myself to those creepy, crawly eyes I still felt all over me, so I tried calling Adria and telling her to meet me out front. She didn't answer my first call, or the second one, and she didn't reply when I sent her a flurry of angry text messages. I really wanted to turn around and head back home, but the fact that she had told me she was feeling funny after drinking with a couple of guys was mixed with my knowledge of the moral-less heathens that populated places like this, and as a result I couldn't talk myself into abandoning her.

I parked the BMW around the corner, sent a little prayer up that it would be there when I got back, and headed for the ware-house that housed the underground club. There was a pretty good chance I wouldn't even be able to get inside. The door had a code and a security system attached to it. Last time I had been here I had gotten inside only because I was with Dovie.

I shivered a little as soon as I shut the door to the car. I could feel those prying eyes on me, could practically hear footsteps falling in time with my own, and it had fear riding hard at the back of my neck. I picked up the pace and walked around the edge of the old warehouse where I knew the dilapidated stairs that led to the inner sanctum were located. As soon as I cleared the edge of the alley, a heavy hand fell on my arm and I burst out a terrified scream. My heart was in my throat and I jolted back so hard, I toppled over on my butt. I didn't stop screaming even when a mysterious liquid that was on the ground started to seep into the fabric of my pants.

The guy looming over me was thin and twitchy. He had greasy brown hair that was hanging in his eyes, and he looked as afraid of me as I was of him. He was dancing from foot to foot and held both of his hands up in front of him like he was trying to ward me away. I snapped my mouth shut on a gasp and glared up at him.

"What in the hell is wrong with you?"

He shifted around some more and his eyes darted to the side.

"I'm sorry, so sorry. Don't tell Race." He sounded legitimately panicked, and when I groaned and lumbered to my feet, he jumped back from me like I was going to stab him or something.

"What?"

"Race. Don't tell Race I scared you and that you fell. I saw you come around the corner and there was this guy, a big guy, and he was following you. I just wanted to warn you not to go into the alley by yourself."

I tried in vain to brush some of the grossness off my pants, but had no such luck.

"What do you mean some guy was following me? What does Race have to do with anything?"

The guy shoved shaking hands through his gross hair and tugged on the oily strands, obviously upset.

"Race told me to keep an eye on you. I owe him so much money I couldn't say no. There's been a guy, I've seen him a couple times. He's watching you. He followed you here tonight and was behind you when you got out of the car. This alley is dark and isolated on purpose. I didn't want the guy to grab you or some shit. Race would fucking kill me for that, so I grabbed you instead. I wanted to warn you."

He took a few steps back from me and pulled out his phone. I was still trying to get my head around the fact that Race was having someone follow me, when the greasy guy muttered, "I'm gonna call him."

Just then my phone went off with Adria finally returning my calls.

"Where are you?"

I was scared and I was mad. It wasn't a good combination.

"What do you mean?" She sounded sloppy and drunk.

"I came to get you like you asked. Where in the hell are you, Adria?" I wrinkled my nose as a whiff of whatever I had landed in snuck up into my nose. What an awesome way to end the night.

"I left with some guys that were really nice. I'm going to an after party back by the university. You should meet me there."

Oh, for the love of all that was holy. I was going to murder her. I gritted my teeth and clenched my phone so hard in my hand that it hurt.

"Why did you ask me to come get you if you were just going to leave with a bunch of random dudes, Adria?" I was starting to really rethink calling her a friend.

"Oh, loosen up, Bry. You need to get out more. I knew you wouldn't come hang out if I just asked you. You need to live a little. Come to the party! Oh, and bring the blond hottie. I saw him floating around the crowd while I was there; yummy."

I hung up on her and had to seriously fight the urge to throw my phone back into the muck on the ground. I growled— actually growled like a beast—and looked back up at the nervous guy watching me.

"What did the guy who has been following me look like?"

"Yeah, Aldo, what did he look like?"

I spun around, startled at the sound of Race's deep voice. His golden head cleared the top of that nasty stairwell, and I couldn't stop my eyes from rolling greedily over him. He had on dark jeans that were rolled up over well-worn, black cowboy boots, a fitted black sweater that had a hood on it, and over that a dark gray blazer that looked tailored and expensive. He looked as out of place in the dingy alley as I felt.

The guy, Aldo I guess was his name, started pacing back and forth in front of me like a nervous little rodent. I came to the rapid conclusion that I wasn't fond of the people Race did business with.

"A bigger guy, like your size but thicker. At first I thought it was a couple different people, which is why I didn't say anything. He wears a hat or glasses, and one time I think he even had on a wig. And he never drives the same car. One day it was a truck that followed her to work, and then a Volkswagen that followed her from school. I'm not cut out for this shit, Race. I just like to bet on sports."

Race's green eyes drifted over me then over the nervous guy. I saw his chest rise and fall in a heavy sigh.

"Fine. Consider your last marker paid."

"For real?" I could practically feel the guy vibrating with excitement.

"Yeah, but next time you're going to have to pay in actual cash, Aldo. No more solids from me."

The guy nodded and practically darted off into the night.

I crossed my arms over my chest and tried not to flinch when he prowled toward me.

"You were having me followed and didn't bother to mention it? I've been jumping out of my skin all week thinking someone was after me."

Race shrugged and moved until he was totally up in my space. I breathed him in and wondered how he could make even this dank alleyway smell divine.

"If Aldo wasn't such a waste of skin you wouldn't have even known he was there. I wanted whoever has been messing with you to know that we know he's there. What happened to you? Why are you all dirty?"

I blushed hotly and hoped he didn't notice. "That Aldo guy grabbed me and freaked me out. I fell."

He lifted a sandy eyebrow and reached out to rub a spot on my cheek. "What are you doing here anyway?"

Wasn't that the question of the night?

"My friend was really excited she got invited to fight night. Like an idiot, I tried to talk her out of coming, so she tricked me into coming down here to give her a ride. Only she took off before I got here and now I'm covered in alley goo and was scared half out of my mind by that creep. It's not an awesome night."

He tilted his head to the side a little bit and just stared at me. I shivered again, and this time it had nothing at all to do with being in the Point after dark, or feeling like I was being followed.

"I can make it better."

Kill me now. I had to physically bite down on my tongue to keep from groaning out loud.

"Aren't you working?"

The dimple made an appearance and I felt my breath catch in my throat.

"One of the guys who was fighting went in the Pit injured. It was pretty brutal to watch, but he somehow managed to pull out a win. Since he was a long shot, most of the bets were placed on the loser. It was a collecting night, not a payout night. I did my part, but now Nassir won't let anyone leave without ponying up."

His world was so different from anything I had ever known, and I hated to admit that it was fascinating, alluring, and dangerous—just like him.

"I should go home." My voice was strained to my own ears. I couldn't have sounded less convincing if I tried.

"There are always other things we should be doing. Come back to my place with me, Brysen."

It wasn't a question, it was almost an order. It shouldn't sound as hot as it did.

"I don't really think that's a great idea. Besides, we haven't even touched on the fact that I do officially have a stalker."

He took a step even closer and the finger he had used to rub my cheek he now used to push some of my hair back behind my ear. It was probably the most kind, most reverent touch I had felt from another person in my life. That it was coming from this complex and troubling man hit me in all of my warm and squishy places.

"You have a stalker until I can get my hands on him. And it might be a bad idea, but it's a bad idea that is going to happen one way or another, so fighting it seems stupid and takes energy I can sure as hell put to better use. Let me take care of you for one night, Brysen. I promise you won't regret it."

Of course I wouldn't regret it. I wanted him, was entrapped by him, and after I ate it all up, took everything he had to give, lived in the pleasure and passion he broke loose inside of me, it would for sure kill me to know I would never be able to have it again. I blew out a breath, lifted a hand to wrap around his thick wrist, and fully intended to tell him no, that it just wasn't worth the impending heartache, but what came out of my mouth was:

"I don't know what to do with you, Race."

His warm hand slid under the fall of my hair at the back of my neck and his head lowered toward mine. His mouth hovered right over mine and my lips parted in their own invitation.

"Yes, you do."

When he kissed me, my mind was made up. I wanted this—wanted him—and I hadn't had anything just for myself in far too long. I knew it was bound to lead to really bad things, but on the way there I really, really wanted to enjoy everything that came with him. Including the way he pulled me close. The way he slid his hands down over the curve of my ass. The way his tongue lured mine out to play, and maybe mostly the way he made everything else that was always hounding me fade away. With his mouth on mine, with his hands roving over me, there was no crumbling home life, there was no failed math class, there was no lurking and unidentified threat . . . all I could feel was heat, burning desire, and desperation. It was such a welcome reprieve from what I usually felt that there was no way I could tell him no.

He took a step back and squeezed the back of my neck. I was breathless and his eyes had shifted to that sexy, deep, opaque forest green.

"I can't offer you anything fancy. You've been on my mind and under my skin for a minute now, but I promise that I'll make it worth your while."

I breathed out a sigh and took the hand he offered me.

"You already have, Race."

He flashed that dimple at me again and inclined his head toward the mouth of the alley.

"Where did you park?"

"Around the corner." He gave me a look that indicated I would be lucky to find the BMW in one piece once we reached it.

"I saw your friend, the one from the party. She doesn't have any clue what she's doing running around in a place like this. She's loud and flashy. Things like that are like bait in the water for predators. Anyone actually from here, anyone who knows how the Point works, knows the less attention you can draw to yourself, the better. She also tried to grab my junk when I walked past her."

That was the last straw. Adria was off the friends list. I looked up at him under my lashes and hoped against hope that the gunk I had fallen into wasn't spreading onto him as he pulled me closer to his side. I loved the way I could feel the ripple of all that lean muscle against me as he moved. Knew I would love it even more when there weren't so many clothes separating our skin.

I jerked to a halt when we rounded the corner. Because my luck was so stellar, and because, of course, that was how my night was going to end, the BMW was sitting on the ground, the tires and rims long gone. The driver's-side window was busted out, meaning my radio and whatever else wasn't tied down was probably missing. Luckily, I had locked all my school stuff in the trunk, and it still looked closed.

"Shit." I breathed out the word and let Race pull me into a tight hug.

"That's what happens out here."

"It sucks."

He didn't argue, but pulled out his phone and started bark-

ing orders into it. It sounded like he was arranging to have someone tow the heap to the garage.

"More minions?"

He gave me a grin that had my insides turning liquid and
slippery.

"Sometimes they serve a purpose. Let's go. The Mustang is
behind the warehouse."

"I need to see if my computer and books are in the trunk
still."

He gave me a hard look and shook his head.

"You shouldn't come down here with that kind of stuff.
People get carjacked for a cell phone, let alone a new computer."

I made a face and went to collect my stuff. "Like I said, I don't
know what to do with you and I have no idea what to do in this
place, and yet I keep finding myself here."

I breathed a sigh of relief when the Mac glinted up at me. I
grabbed it and went back to my sexy escort.

He took my hand again and pressed a kiss to the back of it.
It made me want to literally swoon. No one person should be
that smooth. It was like he didn't have any kind of edges, even
though I knew for a fact that wasn't true.

"Whether you want to be here or not, you have to know
how to take care of yourself once you get here. The Point eats
pretty girls like you alive."

"What about pretty boys like you? Does it eat you alive too?"

He gave me a look that was dark in a different way from the
ones he gave me when he was turned on. There were shadows
there, deep places that had marked him, and it made me a little
afraid, not just *of* him, but *for* him. Getting into bed with Race

Hartman came with risks. I knew it, and the look on his handsome face told the truth of it.

"It does until the pretty boy grows a really sharp set of teeth to bite back."

Yikes. That made him as much of a predator as everything else hiding in the darkness and shadows of this city, and I was about to go willingly with him and let him "take care" of me. It looked like I couldn't avoid messy situations no matter how good my intentions might be.

Chapter 8

Race

I HAD TO ADMIT that so far, this night was turning out to be all kinds of awesome. Seeing the underdog win against that doped-up bruiser had done something good for my soul. Watching a bunch of greedy, overzealous, bloodthirsty people fall apart when they realized they had bet on brawn and not heart also made something warm ooze inside of my chest. This was a bad place, corrupted by bad people, so when the unexpected happened, when something good and just fought its way to a hard-won victory, it was hard not to revel in the aftermath. Plus the amount of money we had cleared on that dirty-ass fight was obscene and more than enough to keep Nassir off my ass for the foreseeable future.

Brysen was in the passenger seat of my car and she was coming home with me. That alone put the night at the top of my list in awesomeness. She was hesitant about it, looking for a way to justify it not going down, but then I would look at her out of the corner of my eye, she would bite her bottom lip and blush, and I knew that even though she still wanted to fight the attraction—deny the pull—she wanted to give in to it even more, wanted to give in to me.

I reached across the interior of the car and put a hand on her knee. She was jittery, I could feel it coming off of her. She was also the only girl I had ever met who could make dirty jeans and a simple black T-shirt look overtly sexy. There was just something about the way she moved, the innate grace and class that she carried with her, that made her so unique and desirable. It was like she knew that she was so much better than what was going on around her, but instead of looking down on it with disdain and resentment, she just stood in the eye of the storm and let all the ugliness and destruction whirl around her, waiting to see where it was going to land. Then she would just gingerly pick her way through the debris and mess and end up safely on the other side of it all.

She put her hand over the top of mine and traced the heavy veins on the back of it with the edge of her fingernail. It was a barely-there caress, but I felt it all the way through my body.

"You look like the kind of guy that would have soft, manicured hands. Not hands that are all scarred up and rough."

I had a wicked scar on the back of one hand from getting into an accident with Bax while we had been running from the cops. My middle knuckle on one hand had been broken so many times it was big and off-center. There were numerous nicks and cuts along my fingers from different fights and different altercations, most recently from the fight for my life when Novak had sent his crew in to kill me.

"You look like a girl who should get to enjoy a night out with an interested boy and not have to rush home to take care of her sister."

She cut me a look and sat back in the seat with a little *humph*.

"I guess looks can be deceiving."

"Why don't you give me the CliffsNotes version of what that's all about?"

She didn't want to, I could see it. Giving me that changed what we were about to do from a quick fuck because we wanted each other into something else. Turned it into something with more depth, and she wasn't ready for that. Still, after a heartbeat, she breathed out a long sigh and turned to look at me.

"I was just a typical college student the year before last. I went to class, partied a little too hard, just did my own thing, and it was a blast. Well, my mom has struggled with depression on and off for most of my life. She usually maintains with meds, but something really bad happened last year and she went off the rails. She quit taking everything prescribed to her and started drinking really heavily. I didn't know what was happening. My dad is a workaholic, spends all his time in the office at work, and the one at home, and pretty much forgets he even has a family."

She made a noise under her breath and I wanted to pull the car over and give her a hug.

"Well, one day Mom went out, I think to pick Karsen, my sister, up from school. Only she had been self-medicating all day with vodka and was shit-faced. She caused a major accident on the highway, hurt herself really bad, and rear-ended a family in an SUV in front of her. She hit the other car so hard that it smashed into the big rig in front of it. The mom and the son made it out alive, but the dad died. It was terrible. Mom was in the hospital for a long time and ended up with all kinds of medical problems. Somehow she was lucky enough to get out of having her BAC taken, either because the cops were distracted or because money changed hands, but either way she missed getting saddled with a DUI and her insurance covered the bulk of the bills, but not all of them. The next thing I knew, we couldn't afford my car or classes anymore, and things at home were a nightmare for my sister. No one was making sure she went to school, or had any food in the house or that the bills for the lights or the heat were getting paid."

She shook her silky blond head and I could see frustration and harder emotions surge in her clear, blue eyes. She might be all frosty and cool on the surface, but underneath a torrent was raging. It made me want her even more.

"I wasn't going to quit school, not when I was so close to being done, so I got a job and took a few loans to get through the last few semesters. I moved home to try and keep things together as much as I could until Karsen is finished with high school. One more year, I just have to hold it all together for one more year, but in the meantime, my mom has added all kinds of painkillers to the booze and my dad is even less present than he was before. I never really know what kind of situation I'm walking into when I get to my own front door, and that sucks. I deserve better and my sister sure as hell didn't do anything to ask for any of what has happened to our family."

I wheeled the Mustang into the compound and watched to make sure the gates swung closed behind us. The security lights flickered on overhead, casting her in an ethereal, bluish glow. Everything about her was refined and pure looking. God, I wanted to mess her up. I wanted my hands in her hair, my marks on her skin, and my taste in her mouth. I wanted her to look as rough as she made me feel on the inside. No one had ever riled me up like that before. Maybe because I was so used to just getting without having to ask, and Brysen never offered that to me. I always had to ask her what the next move was going to be, and her answers often surprised me. She was not a sure bet, and I think the challenge of that made her even more desirable.

"The lengths we go to in order to keep our family safe, to do right by those we love, is often a weighty burden to bear." I got out of the car and went around to let her out of the passenger side. When I pulled her up, I pressed her back into the side of the car with the full length of my body and bent down so that my mouth hovered enticingly over the plump ridge of hers.

"I would do anything for Dovie, anything. I have done things for her that made me hate the man I had to be in order to do them, but it was in her best interest. I admire you being able to put your own life down and pick up a different one out of loyalty to your sister, but somewhere in there, you need to remember she's going to have to learn to take care of herself. She'll eventually have to admit that your parents are fucked and move on with her own life. Dovie found the one person in the world to love who has the ability to insulate her from anything the Point wants to throw at her. Your sister will eventually have to find her stability as well. She won't need you forever."

I saw something flare deep in those cerulean eyes, a spark of pain, maybe of realization that I was right, but then it was gone and she was pressing up on her tiptoes and sealing her mouth over mine. I let my hands glide down her sides and fall under her backside. She had the nicest butt on any girl I had ever seen, the nicest body really. There was no end to all her curves and dips, and anywhere my hands decided to land, they were filled with firm and sexy flesh. The brief glimpse I had had of her out of her towel the last time we were this close together had been enough to burn out the image of any other female I might've seen naked in the last few years. All I could see was Brysen and her pretty, pale skin, her high breasts with perfectly pink nipples, and her most private of places that was just as elegant as the rest of her. She was a blond bombshell and I could feel my body urging me to stop playing around and finally seal the deal with her.

She was sucking on the tip of my tongue, her hands were working their way into the collar of my sweater, and the edge of her knee was rubbing ruthlessly against the very obvious erection straining at the front of my jeans. I was supposed to be making her night better, supposed to be taking care of her, making her feel all kinds of good, and here she was getting me so worked up, so turned on, that if I wasn't careful, didn't pull back a little, I wasn't even going to make it inside that perfect body before blowing a load in my pants.

I gave her a hard kiss and pulled back with a low breath hissing between my teeth.

"As much as I like the idea of screwing you against the side of my car, considering you and it are the two most beautiful things I have ever seen, I should warn you that this entire place is wired like the White House. There are more video cameras watching what we're doing right now than I want to think about. So if you don't want an audience, we need to move this upstairs."

She did that thing where she ran her tongue over the curve of her bottom lip and a soft pink flush heated up the crest of her cheekbones. Maybe the idea of having someone catch us in the act wasn't such a deterrent to her after all. Brysen had a wild streak under all that cool composure, I knew it, had felt it in the bathroom the other night, and I couldn't fucking wait to start melting some of those icy layers surrounding this girl. I had a feeling the deeper I got into her, the more and more things I would find that I really, really liked. Hell, I was already fascinated by her, she had my interest all tied up in her, and no other girl to date could claim that same distinction.

I took her hand and pulled her behind me into the garage. Titus's voice rose up from the other day, taunting me, mocking me. How was I supposed to put the moves on her, seduce her and entice her inside of a place that was practically a hovel? Suddenly, not wanting anything and not having anything to show for what I had been doing in the last few months to take over Novak's reign seemed like a foolish and self-sacrificing idea. I didn't know what I had been trying to prove by not accumulating anything, by not staking claim to anything, but right about now I wished I had at least splurged on a kick-ass bed.

She was steady and sure in front of me. There was no hesitation in her gait, and when we rounded the corner into the loft she turned and put her hands on the center of my chest. I had to admit that I liked the bold streak in her. It matched the bold streak that ran wide through me and I enjoyed the way it contradicted the always polished and prim way she tended to appear on the outside. I think I felt a kind of bond in that. I knew the things that ran in my blood, the things that made me tick and were important to me, didn't necessarily match the refined genes I had been born with. She pushed my jacket off my shoulders and it landed on the floor with a dull thud.

I caught her delicate wrists in each of my hands and started backing her toward the couch. I didn't know that she was ever going to give me an opportunity like this again and I needed to take every second, every moment to prove to her that this thing between us was something she just needed to let happen. I wanted her to feel like it was as unstoppable as I felt it was.

I moved her back until her legs hit the couch and she went down with a little *oomph*. Her eyes were huge in her face, big pools of blue that were filled with anticipation and something hot and needy. I got on my knees in front of her, pushed her legs apart so I was right in the middle of them, and felt her start to quiver against me. I reached for the hem of her T-shirt and was a little surprised when she beat me to it and pulled the fabric off over the top of her head. Her blond hair danced up and around her head like a halo. She lifted a pale brow at me and raised her chin.

"Your turn, handsome."

That startled a chuckle out of me, so I obliged her and jerked my sweater up over my head by the back of the neck. I liked the way she looked at me, like she saw more than what was on the outside. Her gaze skimmed over my chest, across my abs, and then landed back on my face. She reached out a finger and traced over the few scars my last ride with Novak's boys had left. The worst of the damage had been to my leg. It was a gnarly mess of scar tissue and sewed-back-together flesh. If she didn't like the little imperfections on top, what was below that was going to send her running for the hills when she caught sight of it.

I used the edge of my knuckle to trace over the pale crest of each of her breasts where they peeked out over the top of her lacy bra. Her heartbeat was erratic and she inhaled sharply at the touch. I continued the journey around her side to the back clasp. She leaned forward so I could unhook the fasteners and set her free. She wiggled the straps down her arms and leaned forward so that her now-naked breasts were pressed against my own naked chest. She felt so good, like this was where she was supposed to be.

I skimmed my hands down the flawless curve of her spine and leaned in close so I could whisper in her ear.

"Gonna have to lose more clothes than that if I'm gonna take care of you, Bry."

I ran the tip of my tongue along the shell of her ear and it made her legs clamp around the outside of my thighs.

"Okay." It was barely a whisper and it made my dick so hard that it hurt.

I let her pull away far enough to get the top of her jeans un-buttoned, helped her kick off her shoes, and somehow managed to get her all the rest of the way naked without having to move from my really perfect location caught between her long legs and the very heart of her desire. There wasn't a single part of her that wasn't pretty and perfect. She was the kind of girl a guy could fantasize about in a million and one different ways and never have to repeat himself. There was just something about all that cool blond hair and endless amounts of silky pale skin that gave her a dreamlike quality not a lot of girls possessed. She was enough to get a guy off just by looking at her.

I gripped her hips and pulled her to the very edge of the couch. I kissed her hard, tasted the way she was so ready to do this with me. I felt it in the way her hands twined in my hair and gave it a hard tug. She wasn't shy and that was beyond awe-some. I moved down to kiss the side of her neck, licked at her pulse jumping there. I skimmed my hands up along her rib cage and stopped to brush each thumb along the underneath swell of her breasts. I felt her nipples go diamond hard where they were pressing against me. I kissed her collarbone, fought the urge to suck on it, to mark her up with my mouth. She was fair, and marring that pristine landscape with something so barbaric seemed like it should be a crime. I knew that I was going to do it anyway.

I had to give her a little nudge back in order to make enough space between us to get my mouth around the begging tip of her breast. When I did, she gasped and pulled at my hair. I swirled the little pebble around and around until I had her panting, and I could feel her getting wet against me. Her thighs were shaking and her chest was rising and falling in a rapid rhythm. I used my teeth, was a little rougher on the other side and not at all surprised when she seemed to like that even more. She was pulling me closer and mumbling my name. Her hips also lifted involuntarily off the worn fabric of the couch, which totally worked to my advantage. I slid my hands under each side of her ass and lifted her up a little as I pulled back and grinned at her.

"Showtime."

Her eyes got even bigger, if that was possible, and she sank her teeth into her bottom lip, which nearly had my cock coming out of my pants on its own.

I pressed her legs a little farther apart, bent down lower so I could lick around her belly button, kissed her below that on her quivering stomach, and traced the curve of her leg where it led to my intended target. I heard her whimper and could literally feel the way she heated up from the inside out as I got closer and closer to the parts of her that were weeping for me. She was slight enough that I could lift her up to my waiting mouth, my hands holding her still as I used the tip of my tongue to work through her damp flesh. She tasted like she looked, expensive and divine, silky and smooth, and this was the only part of her that didn't seem to have a perpetual chill. All along the edge of my probing tongue she rippled in pleasure, and her fingernails gripped hard at the sides of my head.

"Race . . ." My name was a broken plea, asking for more or asking me to stop, I didn't care which, because I was getting drunk on her taste alone and I hadn't even really started yet. I pulled her up higher, freed a hand from underneath her so that I could put it to better use. I spread her farther apart, breathed her in, and caught the hard nub of her clit between my teeth and gave it a tug. I wasn't exactly gentle and she didn't seem to mind. She arched her entire back up off the couch and squeezed my head so hard between her legs it made me chuckle. Never had I been caught in a sexier trap.

I swirled the pulsing bud around and around with my tongue, used my fingers to play with her, glided them along her inner walls that were flexing and jumping at the barest touch. I lapped at her, sucked on her, used my hand that was holding her up to my face to squeeze her backside, and felt her rising, felt the way her insides were chasing down all the pleasure I was throwing at her. I had never been with a girl who was so honestly responsive. She muttered her approval, said my name when my questing fingers hit her in just the right spot, and she didn't bother to hide or be embarrassed by the physical signs I was drawing out of her body. She was all kinds of liquid and hot and it was enough to have me wondering if I could finish this without making a fool of myself in the process. I couldn't ever remember having an erection so hard, having lust riding me so high that it physically hurt.

She was close. I could hear her making keening sounds at the back of her throat. I felt it in the way she was flooding my tongue with desire. She let go of my hair with one hand and reached behind her to clasp my hand that was holding her up by one firm ass cheek. She squeezed my fingers, I saw her eyes flutter closed and her mouth fall slack in a wordless sound, and then all the parts of her I had my mouth across exploded across my tongue as I continued to eat her up. Her inner muscles spasmed around my stroking fingers and suddenly she was lax in my hands. She went limp, her arms looping loosely around my neck as I lifted my head up from between her legs to look at her. She bonelessly slithered off the edge of the couch so that she was sitting across my legs. My dick practically whimpered when the moist center of her hit my fly.

Her sky-colored eyes were heavy lidded and completely content looking. If I didn't have my arms full of naked woman, I would've smugly patted myself on the back. I didn't get a chance to bask in a job well done because she shifted from compliant and soft to forcibly aggressive before I could get my head around her mood change.

She kissed me, used her tongue to tangle with mine, sucked the leftover flavor of herself off of my lips, and shoved a little hand between us to start working on the buckle of my belt. I bent her back a little so that her shoulders were resting on the edge of the couch and groaned into her mouth when her fingertips brushed across the throbbing head of my cock.

I pulled back so she could pull the zipper down and watched as her eyes flared up in appreciation. She bent forward to kiss me again and a nagging thought barreled into the back of my skull. I caught her chin in my hand and lowered my forehead to touch hers.

"I don't have a condom."

It went along with my current minimalist state. Not having

things meant not missing them when they were gone, including the basic urge to get laid. Only now I was going to murder someone for a tiny piece of latex because if I didn't get inside her ready and willing body in the next second, I was pretty sure I was going to die.

Her fingers on one hand curled around the back of my neck while the other stroked the aching shaft up and down where it was straining at the opening of my jeans. It looked furious and enormous in her tiny grip. God, just watching her touch me was enough to set me off.

"We don't really need one."

I lifted an eyebrow at her and she cocked her head to the side. "I did have a pretty normal and active life before moving back home. I'm covered if you are."

Shit. I hadn't had unprotected sex since one mishap in my teens that had me pissing fire for a month. It was risky, and even though I looked like a choirboy on the outside, I had done things, been with dangerous women, that wouldn't necessarily make me a good bet to take that risk on. Granted, all those careless choices with women had been a while ago and I never made the same mistake twice, so I was as clean as a whistle. I wanted her more than I wanted to keep breathing, but I felt compelled to ask:

"Brysen, that's a pretty big risk to take on me. Are you sure?"

If she said no, my dick was going to fall off, but I had to respect her wishes.

She stared at me for a long, silent moment. I could practically see things turning around and around behind her burning-hot gaze. She leaned closer to me, her breasts brushing enticingly across my chest. She rubbed the end of her nose across my cheek and stopped at my ear. She put her lips right up against it and whispered:

"You make me want to take every risk there ever was worth taking, handsome." Then she sank her teeth into the lobe and I was done for.

I hefted her up enough to get the stiff denim out of the way and pulled her back down directly on my very ready erection. She was already all open and malleable, so she slid right down to the hilt. We were joined closer, tighter than I think I had ever been with any other girl. Her head tilted back, her throat arched up, and I couldn't resist the allure, the invitation to suck on it, to leave a mark on it.

She started to move, used her hold on my shoulders to work herself up and down while I moved up on my knees a little to get better leverage to thrust into her. I tangled my hands in her hair and kissed her closed eyes, her nose, and finally settled on her mouth. I loved kissing her. Loved the way she tasted and responded to me. I had had more sex than I probably should be comfortable admitting to, but I had never had sex like this. The routine was get in, get it on, get off, and then get gone. With her, there was so much more than that. There was the buildup, the erotic burn, the way she pulled at me, asked me to give her more without words. There was the way she said my name over and over, the way she sank her teeth into the top of my shoulder hard enough to make me grunt in pain. There was the way she told me to go harder, faster, and when I didn't respond quick enough she somehow managed to get a hand between us to snake around my balls and give me the proper encouragement. She was being sexually daring and I fucking loved it, and it made me pretty sure I was on the edge of loving her. She was beautiful, and when she came a second time, I followed right behind her, shuddering a naked release into a very special girl I was pretty certain was going to set my already unsteady and uncertain world even further off-kilter.

I let the aftershocks of her soft body ripple along the still-buried length of my cock and shifted so that I could lay her across the threadbare couch. It took some maneuvering to keep us joined together and to get both of us to fit, but the end result was me still nestled in the cradle of her long legs and her arms draped loosely around my shoulders while she gazed up at me through passion-drunk eyes. I pushed some tangled pieces of her hair off of her face and used my thumbs to brush across the planes of her cheekbones.

"I take it back. You are way more beautiful than the Stang."

She rolled her eyes at me and spread her legs a little farther apart so that I could settle more fully into her.

"I feel like I got the raw end of the deal in the checking-out-the-goods department, pretty boy. You've now seen me naked twice, and yet somehow you have managed to stay mostly clothed, both times."

I lifted an eyebrow at her and grinned. Her eyes zeroed in on my dimple and I felt her response where we were still joined. I was stoked that it was as easy for me to get to her as it was for her to get to me.

"Not all of me is that pretty." I put her hand on the scar on my chest. "Novak's guys did a number on my leg when they went after Bax and Dovie. I was lucky they didn't kill me, but they left me with a lifelong reminder of what happens when you think you can take on the Point and win."

She made a face at me and started to wiggle underneath me. It felt awesome but clearly she wanted up. I groaned and pulled out of her heat and let her climb to her feet. She grabbed my hands and pulled me to my feet. I was going to ask her what she was doing but she was suddenly very much all up in my personal space, pulling my jeans and boxers the rest of the way down my legs. The sight of a sexy, naked blonde on her hands and knees in front of me wasn't something my recently satisfied cock could ignore, and she lifted both her eyebrows up at me when it twitched in her direction. I would've shrugged it off, smiled at her and tried to play it smooth because she really was that hot, but I couldn't breathe because she bent her head next to the mangled side of my knee, the part where the scar tissue was the ugliest, the thickest and knobbiest, and pressed the softest, lightest kiss to it. It did something to the center of my chest, made my heart kick hard enough that I was surprised my ribs didn't crack from the force.

She trailed her fingers along the outside of my thigh, kissed the part of my abs that flexed and tightened right below my belly button, and got to her feet in front of me. She twisted her arms back up around my neck and pressed her cheek to the center of my chest. I don't think I had ever been embraced with such care. I put my hands around her back and stroked my fingers up and down her spine.

"I'm glad you're not absolutely physically perfect, Race. Trying to handle all the obvious perfection is distracting and hard as it is. Knowing there are parts of you that aren't flawless makes you so much more human."

I backed her onto the couch again. Covered her with my less than perfect body and started kissing her again.

"More parts of me are flawed than not, Bry. Stick around long enough and you'll see."

She must not have been in any hurry to go because when I wrapped a hand around her knee and put it up over my hip, she slid the other one to the side of my hips of her own volition, making room for me to be able to slide right back inside her body. Her eyes fluttered closed and a tiny smile danced over her mouth. She arched up into me and whispered against the side of my neck, "Thank you for taking care of me tonight."

She didn't have a clue. As I started to move again, started to make her more and more mine, she didn't even know the lengths I would end up going to in order to take care of her, and neither did I.

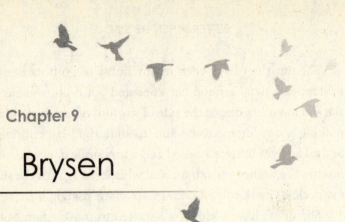

Chapter 9

Brysen

I SPENT THE NIGHT with Race. Not that it was a hardship to have his very talented hands and mouth all over every part of me for most of the night. But in the bright light of the daytime, the fact that I had just put everything down, walked away from what I knew made the most sense, and took something for myself made me feel a little overwhelmed. It was the first time in forever that I actually felt like myself, like I had some part of a life I actually wanted within my grasp, and I didn't want to squander it. Even the fact that I had let him make love to me over and over again without protection was something I should be kicking myself over, but I was on the pill, responsible for my own choices. If I never had the chance to be with Race again, at least I knew I had had *all* of him, and it was better than anything else in the world had ever been. I think the thrill of it, the little unknown that came with being with a guy like him, added to the way it was so easy for him to work me all up.

He had rolled off of me this morning when his phone went off. He had mumbled words like *payout,* and *the spread.* He had pulled on a pair of jeans minus underwear, which was just dead sexy, kissed me hard on the mouth, and told me that Bax was getting the BMW squared away, and disappeared in a flurry of golden gloriousness and hasty good-byes. I didn't know if I would see him again anytime soon, and frankly I was all right with that because I wasn't sure how I was supposed to handle this major change in our relationship. We had never really been friends, didn't know each other beyond the powerful attraction that seemed to pull us together, but the more bits and pieces of him I uncovered, the more I realized he was so much like me. His life looked one way, but underneath the surface there was so much more, so many other things going on. I hadn't meant to blurt out my entire sad tale to him the night before, but after I had, I felt like a small portion of the burden was off my shoulders. It was a relief to have someone else out in the world knowing why I was doing what I was doing at home, that my sacrifice might go unnoticed on the home front by those it was for, but Race would know, and that mattered somehow.

I took a quick shower with the demon-hot water and cringed when I had to put on my dirty clothes from the night before. My face was scrubbed clean of makeup, my hair was damp, and I had a very prominent bite mark right on the center of my throat. I looked like the very image of "the morning after," and I couldn't say that I hated it. My eyes were big in my face, but there was a shine to them that had been missing for a long time—and maybe even a bit of the old me lurking back in the blue depths.

I collected my stuff, braced myself for whatever Bax was going to say, and went in search of my car. The garage was busy and loud. Machines were running, a plethora of male voices were talking, a radio was playing loud rock music somewhere, and over the top of it all engines were running and exhaust fumes perfumed the air. It was hectic enough that I was hoping no one would really notice me, but of course there was no such luck. A freshly showered girl exiting Race's loft wasn't going to go unnoticed, so I blushed when I caught a few knowing looks from the guys covered in grease and motor oil.

I saw Bax's big form come out of the office. He had a cigarette dangling out of the corner of his mouth and his phone pressed against his ear. He caught sight of me where I was walking down the metal steps and inclined his dark head toward the back of the garage. Everything about him was dark and demanding, I had no clue how Dovie didn't run from him every single time he looked at her. Just the look in his pitch-black eyes was enough to make me scamper like a scared little rabbit in the direction he indicated.

The BMW had four new wheels along with a new set of rims that looked way more expensive than the stock ones that had been stolen off of it the night before. I tossed my purse and the laptop on the passenger seat and looked in surprise to see that even a new radio had been put back into the console. I startled when Bax called "heads-up" and tossed me my keys. I caught them in my hand and watched him warily as he sauntered over to me. A ring of smoke escaped his lips and his dark eyes narrowed fractionally at me. He had a black star tattooed on his face right next to his eye, and the way it crinkled and moved was fascinating. He was the embodiment of the kind of man who was honed in the very fires that fueled the Point.

"Have fun last night?" It was crude, and none of his business, but it was a very Bax thing to ask.

I cleared my throat and clasped the keys to the car tightly in my hand. "I did."

He took the cigarette out of his mouth and dropped it on the

ground. He put it out under his boot and ran his hands over his
shorn hair.

"Race has had a thing working for you for a while, but things
with him and the business in the city right now are shaky. The
Point is never really standing on solid ground, and right now the
entire place might fall into nothing. He needs to keep his head up
and his eyes on the prize or really bad shit could fall down on him.
If you're planning on being at his side, it'll pull you under too."

It was a warning that was about as subtle as a bulldozer.

"He's just helping me out a little. I sort of have a stalker problem. I'm not trying to distract him or put him in danger."

The corner of his mouth kicked up in a small grin, and I
could see it, really see the beauty in him that had Dovie so head
over heels in love with him. It almost made me sigh out loud.

"Looking the way you do, him already wanting a taste, and
you should know you don't have to do anything to distract him
but breathe. I'm just telling you to keep all of it in mind when
you decide to walk on the wild side. Here there are more things
to consider than just getting off."

I sucked in a startled breath at his bluntness and lowered my
eyebrows at him in a very prudish scowl. He cocked his head to
the side and considered me for a second.

"Your stalker . . . you have any idea who it might be? No exes
in the picture? Any bad blood?"

I shook my head. "No, no one. I haven't been on a date in
over a year or so. I live at home. I go to work and school and
that's it. I'm boring. I mean I've turned some guys down when
they've asked me out and I'm pretty sure I have a TA at school
that wants to ruin my life, but no one has ever threatened me
outright before."

"You're interesting enough for someone to want to be fucking with you pretty hard, and everyone is a threat."

I sighed and lifted some of my wet hair from the back of my neck.

"The TA is an asshole. He asked me out and I sort of turned him down in a jerky way. Ever since then I've been positive he's messing around with my grades and making this semester a living hell. He's the only person I can think of that I might've rubbed the wrong way lately but I can't prove he's doing anything shady."

Bax rubbed his thumb along his chin and lifted up a dark eyebrow.

"You mention this guy to Race?"

"No. He's just a nerdy math major. He's annoying, and I'm pretty sure he's trying to ruin my grade so I fail my class. I just can't prove it."

"Doesn't take much for a lonely guy to get pushed over the edge by a pretty girl."

I didn't know what to say to that, so we just stared at each other for a long minute until he took out another cigarette and stuck it in his mouth. I cleared my throat a little bit and moved to get into the car.

"Thank you for putting wheels back on my car."

"Thank Race."

Well, I was pretty sure I had covered that last night, but I wasn't about to tell Bax that.

"Hey, Bax." His dark eyes flicked to me. "The things Race is doing, the business he's involved in . . . he'll be okay with everything, won't he?" I didn't really want an honest answer, but I knew I would get one.

Bax lit the end of the cigarette and lifted his heavy shoulders in a shrug.

"Race is the smartest guy I know. He's doing what he thinks needs to be done. The guy makes pretty drastic choices that often affect others around him—and not always in a good way. But he owns them and there has to be something in that, right?"

That didn't sound overly reassuring, but one of his guys called his name and I was dismissed for a blown head gasket or something like that.

I left the garage with my head spinning around the night before and thoughts of the kinds of things that could happen to Race if he wasn't, in fact, smart enough to stay on top of all the things chasing him down in the Point. I liked him. I mean, I really liked him. It was hard not to, he was just so charming and endearing, but it was the surprises, those hidden little corners, that made him irresistible. I wanted to really know him, to get inside that golden head of his and figure out what made him work. Too bad I didn't have the time for it or the space to figure out how things might work between us.

When I got back to my own part of town, my sister was home, my mom was in the kitchen, surprisingly sober and making sandwiches, and as usual, my dad was nowhere to be found even though it was a weekend day. I skittered past, hoping my rumpled and manhandled appearance wouldn't cause a commotion, and put myself back together up in my room.

Karsen might want to pretend Mom was okay, might want to soak up the brief moments of lucidity and sobriety that came between her binges and manic attacks, but that took an effort I wasn't willing to make and a mind-set I wasn't willing to adopt. I ignored an apologetic text from Adria and responded to a snarky one from Dovie. I wasn't going to try and hide the fact I had hooked up with Race from anyone, but I wasn't going to flaunt it either. He was hot, we were both single, I had wanted him for so long it felt like it was a built-in part of me, and I wasn't going to try and explain the need to simply *have* him to anyone, even a well-meaning Dovie.

It actually made me giggle a little that a guy who looked as big and as badass as Bax did was still prone to gossiping about his friend's love life like a girl. He was the only way I could figure Dovie knew I had spent the night with her brother.

I settled on my bed to spend the afternoon knocking out homework and went to work on getting caught up after my computer fail last week. It was only a few minutes later when my sister knocked on my door and stuck her head in. She had one of the sandwiches on a plate and a hesitant smile on her face.

"You don't want to eat lunch with Mom and me?"

She came in and set the plate on the edge of the bed and propped herself up on the corner of the mattress.

"No. Watching Mom putter around the kitchen after destroying it last week just doesn't sit right with me. I'm surprised you're even home. I thought you were spending the weekend with one of your girlfriends."

Karsen finding somewhere else to be on the weekends was becoming more and more common, and it wasn't like I could blame her. If I had a place I could run away to, I would be gone as well. Only I knew distance wouldn't fix the problems currently building inside the walls of this house.

She twisted a piece of her hair around her finger and grinned at me.

"I got invited to a party tonight, so I had to come home and grab something else to wear. Connie and I are going to go together and then I'll stay with her tonight."

I lifted an eyebrow at her and gave her a look. Race's words about her growing up, about her starting to figure out her life on her own without me watching her back, echoed between my ears.

"What kind of party?"

Parties on the Hill were a scary thing. Not scary in the same run-for-your-life way all the things in the Point were, but scary in a much more insidious, underhanded way. Boys from the Hill didn't like to take no for an answer, and rich kids could get their hands on a lot of things they shouldn't be able to. I wasn't Karsen's mom and I knew she was a bright kid, but I didn't give up all I had just to watch her fall victim to a smooth-talking boy with a nice car. I almost rolled my eyes when I considered my current circumstances with my own boy who was originally from the Hill.

"Nothing crazy. Just a couple of friends getting together at this guy Parker's house. I think he's nice. He plays baseball and Connie is sorta hanging out with his best friend."

She blushed and looked a little flustered.

"You like him."

She lowered her lashes and ran her fingers over my comforter.

"Kinda."

I sighed and put my computer to the side. I crossed my legs and leaned closer to her. I had to admit I was a little jealous. It felt like so long ago when I had just been a normal girl with a crush on a cute boy from school. Really, I was just happy and pleased that even with all the upheaval in our lives, all the strain our parents' situation had put on the two of us, she could still just be a teenager who wanted to hang out and have fun like she was supposed to.

"What's he look like?"

She giggled and I picked up the sandwich to take a bite.

"Not nearly as cute as your guy, but still hot."

I almost choked on the bite I had just taken. "I don't have a guy."

It was her turn to give me a speculative look as she climbed off the edge of my bed.

"You weren't here last night. You had wet hair when you came in. And I don't know if you've looked in a mirror this morning, but you have a hickie on your neck the size of Texas and you're smiling. Honestly, I'm glad. There is no reason you shouldn't have a hot guy all over you and I haven't seen you smile silly like that in forever. It's a nice change."

It was highly inappropriate that my little sister was practically giving me a high five over getting laid, and I hadn't realized I was smiling. Oh, Lord, what was I going to do about Race?

"Just be smart, don't do anything stupid while you're out tonight, okay?"

"I never do, Brysen."

I wished I could say the same thing. She left me to my own devices, and I finished a project I had, looked over my Math Theory notes, and somewhere in there fell asleep for a few minutes. I then had to scramble to get up and get ready for my shift at the restaurant that night, because naptime hadn't been planned, but my body was obviously in need of some rest after the paces it had been put through the night before. I don't think I had ever had the kind of sex that left you feeling it long after,

all over, everywhere, before. That alone was enough reason to
be leery of getting into anything deeper with Race. A girl could
quickly become addicted to that feeling, and there was no place
in my life right now for a frivolous addiction.

I was running down the stairs, trying to pin the front of my
hair out of my face with a bobby pin, when I noticed that my
dad had made his way home finally. He was pacing between the
kitchen and the living room, his phone pressed to his ear, while
my mom sat on the couch and watched him with glassy eyes.
She didn't look like she had been drinking, but the calm from
this afternoon was gone from her face.

"What's going on?" I asked the question not really expecting
an honest answer from either of them.

My dad held up a hand and I looked at my mom, who just
ignored me. I wanted to throttle them both.

I was going to just keep going, let them stew in the broth
of unease and discontentment that always seemed to fill the air
inside of this house, when my dad caught my wrist as I reached
the front door. I looked at him in surprise and shook him loose.
His grip was way harder than it needed to be, and up close there
was a scary kind of desperation swirling in his gaze that made
me nervous.

"Brysen, I need you to let me use your car for a few days."

I couldn't help but bark out a laugh. I had given up everything to come home, to be here for Karsen. The only things I
had left were my car and school. The things I had to work my
butt off to keep.

"No way. I have to go to work and I'm not taking the bus or
finding a ride. What's wrong with the Lexus?"

My mom didn't drive anymore. She had lost her license after the accident but Dad had managed to hold on to a nice Lexus SUV.

He scowled at me and looked at his phone as it started ringing again.

"It's in the shop for a couple days. Stop being selfish. I provide for this family, not you. I need your car."

I laughed again but this time I almost choked on it.

"No." This wasn't an argument I was going to have. My car was not something I was going to give up, it was seriously the last tie to any kind of freedom I had. I would rather lick the bottom of my shoe than be stuck in this house with no viable way to get anywhere else. Plus I worked my tail off to keep my car; he wasn't going to get away with trying to make me feel bad about not handing it over to him.

I pulled the door open and marched out of the house without looking back. I heard him follow me and looked over my shoulder to see my mom hovering uncertainly in the doorway. As soon as she could, I knew she was going to grab a bottle and that being alone in the house while Dad locked himself in the office was a major trigger for her. I couldn't work up any concern about it, it was too commonplace now. I was mad, really mad, and when my dad reached for my arm again I actually slapped his hand away, which had him drawing back from me with a scowl.

"Stop it. I'm not giving you my car, Dad. You can take the bus, or walk, or I don't know—hire a rickshaw. I'm not letting you make something else my problem."

"I haven't made anything your problem, Brysen."

"Really? Like letting Mom trash the kitchen and not doing anything to stop her or bothering to make sure Karsen was okay isn't making something my problem? Or how about the fact Mom doesn't go anywhere, Dad, yet she always somehow manages to have a bottle of booze on hand? That's not my problem either, right?"

I shook my head and stalked to the BMW. They were things I had wanted to say to him for a long time, and there was more, so much more, but I could see by the stubborn tilt of his chin and the way his eyes narrowed at the edges that he was only hearing my refusal to hand over my keys. It was the same old story, neither he nor my mother had any idea how hard being here was for me, and they obviously were both too caught up in their own misery and regrettable decision making to care. Which was exactly why I couldn't leave Karsen alone in the house, whether she was going to need me forever or not.

My dad glared at me the entire time I was pulling out of the driveway and his phone was back at his ear. I was mad, I was frustrated, and more than anything, I was sick and tired of all of it. I didn't want to feel like this anymore, helpless and undervalued. I took a minute when I pulled into the parking lot at the restaurant to look around and make sure no one was watching me or following me. I also took an impulsive minute to call Race.

The call rang and rang without an answer and I hated how disappointed that made me. I didn't know what he was thinking after last night, if it had been as mind-blowing and as life altering to him as it was to me. However, with the unease that was clawing at me after dealing with my dad, I really felt like only he could make me feel better.

Ramon gave me a knowing look and a leer when he caught sight of me. Luckily, I was immediately saddled with a huge party and managed to avoid having to gossip or answer questions for most of my shift. I was grumpy, still annoyed at my dad, and admittedly stung that Race hadn't answered my call, when one of the other girls came to find me while I was on break to tell me I had a new table. I didn't understand why someone else couldn't pick it up, but she told me they had specifically requested me. Considering I had someone following me, I was nervous to go back in the dining room, not sure who was going to be waiting for me. As soon as I caught sight of that golden hair and winking dimple, something released inside my chest and I felt like I could breathe again for the first time since he had left me in bed this morning.

I sauntered up to the table and put my hip on the edge of the booth. He looked up at me with those pine-colored eyes and my mouth went dry.

"Hey."

He smiled at me and I had to fight back a dreamy sigh. Race Hartman smiling should be illegal; it was totally a concealed weapon.

"I saw you called. Figured I would stop by and make sure everything was all right."

I blinked in surprise and fiddled with the edge of my apron. No one had ever cared enough to check up on me like that. It made my heart want to be really, really stupid.

"I'm fine. I was just wondering what you were up to tonight. My sister isn't at home, and honestly, I want to be anywhere but there. I know it's the weekend and you probably have a million things going on, but I thought it was worth a shot."

One of his eyebrows danced up and he turned so he could put a hand on my thigh. Considering I was wearing a skirt, that meant he got a handful of skin right above where my torn skin was still healing from the fall in the parking lot. It took me a minute to get my breathing regulated as my blood went warm and thick with just the brush of his palm. I wasn't typically this brazen or this forward. But just like last night, something about him made me want to push boundaries, made me want to just take what I wanted—him.

"I am busy. I was working when you called. I've been working all day. What time do you get off?"

It was on the tip of my tongue to tell him as soon as he got me off but I bit it back on a little laugh. What was wrong with me?

"Around one."

He stood up abruptly and we were so close. He put a hand on the side of my neck and bent down and pressed a kiss to my surprised mouth.

"Meet me at the garage. I'll text you the code to get inside the gates. I might not make it exactly at one, but if you go right there from here, you should be okay in that part of town—even that late."

I wanted to spend the night with him, wanted to feel that return to my old self like I had last night. I nodded silently and his chin bumped my forehead. He brushed a thumb along the curve of my bottom lip.

"I don't have a 'minion' to spare to follow you around tonight, Bry. So you need to keep yourself safe, all right?"

I nodded again and he took a step away from me.

"Race . . ." Those green eyes flared at me quickly and an easy grin played across his mouth. "You keep yourself safe too." I felt like someone should be telling him that while he went off to do God only knew what.

Something crossed his face, something that made a shiver work across the surface of my skin.

"Suddenly making sure everyone is safe seems like more of a priority than it was the other day."

He gave me another kiss and left me staring after him with a breathless anticipation that felt so nice, but also left me with a fair amount of worry about what exactly it was I was getting into.

I ended up with a late table of rowdy guys, so I wasn't able to have Ramon walk me out of the restaurant until almost one thirty. I was tired but made sure I was very aware of all my surroundings as I went to the car. No one jumped out of any shadows. No car tried to run me down, and when Ramon sent me on my way with a little kiss on the cheek and a wink, I actually felt pretty good about things.

The drive into the Point was never fun. It was still sad to see the way things devolved the farther into the heart of the city I went. But now that I was spending more time here, was starting to understand the ebb and flow, the way the city fed off the lives of the people who lived in it, the less terrified I was of every dark thing that moved in the night. I had a moment of almost panic when a set of headlights suddenly shone in my rearview mirror. I squinted at the glare and my hands involuntarily curled tighter around the steering wheel. I picked up the pace, rounded a corner, and breathed a sigh of relief when the metal monolith of the garage came into view.

I wheeled in front of the massive gates and punched in the numerical code that Race had sent me earlier. The car that had been behind me drove on without even pausing, and my heart dropped back from throat into my chest. I settled down even

more when the giant metal gates swung closed, sealing me
inside. As barren as this place was, as industrial and unwelcom-
ing as the façade was, there was no denying it felt like an iron
fortress that could keep the wolves of the street at bay. I took a
minute to get my thoughts in order, stripped off my apron, and
went to walk inside when I halted because the gates were whin-
ing and whirring behind me as someone opened them from the
outside.

The Mustang was loud and kicked up a cloud of dust as
Race pulled into the lot. He pulled in right next to the BMW
and killed the engine. I waved a hand in front of my face to clear
some of the debris and walked around the front of the car to
meet him. I stopped dead in my tracks and felt my jaw fall open
when I caught sight of him. He winced when he saw me, and spit
a mouthful of blood onto the ground.

His hair was sticking up all over the place. His bottom
lip was split open. He had a gushing cut oozing blood out of
one blond eyebrow, and one cheek was puffy and swollen. His
button-down shirt was torn at the collar and streaked with pink
trails of blood. Both of his hands had ugly abrasions and scrapes
all along the backs and knuckles.

"What happened to you?" I sounded like I had sucked on a
helium balloon, my voice went so high in alarm.

He spit again and shook out one of his hands. I cringed as
little drops of blood went flying with the motion.

"Work happened."

He was moving pretty slowly, but seemed steady on his feet
as he made his way toward me. I reached out to grab him, but he
held up his hands and backed away a step.

"Let me clean up first."

I scowled and stalked after him as he went inside the garage. He didn't bother to turn on the lights, and when he stumbled a little as we hit the narrow stairway leading to the loft, I reached out and put my hands on his back to steady him, and felt him shudder at the contact. This was a man of contradictions that I didn't know what to do with. At the moment he didn't look so handsome or regal. He looked as mad and as furious as I often felt.

"Come on, let me help you."

He grunted a little bit but didn't argue as I guided him the rest of the way up the stairs and into his empty home. I kept going straight into the bathroom, flicked on the light switch, and told him to sit down on the toilet so I could clean him up like he had done for me the other night. By the time I had returned with a clean washcloth, he had stripped to the waist, was probing at his face in the mirror, and his expression had turned remote and vacant. It was like he was shutting off his emotions.

"What happened?"

I didn't know if he would tell me about it . . . I mean, not if it would pretty much implicate him in some kind of criminal activity. But as I reached up to rub the dried blood off his eyebrows, he sighed and slumped down so that he was leaning against the sink.

"I'll never understand the urge people have to risk what they can't afford to lose."

"This was from one of your gamblers?"

"No. From someone that the guy who owes me money hired to try and get out of paying. Probably cost him more than he owed to farm out muscle, and the guy he sent was a joke, but still . . ."

I put my index finger on the cut in the center of his bottom lip and blinked up at him.

"Doesn't look like a joke to me."

He made a face and I bent to put my lips on a flowering bruise that was starting to take shape over his ribs.

"It could be worse. It could always be worse. The guy wanted to beat me down, not kill me. I can usually hold my own in a fight, but I wasn't expecting it. Which makes me an idiot and I hate feeling like a fool. I don't know why I keep thinking people will do things the easy and logical way. Nothing works like that here."

"I don't think things work like that anywhere."

I moved from the side of his chest to his breastbone and kissed him there. The firm skin was warm and resilient under my mouth. I felt the way his body started to respond to the gentle caress. His fingers threaded through my hair as I ran the flat of my tongue over the disk of his nipple. His heart kicked in response.

I ran my hands over his ribs and rested them on his hips above where his jeans hung low and provocatively. Race was lean, carved out of hard lines and sharp planes. He had a hard, muscled ridge over each hip that delineated strong and supple flesh. I wanted to lick it, to trace every line and curve of his body with the tip of my tongue. I got my hands under the waistband of the stiff denim and grinned where I was kissing him when I felt the hard edge of his cock bump against the back of my fingers. I loved that even in a sour mood he was still so quick to respond to my touch. It made all of this wildness he inspired inside me feel less one-sided.

"My turn to take care of you," I whispered just as I kissed him right over his heart before pulling back so I could wrestle with his belt buckle.

"Brysen . . ." His voice was husky and rough. "I don't know how much I can take tonight."

Good. I would take him to the edge like he had done to me, make everything better with a soothing touch and all-consuming desire. His belt gave way easily enough and he was so hard that the fabric of his jeans was practically pushed out of the way by his throbbing erection. He was long, hard, and looked so solid and right as he fell into my hands. I saw his stomach muscles hollow out, saw his chest rise and fall in a deep breath, and his eyes did that thing where they shifted from pretty green to intense and needy black.

I got on my knees in front of him, a position that should have made me nervous, should have made me question the lengths I was already going to in order to please this man, but it didn't. It made me feel in control, in charge of what was happening between us, and I liked the way his hands got hard and insistent when they curled around the back of my head as I leaned forward to take the straining tip of his cock between my lips. He made a low noise in the back of his throat as I swirled my tongue around the ridges and lines of the powerfully jutting part of him.

He tasted like Race. Sort of mysterious and lux at the same time. He had a trail of fine golden hairs dusting his abdomen below his belly button that tickled my fingers when I circled the base of his erection with my hand because there was no way the whole thing was going to fit in my mouth. He made another noise and his fingers tangled tighter on my neck and in my hair. I sucked on him, licked him, worked him over to the point that his hips started to involuntarily move against the draw and pull of my mouth. I wanted to use my other hand, wanted to stroke him, fondle him, and push him over the edge so that all that tension, all the coiled tautness running through his body, could leach out, but Race was done with being on the receiving end and not giving in return.

I made a surprised noise when he hauled me back up, spun me around, and put me on the edge of the sink where he had been leaning. I licked my bottom lip, which made him swear at me, and curled my legs around his lean waist when he got his impatient hands under my skirt to strip my panties off under the fabric.

"I wasn't done." I wanted to sound sultry and sexy, but I was more like Minnie Mouse.

He grinned at me and that dimple was enough to make all the things between my legs go hot and damp.

"I was about to be, and that's not what I want. I want you."

He stepped into the cradle of my legs, bent his head down, and sealed his mouth over mine. I flinched a little when I tasted blood from his split lip. A second later he joined us together with one solid thrust and I forgot all about his cut, and smashed my mouth more firmly onto his. There wasn't really any foreplay, wasn't any buildup and tune-up like there had been last night, but still, the press of hard flesh, the burn as he moved inside of me, felt like heaven. I twined my arms around his naked shoulders, trying in vain to be careful of the bruises decorating his skin.

This sex was more primal. More about achieving the end goal and making each other feel better than yesterday's romp had been. It was just as intense, just as potent and impactful. It made my body respond just as fast, heated me up and twisted my insides in all the same ways, but there was something else in it, something that made it more penetrating. There was something working behind those eyes and in his touch that made me feel like this was the other side of Race that I was with tonight. This was the Race who lived and worked in the Point. This was the Race who had taken on a gangster and won. This was the Race not scared of breaking the law. This was the Race who was battered and a little soul-broken because he thought he was doing the right thing and no one else in this place appreciated it. He wasn't going out of his way to try and please me, even though he was just that good, he couldn't help but have me panting and writhing against him with just a few skilled thrusts and the brush of exploratory fingers against wanting flesh. I could tell this was something else.

He got his hands under my shirt and pulled it off over my head. He dropped a kiss to the top swell of each breast and I saw the feverish, burning look in his gaze as he watched us move together. This was about him forgetting what made him mad; this was about him trying to set down the guy he thought he had to be in this place. Being with me made him feel like someone else too, and when he snaked clever fingers between my legs, pulled me even farther to the edge of the sink where I was already precariously balanced, there was no holding out against the flood of sensation.

I whispered his name and came apart in his arms and he bared his teeth at me and did the same. Only a guy who looked like Race could make going over the edge—shuddering his release—look that good. I panted against the side of his throat as he smoothed a hand over the top of my head and down to the ends of my hair.

"All better?" Now my voice was husky and full of sex.

He laughed a little and moved his hands around my back so he could unhook the clasp of my bra.

"No, but you make it easier to forget how shitty things around here can be."

Well, what girl didn't want to hear that from a gorgeous guy as he picked her up and carried her off to ravish her some more? Being with him was supposed to be about making me feel right and normal, but I wasn't going to complain if I could return the favor.

Chapter 10

Race

I HURT EVERYWHERE. EVERY single spot on my body that had suffered a blow from heavy hands, every part of my body that had been used to defend myself, just ached all the way down to my bones. I felt battered and bruised everywhere, from the inside out.

The only place that didn't hurt or ache was the spot on my chest where Brysen's head was resting. In sleep, her ear was pressed to the thump of my heart and her hand was curled around my waist. She was like the cool side of the pillow. Like frost on a windowpane, soothing all the bumps and bruises. Where I should be burning up with all of her sexy and honeyed nakedness pressed up against me, instead I felt like she was a refreshing breeze cutting through the smog and pollution that typically flooded my lungs. Her white-blond hair felt like raw silk where it rubbed against my skin, and with zero effort she had my eager body stirring under the covers.

Since she stayed the night, let me have at her without question while I tried to work out all the dark shit in my head, I thought the least I could do was pull the bed out and let her sleep in semicomfort. Not that I let her get that much shut-eye. There was something unique about her. Something about the way she was when she was with me that made me want to get into her, take her apart, see everything she was working with and put my hands on all of it. She was like the best puzzle, the hardest problem I had ever tried to figure out, and it made me like her more than I already did.

I was just thinking about the best way to wake her up, wondering if she would freak out if I skipped all the preamble and just put my mouth between her legs. So far she had surprised me. She seemed down with whatever I wanted to do to her, do with her, but considering we had just scratched the surface of all the ways I wanted to mess her up, I still didn't know how far she was willing to let me go or where her hard boundaries were. I don't think I had any particular boundaries where she was concerned, and that made my blood thick and my dick hard.

I was running my hand down her side, thinking she felt like all the luxury and finer things I had long since left behind, when my chance to seduce her awake was blown by my phone screaming at me from the floor where it was tangled in my pants. I was used to the damn thing going off at all hours of the day and night. People wanted to give me money or take my money all the time and they never paid attention to a clock. What I wasn't used to was my mother calling me—ever. That was a ring tone I hadn't heard in months and months, including the time I had the life nearly beaten out of me by Novak's thugs and I ended up in the hospital. She had firmly joined the Race-is-a-worthless-piece-of-shit bandwagon as soon as my father had declared me persona non grata at the Hartman castle. She had no clue what kind of man my father really was and saw no issue with believing him and whatever lies he told to justify disowning me and taking away every penny I had to my name.

Brysen muttered something and her eyes fluttered open to look at me. I saw her take a second to take stock, realize where she was, then she stacked her hands under her chin and looked out at me from under a tangle of pale hair.

"Are you going to answer it?"

I hadn't, and now it was ringing again.

"I don't really want to." She was naked and draped across me, my face hurt, and my dick was hard. There were a hundred and one other things I could think of that I would rather do than answer that phone.

"Work?"

I sighed and shifted so I could snatch the phone up off the floor. She rolled to the side and took the single blanket I had thrown over us at some point in the night with her. She looked so sweet all rumpled and thoroughly sexed up but so out of place in the hollow and empty loft. She pushed her hair off of her face and watched me with careful eyes.

"I wish it was work." I swiped a finger across the screen of the phone and moved to the edge of the bed. Only my past could instantly deflate the erection Brysen and her sexy, chilly blondness had inspired.

"Been a while, Mom."

There was no masking the bitterness and anger in my tone and I saw Brysen look at me with concern. I sighed again as she climbed off the other side of the bed, taking the blanket with her as she went toward the bathroom.

"Race . . ." My mother was crying, hysterical even, and I thought I should try to care.

"What do you want?" I sounded like an asshole but I couldn't help it. I reached for my discarded jeans.

"I need you to meet me down at the police station."

I paused. "Why?"

She made a hiccuping noise and then a sound like that of a dying animal. "You father has been arrested."

I didn't mean to but I burst out laughing. I heard her gasp, and as I looked up, Brysen was coming out of the bathroom. She was dressed, which was a damn shame.

"This is hardly funny." My mom sounded devastated.

"What did he get arrested for?" My father was a bad man. A criminal on more levels than I could ever be. I wasn't surprised and I couldn't really believe my mother was either. How could you be married to someone, spend a life with them, and not know about all the dirt and filth they wallowed in to keep you in fur and diamonds?

"I'm not really sure. There were federal agents here this morning before the sun came up. They had warrants and took your father away in handcuffs. I called our lawyer." She broke off in a sob again and I frowned when Brysen nodded her head toward the stairs like she was going to leave without saying anything to me. I shook my head at her and scowled. "All of our accounts are frozen. He won't even go to the police station and help me post your dad's bail. There is no money."

Wow. Fate was a real nasty bitch when she put her mind to it. "It's the feds, Mom. You probably can't bail him out anyway." Not if they wanted to tie him up and use him as leverage against the last of Novak's crew or get him to turn on Novak's suppliers. My dad was neck-deep in that mess, and I was honestly surprised they were just now catching up with his sorry ass.

"What am I supposed to do? I can't even stay at the house."
She sounded lost and scared. I climbed to my feet and walked to
where Brysen was standing, watching me silently. I didn't stop
until I was right in front of her. I slid a hand around the back of
her neck and tilted her face up toward mine.

"I fail to see how that's my problem. You tossed me out in the
cold without a second thought."

She didn't answer me for a full minute, and I took the time
to get lost in a sea of endless blue.

"Your dad said it was what we had to do. He told me that
you were poisoned by that boy, by the lifestyle he dragged you
into. You made the choice to disappear for years, to waste your
college fund on some girl, Race. Your father told me cutting you
out of our lives was the only way you would see what you were
giving up. You were supposed to come back home."

It grated on my last nerve. I gritted my teeth and Brysen
lifted her hands to run them over the swirling black-and-blue
bruises that were painting my ribs on either side. People with
power and money always thought they had the upper hand, that
they could manipulate others with no consequences.

I lowered my forehead so it touched hers, and told my mom
in a tone that was final, "You can come into the city and get some
money, not for Dad. I'll give you enough to get a hotel until you
figure out a game plan."

She started to talk over me, but I cut her off.

"That girl, the one I spent all of my tuition money on, wasn't
just some stranger, Mom. She's Dad's kid, and he tried to have
her killed. Once before she was even born, and then again when
her mom came back around to try and extort money out of him.
He's a fucking monster and I hope he turns on Novak's crew

because he'll never make it to the witness stand alive. He can rot in hell with Novak as far as I'm concerned."

I hung up on her before she could say anything else and bent so I could kiss this girl who always made all the bad things seem less in control of my day-to-day. She tasted like mint and the morning, and when she buried her fingers in the hair at the back of my neck and tugged, I made sure she knew that if she wanted to I was more than willing to take her back to bed. Only I got a little overzealous, and the way my lip was split open started to burn, so I had to lift my head, and when I did she had a drop of blood on the center of her sweet, pink mouth. I used my thumb to wipe it away, thinking that's exactly why I had to be careful with her. I didn't want any kind of blood on her: mine, hers, or the rivers of it that the Point seemed to spill without any thought.

"I'll walk you downstairs. The shop is closed on Sundays, but Bax will be around." I trusted my best friend to keep his trap shut and not give her a hard time, but I felt better, more like a gentleman, if I escorted her through the cavernous monster of the garage. I still had some chivalry inside me, even if it was buried under miles and miles of other, harder things.

I didn't bother with a shirt or shoes, just took her hand and guided her down the metal stairs. It was cold on the garage floor since I was only half dressed, and I noticed one of the big metal bay doors was open. Bax's Hemi 'Cuda was up on the rack but he was nowhere to be seen. I was going to just lead Brysen through the open bay when she suddenly pulled to a stop and yanked her hand free of my loose grip. I was going to ask her what in the hell she was doing when she purposely veered off in the direction where all of the boosted cars were parked along the back wall.

The nondescript fleet of cars Bax had collected for me were

patiently waiting on their owners to pay up. In the dark, with the low interior lights, they were hard to see. However, with the bay doors open, and in the bright light of the morning, it was much more evident that the mismatched collection didn't belong with Bax's works of art and restoration or his high-end repairs.

"Brysen?" Her name was a question but she was ignoring me and moving with clear intent right toward a white Lexus SUV that was parked amongst the other collateral.

It wasn't the nicest car of the group. It wasn't the worst either. I couldn't figure out why she had sought it out like a heat-seeking missile until she turned on me and her eyes went from a pretty summer day to a rolling, thunderous storm at sea.

"Why do you have this car?"

I looked at her and tried to decide what I should say. I could lie, tell her it was just waiting to be fixed, but I had the distinct impression she already knew more about why it was here than I wanted her to.

I crossed my arms over my bare chest and lowered my eyebrows at her. I could do flinty and cold as well as any blue blood.

"I don't see how that's any business of yours, Bry."

She let her mouth fall open and I saw a hot red run up her neck and flood into her face. She stalked toward me and jabbed the end of a finger into the center of my chest. I had a bruise there from the night before, so the jab hurt and made me scowl at her even harder.

"That's my dad's car, Race. The car that is supposedly in the shop, which made him demand *my* car yesterday. So yeah, it very much is my business why you have it here."

I took a step back, and out of the corner of my eye saw Bax

come out of his office. His face was hard, and even with the distance separating us I saw how dark his gaze was as it locked on our conflict. Bax wouldn't let anyone mess with his operation and he didn't care if the threat was a mostly harmless pretty college girl.

I grabbed her by the elbow and hauled her out into the front lot where the BMW was parked next to the Stang.

"You know what I do, Bry. Don't pretend like you don't, because now it might be a little too close to home."

She pursed her lips and narrowed her eyes at me. "My dad doesn't gamble. He's a computer programmer, for Christ sakes."

All kinds of people gambled, and I didn't want to tell her, but computer people were some of the most compulsive. They always thought they could beat the odds, outsmart the rules. Because I couldn't forget, even if I wanted to, I pulled up the image of a middle-aged man, frantic and begging as he gave me the last of his life savings and retirement plan in order to get in on a private game at Spanky's a week ago. He was into me for over three hundred thousand and the Lexus wouldn't even touch his debt. I had no idea he was Brysen's dad, and frankly it didn't matter. My job was to take money, not save families or fathers from themselves.

"Everyone gambles on something. Football, horses, cars, with their lives, with cheap sex and dangerous drugs, with love." I looked at her hard. "I didn't know he was your dad. I don't usually ask names and personal details. I just take the cash and make the wager or let them have at a table."

She blew out a breath and her eyes flicked from me back to the open bay.

"Give the car back, Race." Her voice was low, shaky. I knew she was more in shock about the revelation about her dad than the fact that I had taken the car from him. That didn't mean she understood, or that she would forgive me, but at least I knew the real reason she looked like she wanted to throw up on me.

I shook my head slowly and let her see the real regret in my gaze as I watched her. "I can't do that."

She hissed out a breath between her teeth and stomped away from me to her car.

I looked at her and frowned and told her flatly, "This business isn't exactly one where you make friends, Brysen. I don't ask for full names and stats. I just take the money, and when they don't have the money to pay me back, I take something else." Maybe she didn't need to know the rest, but we were this far into it, so I let her know: "The Lexus doesn't even start to cover the amount your dad is in for, Bry."

Something crossed her pretty face and her eyes gleamed at me with something sad and furious. "If you had known he was my dad, would it have made any difference?"

If she didn't matter to me I would've just lied to her.

"No. I still would've let him sit at the table, still would've taken the Lexus for the debt. It's what I do."

She shook her head and told me in a frigid tone, "Fuck you."

I lifted an eyebrow. "Anytime, anyplace you want, pretty girl."

She opened her mouth like she was going to say something else, I saw her struggle with words that wouldn't come, and then she just shook her head and muttered so low I almost couldn't hear it:

"Your job sucks, Race. What you do is not something I think I can be part of. You ruin lives."

Now she was getting the picture. I didn't say anything as she got into her car and drove away. When the gates closed behind her, it was like watching her get locked out of my world forever. I really never should have let her into the fortress in the first place. This world was bleak and gray. There was no place here for the summer sky.

I felt Bax walk up behind me and smelled the acrid waft of smoke that always clung to him.

"Problem?"

I looked over my shoulder at him and shrugged. "Her dad is in deep and she didn't even know he liked to play cards. Unfortunately, he's shit at it and is in for three hundred K at the very least."

"Fuck that."

"Yeah. She's pissed probably more at him than at me, but I can't give the Lexus back, and that hurt her."

"If you give it back you would look like a pussy."

I frowned at him. "I would look like paying up what you owe doesn't matter, and that can't happen."

"What happened to you anyway? Nassir throw you in the Pit?"

The Pit was the bloodstained circle on the concrete floor where men tried to kill each other with bare hands and college kids danced to bad house music.

"Marcus Whaler didn't want to pay what he owed. Instead of figuring his shit out, he paid some thug half of what his debt was to try and persuade me to let him off the hook." I grunted. "It didn't work, and now Marcus has two broken kneecaps."

"What about the hired muscle?"

"If Marcus had more cash I would be dead. The guy didn't have a weapon, wasn't anything more than a gym rat looking for a thrill and a quick buck. After I put him on the ground, I told him to get in touch with Nassir. He's perfect for the Pit on fight night, and when I started talking money, all he cared about was green, not finishing me off for Marcus."

"You need to start taking a goddamn gun with you, Race. This shit is getting more and more dangerous."

I couldn't argue with him and it was starting to get old. I needed to put on some shoes and a shirt. Standing around half naked in the barren garage was doing nothing to help my injured body.

"Yeah, and I'm going to talk to Nassir about hiring some bagmen. The big-dollar stuff I still want to handle, but the little stuff—anything under ten K—we can have errand boys handle. I'm sick of getting used as a punching bag."

We walked back into the garage. I rubbed my hands through my hair and winced as the motion pulled at my sore sides.

"You gonna be able to deal if that chick doesn't come around?"

I looked at him out of the corner of my eye. I had never really been serious about a girl, but I liked Brysen, would keep her if I could, but my life wasn't for everyone, and she had to want to be here in the trenches if things between us were ever going to be more than fun and sexual games.

"I don't know. Maybe?" It was a question I didn't have an answer for at the moment. "I can't worry about her right now. The feds raided the Hartman castle today and took Dad away in cuffs. They froze all the accounts and Mom called freaking out."

"Bullshit. You are not helping that asshole out." His voice had dropped an octave and I could feel the anger and hate pouring off his big body. My dad had tried to have Dovie killed. It wasn't something Bax was ever going to forget. If he ever got a chance, I knew, just knew he would put my father in the ground and not think twice about it because he loved my sister and that was the only thing that made sense to him.

"No. I hope he turns on Benny and the rest of the crew and they have their people shank him while he's locked up. He'll never make it to a trial date, he's too soft."

"What if the feds try and put him in witness protection like they did to that bitch who sold Dovie out?"

If they put him in witness protection—WITSEC—then I would track him down and let Bax have at him and there would be no guilt when I did it; at least that's what I tried to convince myself I would do.

"If that happens I'll find him and you can do what you need to do."

His dark eyes took measure to see if what I was saying was true. I hated that it was there, the distrust he couldn't shake. I didn't regret the choices I had made that had sent him to prison, it had saved his life after all, gotten him free of Novak the only way possible. I did, however, hate that it had broken the ironclad bond we had always had.

"What I need to do won't be pretty."

"I know that. Speaking of doing things that aren't pretty, you think you can take a few hours one day next week and swing by the university with me?"

One of his jet-black eyebrows winged up.

"For?"

I rubbed the back of my neck. "I think it's time someone had a chat with the TA giving Brysen a hard time."

He chuckled a little and walked to the Hemi. "She gonna appreciate you getting involved?"

"Probably not. But I'm going to do it anyway."

He put a hand on the polished fender of the car and looked at me steadily.

"Do you think the reason you are so hooked into this girl is because she reminds you of what you lost? She's all glossy and shiny, kind of like you used to be before I dragged you down into the gutter."

I prodded at the cut in the center of my lip with a finger and thought about what he asked. She *was* glossy and shiny, but inside she was tough and kind of gritty.

"She had to move home to take care of her kid sister. She has some lunatic stalking her. She's works a shit job with shit hours, but she's committed to it. She's getting screwed over at school because she won't put out for some loser. She just found out her dad owes the guy she's screwing a ton of money, and that I took the family ride for collateral. On the outside she might look like my old life, but on the inside I think she is completely full of my new life."

He dipped his head in a slight nod and I reached out to shove him on the shoulder. It was like pushing against a brick wall.

"Besides, there was no dragging into the gutter involved. I chased you into the streets, Bax. I guess at the time, I always thought there would be a way out if I needed one."

He grunted. "Is that what you're doing? This business with Nassir, the money and the risk? You still looking for a way out?"

Was that what I was doing? Sometimes I didn't even know anymore, but I did know two things that were crystal clear in my mind.

"You're here. Dovie is here. That means if I have any kind of say in the matter, I'm going to make this a survivable place to be."

"You think you're going to single-handedly pull the Point out of the fire, Race?"

I turned away and started back toward the stairs.

"No. But I do think I can control the burn, Bax, and that's all I really want to do."

I didn't wait to see what his response was. I hurt and needed to find some kind of painkiller. I needed to call Titus and see if he could find out what the deal with my father was, and more importantly, I needed to figure out what I was going to do about Brysen.

I had always thought I could take care of myself, that I was smarter than this awful place that I called home. Now I wasn't so sure. The Point had been around for a long time, had seen all variations of evil come and go. The only thing that ever seemed to change here was the seasons.

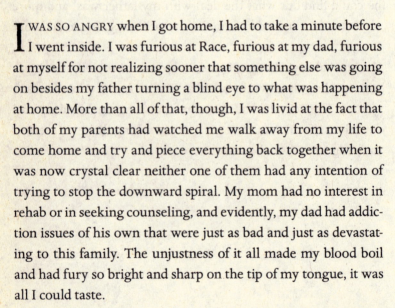

Chapter 11

Brysen

I WAS SO ANGRY when I got home, I had to take a minute before I went inside. I was furious at Race, furious at my dad, furious at myself for not realizing sooner that something else was going on besides my father turning a blind eye to what was happening at home. More than all of that, though, I was livid at the fact that both of my parents had watched me walk away from my life to come home and try and piece everything back together when it was now crystal clear neither one of them had any intention of trying to stop the downward spiral. My mom had no interest in rehab or in seeking counseling, and evidently, my dad had addiction issues of his own that were just as bad and just as devastating to this family. The unjustness of it all made my blood boil and had fury so bright and sharp on the tip of my tongue, it was all I could taste.

I slammed the door to my car way harder than was needed and marched into the house without a plan. I was fueled by new revelations, and all the things I had been swallowing down for the last year or so were breaking free of the stranglehold I normally kept on them. I shoved open the front door and didn't

even bother to close it as I marched with purpose and ferocity to
my dad's closed office door. I didn't bother to knock and didn't
bother to announce myself or make any kind of pleasantries. I
just stormed in and attacked.

His head snapped up from the computer screen and his eyes
got wide. "Brysen?"

I put my hands on the edge of the desk and leaned over so
that he had no choice but to look at me and not at the computer
monitor.

"I know you lost the Lexus because of a gambling debt, Dad.
I also know it doesn't even begin to cover what you owe."

His eyes got even bigger, if that was possible, and all the
color fled from his face.

"What are you talking about?"

I narrowed my eyes at him and pushed off the desk so I could
cross my arms over my chest in a defensive stance.

"I know, Dad."

"You don't know anything, little girl." His tone got sharp,
and where he had been pale a minute ago, now a hot red flooded
into his cheeks. "Everything I have done I have done to keep this
family afloat since your mother's accident. Do you think those
doctor bills were cheap? Do you think the settlement we had to
pay to that other family was pulled out of thin air? I did what I
had to do."

"Yeah, but you didn't stop, did you?"

He just glared at me and I glared at him even harder.

"How much do you owe, Dad?"

He huffed and puffed and pushed back in his chair. "That's
none of your concern. I have everything under control."

I wanted to chuck something heavy at his head. He most

definitely didn't have anything under control. It was glaringly obvious.

"What about Mom? Does she know about this, or is that why you have no problem keeping her in a steady supply of booze? She's already depressed and all messed up, so maybe you think enabling her to self-medicate will keep her off your back while you lose whatever this family has left."

He flinched and I saw the horrible truth of my words reflected in his gaze. What in the hell was wrong with my family?

He heaved a heavy sigh and flopped back in his swivel chair. He covered his face with his hands, and right before my eyes suddenly looked a hundred years old.

"There isn't anything left to lose, Brysen. My 401(k), all our savings, the credit cards, and my car—all of it is gone." His eyes got glassy and he looked really scared when he told me, "The mortgage on the house hasn't been paid for months and months. We went into foreclosure a month after you moved in. Luckily, the banks are still trying to dig out of the rut the recession put them in and are backed up. It's going to happen eventually. We're going to have to leave when the bank takes possession."

I felt my lungs seize, felt everything inside of me go ice cold. I exhaled slowly and saw the room start to fade around the edges of my vision.

"So you are telling me you knew this entire time that you were going to lose the house, that no matter what happened, Karsen was going to have to change schools and end up tossed around and uprooted?"

He didn't answer me, but he didn't need to. The truth was evident in everything that had happened inside these walls over the last year.

I shook my head. "You're disgusting."

I turned and went to go find my mom. I was over it. I was telling her it was well past time that she checked into an inpatient treatment program and I didn't care if I had to get two more jobs to pay for it. The chaos that was the Carter household ended today.

"Brysen." My dad's tone was sharp, so I stopped and looked at him over my shoulder with one foot already out of his office. "How did you find out?"

Well, that was a tricky question, wasn't it? I gave a bitter little laugh. "Race Hartman is Dovie's older brother. We've been spending a lot of time together the last few weeks."

He bolted up in his chair and slammed his hands down on the desk.

"No. I forbid that. He's not a young man you can have in your life. He's dangerous."

I knew that, but so far, all that danger was directed at other people and all he had done for me was try and protect me and take care of me. Right about now, out of the two of them, Race and my dad, Race was by far the lesser of two evils, even if I was seriously pissed at him.

"No, Dad, he's not. People like you, people who don't know when to stop even when it's obvious they are putting their family, their lives, at risk, are the dangerous ones. Race just gives men like you enough rope to hang yourself with."

My dad swore and then the anger in his gaze got speculative. "How close are you to Hartman, exactly?"

Oh my God, he did not just seriously ask me that.

"No. He won't forgive the debt or give the Lexus back on account of me, Dad."

Now it was his turn to bark out a harsh laugh that grated.

"Oh, don't be naive, Brysen. I'm wondering if your boyfriend is invested enough in you that I might make it out of this hole I dug alive. Race has a business partner that doesn't take too kindly to being stiffed. If I don't come up with at least half of what I owe, there is a good chance you'll be getting a phone call to come and identify my body in the morgue."

I didn't even have the words to respond to that, so I just finished making my escape from the office and trucked my way to my parents' room, where I knew my mom was bound to still be in bed. I was surprised, though, that when I came around the corner, she was in the hallway leaning against the wall. She was crying. The crying wasn't anything new, the fact that she was sober, and that her gaze was sharp and clear, was.

"He gambled the house away?"

"That's what it looks like."

She bit her bottom lip and started to wring her hands. "This is all my fault. If I hadn't been drinking, hadn't caused that accident, none of this would be happening now."

I didn't disagree with her, so I didn't offer up platitudes and useless reassurances.

"Well, now you have the opportunity to try and make some better choices, Mom. You need help, physical and mental. You need to be in a treatment program, and you need to see a professional for your depression. All the vodka in the world isn't going to help you get a handle on it."

She started to cry harder. "I can't believe this is happening. How could he do this to us?"

I wanted to shake her. They both had a firm hand in the disaster that was currently unfolding, but it was past the time to start handing out blame.

"Mom—"

She interrupted me with a wail. "What's going to happen to you and Karsen?"

In my opinion, it was way too late to worry about that, so I simply told her the truth. "I'll take care of Karsen, just like I've been doing for the last year."

She sniffled a little and put a hand to her chest. After a moment of silence, she dipped her chin at me.

"Your aunt Eleanor in Texas would probably be willing to take you girls in for a while."

I gritted my back teeth. I wasn't going to Texas. It was hot, it was far away, and as much as I didn't want to admit it because he was currently on the top of my shit list, Race wasn't there, which automatically made it unappealing.

"Mom, worry about yourself right now. I'll be fine and I'll make sure Karsen is fine."

I mean I knew she had her own issues, that she had never been perfectly healthy of mind and spirit, but if there was ever a time to rally and pull it all together and give it her best shot at being a mom, at being a woman who cared for her daughters, now was it.

"What about the money?"

Yeah, that was going to be a problem I was going to need to think on it for a second until I figured out a solution.

"Let's just find a place for you and then we'll figure the rest out as we go, okay?"

She nodded and disappeared back inside of her room. She

came back out a second later and handed me two bottles of vodka. One was almost empty, and the other hadn't been opened yet. I sighed and headed to my own room without saying a word to her.

It had been a crap day and all I could think as I tried to pick it apart and compartmentalize all of it was that I was so thankful Karsen wasn't home to witness the last of our family's flimsy shields of normalcy and happiness being ripped away.

I WAS ACTUALLY LOOKING forward to classes on Monday. I needed to get out of the house and get some space. I dropped Karsen off at her school and could tell she knew something was up, even though she didn't ask me directly. I tried to keep her distracted by teasing her about her date and about the small little hickie she had on the side of her neck, which totally backfired when she pointed out the fact Race had done a bang-up job of leaving his possessive marks all over my pale skin. It was just one more reason to be seriously irritated at his sexy ass.

I went through the day with my mind spinning in circles, and I was short with Drew when he asked me about the weekend with something more than friendly curiosity in his voice. I ignored Adria, completely pretended like she didn't exist when she tried to talk to me, and I almost cried when I saw my latest assignment in my Math Theory class. After everything that had happened, it was the big fat *F* on my most recent project that had me on the verge of breaking down. If I hadn't caught the vindictive gleam in the TA's eye, if I hadn't had far more pressing issues weighing me down, I might have done something rash. This was one more problem on top of my already gargantuan pile that I needed to work on finding a fix for. On the other hand, if I had to drop out of school to get another job, failing this class and tanking my GPA wouldn't matter one way or the other.

I dodged Drew and even skipped out on coffee with Dovie so I could go straight to work and not have to interact with anyone. I wasn't really fit company for civilized people at the moment, and I think even my customers noticed. Ramon was giving me sideways looks, and finally when the shift was over, he cornered me and hounded me until I gave him the glossed-over version of what was going on. I didn't tell him about the gambling and didn't go into minute detail, but by the end of the recap I was shaking and holding on to everything I was feeling until it felt like it was just too much.

I let him hug me as I shook and fought back tears. He kissed me on the top of my head and told me everything would be all right. That wasn't really a possibility, and because I knew it, it made me shake even harder. When he walked me out to my car, I got that creepy feeling like someone was watching me again, and made sure I kept my eyes peeled for any kind of impending danger in the parking lot.

"What about the car?"

I looked at Ramon and frowned. "What about my car?"

He shrugged a little. "It's a nice ride, worth some money. If you're really desperate you could sell it."

I looked at the BMW and then back at him. "I still owe on it."

"Doesn't matter. BMWs are classic. Rich people always want them. Get rid of it, pay the loan off, and then use the rest of the cash to get you and your sister situated. Then you don't have to worry about the payment and you have a cushion to land on. Flimsy as it may be."

Ugh. It made perfect sense and I hated it. I loved my car. It really did feel like my last tie to independence.

"That still doesn't help me figure out what I'm going to do about money for my mom."

He bent and kissed me on the cheek and ushered me into the car. "Honey, your parents are grown-ass adults. It's not your job to take care of them. It was their job to take care of you and they are absolutely awful at it. You have too much on your plate to be trying to save anyone else but you and Karsen at this point."

Maybe that was true, but I didn't know how to let it go after holding on to it all so tightly for so long.

I didn't want to go home, but I wasn't ready to talk to Race yet either. Not that he had reached out to me. I wasn't sure what we had to say to each other, and I hated that things felt so unfinished and unsatisfying between the two of us. I needed to honestly figure out if Race and all the things that came with him were really things I could deal with. I wasn't lying when I told him his job sucked and that I thought he ruined lives. The only thing that kept me from being able to totally walk away was that I could see that even though he knew what I said was true, he took no pleasure in doing what he did. To him, he really was just providing something the Point needed to have in order to keep from cannibalizing itself.

Tuesday was more of the same. I hadn't slept very well Monday night, and it had more to do with wanting to curl up next to a hard, warm body and missing the feel of golden hair against my skin than it did with the stress of trying to figure out the rest of my unsteady life. Karsen told me I looked like crap, and it took twice as much effort to avoid Adria and blow off Drew than it had the day before. It was bad enough that I actually contemplated calling in sick for work, but considering the root of everything wrong at the moment had to do with money, I figured that would be a bad idea.

By the middle of the week, I was exhausted and tired of running in circles. I was going to sell the BMW. I was going to drop the Math Theory class, even if it meant postponing my degree, and I decided I was going to call Race after my shift that night. I was sick of simply letting things happen around me, I needed to take control of my circumstances back. When Drew caught up with me before class, I let him stop me and I was even going to apologize for being so short with him over the last few days, when I was surprised by the professor interrupting us.

I didn't like him. He had ignored me when I tried to talk to him about the TA, and he had refused me time and time again when I asked him to look over the grades that I thought were unfair. I secretly thought the man believed me to be nothing more than a stereotypical dumb blonde, and as such, he believed I was just trying to get special treatment. It didn't help that I had no concrete proof that my work was being graded by much harsher criteria than the others in the class, just my gut instinct. I figured if the professor wouldn't listen to me, then going over his head wouldn't get me anywhere either.

"Ms. Carter, can you make a minute for me after class? I would like to speak to you in my office."

I sighed. I didn't need him to tell me I was failing and that there was no way I was going to graduate at this rate. I tucked a piece of hair behind my ear and nodded.

"Sure, Professor Hammond."

He pushed his glasses up his nose and went into the classroom. Drew frowned at me and followed me to our seats.

"What's that all about?"

"He probably wants me to know just how screwed I actually am."

"That's not cool, Brysen."

It wasn't, but I didn't know what kind of alternative I had. Again, I was going to tell Drew that I felt bad for taking out all my bitchiness and stress over the last week on him. After all, he was a nice guy, and the fact that he liked me and sometimes it made him overstep his bounds wasn't reason enough for me to be mean without reason. However, the words died on the tip of my tongue when my mortal enemy, the TA from hell, came in the room. Normally he looked right at me and smirked, plotting my educational demise, but today he looked anywhere but at me as he walked up to the professor and said something to him in a tone too low for the rest of us to hear.

The professor made a startled noise as he looked at the TA in shock and then cleared his throat loudly enough that the class in all of its entirety watched as the jerk of a teaching assistant walked out of the classroom without a backward glance. I shared a confused look with Drew as the professor got to his feet and began to pace back and forth in front of the room.

"Elliot just informed me that he has asked for a transfer. He will no longer be acting as the teaching assistant for this class during this term. That puts me at a little bit of a loss. Elliot has been solely in charge of all the grading and evaluation of work up to this point."

Yeah he had. The oily bastard. I wanted to breathe a sigh of relief. Maybe with the jerk out of the way, I actually had a chance at pulling my grade up from the bowels of failing hell after all.

The professor cleared his throat again and I felt his gaze land steadily on me.

"Elliot also mentioned that I might want to take a look at a few specific assignments where he might have not understood the concept in the material, and as a result, gave out inaccurate marks. I will have to go through all our past assignments and make sure everyone has the correct grade and that you are all up to speed before we get ready to start the review before finals."

Holy shit! This couldn't actually be happening. I was finally going to catch some kind of break. Was that even possible? I looked at Drew to share my over-the-top glee, but he was watching the TA's hasty exit with narrowed eyes and not paying any attention to me at all. I was so excited I squeezed his arm, which had him jerking his head back around in my direction and a little grin pulling at his mouth. If it hadn't been the middle of class I would've hugged him in my overwhelming glee.

Class flew by, and when I walked up to the professor's desk afterward, he looked up at me over the edge of his glasses and gave me a sheepish shrug.

"Elliot told me he has been unrightfully hard on you this semester, Ms. Carter. Our meeting can be postponed until I have a chance to further investigate the circumstances. I will be going over all your quizzes, tests, and assignments."

I tilted my head to the side and considered him. "No offense, sir, but I told you he was being unfair and that I felt like he had a personal vendetta against me on numerous occasions. You've ignored me and my concerns all semester."

He had the good grace to look apologetic and contrite. "Sour grapes, Ms. Carter. It happens every semester. An attractive young woman doesn't do as well as she thinks she should and it is always my fault, or the TA's fault, never the student's fault. I've learned to turn a deaf ear to it all. This is a good reminder to pay attention and not just go through the motions. If there are inaccuracies, I will make sure they are corrected."

"Thank you."

I wanted to skip to my next class I was so excited. I was running a little behind, so I almost ran over Dovie when our paths crossed as I was racing across campus. She looked windblown and rumpled, and her shirt was buttoned all cockeyed. I stopped for a second and pointed it out to her while babbling about the newest development in my academic drama.

She blushed, her fair skin turning pink as she straightened out her appearance. Her green eyes glinted in humor.

"I ran into Race and Bax when I got here for my first class. Bax wanted to say good-bye properly."

She shoved her orange-ish-colored hair back and asked me if she looked presentable. I told her she did, but I was stuck on her words.

"Why were Race and Bax here?"

It could be any number of reasons, none of them very pleasant I was sure, but then I remembered that the TA hadn't even been able to look at me. In fact, he had seemed terrified to let his eyes even land on me, as if there would be horrible consequences if he did so.

She lifted a shoulder and let it fall. "It was one of those things Bax didn't feel like sharing with me."

I had a sneaky suspicion that I might know exactly what they'd been up to. "That doesn't bother you? It doesn't make you crazy that he keeps things from you?"

She lifted both her copper-colored eyebrows and grinned at

me. "No. If I asked him to tell me what he was up to, he would. Most of the time I feel better not knowing. Bax has a scary and dangerous life, but he leaves it in the Point when he comes home to me, and that's where I want it to stay. I trust him to keep himself safe. I trust him to keep me safe, and that's all that matters to me."

Wow, that was either highly evolved or very shortsighted. She continued in a steady tone.

"The same thing goes for my brother." I flinched a little at that because she was looking at me like she knew exactly what I had been up to with her gorgeous, golden sibling. "These guys will take everything you have, Brysen, but in return, they will give you everything they've got to replace it. That's a huge commitment to make and you have to be willing to let them and that life fill you up."

I blew out a breath that sent my hair floating up around my face. "I don't know that I'm in a place where I'm comfortable offering anyone anything, let alone offering a guy like Race everything. His world terrifies me. My dad owes him a lot of money, Dovie."

Sympathy flooded her face and her freckles stood out across the bridge of her nose.

"It's not just his world, Bry. It's mine. It's Bax's, and if your dad has been gambling, then it's kind of yours too. The Point doesn't discriminate, it will taint whoever touches it to some degree. The trick is not to fear it, but to embrace it and make your own place in it." She nudged me with her shoulder. "It sounds to me like you think your place might be next to Race."

"Sitting next to him on his tarnished throne? Would that make me the queen?"

She laughed and moved past me now that we were both really, really late for our next classes.

"A tarnished throne for a tarnished king in a tarnished kingdom. Can you handle being a tarnished queen? He likes you enough to let you in, Brysen. Either you like him enough to do the same or you don't. Hey, I've got to run, but think about what I'm telling you."

I liked Race; that wasn't the problem. I hated everything that came with him, and I just didn't know that I could separate the two. But I also knew no one else in my life had stepped up to the plate and helped me handle any of the seemingly insurmountable problems that had been piling on me lately, and that alone made the decision to at least tell him thank you a no-brainer.

Now if only I could quiet all the tingly parts of my anatomy that were screaming at me that in order to properly show my appreciation we both needed to be naked and wrapped all around each other, it would be superhelpful.

I might have a ton of apprehension and a million reservations about Race's world and his hand in keeping it running, but it seemed like my hormones didn't share any of those very valid concerns and that my silly heart was caught firmly between the crosshairs of the mixed signals my body and brain were firing at it.

Chapter 12

Race

I WAITED IMPATIENTLY FOR Bax to finish mauling my sister and leaned against the fender of his car. It still surprised me after all this time, the way they were with each other. Bax was so dark, so entrenched in everything violent and unpredictable that came from the place where he had done whatever it took to survive. Dovie was sweet, and even with the hardships she'd been forced to endure, she hadn't let anything poison all the goodness that was inside of her. I knew they loved one another, that nothing on this earth, nothing the Point could produce, would ever tear them apart, and that was beautiful. It also made them a force to be reckoned with. Dovie had given Bax something to live for, to fight for, and Bax had given her something that was completely her own. Not a day went by that I wasn't grateful to have both of them on my side.

Really, I had more pressing matters on my mind than the fact that Bax had his hands inside Dovie's shirt. The weasely little TA had backed down and started babbling as soon as I had cornered him in the empty lecture hall. I don't know if it was the fact I had picked him up by his collar and shook him like a rag doll, or if it was Bax's threatening, silent presence, but the guy had started babbling and blubbering immediately and had rushed to admit within seconds that he was tanking Brysen's grade on purpose. I think if I had pushed any harder, the little slimeball would have peed himself, but the information he was spilling was far more valuable to me than his embarrassment would've been.

I let him go and told him he was going to transfer classes, or better yet, transfer schools, and he didn't argue. I told him to stay the hell away from Brysen. It was then he told me the reason he had been harassing her so furiously, and why he had been dead set on ruining her semester, and it was those reasons that were chasing themselves around in my mind. Yes, Brysen had turned him down when he asked her out and she hadn't been very tactful about it, but then he insisted that she had proceeded to hassle him online about it. He stammered that she had sent mocking text messages, awful e-mails telling him a guy like him never had a chance with her, that she posted nasty stuff all over his Facebook and just generally made him look like and feel like an idiot. According to him, it was Brysen acting like a typical, spoiled mean girl and he was her target. He called her a bully without actually using the word. So he struck back the only way he knew how, by taking it out on her schoolwork.

The problem I had with the scenario he was laying out was I knew how busy Brysen was and I had torn apart her old computer. She didn't even have a Facebook page, and the only e-mail she used was the one all students had access to, which was registered through the university. The correspondence I had been able to retrieve was mostly boring stuff related to school and projects. There had been nothing alarming, nothing lining up with the story this guy was spinning, but his reaction and his immediate agreement to get gone had me wondering what was really going on. Someone wasn't only stalking her, they were messing with her life behind the curtains as well. I didn't like any of it.

I looked up as Bax made his way back to where I was waiting. I was going to give him shit for groping my sister in broad daylight, but didn't get the chance because my phone rang. I didn't want to answer it when I saw it was Nassir, but I did anyways. Business was business after all.

"What's up?"

"I need you to get your ass to the District." He sounded furious.

"Uh, why?" I motioned to Bax to hold on for a second. He leaned on the opposite fender and stuck a smoke in his mouth.

"Because someone kicked the shit out of Roxie and told her to give us a message."

I felt my eyes get big and I looked over at Bax. Roxie was a girl who got around and made a good living at it. She and Bax went way back, well before she started making her living rolling around the sheets. He hadn't kept in touch with her since he and Dovie became a thing, but this was going to piss him off big-time.

"What was the message?"

Nassir swore and I heard someone moan low and painfully in the background. He barked at Chuck to find out what was taking the doctor so long, and then came back on the line.

"That this is just the beginning."

"Fuck. Did she have any idea who it was?"

"She can barely talk. It looks like someone stomped on her face. All I could make out was that she had a normal client, a regular, and when she went to answer the door, it wasn't him. Whoever did this wasn't fooling around. She's a mess."

No one deserved to suffer like that, even if they had a job that was risky.

"I thought you were watching the girls who worked for you, Nassir. How did this happen?"

"Don't even start thinking you can question how I manage my business, Race. I do have people on the streets keeping an eye on the girls. If they take new clients, if they get bizarre requests, if they think something seems funny, I don't let them do anything that might put them at risk, or the operation at risk. Like I said, Roxie said this was a routine date, there were no red flags. Whoever this guy is, he knows how places like the District work. He knew she wouldn't see a new client alone."

I swore again. "Who was the original date with?"

Nassir went quiet and I heard him ask the question into the room. There was more moaning, then a sharp female voice telling him he was a bastard. That had to be Honor, no one else had the balls to talk to Nassir like that.

"I think she's trying to say Marcus something." Well, shit. Marcus was just making all kinds of friends lately.

"Marcus Whaler?"

Nassir repeated the question and then got distracted as the doctor apparently showed up. "Yeah."

I blew out a breath. "Marcus Whaler is in a hospital bed right now because I took a tire iron to both of his kneecaps last weekend. What in the holy fuck is going on?"

"I don't know, but it needs to end now." Nassir went from furious to deadly cold. That was when he was at his most terrifying.

"Bax is with me now. I'll make a stop and see what Marcus

has to say. Do you think this is tied to Novak? Could it be one of his guys the feds missed?"

"I don't give two fucks who it is. This is our town now, and I'll do whatever it takes to protect it."

I didn't disagree with him. "Shoot me a text and let me know that she's okay."

I hung up and looked at Bax. His shoulders had tightened up and his dark eyes had deepened in a way I knew meant he wasn't happy.

I put my phone away and lifted a hand to rub the back of my neck. "Roxie got beat up. Nassir has her down at Spanky's waiting on a doctor. He says it's pretty bad."

He flicked his cigarette away and pushed off the car.

"One of her johns?" His tone was as hard as the look in his eyes.

"No. It sounds like someone set her up to send a pretty clear message to me and Nassir. She said he told her to tell us 'this is just the beginning.'"

He just stared at me for a minute and made his way to the other side of the car. "That's the thing about trying to get the upper hand in a place like the Point: it always fights back, and more often than not, it's the innocent that end up getting hurt."

I got into the car and looked out the window as he pulled out of the parking lot with a squeal of tires.

"Head to the hospital." He didn't respond as the car raced through traffic. "The guy she was supposed to hook up with is there. I want to talk to him."

"Talking is overrated when a girl gets hurt, Race."

I looked at him out of the corner of my eye and told him, "It's the same guy who tried to get out of his debt by hiring the

muscle to work me over. He's not going anywhere, Bax. I shattered both of his kneecaps after I got rid of the thug."

He turned his head to look at me and I saw the edge of his
mouth quirk up in a slight grin. "Didn't know you had it in you."

I snorted at him. "Really? Your wrist didn't snap itself the
night we met, now, did it?"

He chuckled. "Yeah, that did surprise me. I thought you and
all that blond hair and sissy-rich-boy attitude you were prancing
around with was going to make for an easy mark. Funny, with
you nothing has ever been easy."

"No, it hasn't. Do you think it's worth it? After everything
we've been through?"

He lifted a shoulder and let it fall as he pulled into the parking lot of the hospital. "Your sister is worth it. The garage is
worth it. Novak being gone is worth it. You and Titus making
it out of that shit storm of beatdowns and bullets is worth it, so
I guess it's all in how you look at it. I've been here too long to
think it's ever going to get easier, but now being in the thick of
it means something different. I have a reason for doing what I
do."

"What's that?" I figured I knew the answer already but hearing him say it would put a lot of that trepidation I had about him
and my sister to rest.

"Dovie. Good, bad, and everything in between, I do for her,
because of her."

"Me too, Bax. Me too."

He looked at me and we had a moment where I think we
were finally on the exact same page about what was happening
in our world right now and our roles in it. We would both sacri-

fice everything for those we loved, and it didn't matter what kind of men that made us.

Finding Marcus was easy enough. All I had to do was ask where the whiny and sleazy guy with two broken legs was. Plus, Marcus was kind of a tool and wasn't really the type of guy who endeared himself to anyone. Especially to the pretty nurses in charge of his care, to him they were just prey. When we walked into the room, it was clear they had him on some intense pain medicine, because instead of freaking out or calling for help, he just gave me a dopey grin.

Both of his legs were encased in plaster from midthigh to his foot. They were suspended from the ceiling on some kind of contraption that kept them elevated above his heart, and he looked more like a mummy than a man. One of his eyes was still swollen shut from where I had socked him, but a big, sloppy grin was on his face, making me wonder how much help he was going to be.

"Rasssssssse." My name turned into a long-drawn-out sound and his glassy eyes flicked to Bax. "Did you bring him in to finish the job?"

Bax grunted and propped a shoulder against the doorway. "Looks like he took care of it just fine on his own from where I'm standing."

"Fuck you."

Bax lifted a black eyebrow. "Sorry, man, you aren't my type."

"Marcus, who did you tell about your date with Roxie today?"

Those pain-medicine-glazed eyes shifted to me. "How did you know about Roxie?"

On top of being a really shitty poker player, Marcus was

married and had two little kids at home. He was a real prince of a guy.

"Someone showed up at her place because she was expecting you. He hurt her real bad and now there are a lot of people seriously pissed off about it. Two of them are in this room right now, and you don't even want to know what Nassir will do if you don't give me some answers."

He tried to shake his head but it really just lolled from side to side. "I don't know anything. I haven't been able to move since the ambulance hauled me here. Besides, my wife has been in and out with the kids, so there was no way I was going to risk a phone call to a hooker when she might overhear."

I lifted an eyebrow and curled my hands around the rail on the end of the bed. "It was a long-standing date, Marcus. Who knew about it?"

His eyes drifted closed and I saw him wince a little bit. "I had to lie to my wife and tell her I got hit by a car. Fuck you, Race. What else can you do to me? I'm not going to be able to walk for four months at least, and then I'll be in a wheelchair for who knows how long."

Typical addict. It was always someone else's fault. It was my fault Marcus went all in on a shaky hand and tried to bluff. It was my fault he risked forty grand he didn't have to lose. And of course it was all my fault I hadn't just sat back and taken a beating, letting him walk away scot-free. There was nothing more irritating than someone else trying to make me shoulder the blame for their bad decisions. I was going to tell him as much when Bax suddenly shut the door behind him and stalked to the head of Marcus's bed. Even doped up as he was, I saw Marcus's eyes widen and fear flood in behind the pain meds.

Marcus opened his mouth to scream, but Bax was faster. He slammed a heavy hand over the immobile man's mouth and yanked one of the pillows out from underneath his head. He snatched the nurse's call button so that it was out of reach, and took matters into his own hands. I should've winced or at least protested when Bax put the flat hospital pillow over Marcus's face and pushed down. Marcus clawed at Bax's arms, thrashed his upper body on the bed, and made garbled noises from behind the pillow. His encased legs rattled the contraption holding them aloft. Bax looked at me and I just shrugged. What was I going to say at this point?

Bax lifted the pillow up and I could hear Marcus's sucking breaths from where I was standing.

"A jackass who doesn't pay his debts is one thing. A piece of shit who cheats on his wife is another, but anyone who idly stands by while a woman is hurt has no use walking around with the rest of us. I have no qualms about putting you out of your misery, asshole."

Bax was scary without trying. When he really put his mind to it he could rival Satan for his spot at the top of the evil and petrifying food chain.

Marcus had tears leaking out of his eyes and snot dripping out of his nose when Bax released his smothering hold with the pillow.

"You're both out of your fucking minds."

I sighed. "No, but I am out of time." I nodded at Bax and he loomed over Marcus again, making the injured man hold up his hands and shake his head violently back and forth.

"This guy came in to see me the night after I ended up here. He told me he would give me enough money to pay off the debt

I owe you if I could give him a way to get to one of Nassir's girls. I told him Nassir is careful, he knows what he's doing, and he would never let one of the girls take a new client unescorted." Marcus's eyes darted between me and Bax and he gulped. "I told him I would keep my date with Roxie. That he could go in my place if he gave me another five Gs."

Bax growled low in his throat and Marcus held up his hands like that would ever be enough to ward off the dark and dangerous man.

"I didn't know the guy, had never seen him before. I don't think he was from around here."

"He was from the Hill?"

Marcus blinked at me like the question made no sense.

"No. Like, he was from a different country. He had an accent."

Bax and I exchanged a puzzled look. No one came to the Point from somewhere else on purpose.

"An accent from where?" Bax's voice sounded like gravel.

"I don't know . . . really. Irish, Scottish, British, South African—something. Please leave me alone." He whimpered and Bax gave him a disgusted look and moved to the end of the bed where I was standing.

"Where's my money?" I asked.

Marcus looked at me and his eyes got huge. "What?"

I crossed my arms over my chest and narrowed my eyes at him. "You said he gave you enough to pay off your debt and extra five. Where is my money, Marcus?"

It was a tiny little room and there was no missing his eyes trying to land anywhere but on the black weekender bag someone had haphazardly tried to shove under the chair next to the bed. I inclined my head at it and Bax walked over to grab it. I heard the zipper and then he nodded at me. I put a hand on the top of Marcus's foot and gave him a smile that was anything but sincere.

"I'm done with you. I won't take any more action from you. You stay the hell away from Nassir's girls; stay out of the Point altogether, Marcus."

I pulled as hard as I could until the cable holding the leg I was leaning on gave way from the pulley device that was keeping it elevated. There was a popping noise and then the leg and the cast thudded down on the bed with a jarring force, making Marcus scream at the top of his lungs. Bax and I left just as a couple of nurses came running toward the door. Bax hefted the bag over his shoulder and I followed behind him to the parking lot without either of us saying a word.

When we were back in the car headed back to the garage, I couldn't help but ask, "A guy with an accent?"

He didn't say anything for a long minute and then shook his head a little. "I have no idea."

"I'm getting together with Titus tomorrow to see what he knows about my dad. I'll ask him."

"I don't like it."

We were so used to knowing who the enemy was, knowing what was waiting for us in the dark. This new twist wasn't welcome.

"Me either." And I didn't even want to speculate as to what Nassir's reaction to this new unknown was going to be. We were supposed to be the new big-bad in the Point, not some shadowy figure with revenge on his mind and an accent who was just as good at moving through the shadows as we were.

We made the rest of the way into the city in a brooding silence that was only broken by the tapping on my phone as I texted Nassir the newest updates on our situation. His response was just a bunch of four-letter words. I was going to put my phone away when I was surprised to see that Brysen was calling me. I figured she was still mad at me and I was planning on giving her until the weekend to stew. Then I was going after her whether she was over it or not.

"Hello?"

"Where are you?"

No preamble and she didn't exactly sound happy.

"Headed back to the garage for the night."

"Good. I'll meet you there."

"Uh, okay." She hung up without saying anything else, leaving me staring at my now-dead phone in bewilderment. I looked at Bax and he just grinned at me. "She's meeting me at the garage."

"She probably found out about our visit with the TA."

"Shit."

"She sound pissed?"

"No . . . I mean, not really. With her it's kind of hard to tell."

"I'm going to drop you off and head to check on Roxie."

I made a noise of agreement. "You better tell Dovie that's where you're going."

"Seriously, dude, you need to get it through your head that your sister and I are the real deal. She trusts me. She knows Roxie isn't a thing anymore and never will be. No one matters except for her."

He might be stupid in love with my little sister, but he was an idiot sometimes when it came to basic human emotion.

"Bax, you used to sleep with Roxie and she was the first person you went to when you got out of prison. Yes, Dovie trusts you, but it would hurt her to hear from someone else that you were going to the District in order to see a chick you used to hook up with. Just explain to her the situation to save her some heartache, all right?"

He just grunted at me, but when the Hemi pulled to a stop in front of the gates, I shoved the door open and noticed he was pulling his phone out of his hoodie pocket. I told him we could touch base later, instructed him to hand the cash we collected from Marcus off to Nassir, and punched the code into the security gate just as Brysen's BMW pulled around the corner. She glided through the gates and I had just gone to follow her in when another car raced by on the street. I wouldn't have thought anything about it normally, but with everything else circling around the icy blonde like a hungry vulture, I couldn't just chalk it up to coincidence. I waited a minute to see if the vehicle would turn around and drive back by, but had no such luck.

The gates swung closed behind me and I walked to where Brysen had parked. The car was empty and she was nowhere to be seen. She had been on the compound enough to make her way through the side door and into the garage. I wasn't sure if it was a good sign or a bad sign that she was waiting for me in my space, but I wasn't scared of her and it didn't matter to me what she had to say. I wasn't ready to let her go. I knew there were serious obstacles standing in the way of just claiming her for my own, but that didn't stop every primal thing inside of me from wanting to do it anyway.

I made my way into the loft and stopped short once I hit the entrance. She was sitting cross-legged in the center of the bed I hadn't bothered to fold back into the couch. She had the frosty bottle of Scotch from the freezer in one hand and a glass half full of the amber liquid in the other. She had her platinum hair tucked behind her ears and her powder-blue gaze locked on mine. All of that was enough to make my dick twitch as it was, but the fact that all she had on was one of my button-up shirts and apparently nothing else had my vision narrowing to fine points and all the blood in my body surging out of my brain and pooling below my belt.

She took a swig of the amber liquid and I had to bite back a groan when her tongue darted out to scoop up a stray drop off her lower lip.

"Are you going to hurt my dad, Race?"

I heaved a heavy sigh and sauntered over to the bed so I could snag the bottle from her. I looked down at her and muttered, "I haven't lied to you yet, Bry, and I'm not going to start now. Even if it means you start putting clothes back on and walk out the door."

She cocked her head to the side and finished off her drink. "I need to know the truth."

"I don't know what's going to happen with your dad, Brysen. He owes a lot of money, and eventually he has to figure out a way to pay it off. I'll tell you this: dead men can't pay, so even if we eventually have to have a talk, making it real clear he better come up with the cash is as far as it's gonna go—for now."

That was so far from reassuring that I was sure she was going to freak out again and leave, so I snapped the cap off the Scotch and finished the remainder of the bottle in one, burning chug. I had to hiss a cooling breath through my teeth. It was smoky and earthy tasting.

"There isn't any money, Race. The house is in foreclosure, he gambled away his retirement, and you already have the car. There isn't anything left."

She sounded so sad, so defeated, that all I wanted to do was snatch her up and tell her everything was going to be all right, but like I said, I wasn't going to start lying to her now.

"That happens more than you think." It sucked but it was the cold, hard truth and it had long since stopped making my head hurt when I heard the same story over and over again. Only this time there was something there, something deeper than judgment and disappointment in her blue eyes that had a twinge of remorse poking at the iron shell I wrapped myself in when it came to business. I kept telling her I wanted to take care of her and keep her safe and yet here I was indirectly causing her all kinds of grief. It made me feel the first real stirrings of regret about what I was doing in the Point, considering all the suffering she had already been forced to endure as the result of so many poor choices made by others.

It was her turn to sigh and she bent over to the opposite side of the bed to put her empty glass on the floor. The motion gave me a perfect view of her very naked backside, and this time I couldn't hold the groan in. She lifted her eyebrows and rose up on her knees so she could make her way to the edge of the bed where I was standing. She didn't stop until she was right in front of me. Her chin tilted and those blue eyes bored into mine with unflinching directness.

"Are you the reason the TA from hell suddenly switched classes? The professor is reevaluating all of my work for the entire semester and now I'll probably pass."

I lifted the hand that wasn't holding on to the chilly bottle and cupped her cheek. I used my thumb to brush across the velvety-soft curve of her bottom lip.

"You're a good chick and a sweet girl. I'm tired of life trying to kick you around. We have to talk about that TA, Brysen. Shit doesn't add up."

She made a face but turned her head and put a kiss in the center of my palm that I felt all the way down to the last pieces of my soul that were untainted and unmarred by the life I chose to live.

"Are you trying to take care of me, Race?"

"Trying. So far my success rate is only about fifty-fifty."

She laughed drily and put her hands on either side of my waist.

"Why? Why, with everything else in your life, do you want to add me to the mix, knowing I might not be able to stomach this? I'm not Dovie. I'm not from the streets, Race. Your life scares the hell out of me."

I let the Scotch bottle fall to the floor, not caring if it broke. I threaded my fingers through the supersoft hair at her temples and tilted her face up so we were looking at each other and she couldn't pull away.

"I know it does, but you're here anyway and that's why I want you in the mix. You make all the ugly things a little less nasty to look at, and really"—I leaned even closer so she was feeling my words against her parted lips rather than hearing them—"your life is just as scary as mine at the moment."

She let out a breath and then lifted herself up on her knees so that our mouths were hovering a fraction of a breath apart.

"I really wanted to convince myself that I could hate you. I wanted you to be the worst thing in the world for me, but every time I turn around, you end up being the best thing in my world at any given moment."

I brushed my mouth across hers, let the very tip of my tongue touch the little divot in her upper lip, which had her shuddering and had her fingers curling into the fabric of my shirt.

I told her in a rough rush, "I'm not a very good person, but I do know right from wrong. I'm tired of the wrong always winning in this place, and I'm tired of the wrong trying to eat you alive, so I will do anything and everything I can to make sure it doesn't get its teeth into you."

I was done talking. She was almost naked, she was beautiful, and she had come to me. I had every intention of kissing her and taking her backward to the bed, but she circumvented me by lifting her hands higher on my back, pulling herself up straighter, and sealing her mouth over mine. She tasted oaky and intoxicating from the booze, but under that she tasted tart and sweet, like the best treat I could ever ask for. My thoughts from earlier rang even more true now. I wasn't done with her by a long shot, and at this rate I was doubting that I ever would be. I was more than willing to fall for her, and as she leaned backward and pulled us both down onto the bed, I literally fell for her, and nothing could've made me happier.

Chapter 13

Brysen

M Y INTENT HADN'T BEEN to seduce or to tempt. But when I saw him standing at the gate, a perfectly composed, gleaming gold, and shining light in a place that was so dreary and dark, my motivations had instantly shifted. There was something about how effortless he was in both the skins he wore—the one of a stunningly handsome young blue blood, and the one he more typically wore as the ruthless and broken king of the streets. They both just got to me.

There were so many unanswered questions and so many obstacles that seemed to stand between us. Really, when I broke it all down in my head, as I stripped on my way to the barren little room that now felt more welcoming and more like home than the house of lies I had been living in for the last year, I could see that Race was the only person who had been unfailing in his honesty with me. He was also the only person in recent memory who'd gone out of his way to do something for me, instead of expecting me to swoop in and hold it all together for him. I could no longer deny that this alone had me ready to crawl all over him and wind myself around him so tightly neither one of us could ever get loose.

I was impatient to get him at least to the same level of undress as I was, but when his shirt came up and off over his head, instead of admiring all the ripped and corded muscle pressing me down into the mattress, I got caught up skimming hands over bruises that had mottled to an ugly yellowish-green color. It was always there under his polished and glossy veneer. The ruthlessness of who he really was. The dual parts of the man that made Race Hartman who he was. I shifted my legs apart as he nudged them with his knee and gasped a little as he settled his hard body more fully into mine. I twined one arm across the breadth of his shoulders and let the other one snake between the very limited space between us so that I could go to work on his belt and the front of his pants. I could feel him pulsing in time to our racing hearts and could feel how hot and ready he was. When the backs of my fingers got inside his waistband, I heard him groan as they immediately encountered eager and willing flesh. Nothing ever thrummed and burned with life and vitality the way Race did. I wanted to eat them, and him, up.

He shoved the shoulders of the shirt I had commandeered off of me and bent his head so he could lick from one side of my collarbone to the other. He repeated the process back the other direction and stopped in the center at my breastbone. When he lifted his head and flashed that sexy dimple at me, I felt a full-body shiver overtake me. I could tell by the way the green in his eyes darkened that he felt my reaction as well. I needed to get his pants out of my way before he rendered me mindless, which I was pretty sure was his intent, when he lowered his head and captured the tip of one straining breast in his mouth.

It wasn't just the heat of his mouth or the swirl of his tongue around my nipple that had my entire spine arching off the bed. It was the way he touched the other one with reverence and hummed against my already tingling skin like I was some kind of delectable dessert he had been deprived of until now. It was like he was going to use every sensory tool he had to savor me, and it made my hands shake, which had getting that throbbing erection free from its denim confines harder than it should have been.

"Race?" His name was a question and a plea.

He just grunted in response and pulled his head up off of my breast as he levered himself up in a one-armed push-up so that he could help me shove the rest of his clothes out of the way. My arms were still tangled in the sleeves of his shirt, and when I went to wiggle out of it, he shook his head, sending gold strands of hair into those eyes that were gleaming dark with arousal.

"I like you all twisted up in something of mine."

He caught both of my legs, which were splayed on either side of him, and lifted them up so that they were wrapped around his lean waist. When he leaned back down on the bed over me, everything about him that was hard and hot was pressed up against everything in me that was warm and melty. I wanted to lift my hips up to force him inside, but he put a hand on the side of my face and used his index finger to trace over the curve of my eyebrow, which was arched in question.

"That's not how we're going to do this, Bry." He bent his head and kissed the high curve of my cheekbone and then my temple. I ran my hand up and down the sides of his ribs, careful of his still-healing body.

"What do you mean?"

He moved to the other side of my face and repeated the gentle, lulling kisses at the same time as my body involuntarily arched into his. I could feel how ready he was, evident by the beads of arousal, wet and warm against the inside of my thigh, but for some reason, he held himself just out of reach.

"Get in, get off, and get out. We aren't going to do that to each other. I don't give a fuck what the reasons end up being, in the long run all I care about is that you are here, and when you are, I'm not going to ever give you a reason to regret it."

His eyes burned into mine and then he kissed me. He kissed me with his mouth. He kissed me with the rest of his body as he finally sank inside of me. He kissed me with his hands as they trapped my face between his rough palms so that I was still and couldn't look away from him, and he kissed me with something deeper, something more significant than that, as I felt his heart trip and dance against mine. I lifted my hips up to take him inside my clamoring body even farther, and curled my legs up higher along his sides.

"It isn't always easy. You aren't always easy, but I have yet to regret any of it, Race."

I tasted the words as he breathed them back into me and we panted against each other as he planted his hands on either side of my head and started to move. Having sex with Race never felt the same, each time our bodies connected I felt like both of us were leaving pieces of ourselves behind with the other. I saw the darkness in his gaze deepen, felt his breathing hitch a little as the slick surface of our skin rubbed together.

I used my teeth on the lobe of his ear, kissed the sensitive skin behind it, and buried my nose in the hollow of his throat as

I felt my body start to quake and flutter around him. His rhythm picked up, and one of his hands disappeared between us, his sensuous pace picked up a little, and muscles and veins in the arm that was holding him up bulged and flexed in a heady show of strength. I wanted to tell him not to bother with the added caress because I was already there. His words and the way he was looking at me, the way he kept bending to kiss me, to make love to my mouth as thoroughly as he was making love to the rest of me, had me already on the edge. I could feel how liquid I was, how needy my inner walls were, as they pulled at him, and the entire room smelled like sex and expensive Scotch. It was indisputably sexy.

Race being Race had to go the extra mile, though. He tickled the indentation of my belly button with his finger, which had me giggling into the curve of his shoulder, and then he was there, right at that center of me, where coiled pleasure writhed and begged to be released. Clever hands delving into the place where we were joined, into the damp fold of my sex and right on target. He used his thumb to press down and simultaneously levered his hips so that he was driving as hard and as deep as he could. I lost my breath and couldn't keep my eyes open under the onslaught of pleasure and emotion that engulfed me. I might have screamed his name, or maybe I blacked out for a second, because the next thing I knew he was grinding his way to his own release and groaning his completion into my mouth as he dropped down and sealed our lips together in one final soul-entangling kiss.

We stayed like that for a long time. Replete and quiet. I could feel the weight that it always felt like so much more than sex when we were together settling pretty solidly on top of both of us. Finally I had to wiggle a little in order to breathe, because even though he wasn't bulky, he was still big, heavy, and I didn't want to be stuck in the wet spot on the mattress. He laughed when I told him that, and rolled us over to the other side of the bed, landing with him on the bottom this time. He helped me pull out of his now hopelessly wrinkled shirt and I don't know how he did it, but he kept us joined together. I wasn't going to complain about it and I liked the way he was twisting strands of my hair around his fingers as he stroked my spine up and down in long, smooth brushes of his palm.

"Can I ask you a question?"

I had my cheek resting right over his heart, so when he asked, I heard it rumble all the way through me. I yawned and rubbed my nose against the rock-hard plane of my pillow.

"Is it going to make me mad? Because I feel pretty great right now and that doesn't happen very much for me anymore."

He swore and his wandering hand landed on my naked rear end. He gave it a little tap and chuckled. The vibration made my insides all squishy and happy.

"Why did your parents give you a boy's name? I mean, you are clearly a girly girl and Brysen sounds like a guy who takes your lunch money in elementary school." I wiggled a little and sighed against him as his hand wandered even lower.

"I was supposed to be a boy. On the last ultrasound, the tech thought they saw a dangler, so my parents weren't prepared for a little girl. They had a blue nursery, and a name already picked out. Then out I come and I guess they were too lazy or too unconcerned to change it." I shrugged a little and kissed him on his breastbone. "I hated it when I was little but I grew into it. I kind of had to own it when Karsen came along and they gave her a boy's name too."

He shifted his legs a little and I felt the lower half of him start to stir. I was ready for a nap, but it seemed like Race, in all his otherworldly amazingness, was up for round two. I lifted my head and rested my chin on the back of my hand that I had crossed over his heart. I lifted both of my eyebrows and smirked at him.

"Really?"

He flashed that dimple at me and I groaned because it was a surefire way to get me to react. I felt the walls that he was nestled so snuggly in already clench in response. He moved his arms up above his head, treating me to a visual feast of sinew and skin flexing and rippling in the most mouthwatering way.

"Like I said, you might have a boy's name, but you are *all* girl." He said it with a leer that made goose bumps break out all over my exposed body. "So your parents were always kind of half-assed?"

I couldn't keep up with how he turned our post–sexy time into a share-all about our pasts, but he was soothing me along with turning me on, and I was too mellow to argue about the timing or setting.

"I never really thought about it. We always had a nice house, and Karsen and I always had new clothes and went to an all-right school. We were never Hill rich, but we were far from being poor. I didn't know anything about the Point or the other side of the street until my mom's accident. When the family lost her income, I think things really went downhill for my folks. It was always kind of just me and Karsen anyway. So I just did what I thought I had to do."

"You were trying to hold the family together."

I nodded and wiggled my hips a little, which had his pretty

eyes rolling up in his head. I liked that I had the same kind of power, same kind of control over someone who could dismantle all my reservations and objections without trying. It was also kind of intoxicating to know that I had that kind of sexual pull over someone who seemed as powerful as Race.

"I thought for a long time that I owed it to them. They took care of me, at least on the surface. So it was my turn to go home and take care of them, only I didn't realize they were bleeding from self-inflicted wounds."

He grunted and shifted his hips in an impatient way under me. It made my stomach flutter. This was the most intimate kind of flirting, the most heady kind of foreplay. I turned my head and brushed my lips across the flat of his nipple and watched it bead up in response.

"How did your mom escape getting charges leveled at her if she killed someone while drinking and driving?"

I rubbed the tip of my nose against his pebbled flesh and blew out a heavy sigh.

"She hurt her back. She was in the hospital for a really long time. I don't think anyone ever actually proved she was drunk. There was never a blood alcohol test done on her. The victim's family got a settlement and I think my dad offered them a payoff. They were from the Point, so I think they took it and looked the other way. I was living on my own when it all went down, so I only know the aftermath. All of it has been ugly."

His hand went back to cupping my ass as one of his legs moved my knee so that I bent it up and out to the side. I felt him expand and get harder where he was still planted inside of me.

"Was your mom always a mess like that?" His other hand slid under the curtain of my hair where it rested on the back of my neck. He used his thumb to rub on the tendon there, making me lean into him like a cat.

"She was always moody and unpredictable. It actually made her kind of fun when we were little. I didn't know it was depression or how dangerous it could be until I got into my early teens. She was medicated for a while, but when my dad started working all the time, I think she stopped taking pills and switched to booze in a bid for his attention. She knows about his gambling and agreed to get help for her own addictions. Now I just have to figure out how to pay for it. The least expensive place that can help her is still fifteen grand per patient."

He made a noise low in his throat and I could practically hear him thinking. I should've known Race's brain was just as golden and complex as the rest of him.

He kissed the top of my head and trailed his hand across the curve of my backside and along the slope of my hip. His touch was light and left tingles and shivers in its wake. I felt my inner muscles start to tense and squeeze him involuntarily. With a little whimper I pushed up with my hands planted on his chest and looked down at him. I loved the way his eyes shifted from one color to another. He would never be able to hide how much he wanted me, and that made my heart swell. He was holding on to both of my hipbones now and fully erect where we were joined. A flush worked into his face and he grinned up at me. He looked like some ancient ruler satisfied after conquering a foreign land.

Before he could move me up and down, wind us back up all over again, I reached out and cupped his too-pretty face in my hands. I ran my thumb over that dimple and lifted an eyebrow at him.

"What about you?"

His sandy eyebrows dipped low over his eyes and I saw his nostrils flare out a little bit.

"What about me?"

Why did all boys have to be obstinate? Granted, he was rock hard and ready to go, but I wasn't going to lay all my past out at his feet and not get something in return.

"What about your family?"

He sighed and gave his head a little shake from side to side. "Bax and Dovie are my family. Even Bax's brother, Titus, to an extent, but that's where it ends. My dad is an amoral, murderous piece of shit and I thought my mom was just too delicate to deal with it. Turns out she actually loves that monster to the exclusion of all others. I tolerate her at best. I'm ashamed I have their blood inside of me."

Wow. I knew there was dissension in his family, that he had been disowned and that there were issues with his father's refusal to claim Dovie as his own, but I had no idea how strongly or how deeply Race's dislike of his parents ran.

"I'm sorry."

"Don't be. I was an asshole and a spoiled brat when I lived like them. It took making my own place in the world, finding my real family and my real place, to understand what life was really about." His eyes glittered mischievously at me and one of his hands skated from my hip around the curve of my thigh and disappeared inside the damp folds already open and situated to accommodate his girth. "I know how to appreciate a good thing when it falls in my lap, Brysen. Don't doubt it."

I would have answered but he was using his fingertips to play with my clit and all my reason shut down to focus on the pleasure he was giving me and the lusty way he was now leering at me. I couldn't just sit on top of him anymore while we rested together and teased each other. I think that was his intent. I moved my hands so they were resting on the defined cut of his abs and started a slow glide up and down that had his fingers dragging through the excitement our bodies moving together was generating. I felt his stomach contract and he moved the hand that was up behind his head to pinch the achy point of my breast. Man, was he good at multitasking. He seemed to be damn good at everything he did, and as I rode him, and he petted me and stroked me into yet another mind-bending orgasm, I wondered if that goodness made up for the badness that I knew wasn't too far behind it.

HE WORE ME OUT. We were up all night, and the only time he let up on me was when I told him I had to at least text Karsen to let her know I wouldn't be home. I didn't get to sleep until well after the sun was up, and it was a testament to how exhausted I was that the noise coming up from the garage as the guys went to work in the morning didn't even make me stir.

I finally pried my eyes open when the mattress dipped by my shoulder and a mug of coffee appeared in front of my blurry eyes. A kiss landed on my temple and I struggled up and shoved my hair out of my face.

Race was dressed in dark jeans and a gray pullover with a V neck. His hair was damp and he hadn't bothered to shave. He looked delectable but had a serious expression on his face.

"Morning."

I gulped the coffee and realized I was sitting naked in bed

while he was fully dressed. I tried to pull the blanket up around myself but he laughed and moved it out of reach.

"More like afternoon. If you had early classes you missed them."

Well, shit.

He crossed his arms over his chest and looked down at me with what I was learning was his something-isn't-right face.

"Remember last night when I told you we were going to have a chat about the TA?"

How was I supposed to remember anything beyond all the wonderful things his hands and mouth had been doing to me all night long?

"Wanna throw me a shirt or something and maybe that will jog my memory?"

He raised an eyebrow at me but turned and went to rummage in the single storage closet. He came back with a black T-shirt that I slipped on over my head. Next time I stripped and waited for him in bed, I would have to remember to leave my own clothes closer at hand.

Once I was covered, I tucked my hair behind my ears and gazed up at him questioningly.

"What about him?"

"He admitted right away that he was purposely trying to tank your grade and mess with your GPA. Any little thing he could get away with for lowering your grade, he was finding it and taking away points."

I snorted. Race was a good five inches taller than my nemesis and there was no way a guy who was academic and used to scholarly debate could stand up to all the self-confident swagger and intensity of a guy like Race. Add in Bax, who looked like a criminal without even trying, and I figured it was impressive that Elliot the TA hadn't packed his bags and moved to a different state after they threatened him.

"What a dick. Just because I wouldn't go on a date with him."

Race made a face at me. "No, that's what I want to talk to you about. He was bummed you said no, but it wasn't a big deal until someone started sending him texts and e-mails making fun of him, putting his personal business out in the world to mock and ridicule."

I was stunned. "What?"

"Someone claiming to be you sent him some really jacked-up shit. Nasty stuff that would piss anyone off. It was all over his social media, all up in his face. He was tanking your grade in retaliation."

I almost dropped the mug of coffee all over the bed.

"I didn't do that. I would never do that. I don't even have Facebook or Twitter and I've never once texted him. I may have e-mailed him about school, but that's it."

I was desperate for him to believe me. I didn't want him to think I had brought any of this upon myself after he had gone out of his way to intervene on my behalf.

"Bry, calm down." He reached out and ran his hand over my hair and let it fall on my shoulder. "I went through every inch of your computer trying to pull data out of it. I know you didn't do any of that stuff, but it doesn't change the fact that someone pretending to be you did. Someone tried to run you over and now someone is messing with your life in a more subtle way. There is obviously someone out there with a serious hard-on for you, and I need to figure out who it is."

"This is crazy."

"I know. I have to meet with Titus about some stuff, and then I'm taking your old laptop to a friend to see if he can pull more off of it than I managed to. I'm also going to ask him if he can figure out where the stuff from 'fake you' originated from."

All I could do was look at him dumbly. I didn't know what to say. He tapped me on the chin with the edge of his knuckle and clicked his tongue at me.

"Don't worry, we'll get a handle on it."

"Before or after I lose everything?"

"If anyone wants to take anything else from you, they are going to have to get through me." He dropped his mouth on mine then rose and shoved his hands through his hair, sending the blond strands sticking up all over the place. "By the way, I think I might have an idea to help you out with your mom getting some help."

I recoiled automatically and swung my legs over the side of the bed.

"I'm not borrowing fifteen grand from you, Race. I'll never be able to pay it back, and the idea of taking that kind of money from you while we're sleeping together makes me want to throw up."

He swore at me and leaned back and crossed his arms over his broad chest.

"We are doing more than sleeping together—get that through your pretty head right now. And you know I didn't mean it like that. I know a guy that owes me and I think he might have some pull with a rehab center in town. It won't be in the best part of town, but I think I can work something out."

I let my head fall so that my forehead touched my knees. "Sorry. I'm just not used to anyone trying to help me out. My knee-jerk reaction is that things are all messed up, I don't mean to automatically drag you into it." I laughed a little and rolled my head to the side to look at him. "More minions?"

He grunted and moved to the tiny kitchenette to grab his keys.

"No. A fairly decent guy who likes to gamble on baseball, only his team had a shit year and now he's in trouble. He's been trying to get on top of it, and so far, all he's done is dig the hole deeper, but if I let him square up by working out something with your mom, I think he would jump at the chance. I'm not promising anything, but it's worth a shot." He came back over and gave me a kiss that had me squirming against him, and not just because I was freaking out about murdering him with my morning breath. "I'll give you a call in a bit to let you know what I find out."

I just watched him saunter away and was left to ponder how I had gone from being so frozen and stuck in a life that felt like a shadow of what it should be, to being right in the center of a life full of danger and risk with a guy like Race at the heart of it. It felt so good that he wanted to step in and try and tidy up everything that had spilled over in the last year or so, but it also made me wary.

Race was obviously a problem solver, he always had a ready answer, but when I'd asked him about my dad's future, he had been vague. I liked Race, probably was right on the cusp of being in love with him, but I didn't know what that looked like if I had to process what happened if he ended up hurting my dad. It was that contradiction that I always seemed to wrestle with when it came to him. He would do something wonderful like try and get my mom the help she so desperately needed, then turn around and have to take out street vengeance on my dad. I couldn't get my head fully wrapped around having feelings for the man capable of doing both of those things in the same breath.

Deciding I wasn't going to have a concrete answer to that dilemma right at the moment—or maybe ever—I hauled myself out of bed and went to take a shower and get presentable for the day. I climbed back into my outfit from yesterday and decided I was skipping school for the rest of the day and that I would just go to work later on. I searched high and low in Race's minimal space for something to eat, only to come up empty. I didn't know how he could live like this. There was something to be said for living simple and not acquiring unnecessary things, but he kept that amazing car and I saw the way he dressed. He was taking minimalistic living to the extreme, and by now I had a firm enough grasp on how he worked to know there was a reason behind it.

My growling stomach wouldn't allow me to hang around the loft without some kind of sustenance, so I made my way down the stairs and into the garage. Bax immediately popped his head out of his office when he caught sight of me. It looked like Race wasn't the only person keeping an eye on me around these parts. He tilted his chin at me and looked like he was going to retreat back inside when I called his name. He turned around and propped a heavily muscled shoulder on the doorframe.

I walked up to him, and putting all the old fear and questions I had about him aside, wrapped my arms around his lean waist and gave him a hug. I felt him go stiff and pull back.

"What in the hell was that for?"

Both of his black eyebrows were raised to his hairline and the star tattooed by his eye was twitching. Bax was not a guy you just randomly squeezed out of gratitude, apparently.

"I just wanted to tell you thanks for getting that creep in my class to back off. I really appreciate it. Also, if you know anyone who would be interested in buying my car, could you maybe feel them out for me? I still owe money on it but I need to make enough on the sale to get a small apartment somewhere for me and my sister."

"Say thank you with words, not hugs. All I did was lurk around. Race was pissed and the guy knew it. Someone messing around deep in your life like that"—he gave me a pointed look—"means someone wants to not only hurt you but make your life crumble from the inside out."

I bit down on my lower lip. "Race says it's someone with a hard-on for me."

He nodded, dark eyes serious and steady. "Sounds like it."

Well, there wasn't anything I could do about it now, not until I had some idea who it was at least.

"Will you let me know about the car?"

"I'll keep an eye out. BMWs always sell, but you know Race will lose his mind if you get rid of that car and take up residence in some slum down here."

"Race can't fix every problem I have right now. The ones he's already helping me with are enough."

Bax grunted at me and turned back around to go into his office but not before telling me very matter-of-factly, "You bring him a problem, he's going to try and fix it. It's what he does for the people he cares about, and if you don't let him help you with it, he'll take matters into his own hands anyway. Don't make him go around you so that you have an excuse to be mad at him later. That isn't fair and you're both too smart for it."

"Why do you even care, Bax?"

He glared at me over his shoulder and I saw him dig in his pocket for his smokes. "Race and I have a shit ton of history. Most of it good, a pretty big chunk of it bad. I'm in love with his sister and she makes me appreciate having someone that you're willing to destroy an entire city for. Race will tear apart anything and anyone he thinks is a threat to you, so you need to handle him carefully. Being with guys like us . . ." He shrugged and put the end of his cigarette in his mouth. "It's like being in love with a loaded weapon and you're the safety."

I wanted to tell him I wasn't in love with Race and that I didn't have anything left in me to be the safety for him, but Bax's dark eyes saw the truth so I didn't bother to lie. I just turned around and walked away wondering how I could be Race's safety if I didn't even know how to handle a gun.

Chapter 14

Race

Y OUR OLD MAN IS a piece of work."

I was impatiently tapping my fingers on the tabletop and staring balefully at Titus while he shoveled a burger and fries into his face. He had his tie thrown over his shoulder and mustard on his chin, but he still managed to look tough and no-nonsense in a totally different way from Bax. He also looked extremely worn out, like he hadn't seen a bed or a good night's sleep in days.

"You're telling me." I muttered it under my breath.

We were at a run-down diner across the street from his station house and the place was crawling with cops. Some in uniform, some out, all of them giving me the side eye and clearly wondering what I was doing in their midst. It was like inviting the wolf to dine with the flock and they didn't care for it one bit. I might have been more concerned if Titus seemed to care about it, but he was just eating away while I tried to pull information out of him about my dad. A task that would've been easier if he didn't keep changing the subject to the dead bodies and to whoever it was that had assaulted Roxie.

"You really have no idea who might be behind it?" Titus asked the question around a mouthful of fries, making me roll my eyes at him.

"Do you really think if I had any clue who it was that I wouldn't have told you, or Bax? He's mad as hell about Roxie, and Nassir doesn't like anyone trying to disrupt his business, so there would be a body somewhere."

He choked a little and reached for his drink. "You can't say stuff like that to me, Race. I'm a cop."

I just shrugged. "It's true."

"It might be true, but talking like that makes shit premeditated."

"No one knows anything, Titus."

He considered me silently for a second and flipped his tie back down. He wiped off his face and hands and pushed the now totally empty plate to the side.

"Your dad thinks he can play both sides. He thinks he can give the feds just enough to guarantee him a place in WITSEC, but not the entire bag of tricks so that his ass is covered from the last of Novak's guys."

I snorted. It sounded like my dad. He was always looking for some angle to work to his advantage.

"The feds froze all of his assets."

"That's pretty standard in a RICO case. Criminals aren't allowed to use dirty money to pay for their criminal defense."

"What are the chances of him wiggling out of everything and getting put in the program?"

Titus swore and his dark brows dipped sharply over his eyes. "With Novak gone, the D.A. is less eager to go balls to the wall on Benny and the rest of his crew. He has his sights on fresh meat." I didn't miss the hint in his tone or the way his blue eyes sharpened on me. "Your dad very well may give his testimony to a grand jury, and then disappear."

I felt my back teeth grind together. "He tried to have Dovie killed."

Titus leaned back in the booth and nodded. "I know, but the justice system is more interested in cutting off the stream of guns, drugs, and sex that Novak handled than they are anything else. They want his network connections and suppliers, and the way they get them is to offer deals to people like your dad and Benny to entice them to talk."

I groaned out loud. "Setting my dad up with a new life is bad enough, but if Bax finds out Benny is getting a deal, he's going to lose his mind."

His mouth turned down and a harsh look crossed his face. "I know. That's why I haven't told him anything yet. The feds think your mom knows more than she's saying. They've pulled her in twice for questioning."

"I don't think she knew. I think she just followed him blindly."

Titus just stared at me. Fuck me. It was bad enough to think that my dad was capable of killing his own flesh and blood; if my mom had known and just sat idly by . . . my family was such a goddamn mess.

"Either way, my dad doesn't just get to walk away with no consequences."

"He does if he cuts a deal."

I just lifted an eyebrow. "The feds can put him in the system, Titus, but I'll find him."

He swore under his breath at me. "Like I said, don't tell me that shit, especially since I know anything you cook up will involve my boneheaded brother."

With that I changed the subject, because like I told Brysen the night before, I was tired of the wrong always winning, and my dad was definitely wrong.

"So my girl's stalker has upped the game. Instead of just trying to physically hurt her, he's been messing with her life from the inside out. He almost managed to screw with her entire semester, which would've screwed with her graduating."

He cocked his head to the side. "Your girl?"

"Yep, mine." And she was. She was the perfect bridge between who I was and who I had to be in order to survive, and there was no way I was letting her go when she made getting back to myself so easy and so pleasurable.

"Are you sure she doesn't have some kind of pissed-off ex or maybe an old friend she screwed over? When a stalker makes the effort to take an object of their obsession's life apart like that, it's usually because they are trying to isolate the victim, forcing them to be the only person that the victim can then turn to for support."

"She swears up one side and down the other that there isn't anyone from her past that would be this interested in ruining her life."

He rubbed his thumb along the curve of his jaw and I could practically see his cop wheels turning in his head.

"Whoever it is has a lot of anger built up toward her, whoever is after her clearly sees her as a target, as some kind of important figure in their life. What about the rest of her family? Could the stalker be trying to get to her in order to punish them?"

I blinked once, then twice, and felt dread settle heavy and hard in my abdomen. "Her dad owes me over three hundred grand and her mom is an emotional and drunken mess. There's all kinds of room in there for someone to be good and pissed at them and taking it out on Brysen."

He nodded, looking grim.

"Will she let you dig into her family's dirty laundry to figure it out?"

"She already knows about her dad and the money. She said her mom is looking at getting help. I guess she caused a really bad accident a year ago that killed some guy."

As soon as the words left my mouth, we both stopped and awareness dawned. I swore and Titus leaned forward in the booth.

"Were there survivors?"

"Yeah. Brysen said the dad was the only one killed."

"A grieving family is as good a place to start as anywhere. Let me pull the accident report and I'll see what I can dig up."

"I appreciate it, Titus."

"In return, you will pass along any info you get on the mystery man with the accent."

"If I hear anything, I'll let you know."

We both went to slide out of the booth when he stopped me with a heavy hand on one of my shoulders.

"This business with your dad—I would let it go, Race. The worst punishment a guy like him can experience is living in Iowa somewhere, living a middle-class life on an allowance the government gives him. He'll be no one and have nothing, and that is far worse than death for a man like him."

I was going to respond that only death was appropriate for a man who was so ready to murder his own child simply to avoid uncomfortable questions, when the front doors to the diner slammed open and a uniformed officer came running inside.

"Who owns the red Mustang?"

I exchanged a look with Titus and got to my feet.

"The '66 is mine."

"I already called the fire department, but you might want to get out here. The whole goddamn thing was in flames when I pulled into the parking lot."

I used every bad word I could think of as I raced out of the diner with Titus hot on my heels. Sure enough, there was a crowd gathered around my car as yellow-and-orange flames danced over the cherry-red paint. The smell of gasoline and smoke was almost suffocating as a couple of uniformed officers tried to move everyone back from the blaze.

"Race."

I looked at Titus out of the corner of my eye.

"Don't say it, Titus. I fucking love that car."

He ignored me as sirens wailed in the background.

"When you have so many enemies that you can't even tell what direction to look in order to watch your back . . ." He paused to make sure I understood what he was saying. "That's a really dangerous place to be."

I grimaced as the fire got so hot, the front windshield shattered and collapsed inward. The car was going to be a total loss and it broke a little piece of my heart. It was the first car I ever bought for myself without my dad's money. It had been in rough shape until Bax worked his magic on it. It was the one thing that was mine, had been mine from the get-go, and now it was just a blackened, smoking pile of scorched metal and melted rubber. It made my heart hurt and my blood thick with rage.

"Is this the mysterious man with the accent, or about your girl?"

I had no idea, and it didn't matter either way. Whoever was behind it was going to pay. I didn't say anything, just locked my jaw as the fire truck wheeled into the lot and added high-pressured water to the mess that was once my beautiful ride. The crowd dissipated and left me and Titus standing there in the parking lot. He clapped a hand on my shoulder and gave me a little shake.

"The station has cameras. I'll see if we can pull a visual or a license plate. Let me take you back to the garage."

I blew out a breath, low and shallow, and ran my hands over my face. "All right."

I still had to go see my techie friend about Brysen's computer, but I couldn't do it without wheels. Good thing there was a surplus of them around the garage.

I climbed into Titus's boring cop sedan and closed my eyes and rubbed my temples as hard as I could. Losing the Mustang brought back all those thoughts and fears I had about losing things that mattered to me running in furious circles around in my head. I was all caught up in a girl who had a psycho after her, my sister was in love with the most dangerous person in the Point, and my business partner would kill me just as soon as look at me. All of it made my skin feel too tight for my body and had a buzzing nervousness popping and snapping right under the surface of my control. My fate was going to be whatever the Point decided for me, but if anything happened to Dovie, to Brysen, or even to my seemingly invincible best friend, it would break me, and I knew it.

When we got to the garage it was late afternoon and most of Bax's crew was headed out, but his Hemi was still in the lot. I didn't want to try and explain why I was riding with Titus and not in my own car, but Bax was already walking toward us smoking a cigarette and talking on the phone. He gave the nondescript sedan a dirty look and then glanced between me and his brother.

"How are you going to outrun anyone in this piece of shit?"

He kicked the fender and then had to duck as Titus swung at his head.

"You wouldn't be talking so much trash if you saw what was under the hood. It's a cop car, dummy, it's supposed to blend in."

Bax snorted and flicked his cigarette onto the ground.

"Where's the Stang?"

I shoved my hands through my hair and tugged on the pale strands in frustration.

"Melted into the parking lot of the diner across the street from the cop shop."

His dark eyes nearly bugged out of his head and he just gaped at me. I sighed and told him curtly, "Titus is gonna see if they caught whoever torched it on tape, but I don't know if it's about me or it's the whack job that's after Bry."

He lifted an eyebrow at me. "If it weren't for bad luck . . ."

"I wouldn't have no luck at all. Tell me about it. I need to snag a car for the rest of the night. I have some stuff I need to do."

He rubbed the edge of his chin with his thumb in a move

that was eerily similar to Titus and told me in a flat tone, "Why don't you ask your lady to sell you the BMW she asked me to find a buyer for today?"

My spine snapped straight and I felt my teeth grind together. "What?" There was no missing the surprise and irritation lacing the single word.

He smirked at me and told Titus to pop open the hood of the sedan.

"She said she needs to sell it so she can get an apartment for her and her sister due to the fact her dad is a worthless fuck and whatnot. I told her she needed to talk to you about that stuff, because the only place she can find with what she would make on selling the BMW would be crap."

"She's not moving into the slums with her sister." Hell no she wasn't.

"I told her that was what you were going to say. I think she's pretty badass for just trying to figure out a crap situation and being willing to sacrifice. She looks a little too fancy to be the type to get her hands dirty. Glad I was wrong about that if she's going to be in this with you. Blood is hard to wash off. It stains."

"Jesus, Bax." Titus growled the words.

Bax just lifted a shoulder and let it fall. "It's the truth."

"Hanging out with the two of you isn't any good for my blood pressure or my career." Titus's voice indicated he wasn't joking.

I narrowed my eyes at my friend. "Is that what you tell Dovie? The blood is hard to wash off?"

His dark gaze was like looking into a bottomless pit. There was no end and there was no light.

"Your sister knows all about how hard it is to get blood off,

Race. She sees it every time she gets dressed and covers up that scar Novak left on her chest. She sees it every time I come home from somewhere I shouldn't have been and she doesn't want to ask me where I was at because she knows the answer will scare her. Blood is just part of living this life, and Brysen needs to know that if she's here to stay."

I didn't know if she was here to stay but I had no trouble admitting to myself that I wanted her to be. I knew coming home to her after all the ugly stuff that surrounded me all day long was one surefire way to keep my head in the game. Having something to lose like her love . . . it was a huge motivation to make sure I kept the parts of me that were still just Race intact. With her I didn't have to be Race the bookie, Race the loan shark, Race the enforcer, I just got to be a regular guy concerned about making a regular girl happy.

"Shouldn't the goal be to keep the blood away from the people you care about?"

I didn't think he heard me at first because his head was buried inside the engine compartment of the sedan. When he leaned back, he was grinning at his brother.

"That's a V-10. Who dropped that in there and did the work to make this junker able to handle all the torque it puts out?"

A shadow crossed over Titus's face. "Gus."

Bax's dark eyes went even darker.

Gus was the man who had been a father figure to Bax. He had owned the garage and given me a place to hide out when I came back to exact my revenge on Novak. He had also run Novak's chop shop for him, so when the now-deceased gangster had found out about the crafty mechanic's betrayal, he had had Gus murdered. Right in front of me. While Benny and the rest of his boys had beaten me, broke my leg, smashed my head over and over again into the concrete until I couldn't see through the blood in my eyes or the blackness flooding my mind, I had somehow still managed to make out one of Novak's goons pointing a shotgun at Gus and blowing a hole right through the middle of him.

Bax made a noise low in his throat and ran a hand over his face. He closed the hood to the sedan and dug out a smoke. He pointed it at me.

"That's exactly why it's better to get the ones you care about used to the blood, Race. Even if they know about it, about how this place works, bad things will happen no matter who the gate-keeper happens to be."

This conversation was depressing and I was already bummed out because of my car. I walked away after telling Bax he better not even think about helping Brysen get rid of her car as the brothers started talking about engines and horsepower like death and blood weren't major topics of interest to either of them. I mean, I knew logically that dealing with things like the loss of someone you admired and respected, and losing them well before their time, was just a brutal part of the reality of living in this place, but not even taking a minute to acknowledge how much that sucked was hard for me to get my head around.

Maybe it was because I had actually watched Gus die, maybe it was because I still had a bunch of guilt swirling around that the only reason Novak had set his sights on the mechanic was because of me, but thinking about him and the reasons why the garage was now Bax's made me depressed and brought up a bunch of bitter memories lingering behind everything else I was dealing with.

I snagged a set of keys out of Bax's office and decided on a brand-new Chevy Stingray that belonged to a dermatologist who had foolishly borrowed money from me to pay his student loans. Considering I charged a thirty-five-percent interest rate on money I loaned out, I had no idea what he was thinking, but the car was sweet and looked all kinds of sexy and fast. If the skin doctor didn't come up with the cash he owed, maybe I would just keep it. I didn't have the heart to try and rebuild another classic. It hurt too much to watch it burn.

I grabbed Brysen's dead laptop and called my buddy Stark to tell him I was on the way. Stark was the ultimate computer nerd. I don't think he had seen the light of day in over five years, considering he was always glued to this game or that, but he could find anything I had missed in her computer, so I was willing to brave his Cheetos and Mtn Dew–filled domain for some answers. Stark was actually the only person from the Hill I still stayed in contact with. He was also an erstwhile rich kid who had been tossed aside by his well-to-do parents. Granted, Stark's disownment followed on the heels of him getting declared a threat to national security after a raid from Homeland Security that had been all the talk in the upper elite for months. Turns out hacking into a secure NSA database to see what the government was actually monitoring wasn't an awesome idea.

Fortunately for Stark, he was a veritable genius and had managed to find a software development company that paid him bucketloads of cash just to have access to his superbrain. He made almost as much money as I did just by answering e-mails when the company sent them.

I pulled up in front of a perfectly respectable town house that was located just at the base of the Hill. When Stark answered the door, I had to admit he didn't look like any computer hacker or gamer guy I had ever seen before. He was shorter than me by a few inches, had dark hair that tended to lean toward a reddish tint, and he wore black, Buddy Holly–style glasses over a sharp gray gaze. All of that was pretty normal and basic; what wasn't was the fact that the guy was jacked. I mean ripped like an action-hero movie star and big enough that he could probably hold his own in the Pit against any of Nassir's juiced up brawlers. The other thing that would never have people pegging him as an über-nerd was the fact that he was covered in ink.

Colorful tattoos started at his collarbone and wound and twisted all the way down his massive arms and across the backs of his hands. I didn't get the theme behind all of the designs and characters, but it was all very bright and detailed and totally belied the fact that Stark was a mellow, mild-mannered guy who played around on the Internet for a living. He really looked like as much of a thug and a criminal as Bax did.

"Hey, man. Thanks for taking a look at this for me."

I handed the laptop off and followed him into the darkened town house. There were electronics and wires, as well as monitors and a variety of TVs everywhere. It resembled what I figured a command center of a spaceship had to look like. I accepted the beer he offered and took a seat in a giant leather recliner that was placed in front of a TV that was the size of a movie-theater screen.

Stark sat on the couch and started poking at keys on the computer.

"What exactly am I looking for in here if the hard drive is shot?"

I shrugged. "Anything that doesn't belong there. My girl has a stalker, and whoever is fixated on her is messing with her life. They made a fake e-mail, a fake Facebook, and even a fake phone number, all pretending to be her. Whoever it is has managed to get pretty deep inside her life already."

He looked at me over the top of the computer. "You got a girl?"

"Why does everybody keep saying that?"

He snickered at me. "I've known you a long time, Race. I remember the way you ran through girls before you fell in with Bax and started screwing around with cars instead of cheerleaders."

I slumped in the recliner and scowled. "I guess when I found out I had a little sister and that she had been living in squalor, was fighting to survive every single day, it made me have a new insight into the chicks I was wasting time on."

Not that I had lived like a saint at any point in my life, but from the second I met Dovie, took her under my wing, I made sure that any girl I hooked up with, messed around with, knew the score. I was in it for one thing and one thing only and they had to be okay with that. That was one of the major reasons I knew Brysen was different from the get-go. She hadn't bought into my charm, into my practiced flirtation, and that alone made me want to get to her. But it was the fact that even with her feigned dislike of me, I knew, just simply knew, that I wanted her for way more than just sex. I wanted those sky-blue eyes to look at me like I was her hero, I wanted her to smile at me because I made her happy, and I wanted all that pretty, pale skin to get pink and warm because I turned her on and she wanted me just as much as I wanted her.

"How is Dovie?" More rapid tapping on the keys followed by a noise and his eyebrows dipping under the rim of his glasses.

"Good. She has a job she loves and makes pretty good money doing it. She's going to school to get a degree, and despite everything I thought I knew about her and Bax, they seem to be a perfect couple. They're making it work. She's happy, she makes him happy—well, a Bax version of happy—and I guess that's all I can ask for as a friend and a brother."

He shook his head and laughed a little. "You getting serious about a girl is surprising, Bax settling down is downright unbelievable. I thought for sure he would be in prison for the rest of his life by now, not playing house."

I replied easily, "He's a lucky guy and I think he has more than nine lives."

Stark muttered his agreement and then looked up at me with a frown.

"There is all kinds of trick software loaded on this computer, Race. The hard drive ate a bunch of it when it went down, but there are traces of it all over the place."

"What do you mean?"

"There's key-tracking software on here, there's code written in here that allows someone to remotely view whatever the front camera is looking at. There's mirroring software on here so that whatever she was looking at on her monitor was being projected onto the other user's computer. Whenever she used this computer every single thing she did was being tracked. This is a wide-open doorway into your lady's life."

All I could do was stare at him stupidly. How had I missed all of that when I went digging in there for her school stuff?

"You've got to be kidding me?"

"No way. If anyone tried to track where all the stuff that was sent out from the fake her was coming from, it would point back to this computer and her IP address. Who is close enough to her that they could install all of this on here without her knowing it or questioning it? Programs like this take up a lot of space, and take forever to install. She would've had to hand over her computer willingly for them to download this stuff."

"I can't believe this."

"Me either. This is some serious Big-Brother-eyes-everywhere-shit on here. I haven't seen anything like this outside of military or government use. This is one obsessed freak you are dealing with."

I wanted to grab the laptop and smash it into a million and one pieces, but more than that, I wanted to find whoever was behind terrorizing and violating Brysen and choke the life out them with my bare hands. Once I found out who it was, a tire iron and some broken kneecaps would look like child's play.

"Is there any way for you to backtrack to the other computer?"

"If the hard drive wasn't a wasteland I probably could. She's lucky this thing is old and crapped out on her. There's no telling how long all of that software was running in the background."

There really was no telling how long Brysen had been in the crosshairs, and that made me feel murderous. I always liked to use my head first, but right now my heart and the most primal part of me were calling for blood. I would do whatever it took to keep her safe, brains be damned.

Chapter 15

Brysen

THIS WAS A LOT harder than I thought it was going to be. My mother had long since ceased being one of my favorite people. However, my heart still twisted as I watched her sign all the paperwork that would lock her away in this facility for three months with no contact from the outside world. She looked scared and her hands were shaking, Karsen was trying to unobtrusively wipe tears off of her cheeks, and I was just trying to hold it all together. This was the only time the facility had to process her in, and Karsen and I still had a full day of school looming in front of us right afterward.

The guy Race had set all this up with was begrudgingly helpful in expediting the process of getting my mom into treatment. It was clear he was breaking some major rules and could get into some serious trouble if anyone found out just how my mother had scored a spot in this treatment facility. I think he reiterated no less than five times that if she broke any of the rules, didn't stay on her meds, or slipped up in any way, she was out on her ass and the debt he owed Race was still going to be considered clear. My mom just nodded like a puppet and assured anyone who would listen that she was ready to get help.

I wondered if she realized getting help meant delving into the fact she had stolen a man's life with her actions and coming to terms with the fact there would be nothing left for her to return to by the time she was out of the facility. I hadn't seen much of my dad since the gambling revelations, but now there was no trying to hide the foreclosure notices and warnings filling up the mailbox from the various banks and mortgage lenders.

It had been two weeks since things had turned into something different between me and Race. Two weeks in which he had maneuvered things so that my mom could get into this place. Two weeks in which he had insisted that a monster of a man with a scar on his face and a permanent glower—who simply went by the name Booker—follow me to and from every single place I went. Two weeks in which the bank had sent the final notice of nonpayment on the house, letting us know we had only to the end of the month to pay or get out. And maybe most importantly, it had been two weeks in which I realized that when I didn't see my golden god it really sucked and made me miss him something fierce.

Between handling things with my mom, trying to figure out what I was going to do about where Karsen and I were going to go, and getting everything squared away with school now that I was a hundred percent back on track, there hadn't been any time to see Race. I wanted to this weekend, but it was fight night at the Pit and there was some kind of playoff game going on, so he hadn't been around. When I did manage to get him on one of his many phones, I was happy to hear that he didn't seem any more pleased with the separation than I was, and then he demanded that if anything felt off I tell Booker about it. I had already had to hand my new laptop over to the giant and wait anxiously while he pawed at it and searched for God only knew what. If there was spyware downloaded on this one, the giant couldn't locate it, which seemed to make Race a little less anxious, but didn't make me feel any less violated.

It wasn't that I was opposed to having a man at my back who looked like he could rip someone's head off simply because they looked at him wrong, it was more the fact that he didn't talk and didn't seem too stoked at being my babysitter that bugged me. He was a few years older than me and way taller than both Bax and Race. He had short dark hair that he slicked up off of a high forehead and made the scar that started above his eyebrow and cut straight down the side of his face to his jaw look even more prominent. It was really a shame considering he was a really handsome man. His eyes were a pretty, sharp, gunmetal blue. They were so pale they looked silvery and reflective, and they sat in a face that was strong, defined, and chiseled in a supremely masculine and hard way. If it wasn't for that scar, he could give Race a run for his money in the heartthrob department, and I wasn't excited that my little sister kept sneaking furtive glances at him when she thought no one was looking.

"Don't be nervous, Mom. They'll get you on the right meds and help you get straight." I put a hand on her shoulder and tried not to flinch when I felt her shake under the light touch. "It's what has to happen."

Karsen nodded and bit her lip. She looked so young, so fragile, that I hated that she had to be part of this. My mom saw where my gaze shifted and whispered so I was the only one that could hear her, "What are you going to do? The house . . . there is no money."

She sounded genuinely distraught about the circumstances, so it took every ounce of self-control I had not to remind her that this was all a little too late. Maybe if she hadn't been drinking and driving in the first place, maybe if she had fought harder to stay medicated, maybe if she had left my oblivious and selfish father before it all had reached this point, I would be able to buy into her regret and shame. Now it just made my stomach hurt and had disbelief and aggravation struggling for dominance under my skin.

"Don't worry about us. I'll figure something out."

She finished the paperwork and handed off the thick stack to a woman dressed in scrubs who had been lurking off to the side watching our awkward family moment. The employee told us that we had five more minutes to say our good-byes and then Mom would be assigned a room. Karsen stopped trying to hide her tears and wrapped her arms around our mom's shaking frame. I heard her tell her that she loved her and my mom echoed the sentiment. When they separated, my mom turned to me and I just shook my head. I wanted her to get help and to be able to offer my sister some kind of healthy parental figure, but I wasn't about to pretend like we weren't here at this place without reason.

I reached out and squeezed one of her hands and told her, "I really want you to get the help you need, Mom. Please don't waste this opportunity. You won't get another one."

Race was eventually going to run out of people he could wiggle favors out of, and if my mom squandered this chance at patching up her disrupted life and mental state, there was nothing else I could feasibly do to try and set this family to rights.

Karsen leaned against my side and I wrapped an arm around her shoulders and we watched as my mom was led away. She looked back at us over her shoulder and I felt the way Karsen's thin body quaked against mine. She was too soft for this. How on earth was I going to drag her away from a nice suburban home into a dive located in the heart of the city if she couldn't even handle the reality of who our mother really was?

"It'll be all right." I wanted to sound reassuring, but I just sounded tired and sad.

"I hope so. Things haven't been all right in a long time."

Hearing that twisted my guts into knots, so I tugged her closer. "I'm so sorry for that."

She sighed and jabbed me with her elbow like we used to do when we were younger and roughhoused with one another.

"You've always done whatever you could to make it all seem okay, Brysen, but if no one else in the family is willing to keep up the façade, then the cracks show. It's not your fault."

"No, but I'm not giving up on us."

Her mahogany eyes flashed at me. "I know you won't."

I guided her out of the waiting area to the front doors of the facility. It looked less like a hospital and more like a nice spa that middle-class ladies would spend an afternoon at. When we hit the parking lot I put my sunglasses on and noticed that Karsen's gaze immediately went to the big black truck that was parked a few spaces over from my BMW.

"Why is that guy following you around again?"

She made no secret of the fact she was staring at the brute in the driver's seat and I didn't like the way he flashed his teeth at her like a hungry wolf. She had asked me repeatedly why the darkly brooding man and his massive truck always seemed to be around when we went anywhere, and pat answers weren't cutting it anymore, so I told her the truth.

"Because Race is worried about me. Someone was spying on me through my old computer and then tried to hurt me after work. Race knows some pretty scary people, Booker is apparently one of them, and he's hoping that having a pseudo bodyguard will keep my stalker at bay."

The news about my computer had literally made me break down. I cried for an hour and then yelled at Race when he asked me who could've possibly downloaded the spyware onto it. If I knew the answer to that I wouldn't be in this mess in the first place. After I hung up on him and then paced a hole in the floor, I started to feel guilty for taking out my frustration on the one person trying to help me out. Before I could call him and apologize, he had sent me a text with Booker's picture attached and told me I had a new shadow. The mountain of a man was going to follow me everywhere whether I liked it or not. Then Race texted that if I ever hung up on him again, he would be at my door within ten minutes and I wouldn't love the results. It irked me that he was threatening me, but I got where he was coming from, so I just said I was sorry and told him I couldn't wait until he *did* show up at my door.

Of course, Karsen, with her romantic and unfettered mind, focused on the part of my statement that was the least important.

"So Race is like your boyfriend now?"

I cut her a sideways look and popped the locks on my car. After we slid inside and fastened our seat belts, I told her, "I don't really think Race is the boyfriend type."

She rolled her head to the side and looked out the passenger window. It took me a second to realize she was staring fixedly at the mirror and the truck behind us.

"But he has someone protecting you and he helped you with Mom, plus he calls and texts you all the time, and I know those nights you don't come home after work you're staying with him. So if he's not your boyfriend, what is he?"

I wasn't really sure I had an answer to that question. He was a lot of things, not just to me, but in general.

"He's important to me and I know he cares about me. I've had a pretty big crush on him for a long time, but he's from a different type of world than I am, and I'm still trying to figure out if I can fit into it."

She turned her head back to look at me and I saw her start to pick at the threads on her jeans where there was a hole on her knee.

"Because he lives in the Point?"

I snorted. If only it was that easy to explain.

"No. Race didn't start out in the Point, but now that he's there, he's kind of decided that he's going to be in charge of what's going on in the place. He's not exactly a law-abiding citizen, and even though I think at his core he is a good man making hard choices, those choices suck and they affect more than just him. I'm not sure I can be part of that, even if I want to be with him."

She shifted her gaze back to the mirror and her voice dropped.

"If he's nice to you, takes care of you, and makes you happy, the choices he has to make that affect others shouldn't matter. People are always hurting each other, and if you have a guy going out of his way to not hurt you, well, that's what matters. Rich, poor, and everything in between."

"That's a pretty bleak view for a sixteen-year-old girl to have, Karsen."

She tucked her hair behind her ear just like I did and turned back to look at me.

"Mom and Dad loved each other at one point, but they ended up hurting each other and us. The boys from my school think they are entitled to anything and everything they want because they live in a particular zip code and they don't care who they hurt. Dovie almost died because of bad men and other people's actions that had nothing to do with her. Pain is everywhere, Brysen. I'm not blind. Everyone's choices affect other people. Look at where we just left our mom."

Well, fuck me. Here I thought I had been insulating her and protecting her from all the evils at our doorstep and she was looking at them far clearer than I ever had.

"That's a very good point."

She lifted the side of her mouth in a little grin that turned my heart over. I just adored every single thing about this kid.

"Besides, Race is a total babe. You'd be an idiot to pass on your chance to get with someone that hot."

That made me laugh, mostly because she wasn't wrong. I would be an idiot to pass up on taking advantage of everything Race seemed willing to offer me, his sexy self included.

As we got closer to her school so I could drop her off, her words nagged at me. Karsen was a peacemaker, a girl who just wanted everyone to get along and be happy. Her statement that the boys at her school felt entitled made me uneasy.

"Hey, that boy you liked, whatever happened with him?"

She lifted a shoulder and let it fall. Her eyes locked firmly on the mirror and the truck.

"He wasn't as nice as I thought he was."

That made my jaw clench and my hands tighten reflexively on the steering wheel.

"What does that mean, exactly?" My voice was sharp and I saw her flinch from the lash of it.

"It means that because I don't really live on the Hill, just at the base of it, I'm good enough to fool around with but not good enough to date. Once I figured that out and walked away, he got kind of nasty. He was mean and tried to drag me down to his level time and time again." She whipped her head around and met me stare for stare. "Guys like Parker are exactly the kind of young men the world doesn't need making the hard choices, Brysen. He's a terrible person through and through, and he's just going to end up more evil and more hateful as he gets older. We're all better off when the bad things in the world are being managed by guys like Race. At least he has good somewhere inside of him."

We were finally at the high school, and as we rolled to a stop, she leaned over and gave me a smacking kiss on the cheek. She shoved open the door and ducked her head down to look at me one last time.

"From the outside looking in, Race is giving all of us a chance at a new start. Take the advice you gave Mom and don't squander it, Brysen. Love ya."

She slammed the door and I turned to watch her blend in with the crowd of similarly dressed teenagers. I didn't miss the jaunty wave she shot, not to me but to the behemoth in the truck behind me. There was no clean slate for the Carters. Not with the spectacular way our parents had managed to break it.

I pondered Karsen's words, how wise beyond her years she seemed, and how futile my efforts to shield her from the harsh realities of our family and the world really had been. It rubbed me raw that my baby sister seemed to have a better handle on what was really rotating around us than I did. I got out of the BMW in a huff and walked over to the truck where it idled behind the parking space. I shoved my sunglasses to the top of my head and forced myself to look directly into those pale eyes without once glancing at that wicked scar.

"I'm in class all day today, so you can take off until seven or so."

Booker let one of his beefy arms dangle out of the window and arched a dark eyebrow over the eye with the imperfection. It made him look all the more sinister.

"Sure you don't want me to walk you to class and carry your books?"

The sarcasm in his voice was thick enough that I could almost touch it. I cocked my head to the side and lifted an eyebrow right back.

"You obviously don't want to be doing this. What exactly does Race have on you?"

He barked out a dry laugh and smoothed a hand over his hair that was shiny with product. "I might look like a dumb-ass, but I grew up in the Point, so I know which horse to pick in the race if I want to get out with my vital organs intact." I rolled my eyes at his clever turn of phrase. "Race doesn't have anything on me and I don't owe him a goddamn thing. I offered to be here,

Blondie, because I want that pretty boy of yours to *owe* me in the long run. Plus, following two beautiful girls around isn't a hardship, even if it is boring as hell so far."

Jesus. No one in Race's world did anything out of the goodness of their heart. In fact, I was starting to think my golden god was the only one walking amongst the shadows who was plagued with that particular body part.

"My sister is just a kid, so keep your eyes to yourself, Gigantor." I adjusted my school bag on my shoulder and narrowed my eyes at him. "Whatever your reasons, I appreciate you keeping an eye on me."

"Honey, I got out of the pen not too long ago. I have no intention of going back for a pretty young thing, and I also have no desire to have all my bits and pieces cut off and scattered across the city if I get on your boy's bad side. Like I said, I might look like a dumb-ass, but looks can be deceiving."

He was preaching to the choir with that, so I just waved him off and headed toward the building where my statistics class met. One thing was for sure: the characters that were now a part of my life since hooking up with Race were hands down some of the most interesting and terrifying people a girl could ever come across. I wondered what it said about me that I preferred them over the frat guys and academics that were swarming by me as we all pounded up the staircase to the second floor of the building.

I was so lost in thought that when I was jostled from the side, I just shook it off without turning to see who the culprit was. The staircase was packed with students and all of them had cumbersome bags full of books and school junk, so I was sure it was just an accident and I had accidentally been bumped by someone careless and in a rush. I made a move to see if I could get out of the center of the swarm when I felt another bump, only this one was harder and had me whipping my head around to tell who-ever the offender was to be more careful. That was a mistake.

I had one foot on the steps getting ready to move up and my balance was off because of my own heavy school bag. I was no-where near the railing and didn't have anything to grab on to or any kind of traction to keep me from toppling backward when someone nailed me hard in the side and sent me careening in the wrong direction as startled groups of people split up around me and just let me fall. It wouldn't have been such a big deal, people fall down the stairs all the time, but when hard hands appeared out of nowhere and gave me one last shove to ensure I went flailing to the hard, cement floor a story below with the most force possible, the outcome wasn't going to be pretty. I let out a scream that died on a short breath because I knew the impact was imminent.

Luckily, somewhere toward the end of my free fall, an un-suspecting and oblivious kid that had to have been unaware of the impending impact didn't move fast enough and ended up braking my descent. I landed half on him, half on the floor. Un-fortunately for me, it was my top half that cracked onto lino-leum covered concrete. My head made a sickening sound and pain exploded in starbursts across my vision. I could smell my own blood and the dull roar of concerned voices as a crowd gathered around me. I heard someone call my name and I tried to turn my head in that direction, which had fire and electric agony racing through every nerve ending I had. Darkness was starting to fill my cloudy vision, and I wanted to call out that someone had pushed me, that someone was trying to hurt me.

But more than anything, I wanted to tell someone to call Race. I wanted him.

I heard someone mention a fall and I wanted to bellow that no, I had been pushed, but the coppery, iron tang of blood was getting stronger in my nose and I think I was starting to taste it. It was so much easier just to close my eyes and let the blackness that was covering me like a blanket take over. Finally letting go was so easy and I just let the dark fill me up and surround me.

"I'M NOT LETTING YOU two go back to the house after this."

I couldn't pry my eyes open but I heard Race's voice and the anger that was tight in it from somewhere in the hazy cloud I was floating in. Karsen's voice was shaky when she answered him.

"Nowhere seems safe anymore."

Race swore and I felt gentle fingers dance across my forehead. Even blacked out and consumed with pain, I would know Race's touch anywhere.

"I'm going to change that. As soon as she wakes up I'm headed to that school. Someone had to see what happened, and if I have to give every student on that campus a black eye or broken nose to get answers, I will."

Karsen sniffled and I wanted to open my eyes to tell her there was no need to cry, but I just couldn't do it. The dark was warm, it was welcoming, and while I was here I didn't have to worry about things like losing the house, falling in love with a criminal, or the fact someone was obviously trying to kill me. It was a nice change of pace.

"When she wakes up, the doctor is going to want to do a CT scan. She hit her head really, really hard." Karsen's voice was shaky.

I felt the light touch caressing my forehead flitter over my eyebrows. I wanted to turn into it, to just let him soothe me and take care of everything from here on out. I knew that he would if I just let it all go and handed some of it over to him. That terrified me. I didn't want to think about what it meant to rely on Race when he already had the fate of an entire city balanced precariously in the palm of his hands.

"It's a good thing your sister has a hard head, then. She'll be okay. She just has to open her eyes. I know you can hear me, Bry. Get those baby blues open for me."

Karsen laughed a sad little sound that made me want to hug her. "She's going to freak when she sees what they had to do to her hair in order to stitch the back of her head closed."

My hair! That had my eyes snapping open and a groan ripping out of my chest when the lights assaulted me. I hurt everywhere there was to hurt.

"What happened to my hair?" Sure, it was shallow of me, and there were far more pressing things at hand, but dammit, I had awesome hair. It was just one more reason to be furious at the way this stalker had invaded my life. My voice was raspy and it rattled in my ears all tinny and thin.

Race's tender caress stopped midstroke and his dark green eyes were suddenly all I could see as he loomed over the edge of the bed. His mouth was tight and there were scary shadows dancing behind the concern in his gaze as he looked down at me.

"There she is. Karsen, why don't you grab a nurse and let them know she's awake."

The forest got closer and he brushed his mouth over mine.

"Can't tell you how worried you had me, Brysen." His voice was gruff and I wanted to touch his face, but even moving my eyelids sent pain shooting across the surface of my skin.

"I got pushed down the stairs."

"I know. You fell down an entire flight of stairs onto the floor. The back of your head split open. You lost a ton of blood and have been unconscious for four hours. The doctor was worried you bruised your brain."

That all sounded pretty serious. I groaned again and focused on something that I could actually get my head around. "What happened to my hair?"

He sighed against my lips and straightened up. He cupped my cheek in his palm and flashed that killer dimple at me.

"You're gonna need a haircut when you get back on your feet. You have no less than thirty stitches holding the back of your head closed. You cracked your noggin good, pretty girl."

I swore under my breath and blinked up at him.

"This sucks, Race." I knew that he would know I meant more than having my hair butchered.

"He's escalating. I don't think you're safe, even with Booker on your ass. I'm finding somewhere to move you and Karsen until I can get a bead on this guy. I'm done playing around and waiting to see what he has in store for you next. You aren't something I'm willing to risk."

Well, wasn't that enough to have my heart melting, or it would have been if I could feel my heart through all the pain and agony flooding my entire system.

"What am I supposed to do now?"

His head dropped down again, and this time his kiss had a fierceness behind it I could taste.

"You're stuck here for a little while. We need to make sure you're a hundred percent. I'm gonna ask Booker to stay here with you, and I'm going to find somewhere safe to stash your sister.

Then I'm going to rattle every cage I can find until this asshole falls out of it."

He straightened up and reached for my limp hand. I squeezed his fingers and let my eyes drift closed.

"You can't take my sister to a chop shop. Thank you for wanting to keep her safe, but that isn't any kind of place for her, Race."

He chuckled a little. "It's only a chop shop sometimes, but I know she can't go there. I have something else in mind. Just trust me, Brysen."

I pried my eyes back open so he could see what I was feeling inside of my gaze. I hoped it showed through the pain.

"I do. I didn't think I could, but more than anyone else in my life right now, you are the one constant I trust."

"I'm going to take care of you."

I let my eyes slide back closed and squeezed his fingers again. Karsen's voice was right outside the door and I heard the low rumble of another voice asking her questions. I was ready to let it go. I couldn't hold on to everything anymore, and I wasn't lying. I did trust Race and I knew he meant it when he said he was going to take care of me. I think I was finally ready to let him do it, and even more than that, I was ready to let him help me take care of my sister. I just hoped he didn't let either one of us down because I knew, just knew, if Race failed, no one was going to make it out of this situation alive.

He whispered a soft good-bye and told me he would be back as soon as he could. He also reminded me that Booker, in all his hulking and threatening-ness, would be right outside my door, so I should rest easy and not worry about anyone getting to me while I couldn't move. That, of course, was easier said than done.

He was gone and my sister replaced him. I forced a wincing smile for her but couldn't pull my heavy eyelids back open. I tugged on her hand when she picked mine up and demanded, "How bad is my hair—really?"

Her quick intake of breath was all the answer I needed. I hoped when Race finally did unearth my stalker I got a minute alone with whoever it was and some scissors. Payback was a bitch.

Chapter 16

Race

I WAS GETTING FRUSTRATED, and as a result I was getting care-less. It was Saturday night; I was tired and I was sick of no one having any of the answers I needed. I was pissed off that Booker had been the one to take Brysen to the location I had secured for her and Karsen. The doctors at the hospital had kept her under observation for three full days, but she was out of the danger zone now, and the only lasting effects of the fall were a dull head-ache and a terrible haircut. I wanted to be with her, but between fight night happening on Friday and the burning need to find whoever it was that was terrorizing her, all I had managed was a few quick visits and a few rushed phone calls. It made me feel like an asshole, but her safety was more important to me than anything else. I should be the one taking her home from the hos-pital. I should be the one guiding her to safety—not Booker. It sucked that I had other things I had to take care of. So here I was, back at a university party. This time, Bax was with me, and this time, I was a hundred times more dangerous because I wasn't here to get paid. I was here for information.

I was on the back deck, the same back deck I had dragged

Brysen across what felt like a lifetime ago. The back door had been fixed, but these college kids obviously hadn't gotten any smarter. The one I picked to shake down was friends with the frat guy who had pulled the gun on me and subsequently ended up with a broken neck. When I hauled his drunken, struggling ass through the party crowd to somewhere that was more secluded, he had made a big production of calling me names, telling me he didn't owe me shit, and trying to posture like he was some kind of big shot. The moron had already seen what happened when I got a gun pulled on me, and like his friend, he was too young and arrogant to have any kind of redeeming qualities as far as I could tell. When he took a sloppy swing at me, my paper-thin patience shredded.

Now I had the frat guy on his back with my knee firmly planted in the center of his chest. I had my forearm braced across his throat while he clawed at me with frantic fingers. His cheeks were billowing in and out as he struggled for air, but I refused to lessen my choke hold. His eyes were bugged out in his face and his skin was turning a sickly shade of blue, but I had no intention of letting him up.

"If he passes out he won't be able to tell you anything."

Bax sounded bored but he was right, so I lifted up my arm and balled up a fist. I cranked the college guy in the mouth with a sickening thud that immediately had his lips splitting in half and rivers of bright red blood coating his teeth and his chin. I made sure my knee ground as hard as it could into his breastbone as I climbed to my feet. The guy grunted and spit out a mouthful of blood.

"What do you want, Hartman? I don't owe you any fucking money."

He hoisted himself up on his elbows and glared at me from

his prone position. I looked over at Bax, when his phone started to ring. He pulled it out of the pocket of his hoodie and lifted a dark eyebrow.

"Titus."

I nodded as he took a few steps away to answer the call from his brother.

I crossed my arms over my chest and glowered down at my prey.

"You know Brysen Carter?"

Another mouthful of blood got coughed up and spit out. "Sure. She's a babe, but she doesn't party much and doesn't come across as very friendly, so no one really messes around with her."

"Someone shoved her down the stairs while she was going to class a few days ago. Who would want to do that to her?"

He groaned and levered himself up into a sitting position. "Fuck if I know. Like I said, she keeps to herself, she comes across as kind of a bitch, in all honesty. Maybe she pissed the wrong guy off."

I narrowed my eyes even further. "What guy?"

"What's it matter to you anyway? You screwing her?"

Seriously, this guy must have had a giant bowl of stupid for breakfast. I didn't even think, I just leaned down a little and clocked him as hard as I could on the left side of his face. I felt my middle knuckle split open and the force of the blow had him yelling in surprise and listing off to the side. I shook my hand as I straightened back up and asked him again, "What guy?"

He lifted his hands up in surrender and gripped his head in his hands.

"She hangs around this guy named Drew Donner. He follows her around like a puppy. It's pretty obvious he wants out of the friend zone, but Brysen isn't budging. The guy is kind of intense and a little off. He transferred here a year ago and hasn't made any attempt to hang out or party. All he does is tag along after Brysen. There was even a rumor going around for a while that he had some kind of breakdown when he couldn't get himself into all of the same classes she was enrolled in because he didn't have the right prerequisites. I don't know about you, but I wouldn't get all worked up over some chick that doesn't put out."

I just stared at him for a minute, trying to weigh the validity of his statements against everything I already knew. Brysen hadn't mentioned this Drew guy at all.

I was going to ask the frat guy where I could find Drew when Bax's hand landed on my shoulder. When I turned to look at him, my heart sank because his dark eyes were even blacker than normal. That meant bad news—really bad news.

"We have to go. Now." His tone left no room for argument.

I dipped my chin down to indicate that I understood his unspoken urgency. I pointed at the college kid still sprawled at my feet.

"If you notice anything off, anything out of the ordinary with this Drew kid, you call me and let me know." I turned on my heel and followed Bax back through the throng of drunken partygoers.

When we got to the Hemi, Bax looked at me over the roof of the car as we both pulled the doors open.

"That was Nassir. He's been trying to call you for an hour."

I bit off a string of dirty words. "Fight night was last night. He's probably waiting for the payout. I had other things on my mind."

"No. That's not what he wants." Bax arched an eyebrow until it almost reached his hairline. "The Pit exploded."

I just stared at him like he was speaking a foreign language. "What?"

"Nassir said the entire place just went up in flames. The cops are on the scene and so is fire and emergency. He said the place was packed since it's Saturday night." He sighed and shook his head. "They're pulling bodies out."

Holy shit! That was majorly stepping up the game to show Nassir and myself that we didn't have control of anything. That was making a point in a deadly and drastic way that couldn't be ignored.

"How did someone get by all the security Nassir has surrounding that place?"

We both got into the car and the engine roared to life with the ferocity of a wild animal. Soon the manicured lawns and expensive houses that dotted the Hill were nothing but a blur as we raced back into the heart of the city.

"He doesn't know. Early reports are indicating that heavy-duty explosives were used. Nassir said the entire place is nothing but a fireball and ashes."

"How did he get out in one piece?" I didn't like Nassir, but I was glad he was okay if the destruction was as bad as Bax was describing.

"He was at Spanky's."

I looked at Bax across the dark interior of the car. He had one hand on the wheel and was tucking an unlit cigarette between his lips with the other. His heavy brows were lowered in concern and there was a telltale tick behind that black ink by his eye.

"Why was he at Spanky's instead of the club on a Saturday night?" Belatedly I wondered if all the hundreds of thousands of dollars we had been funneling through the club had managed to survive the inferno.

Bax cut me a hard look and lit his smoke.

"I imagine he was there for the same reasons you were kicking the shit out of some dumb-ass college kid instead of being at home with your lady."

"He's worried about the girls."

"Yeah, more like one girl in particular. No one wants all of this shit to land on the girls, our girls in particular. We need to figure out who's behind it. No one is coming forward, no one is making moves on the Point, it's just like they want you guys to know they can get to you, they can mess with you, and there's nothing you can do about it. It seems like it's all one, big, seriously fucked-up game."

It didn't feel like a game. It felt like life and death. It felt like rocks in my gut and fury in my blood. The Point wasn't much, it was hard to justify wanting to fight for it, to keep it alive after all the misery and pain it had brought to so many. But it was mine. It was home. It might be a kingdom no one else wanted to reign over—but I was going to do it until it killed me, and I wasn't going to let some unknown intruder tear it apart from the inside out. Not if I could help it.

While I pondered what my next step should be, I sent Stark a text message asking him to dig up every single thing he could on Drew Donner. It was the first solid name I had to go on. I just hoped something finally came out of it so I could put all that was going on with Brysen to bed.

When we pulled up in front of the warehouse, the scene was

like something out of a movie. The old factory had never been very pretty, the graffitied walls and crumbling brick providing perfect camouflage for all of the excess and debauchery housed inside the disintegrating walls. Now it looked even worse. The walls that were still standing were charred black, the metal fixtures twisted and melted, all of the barred windows were broken out, and the entire building was a burned-out shell of brick and mortar. The smell of smoke and something far worse permeated the air. There were cop cars everywhere, and I tried not to cringe when I saw more than one coroner van parked in front of the wreckage.

Bax and I both climbed out of the car, a heavy silence floating between the two of us as we watched the emergency crews rush around. I didn't see Nassir anywhere, but Bax let out a low whistle and inclined his head in the direction of where Titus's nondescript sedan was parked. The detective and my errant business partner were standing together and they both had looks of absolute fury etched on their faces. Titus was talking rapidly and gesturing with his hands, Nassir was staring fixedly at what used to be his club. His jaw was working back and forth, and even with the distance between us, as Bax and I made our way over to them, I could see the fury blazing in his caramel-colored eyes.

"This is no joke. We're talking military-grade explosives, Nassir. This goes beyond a couple of bodies in a back alley. They've pulled out six people so far. None of them are any older than Dovie, for God's sake. This isn't just going to get swept under the rug."

A tick worked its way into Nassir's jaw and his gaze shifted to me and then back to the destroyed building.

"It shouldn't get swept under the rug. Find out who's behind it, cop."

That didn't sound good and there was no way Titus was going to locate the culprit and turn him over to Nassir for him to render his own form of justice. Bax's brother didn't operate by the rules of the Point, he only cared about the law.

"How did he even get in?" I asked the question to both of them but Titus was the one to answer.

He turned to look at us and reached up to pull the knot of his tie loose. He ran his hands through his hair and bit out, "Not in, *on*. The point of origin appears to be the roof of the building. It looks like there was an explosion on the roof and then a series of smaller explosions detonated inside the building, which is why there are so many casualties. Surprisingly, this guy"—he hooked his thumb in Nassir's direction—"actually had the place completely up to fire code. The sprinkler system kept the body count to a minimum."

Six people dead wasn't a minimum as far as I was concerned, and I could see by the way Nassir's eyebrows dipped down over his blazing eyes that he didn't think so either.

"One of the dancers called me and told me that there was a rowdy group of guys at Spanky's. She said Chuck had his hands full, and that they were scared. I got to the strip club and wasn't even in the door when I got the call that the Pit was on fire. Whoever is doing this didn't want me here. This was a setup so I could watch everything I have worked for burn to the ground."

Titus sighed and I asked, "All the money?"

Nassir shook his head and pushed off the sedan. "The money is fine. I'm a cautious man by nature. That's how I've managed to stay alive so long." He cut a hard look at Titus. "I'm serious, cop. If you get a name, I want it."

Titus didn't say anything as Nassir wandered off with his phone pressed tightly to his ear. I looked at Bax, who exchanged a look with his brother and shrugged.

"Nothing else for us to do here."

Titus grunted. "No. Go home and be glad you were somewhere else tonight or else you might be in the back of one of those vans, or down at the station for questioning."

I couldn't help but cringe as my gaze automatically shifted to the stark white coroner vans. I didn't want to think about the people ending their Saturday night with a trip to the morgue, but it was kind of impossible not to. This was the kind of price the Point required people to pay for venturing into its depths. I got lost in my dreary thoughts, started to feel like no matter how hard I worked, how much of a stranglehold I had on this place, the worst of the bad things and bad people were always going to win.

I was startled out of my reflections when Bax knocked me on my shoulder.

"Let's get you home to your lady. This night is done for." He sounded like it was just another day, just another glitch in the wiring that made this place run. It sent chills running down my spine.

"All right."

Once we were back in the car headed the few blocks to the garage so I could grab the Stingray, he asked me if I was all right. I took my time answering.

"I'm not sure. This is the Point. It's supposed to be a place that takes care of itself. Nothing and no one is supposed to be worse than the Point. I don't know how I feel about it being under attack and losing."

He made a noise low in his throat. "It's more than the Point. This place is more than a warning to spoiled kids and one wrong turn away from the Hill. It doesn't matter how ugly it is, how vicious and hard it is to live here, it's still home. It's my home, it's your home, and when you see it getting torn apart, when you know the threat is real and coming from outside, it makes you want to fight for it, even if you know it would watch you rot and not give a shit."

He was absolutely right. The Point might be a rotting kingdom, but it was *my* rotting kingdom and I couldn't abide by an outsider trying to tear it down. As much as I never thought it would happen, I was with Nassir on this one. When we had the person behind the destruction, behind the bloody and murderous message directed right at the heart of my city, there would be no long arm of the law, no pursuit of justice—there would only be retaliation and payback in the name of this place that was not nearly as unbreakable as it seemed.

I told Bax good-bye before he raced home to my sister. I understood the clawing need a little bit more, now that all I could think about was Brysen and keeping her safe and in one piece. She was my tether to the reality outside of the violence and machinations that made up my day-to-day life. I needed her if I was going to win this war that was being waged. She kept my head on the end game.

I got to the condo that was built on the docks right on the edge of the city. It was far enough out of the heart of the Point to be safe, but still far enough away from the Hill and burbs that no one would think to look for two upper-middle-class girls to be using it as a hideout. The condo had been my dad's secret love shack. It was where he took all the women he cheated on my mom with. He paid for the place in cash, so it had managed to escape the feds' lockdown on anything with the Hartman name attached to it. The only reason I knew it existed was because Novak had taken great pleasure in not only pulling all of my strings, but also in letting me know just how much dirt he had on my dad in order to keep me in line. A few handshakes and a greased palm belonging to the property manager, and all traces of my dad's ownership were gone. I had no second thoughts about having the title to the condo put into Brysen's name. Sure, if it ever got dragged to court, the legality of her ownership of the property would fall apart, but for now, the place was hers, even if she didn't know it or ended up not wanting it.

I parked in the underground garage and took the elevator up to the top floor. The condo looked out over the water, onto the shipping docks. If the Point had been in a better place, been in a prettier city, the view would be awesome. As it was, all anyone could see for miles was smog, rusty ships, and crusty dock workers. When I pushed through the door, I was greeted with the open end of a gun pointed at my face. Booker wasn't messing around since Brysen's tumble at the school. I knew he wasn't the sentimental or sympathetic type, but he also wasn't the type that liked to look like anyone had gotten the better of him. He was taking Brysen's attack personally, which was fine by me.

He lowered the gun and the scar that covered half of his face twitched.

"I didn't know you were coming by tonight."

He stashed the gun back wherever it had been before he pointed it at me as I shut the door behind me.

"My girl is here. Where else would I be?"

He snorted and picked up an open beer that was on the coffee table. "You better tell her that. She wasn't thrilled I was the one taking her home from the hospital today. She's been a real peach to be around all day."

I winced a little. I should have freed up the time to get her here. I sucked at this relationship stuff. She should always come first.

"And the little one . . ." He lifted his eyebrows up. "She's going to get herself in trouble. Always walking around with those big puppy-dog eyes like she's looking for a master to give her a good home. I would keep her locked up until she's legal."

"I'll keep that in mind."

"You want me to stick around, or you okay on your own?"

"You can take off."

He chugged back the last of the beer. "A little birdie told me that you've taken to rolling around unarmed." Dovie. My sister was always worrying about everyone but herself. He walked over to the gun that he had pulled on me that was placed on the counter. "You know how to use it?"

I just lifted my eyebrows at him. I had been in the Point for a long time now. I was in business with Nassir, and Bax was my best friend. Of course I knew how to use a gun. I just preferred not to.

"Okay, then. Good luck with your lady. I think you're going to need it."

I watched him walk out the front door and looked down at the gun. There was no denying that my life was changing. Some parts for the better, and many parts for the worse. The trick was just going to be finding the right balance. I took the gun and stashed it on the top of the fridge to keep it out of sight for now and made my way to the flight of stairs that led up to the master bedroom, which took up the entire top level of the condo. The lights were on, and when I walked in I expected Brysen to be on the bed watching TV or something. I actually faltered a little when the big room proved to be empty. I walked farther into the room, looking around like maybe I had somehow missed her, when I heard a soft noise from the open door to the master bath that was located off to one side of the space.

I kicked my shoes off and unbuttoned my shirt and went to go find my girl. She was standing in front of the mirror, a pair of scissors in one hand and a comb in the other. Her platinum-blond bob was no more, and her bright, blue eyes were locked on me when I crowded her reflection in the mirror. She set the scissors down and self-consciously ran her hands over her shorn hair. The army of little black stitches decorating the back of her head made my teeth clench as we watched each other silently in the reflective surface.

"This is the best I could do." She sounded nervous and unsure.

It actually didn't look too bad from the front. It was really short, angled close to her face with superstraight bangs across her forehead. The back was almost all clipped close to her head, except for a little part that was just long enough to cover the top of her injury. It was edgy and retro at the same time. She kind of looked like a modern-day flapper. She could pull off being the Bonnie to my Clyde any day of the week.

"I'm sorry I wasn't there today when they released you. I've been chasing my tail trying to find out who might have pushed you down the stairs. I should've been there to bring you home."

She turned around and leaned back against the sink so I was

looking at her and at my own reflection in the mirror behind her. I could see the way my eyes got darker just by being in the same room as her.

"Home? I don't even know where I am, Race. What is this place? How can we even be here? I have a million questions and you haven't been around to answer any of them. Not to mention I can't turn around without running into Booker, and that isn't fun for either of us. I hate this."

All I could do was look at her because she *should* hate it, but I was doing my best. Her eyes dropped down and she took a step forward to grab one of my hands. I had forgotten all about my busted-open knuckles and the dried blood that was caked on the back of my hands.

"Your hands are all bloody."

I choked on a laugh. "You have no idea."

She scowled at me and I sighed as I moved around her to scrub off the blood. I was always doing that—washing the blood down the drain.

"My dad used this place to hook up with his mistresses. It's far enough away from the Hill that my mom never knew about it. The property manager is shady as hell, so I paid him off and now there is no paper trail that can tie this place back to anyone in my family. I asked him to transfer the title over to your name. It's not on the up-and-up, but for now, you and Karsen can stay here, even after we get this shit with your stalker on lockdown. I know you were worried about what was going to happen with your old man putting your house in foreclosure. Now you have a place to stay."

I heard her make a little noise in her throat and then her hands were over mine in the sink and she was helping me wash the last remainder of this terrible night away. Her eyes met mine in the mirror, and I could see all the fear, all the uncertainty, all the questions she had shining out at me, but I could also see the gratitude, the hope, and something even deeper, and that's what I was going to latch on to.

"I should have been there today."

She shut off the water and rested her cheek on the back of my shoulder. "No. I understand you have a lot going on and that you're trying to find whoever did this to me in the first place. I just missed you and feel better when you're close by. I get that I have to share you with the Point."

I lifted a hand to run it over her newly chopped hair. It might be short and a little crazy, but it was still soft and felt like silk where it clung to my wet fingers.

"You shouldn't have to."

She laughed and there was no humor in it. "In a perfect world, maybe, but so far not the Hill, not the Point, and nowhere in between is perfect. We just have to make the best of what we have."

I curled my hand around her neck and asked, "Are we falling in love, Bry?"

She laughed again and pulled away from me. "Probably. Why wouldn't we? Life is a mess, I have someone trying to kill me, and you're right in the thick of a war on the city. What better conditions could you think of to fall in love?"

Definitely the Bonnie to my Clyde. I turned to follow her as she walked into the bedroom.

"You think we'll survive it?" I hadn't ever been in love before, and so far, it was like its own special kind of battle I was trying to win.

She sighed at me. "I don't know, but I sure hope so."

I needed to change the subject before one of us let good sense talk us out of what was happening between us.

"What do you know about Drew Donner?"

She was working on folding down the comforter on the big king-size bed, so she just answered me over her shoulder. "We have a bunch of the same classes this semester. He's nice enough, so we study together sometimes."

"He never asked you out or anything?"

She stripped out of the black pants she was wearing, leaving her in nothing but a tank top and a pair of barely-there panties. This was serious conversation, but my mind immediately went blank and all I could do was stare at her long legs as she climbed up on the bed and sat on the edge. She still had a little red mark on her knee from her close call in the parking lot, and the reminder of her being injured now and before was enough to get my mind back on track as she studied me for a minute before answering.

"He's made it pretty clear he would like to be more than friends, but I was never into it and I told him so. He doesn't love it, but he never pushes the issue."

I stalked toward her and didn't stop until I reached the side of the bed and had positioned myself between her legs. I leaned over her until she was propped up on her elbows and I was just a breath away from being laid out on top of her.

"And why weren't you into it?"

Her chest rose and fell and she let her weight drop so that we both collapsed on the bed and I was completely covering her. She twisted her hands into my hair and met my serious look with one of her own.

"Because I was into you, even if I didn't want to be, and I knew no one else was going to compare."

Damn straight no one was going to compare. This girl got to me in a way nothing else had in a very long time, and the pull between us was something that people looked a lifetime for. It didn't matter that my world was dangerous, that she was going to have to take a risk by being with me—we were supposed to be together—and no deranged stalker or better judgment was going to keep us apart.

I kissed her hard and fast and went to move up and off of her. After all, she was hurt and there was no way I was going to do any more damage to her, but her grip in my hair tightened and she didn't let me go.

"I'm having someone check him out. The guys at that school seem to have a hard time when you turn them down. I want to know what his deal is."

Her eyes glittered up at me, and she curled one of her legs around my waist, which had my hands reaching for bare skin against my will.

"He doesn't have a deal. He's just a typical college guy. He wouldn't hurt me. He has no reason to."

My fingers stroked her thigh and I felt my heart rate speed up a little. I had to remember her head was probably killing her. I kissed the outside curve of her eyebrow.

"I'm still looking into him. Brysen, you just got out of the hospital this morning. Let me up and we'll go to bed. I told you, I want to take care of you."

One of her hands let go of its death grip on my hair to twine around my shoulders as her other leg joined the first, meaning I was now fully cradled against the center of her and the only thing between my growing erection and her warm center was her panties and my jeans.

"I missed you, Race. I want you to take care of me. Just do it this way instead."

The argument I had about her being hurt got lost when she kissed me like we had been apart for months and not just a long couple of days or so. I let myself fall into her lips, into the seduction of her tongue as she coaxed mine to dance. I hopelessly gave in to the demand of her teeth when she used them to make her wants and needs clear. I put my hands on the curve of her hips and used the leverage I had to move us both to the center of the bed, her hands grasping at me the entire time like she was afraid I was going somewhere. She was almost naked and underneath me; there was nowhere else in the entire world I ever wanted to be.

I wrestled her top off over her head, careful of the delicate skin on the back of her head, and let her grapple with my jeans until she had them open and was using both her hands and her feet to get them out of her way. I grinned at her and climbed up onto my knees so I could strip the rest of them way, and felt my heart turn over when she used her index finger to dip into the dimple on my cheek. She smiled up at me as I hooked my fingers under the edge of her panties and started to work them down her legs. She would always be my absolute favorite present to unwrap.

"You're something else, Race Hartman."

Her stomach dipped and quivered a little when I bent my head and stuck the tip of my tongue into the concave little divot of her belly button.

"I was just thinking the same thing about you."

I had to be mindful that she was fragile, breakable, and all too human. I couldn't unleash on her all the things I normally did when I took her to bed. Normally she was my port in the storm while everything raged around us, but tonight she needed care, she needed delicacy and for me to show her she was safe with me.

I trailed my tongue down from her belly button and across the jutting ridge of her hipbone as she squirmed impatiently underneath me. She already had her legs open to accommodate where I was sprawled between them, so it was no work to get my mouth on all the parts of her that were already wet and slick with desire. I loved that she was as ready for me as I always seemed to be for her. There was passion, there was hunger, there was desire that made my balls tight and had my mouth watering for a taste of her.

She gasped my name at the first swipe of my tongue through her folds. Her fingers locked in a painful grip on my ears when I used my shoulders to move her legs farther apart so I could add my hands to the mix. I heard her whimper but was so focused on what I was doing, so drunk on the way she just melted into my mouth, that I didn't stop to think if it was a sound of pleasure or pain. Her inner walls pulled at my fingers, her clit pulsed as I snagged it with the edge of my teeth, and her thighs shifted restlessly against my head as she moved with my caress. I felt her insides get tight, felt the moisture gathering against my fingertips, and ate her up as she broke over the crest while saying my name on a sobbing breath. If I was lucky enough to get her to react like that for the rest of my life, I would take all the other shit my life threw at me on a daily basis with a smile.

Her legs went slack over my shoulders and I pulled them

down along my sides as I crawled back up over her. I stopped
along the way to suck each of her pretty, pink nipples into my
mouth and to nuzzle into the beautiful curve of her neck. My
dick was rock hard, my balls were achy, and all I wanted to do
was sink into her and stay there forever and ever. I held myself
up over her on braced arms and waited until those sky-blue eyes
peeled open and locked onto me. She had a hot flush on her
cheeks and a soft smile on her mouth, and never had anything
looked more beautiful. I would give up any fortune, fight any
war, and bleed over and over again if she was my reward.

She ran her hands up and down my ribs and curled her legs
back up around my waist. She used her hold on me to pull herself
up so that just the tip of my straining erection slid through her
welcoming heat.

"I need you."

Her voice was husky and a little broken. I put one of my
hands under her and clasped the curve of her ass and held her to
me as I slowly allowed myself to settle into the cradle of her legs.
As we both sank back onto the mattress, I found her mouth with
my own and whispered to her:

"I need you too, Bry."

I kissed her with everything I had, let her feel my heart in
it, let her know with my mouth that she was the end of the road
for me. There was nothing else beyond her. And then as I started
to move, thrusting inside of her, moving against her, I used my
tongue to mimic what the lower half of my body was doing,
which had her writhing against me and digging her fingernails
into the skin of my shoulders. I wanted to drive into her, to fuck
her like I normally did, but I didn't want to hurt her, and even

through the pleasure, the hot and sexy burn of the blue in her gaze, there was a shadow of discomfort that kept me firmly in check. Her head was probably killing her.

Her inner walls trembled along my cock, her heart thundered along next to mine, and her nipples were pebbled and sharp where they rubbed against my chest. Her tongue twisted and stroked along my own and her hold was just as desperate, just as needy, as mine. I could feel my pleasure coil and tighten at the base of my spine, felt my body start to shudder. I lifted my head from where I was devouring her and told her:

"You have to come with me."

She tossed her head side to side and I felt her grind her hips up against mine where I was trying to hold off rocking into her with everything I had.

She curled her arms around my sides and lifted an eyebrow up at me.

"Then stop messing around and give it to me."

That startled a laugh out of me, which had me grinning down at her. "I don't want to hurt your head, smartass."

"So give me something else to think about, pretty boy."

Shit. That was a challenge I had no trouble meeting. I braced my hands on either side of her head, made sure her gaze focused on mine, and did just what she asked—gave it to her.

I thrust into her, moved over her, ground our bodies together in a way that made it feel like I was trying to meld us together—and maybe I was. Considering I was already close, already on the brink of coming just by looking at her naked and willing under me, it only took a few minutes before I was breaking apart inside of her and not aware if she was there with me or not. Luckily she was a vocal lover and easy to read, because by the time I was done grunting and jetting into her, I could hear her whimpering and feel her pulsing around me.

I gave it a second, until both of us were breathing more normally, and rolled onto my back so that I was sprawled out across the bed next to her. She laced our fingers together and kissed each and every single one of my busted-open knuckles.

"Thank you for taking care of me, Race."

Of course she wasn't talking about the sex, even though that would be an awesome stroke to my ego.

"Thank you for giving me something good to always come back to, Brysen."

She was the balance I so desperately needed.

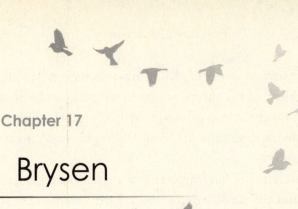

Chapter 17

Brysen

Considering my extracurricular activities the night before with Race, I was surprised that my head was only aching with a dull throb when he woke me up and told me he had to go. I was still sleepy, a little fuzzy, so while I thought he was saying something about Nassir's club burning down, I couldn't be sure. I thought maybe it was a dream, and as soon as the bedroom door closed behind him, I went back to sleep. I didn't wake up again until I heard my sister's breathy, high-pitched laugh and smelled bacon cooking from somewhere in the condo. I wasn't supposed to scrub my head for another day or two, but the stitches were itchy, so I decided to go against the doctor's orders and took a fast shower. I had a hard time looking in the fogged-over mirror when I got out.

My hair didn't look like the worst thing on the planet, but there were dark shadows under my eyes and hard lines next to my mouth that had never been there before. Having someone out for my blood, having a sinister shadow hunting me, getting the better of me, was starting to take its toll, and that was obvious on my face. Even with Race stepping in and handling all

the other major issues life had thrown at me—my mom, finding Karsen and me a place to stay so we wouldn't be homeless,
trying to keep the two of us safe—it was still a lot to handle, and
I think living through it all had me looking well over my twenty-
one years.

Since I didn't have anything at the condo aside from my
purse and the small bag Karsen had thrown together for me
while I was at the hospital, there weren't even any magic tricks
I could do with makeup to make myself look better. Not that I
had anyone to impress. Karsen had seen me at my worst, and
the brooding giant that was Booker had made it perfectly clear
we were never going to be friends. He acted like getting thrown
down the stairs was all my fault and I had just cracked my skull
open to make him look bad in front of Race. He was even more
scowly and growly than he had been before, and for the life of
me I couldn't figure out why the more brash he was, the more
my sister wanted to fawn all over him. I didn't like anything
about that.

I pulled on a pair of yoga pants and a sloppy sweatshirt and
went to rain on my little sister's inappropriate flirting parade.
When I came down the stairs and rounded the corner, I was surprised to see Booker at the sink washing dishes and my sister sitting at the island with a sandwich in front of her. Her dark eyes
got huge when she saw my chopped-up hair but they glimmered
at me in approval.

"It's cute, edgy, and a little punk rock. I can't believe you did
that yourself."

My sister would never have anything bad to say about anything. She was too sweet.

"It's a mess, but it's better than the hack job that the hospital gave me. Did Booker make you lunch?" I hopped up onto the stool next to her and snagged the other half of her BLT.

"No. I cooked and he said he would clean up." The big guy grunted from his position at the sink without turning around. Karsen smiled at me and indicated the modern, beautifully decorated condo. It wasn't in the greatest part of town, but I had to admit it was leaps and bounds better than the loft in the garage. "Isn't this place awesome? Race said we could stay here as long as we need to."

"Race is full of surprises." My tone was dry and I heard Booker chuckle.

"He was in a big hurry to get out of here this morning. He was asking me a million and one questions about your friend from school."

Booker turned around from the sink and gave me a look.

I shrugged. "He's just a friend."

He snorted and crossed his beefy arms over his chest.

"Girls that look like you don't have dudes as friends. Hell, even girls that don't look like you don't have guys as friends. Trust me, Blondie, any guy hanging around any girl for any amount of time is just waiting for his chance to get it in."

I coughed a little on the sandwich I was chewing on and shot a look at my sister, and then glared at Booker.

"That's not true. Not all guys are Neanderthals like you."

He lifted the eyebrow that was bisected by the ugly scar and gave me a pointed stare.

"Yes they are. Some are just better at hiding it when they want to get laid."

"Anyways . . ." I changed the subject and turned to Karsen. "Drew is harmless and he was never around my computer, so all of that creepy surveillance software couldn't have come from him."

Karsen made a strangled noise in her throat that had Booker frowning and me turning to look at her in concern. She grabbed my forearm and her brown eyes took up half of her face.

"That's not true. Remember a few months ago when you needed to borrow my computer because you loaned yours to Adria when hers crashed for a week or so? Well, you were all mad that Drew was the one who gave it back to you, considering Adria was the one who borrowed it. He told you that she gave it to him because she was too busy to return it. You even complained it was running really slow and blamed Adria for downloading a virus or something. You were totally jealous when she got a brand-new laptop to replace the one that crashed."

I didn't remember that at all, but there had been a lot on my mind the last few months and Adria was selfish and needy a lot, so it wasn't a request that would stand out in my mind or seem unusual. Though now that Karsen mentioned it, I did remember Drew giving me back my computer and seeming extra excited about being the errand boy for the task. Like a typical teenager, being separated from her computer and social media meant that Karsen probably recalled the exact events.

"Well, shit."

Booker uncrossed his arms and his hard face looked slightly murderous.

"I need to call Race and let him know that before he heads to the school to corner the guy."

An uneasy shiver slipped down my spine. I really didn't think Drew had it in him to hurt anyone. He was just a preppy college guy with a little crush, but at this point the only people I knew weren't trying to end my life were Race and Karsen—and maybe Booker, even though I was still on the fence about him.

I turned to Karsen and shared the concerned look she was giving me as Booker took his phone and wandered into the living room to make a call. She looked like she was on the verge of losing the lunch she had just been eating, so I told her in my most authoritative tone:

"It'll be fine. Race will figure it out and then life will go back to normal."

She opened her mouth to retort but was interrupted when my phone started to ring from the bedroom upstairs. I had no clue why Dovie would be calling me when she knew I was supposed to be on lockdown, and immediately had visions of Race hurt—or worse.

"Hello." I was breathing hard when I answered, but even the noise of my own wheezing wasn't enough to drown out the sobbing on the other end of the line. Dovie had never struck me as the hysterical type, and immediately my mind started racing with worst-case scenarios involving Race and Bax.

"Dovie, what's wrong?" I didn't mean to snap the question at her when she was so obviously upset, but I couldn't help myself.

"I . . . Bax and I . . . we had a fight. It was bad."

I sat down on the side of the bed and let out a relieved breath. "A fight about what?"

She made a hiccuping noise and my heart squeezed for her. She didn't sound anything like the tough-as-nails girl I knew her to be.

"I told him he had to stop working with Race, that I wanted him out of all of it. Nassir's club was burned to the ground last night. People died, Brysen. I don't want to live every single day of my life wondering if he's going to make it home. I can't do it any-more. It's killing me, worrying about him and Race all the time."

Whoa, that was pretty heavy and I could totally understand why it hadn't gone well. Bax didn't seem like the kind of guy that took to ultimatums, even if he really did love Dovie.

"I'm sorry, Dovie. I'm sure when he has some time to think about it he'll calm down and you guys can talk it over."

She sniffled again. "I don't know. He stormed out this morn-ing and I haven't seen him look that pissed since the night things went down with Novak."

I swore under my breath and ran my hands through my su-pershort hair. I didn't know what to say to her to make it better. As it turned out, all she wanted was a shoulder to cry on.

"Brysen, I can't concentrate on classes right now and I don't want to be at the house all alone. I know Race has you on lock-down, but can you tell me where you're at so I can come over and we can talk?"

Of course I would never tell her no. Dovie was a great friend and she sounded so stressed out and sad that all I wanted to do was give her a hug.

"I don't know the exact address. We're on the docks, though, and the condo complex is pretty nice. I mean way nicer than you would expect for a place in the Point. It's right across the street from some bar called the Rabbit Hole. We're on the top floor."

She made a strangled noise and I heard her gasp. She was be-having superweird and suddenly a tingle started to lift the newly shorn hair on the back of my neck. I trusted Dovie implicitly, but everyone and everything in my life had been out to harm me lately and I needed to remember that.

"Ummm . . . who is 'we' exactly?" She sounded like she had a frog in her throat.

"Karsen and the guy I affectionately call Gigantor. His name is Booker and he's my unofficial babysitter until Race gets his hands on my stalker."

She made another noise, and this time it sounded like she was in actual physical pain. I was really starting to worry about her.

"Are you okay, Dovie? You don't sound very good."

She coughed again. "I'm fine. Just freaking out is all. Hey, is the guy watching you armed by any chance?"

That was a pretty specific question, and the entire off tone of the conversation had me debating whether I should answer honestly or not. I decided to give a nonanswer instead. "I don't know. Probably. He looks like a modern-day executioner or maybe a hit man. I'm pretty sure everyone Race associates with runs around armed. Your boyfriend included."

Her voice changed a little when she told me, "Yeah, Bax carries a weapon and we've both been all over Race to start carrying too. Sometimes in the Point the only thing you can do is be ready for the worst." She made another gasping noise and I got really worried. All my instincts were screaming at me that something was really wrong here, I just wasn't sure what was going on or what I could do about it over the phone. "Brysen, I'll be there in a few. Uh . . . be ready for me, okay?"

The phone went dead and I just stared at it for a long second. I got to my feet and suddenly bolted back toward the kitchen, which did nothing for my throbbing head.

"Who was that?" Karsen sounded alarmed and I realized I must look a little crazed as thoughts about how wrong and how off everything about that phone call felt started whirling and tumbling through my mind. The hair on my arms rose up and ice started to form in my veins.

"Dovie. She sounded really bizarre, though. She said she got into a big fight with Bax and needed to come over and talk about it." I started frantically pacing back and forth as I shoved my hands through my hair, wincing as the motion pulled at my stitches. I played the conversation over in my head again trying to put my finger on why it didn't sit right with me and decided all of it was just wrong.

At that moment Booker swore loud enough to rattle the walls and stalked over to where I was moving back and forth. I came to an abrupt halt as he put his hands on my shoulders and forced me to stop and look up at him.

"Did you tell her where you were at?"

I met his razor-sharp glare with a grimace. "She's my best friend and she sounded really upset. Of course I told her where I was at." But now I regretted it on a soul-deep level.

Booker reached around me and pointed at Karsen. "All right, little puppy, you get your ass in that room and stay put. Lock the door, put all the furniture you can move in front of it, and don't come out for anything. Not for me, not for your sister—not anything. You understand me?"

Karsen's eyes bugged in her face and she looked at me with panic in her gaze. Booker's voice sounded harsh and left no room for argument.

"Why? What's going on?"

He let go of me and moved to nudge Karsen as I slowly shook my head from side to side, furious at myself and my own stupidity. "I think Dovie is in trouble and I'm pretty sure she's bringing it this way. Do what Booker says, Karsen. When it's safe to come out I'll text you. Until you get that message, you stay put."

She shuddered. "I don't understand what's happening. Dovie would never hurt anyone."

I frowned really hard as the pieces of the puzzle started to lock into place in my head and all the wrong things with the situation started to burn bright and clear behind the fear that was coursing through me. "She wouldn't. She also wouldn't have a fight with Bax and call to blab to me about it. That isn't how she works." I put a hand on my sister's shoulder and squeezed. "Please do what Booker is telling you to do."

We stared at each other for a long minute, her brown eyes full of things far beyond her tender years. Finally she nodded and disappeared down the hallway. Booker walked to the closed door and waited until the sound of furniture scraping across the floor could be heard throughout the condo.

When he stalked back toward me I don't think I had ever seen anyone look scarier or more ready to handle business.

"Dovie is part of this place. She knows Race was freaked out about anyone knowing where you are. She's too smart to ask for that info. None of this is right. You need to go upstairs and do the same thing I just had your sister do." He produced a nasty-looking gun from somewhere behind his back and held it out to me. "Do you know how to use this?"

I shook my head numbly. I had never actually been up close with a weapon before. Like everything in my life since I got tangled up in the Point, it looked cold and deadly, yet seemed so totally necessary.

"No. I've never touched a gun in my life."

He swore some more, got really creative with every dirty word in the book, and then opened and closed a series of kitchen drawers until he produced a wicked-looking butcher knife. He slapped it on the counter in front of me and stated in a tone that left no room for argument, "Take that. If you need to use it then shit is fucked and I don't know what else to tell you other than good luck, Blondie. Now get your ass upstairs."

The last of his words were drowned out by a knock on the door. I felt my eyes widen and gulped when he moved around me all tense and coiled to attack like a predator. More knocking rattled the door, and I still hadn't moved, so I shook myself loose and ran toward the stairs with every intention of barricading myself in the master bathroom until I got the "all clear" from Booker. Only before I hit the first step there was a series of loud pops and the sound of splintering wood. Blood bloomed furiously scarlet across Booker's chest and I saw him turn around to tell me to run when the door was kicked open with a resounding thud. I watched in horror as Booker pulled his own weapon and the sound of more shots filled the space. It sounded like a gun range or an Old West shootout, but it was the middle of the day on the docks and this place obviously wasn't on the up-and-up if Race had managed to get it put in my name so easily, so I didn't expect any help from the neighbors in the other units. Especially with the entire place smelling like gunpowder and blood.

In the Point everyone only knew how to look out for themselves and how to look the other way. I backed up a few more steps as Booker's giant frame teetered to one side and a circle of crimson started to bloom rapidly across his back as he fell to his knees. Another shot popped off and I saw him fall face-first right at the doorway as the gun in his hand clattered uselessly to the floor. I screamed but was smart enough to turn and bolt up the rest of the stairs. I needed to call Race. I needed to find help, and all I could think was I needed to put as many doors and as much space between me and the shooter as possible.

I was worried about Booker. I was worried about Dovie. I was worried about my sister, and I was worried about myself.

My phone shone like a beacon where I had left it on the bed after talking to Dovie. I dove for it with every intention of taking it into the bathroom with me so I could call for help, only a heavy weight hit me from behind and knocked me to the floor. I yelped as pain exploded in my already injured head and tried to scramble away as I was yanked onto my back and straddled with a heavy weight across my chest. I went to scream again as my arms were yanked ruthlessly above my head and then I went deathly silent as the barrel of a handgun was pressed directly between my eyes.

I made myself be absolutely still, shock and recognition rippling through me like a tidal wave as I gazed up into Drew's deranged blue eyes. My head was aching, my reality was spinning around and turning upside down, but there was no mistaking that the guy who had just shot Booker and was now pointing a gun directly to the center of my forehead was someone I had considered a friend up until moments ago. Gone was the guy I walked to class with. Gone was the easygoing guy I borrowed notes from. Gone was any semblance of a stable and caring human being. He looked enraged. His cheeks were bright red and his breath was *whoosh*ing in and out like bellows, and I could feel the hatred pouring off of him as he jammed the gun even harder into my forehead.

"Thanks for warning me about your bodyguard, Brysen. That'll make this so much easier for me."

I gasped and stared up at him in shock. "Where is Dovie?" My voice was thready and I could hear how scared I sounded. He laughed like a lunatic and bent over me so that our eyes were locked right over the gun. I saw his finger twitch on the trigger, and I was pretty sure I was going to die.

"She served her purpose. This has nothing to do with anyone but you and me. I just needed the guy guarding you out of the way. He's just one more body you have laying at your feet."

I had no clue what he was talking about. "What?" I tried to wiggle my fingers because they were going numb, but that just had him yanking my arms higher up over my head and the gun pressing even more tightly into my skull. It was like he was trying to shove it through my face. Drew sat up a little and dragged the gun across my cheek, down my nose, and stopped with it shoved into the soft skin under the curve of my chin.

"You're never responsible for the people you kill. Never stop to wash the blood off your hands, do you, Brysen?"

I still wasn't following, so I just kept my mouth shut and stared up at him. I could feel tears burning in the back of my eyes, but after everything he had put me through, after he had pretended to be my friend just so he could torment me, there was no way I was going to give him the satisfaction of crying. I gave my hips an experimental wiggle to see if I could dislodge his weight and almost threw up when the action made him leer at me.

"I don't have blood on my hands, Drew. You're the one who

tried to run me over, spied on me, and pushed me down the stairs. You're the one covered in blood. What did I ever do to you to deserve this?"

I hollered out in pain as he lifted the gun and brought the butt of it down on the side of my head. I saw another galaxy. I felt agony, sharp and blinding from the strike, and immediately I had black spots dancing in front of my eyes. Drew used his hold on my hands to pull me up into a semi-sitting position and loomed over me.

He barked right into my face, "You don't play by the rules. You think you're better than everyone else and that you're special."

I absolutely didn't think that, but it seemed stupid to argue when I heard bells ringing in my ears and had starbursts of pain exploding in my head. "This is because I wouldn't date you? You want to kill me because I don't have romantic feelings for you?"

I sounded confused and it wasn't all because of the echoing hurt rattling through my brain. None of this was adding up and I needed to shake the cobwebs loose and figure something out. My sister needed me, Race needed me, and I wasn't about to let either of them down by continuing to be a victim at the hands of this madman.

"No, you dumb bitch." The gun clattered on the side of my head again and this time I felt my skin split open. The coppery and rusty scent of my blood wafted into my nose. My neck no longer felt like it could hold my head up and it flopped back heavily to smack into the side of the bed. "This has to do with you and your family thinking you're above the law. That because you have money and connections, the law and justice don't apply to you. Your mom ruined my life by being a dumb, drunken piece of shit—and what happened? Not a fucking thing. Your dad threw some money at the situation, at the pitiful, pathetic family from the Point. He talked to some people, and poof, it all went away. Meanwhile, my mom is strung out on painkillers and my little brother ate a bullet because he couldn't stand the thought of being in a wheelchair for the rest of his life. And what happened to the Carters? You just get to go on living life like nothing happened. Your dad and your mom, even your perfect little sister, all happy and secure in a fucking bubble. You think you're untouchable."

Well, hell. I would be furious at my family if I was him as well. He let go of my hands, which had me falling back and raising shaking hands to hold my temples. If my head hadn't been so fuzzy, I might have been able to use my legs to clamber away, but I was still having trouble fighting back the blackness that was trying to suck me under, and then he set the gun to the side and wrapped both his hands around my throat and started to squeeze. There was no way I was going to be able to fight. I tried clawing at his hands but he was intent, lost in his fury and rage. I wasn't a person to him; I was just a means to an end.

"I left NorthCrest to come back home and try and help out my mom. She took the blood money your dad gave her, as well as my dad's life insurance, and used it on pills instead of thinking about the future. Instead of thinking about me. NorthCrest is an Ivy League school. But with my dad gone and my mom strung out on opiates, there was no way I could afford to stay there. I came home, saw what your family had done to mine, and knew I had to take action. I transferred to the university under my mom's last name and made sure I ended up in all your classes."

While he talked he squeezed and squeezed and the darkness started to win. I couldn't breathe, couldn't feel anything below my neck, and my hands started to fall limply to either side of me.

"I saw through the cracks. I knew your dad was a gambling addict and owed all the wrong kinds of people a lot of money. I knew your mom was as bad as my own—drunk, sloppy, and one step away from the edge. I knew your sister gets picked on at school because the almighty Carters aren't really from the Hill and the other kids at her high school can tell. Everyone was failing, miserable, and bound to end up just like my own family; all of them, except for you." As he said it he gave me a little shake like I was a rag doll and I squeaked weakly in response.

"You were supposed to fall in love with me. I was going to sweep you off your feet and then destroy you, ruin you, and leave your life in ashes, but you never let me in the front door. Then you moved home and slapped a big enough Band-Aid on things so the rest of the world could forget just how awful the Carters were. You held everything together when I wanted to watch it crumble, and for that you have to die. You have to suffer, and when I'm done with you I'm going after your sister."

He shook me again, and I knew if I didn't get loose he was going to choke me to death and go after Karsen. I couldn't let that happen. I was trying to stay awake, trying to muster any amount of energy to fight back, when Drew suddenly let out a loud bellow and let me go. He scrambled to his feet above me, which gave me the space and opportunity to lurch to my hands and knees and crawl away from him.

Karsen was standing behind him with her hands over her mouth and her eyes leaking tears while she shook like a leaf. The butcher knife I had forgotten on the kitchen counter was embedded in Drew's shoulder as he swore and danced around.

Karsen grabbed my hand and pulled me to my feet as I yelled at her to run. The gun Drew had brought with him was too close to him for me to try and grab as I hobbled to my feet and let my sister drag me down the stairs. My vision was flashing in and out, and it sounded like a river was rushing between my ears, but I knew I had to at least get her out of the condo before I passed out.

She shrieked when she saw Booker lying facedown and bloody on the entryway floor. She stopped, which had me slamming into her, and made both of us stumble.

"He's hurt."

"I know, but you have to go!"

She wouldn't budge even as I shoved her from the back. I heard a roar that sounded like it came from a wounded animal and knew our window of opportunity was about to slam shut.

"Karsen, move! You have to get out of here!" I grabbed her arm and tried to drag her toward the broken door that was hanging drunkenly on the hinges.

Thundering footsteps were pounding down the stairs and there was no time left to think about anything. I wasn't going to let Drew hurt either one of us. I felt awful for the tragedy that tied us together, but I wasn't about to pay for the sins of my parents, and I sure as hell wasn't going to allow Karsen to suffer for their mistakes any more than she already had.

The gun that Booker had pulled out when Drew started shooting through the door had landed by the back of the couch. I might not know how to use it, but I figured the sight of it might buy us enough time to get out of the condo and call for help.

Karsen pulled free of my frantic attempts to move her out of danger and was now on her knees next to Booker, her hands on his back and covered in blood, while she whispered his name.

I picked up the gun and pointed it at the base of the stairs, making sure I put myself directly in front of my sister and Booker even though he was already down and bleeding. I had never fired a gun before, but I would do it to put an end to this madness once and for all.

Drew tripped and staggered drunkenly down the stairs. He had the gun dangling from one hand and the bloody knife in the other. One of his shoulders was drooping down at an odd angle and the look on his face was monstrous and inhuman. He was literally unrecognizable.

He lifted the arm holding the gun and narrowed his eyes at me.

"Which one of us do you think is faster, Brysen?"

I didn't want to find out. I curled a finger around the trigger and had to narrow my eyes to focus because wavy lines and black stars were dancing all across my vision. The river rushing between my ears had turned into a waterfall and I was having to concentrate really hard to stay up on my feet.

"I don't want to find out, Drew. Hasn't enough damage been done? Haven't both of us lost enough?" My finger twitched on the trigger and I told myself I needed to pull it even if I really didn't want to.

He roared again and I saw the muzzle of his gun flash right before an explosion blasted next to my head. I felt hot air buzz across my cheek, swore I could see the bullet as it zipped by me, but instead of feeling even more pain, or recognizing I had been shot, I saw a perfectly round hole appear right above one of Drew's eyes as he toppled forward and landed on his knees. He gasped and wheezed as the knife and his gun clattered to the carpet and he pitched all the way forward to land on his face as blood started to trickle out of the bullet hole in his head.

I spun around and promptly burst into tears when I saw Dovie standing inside the broken doorway clutching a small black pistol.

She looked awful. Both of her pretty green eyes were ringed in black-and-blue bruises, her nose was bleeding, and she had an ugly gash decorating her cheek. She was paler than normal and her freckles were standing out in stark relief on her nose and cheeks. She looked like she'd had the crap kicked out of her, but the gun in her hands was steady and the line on her mouth was hard.

When she saw me gaping at her, she shook herself a little and gasped when she saw Booker.

"I already called Bax. He and Race are on the way." She threw the phone to Karsen and told her to call an ambulance for our bleeding bodyguard. She made her way over to me and gently grabbed my arms and forced me to lower the gun I was still clutching like a lifeline. She took the weapon from me and looked at it with a frown.

"You had the safety on."

I stared at her for a split second before bursting into a torrent of hysterical tears. I felt her wrap her arms around me and I let her hold me while I shook and shook.

There were two shot and bleeding men at my feet. I had seen my life flash before my eyes, and my sister was more worried about an injured thug than she was about her own safety.

I couldn't believe Dovie was acting like this kind of thing just happened every day. I couldn't take it.

"I thought he might have hurt you."

She dropped Drew's gun and tucked her own into her pants as she rubbed her hands up and down my arms.

"He jumped me in the parking lot of the university. Bax told me Race was on the warpath about him, so I knew immediately what was going on. He shoved a gun in my face and made me call you. I was hoping you could tell something was wrong, but I didn't want to be too obvious. The idiot wanted to take my car in case there was an outside camera on the condo. He pistol-whipped me when we pulled up out front, which knocked me out for a few minutes. But I've been in the Point long enough that I don't go anywhere without some kind of firearm. I got the gun out of the glove box and prayed I wasn't too late. Looks like I was for Booker, but I got to you in time. You need to learn how to use a gun, Brysen. Have Race teach you."

I couldn't believe how calm and collected she sounded. All I could do was cry and let her try and soothe me.

Somewhere in the distance sirens started to howl, and it was just in time because Booker let out a low moan.

Karsen's head snapped up and she screamed, "He's alive!" just as thundering feet and male voices barked, "What in the fuck!" and "Holy fucking shit!" as Race and Bax shoved each other to get into the room.

Bax bolted to Dovie, took one look at the gun in her pants and Drew's still form, and cocked an eyebrow at her.

"This is getting to be a habit." He put a finger under her chin and looked at her battered face with a scowl. "Ouch, Copper

Top." He snagged the gun from her waistband and made it disappear.

I fell into Race as he scooped me up into his arms. He cradled me to his chest and rubbed his cheek against mine.

"I tried to call you to warn you about him. I knew something was up when I couldn't get ahold of you, and Dovie wasn't answering the phone. Thank God you're okay."

I squeezed him as tightly as I could as the sirens got closer and closer.

"I don't think I'll ever be okay again."

All I could think about was the tragedy that could have been avoided all the way around. It was heartbreaking.

"What are we going to do about him?"

I didn't even want to use Drew's name. He seemed totally inhuman to me now so something as simple as a name felt wrong when referring to him. I cuddled into Race's embrace even harder and felt his hand rub over my hair.

"Bax called Titus already. He knows about the stalking and the attempts on your life so he's on the way and will take care of everything. Don't worry, Brysen. I know I've done a shitty-ass job so far, but I promise to take care of you."

I snorted a little into his neck. "You've done a better job taking care of me than anyone else ever has, Race. You can't be everywhere at once, and who would've predicted Drew would go after Dovie? He was crazy, and it's unfortunate he kind of had a reason to be."

I think he was going to say something back but just then a swarm of paramedics flooded into the room and a tall guy who looked like a slightly older, more polished version of Bax strode into the room like he was automatically in charge of everything that was going on. He had bright blue eyes that looked like they had seen everything and nothing would surprise him anymore. He mechanically searched out Bax and Dovie then landed on me and Race.

"Every single time I get a call from you in an emergency, Bax, I expect you to be the one with bullets in you by the time I show up."

I heard Bax snicker, saw Dovie roll her eyes, and I realized that to everyone else, this really was just another day in the Point. How on earth was I ever going to adjust to this kind of life? I closed my eyes and buried my face in Race's neck and let the floaty and drifting darkness that had been pulling at me take over. I just needed a minute in the darkness to wait until all of this passed and then I would deal later with the fact that this was how things worked in the Point.

Chapter 18

Race

WHEN BRYSEN WENT LIMP in my arms, my heart stopped and I almost dropped her. I bellowed for one of the paramedics that were hovering around Booker as they loaded him onto a stretcher. Titus had declared Drew DOA so there wasn't as much focus on him from the emergency service workers. I laid Brysen down on the floor and let out a relieved breath when her eyes popped back open as soon as she was flat.

I went to put her down so the EMTs could get to her, but she wouldn't let go of the stranglehold she had on my neck. Now that some of the fear and panic was beginning to recede, I could see the wicked-looking bruise blooming on her temple and another one on her cheek.

"My head hurts." She sounded like she had been eating glass for a month and I could see that her eyes were fuzzy and unfocused.

"I know. Let these guys look at you, Bry. You need to go back to the hospital." I told the young paramedic that was closest to me, "She just suffered a major concussion a couple of days ago."

He nodded and tried to get to my girl but she just wouldn't let me go. "She probably needs another CT scan."

Brysen whimpered and I felt it like a fist in the gut. This was just one more time I had let her down and hadn't been where she needed me to be. Stark had called earlier while Bax and I were busy moving all of our ill-gotten assets from Spanky's to the garage.

Nassir had shut down. He was always kind of cold and reptilian, but now that an unidentified threat was striking close to home, he had turned into a full-fledged, violent predator. He wanted revenge, he wanted blood vengeance in the form of bodies and blood, and there was nothing that was going to stand in the way of him getting it. He didn't seem at all worried that Bax and I were moving close to two million dollars out of his sight. Whoever thought crime didn't pay had obviously never tried to make a living on the wrong side of the law. Crime paid big—that's why there was so much of it in the modern world. I figured it was smart to get the business straight while we waited to hear back from Stark on the info I asked him to get. After I had gotten all I needed to know about Drew Donner, I had fully intended on heading over to the college.

Stark declared that there wasn't anyone named Drew Donner on the books. The guy didn't exist before he showed up at the university a year ago. It was like he had popped up out of thin air. I asked Stark to run a check on just the name Drew or Andrew that might have any link with Brysen and her family. It had only taken him a second to come back with Andrew Bohlen, as in the son of the guy Brysen's mom had killed while drinking and driving. The fucker had a pretty sound reason for going off the deep end, but that didn't mean he had a right to hurt my girl.

I dropped everything, told Bax that we had to go, and we started back to the condo. Things had amped up, tension had exploded thick and heavy when I couldn't get Brysen, Karsen, or Booker on the phone. I thought Bax was going to put the gas pedal through the floor when he called Dovie not once, not twice, not even three times but ten, and they all went to voice mail. Things were not right, none of it was right, and when we had reached the condo and encountered the unmistakable Road Runner that she drove parked haphazardly and with the doors left open, all I could think was that my sister and my girl were going to be lying in puddles of blood because I wasn't where I was supposed to be at.

The sight of Karsen crying over Booker while blood leaked steadily out of bullet holes decorating his back had made every single drop of blood in my body freeze. Bax had no qualms about running me over as he pushed past me through the broken doorway. I had to force myself to find Brysen, terrified of what I might see.

She was shaking and she looked like a ghost, but she was upright and only bleeding from the cuts on her face and head. She was staring at Dovie in shock, and when Bax pulled the gun out of his girlfriend's hands and stashed it, I could see why. My sister had obviously been beaten pretty soundly, but rather than look broken, she mostly appeared pissed off and annoyed. Like saving Brysen's life and getting smacked around by a guy twice her size was just a minor inconvenience in her busy day. When she looked up at Bax and gave him a wry grin, I realized how fully my little sister had integrated herself into this place and into this life. She was as much a part of the Point as Bax was.

As I scooped Brysen up into my arms and held her while she quaked and shook apart, I knew that eventually she was going to have to make a decision about how much of herself she was willing to give to this place as well. Just like my sister had.

"Don't let me go."

Her whisper was so soft I thought I might have dreamed it, so I bent down to kiss her and told her against her trembling mouth, "Never."

Titus was barking orders and trying to direct traffic as Booker and Brysen were loaded up and moved into ambulances. He told me that he was going to need to get statements from the girls and he took the gun from Bax as a bunch of people with jackets with CORONER printed on them joined the chaos. I blanked it all out and climbed into the back of the ambulance with Brysen and Karsen. The younger Carter wanted to ride with Booker, but Brysen gave me a hard look, so I gently told her no and guided her into the waiting vehicle with us. I didn't know if Booker was going to make it or not, but he wasn't my concern. He knew how things happened here, and yet he signed on for it anyway.

Brysen let out a little whimper when the ambulance started moving, so I made my way to her side and wrapped her frozen fingers in my hand. Karsen huddled herself into my side as we both gazed down at the injured and battered person we loved.

I sighed and put an arm around the younger girl's shoulders.

"I should have stayed home. Should have been there." Or at least told Brysen I had left the gun Booker gave me on the top of the fridge so she could have had some kind of protection against her tormentor.

Brysen opened her mouth to say something but it trailed off in an awful-sounding groan. The paramedic looked at me and then back at her.

"Stay still and try not to talk. You have a really nasty knot growing on your temple and I noticed you pulled some stitches in the back of your head. Try and relax until we get you in front of a doctor."

I squeezed her hand and looked down at Karsen when she quietly told me, "You can't live your life like that. Brysen's been trying to protect me from the fact that our family was falling apart for a year. I'm not blind and I'm not stupid. Sure, her coming home postponed the inevitable, but all the bad things were going to happen whether she was there or not. Same thing with you. If you had been there today maybe that guy wouldn't have shown up, maybe he would have waited until Brysen was alone at school and forced her into a car like he did Dovie. Maybe he would have tried to run her over again, or pushed her down an even bigger set of stairs. Bad things happen, and we just have to figure out how to deal with them when they do. He wanted to hurt her and he would have gone through you just like he did Booker to get to her. None of this is your fault, it's none of our faults. I refuse to feel accountable because my mom—who is a functioning adult—made the choice to drink and drive and ruined that boy's family. That's what happens when bad people are making the hard choices. It isn't right that Brysen had to pay for someone else's mistake."

I saw Brysen's eyes flicker to her sister and then tear back up. I let out a breath I didn't realize I was holding on to.

"Should you be this cynical at sixteen?" I asked it as a joke, but I kind of really meant it.

Karsen snorted into my side. "I'm not cynical. I'm realistic."

She could call it whatever she wanted. She was way too perceptive and way too aware of the ways of the world for a pretty young thing from the suburbs.

The ambulance rolled to a stop and they wheeled Brysen into the emergency room. I trailed after them and noticed Karsen frantically looking around the busy unit.

"They probably had to take him into surgery."

She blushed bright red and fiddled with her hair just like Brysen did.

"Don't you want to know if he's going to be all right? He got shot trying to keep us safe."

I didn't know Booker well, but I knew the cloth he was cut out of. It was the same unbendable steel that Bax was hewn from. Guys like Booker didn't take a bullet because they were chivalrous, or because they were altruistic and brave. Guys like him jumped in front of hot lead because they thought they were going to end up there anyway. They took that risk every time they left the house and hit the streets, it was a living, breathing part of who they were, but I wasn't positive I could explain that to Karsen in a way a sixteen-year-old with an obvious crush would understand. Or that she would believe me if I did find the right words. I could see her tender heart shining out of her dark eyes when she talked to me about the big brute.

"I'm not going to leave your sister but I'm sure she would understand if you took a minute to go check on Booker. Don't be gone too long, all right? Once we know Brysen is all right, I have to get in touch with Titus so you can give him your statement about what happened."

I was pretty sure it was a clear-cut case of self-defense, but I guess when there was a dead body I could see why Titus felt the need to handle the situation by the book. I had no worries that he would draw it out, not with Dovie right in the center of another shooting. There was no way Titus would risk pushing Bax back out onto a ledge by messing with my sister. Karsen nodded her agreement and took off toward the busy nurses' station.

I went into the little area where they had stashed Brysen and pushed aside the privacy curtain just as a nurse was jabbing a needle in her arm. She winced and jerked her gaze up to mine.

"I have to get my brain looked at again."

"That's probably a good thing." I walked up next to the bed and grabbed her chin in my hand. I brushed my thumb along her battered cheek. "He smack you around with the gun?"

Her blue eyes flashed and got stormy. "Yeah, and I couldn't do anything to stop him. My little sister had to get him off of me and my best friend had to save me. How pathetic is that? I just did nothing and let everyone else ride to my rescue."

She sounded disgusted and I let go of my hold on her face to brush the backs of my fingers across the nasty purple-and-black ring of bruises around her neck. I swore that if I looked close enough I could see the indentations of that asshole's fingers in her delicate skin.

"You stayed alive, and when I got into that room, it was pretty clear you put yourself between him and your sister. You did what you could and you made it out in one piece. That's all that matters."

She caught my wrist and pulled my hand up to her mouth so she could put a little kiss on the back of it and then curled it back around her cheek.

"Then that's all that gets to matter to you too as well. It's not your job to save me, Race, and it's not your job to save the Point. I know you nominated yourself for both those roles, but it isn't required."

I sighed. "I keep telling you that I'll take care of you, and yet

I seem to be doing the exact opposite. I'm never there when bad shit happens."

She rolled her eyes and it made her wince. "No, but you rushed me away from gunfire and took me home and cleaned me up so I wouldn't freak Karsen out, you bought me a new computer, you got my situation at school handled, you fixed the BMW, you got my mom the help I never would have been able to afford, you found me a place to stay, and you make me feel normal and happy, which no one else has managed to do in a very long time. I don't need a hero, Race. I just need you to want to be with me and to love me. I need someone that will be there for me when all the little things start to add up, because that's what real life looks like. There isn't always going to be a stalker or a major crisis for us to navigate, but there will always be hiccups and bumps because that's what being together looks like. We just have to want it bad enough to make it work."

I smiled at her and saw her eyes brighten when my dimple appeared in my cheek. "Bry, this is the Point, it thrives on things like major crises and lunatics hell-bent on vengeance. I get what you're telling me. The little things matter just as much as the major things. I will always choose to be with you, Brysen, but I can't just walk away from what I'm doing here, even if it means you can't stay." She gaped at me and I brushed her bangs off of her forehead. "I do love you and I need you to keep me from turning into something I hate, but I can't ask you to give yourself to the streets, to this life, if it's not what you want."

She narrowed her eyes at me and rubbed her lips against my palm. "Then don't ask."

I felt my insides seize up and something in the center of my chest twist so hard, my heart couldn't find a way to beat around it.

"All right, I won't." Even if it felt like it would kill me.

"Good, and then when I'm there—on the streets in the city, when I'm there every time you come home, you'll know that's the only place I want to be. It's where you are, Race, so it's where I have to be."

I wanted to collapse in relief, but all I could do was lean over and kiss her in a way that probably wasn't appropriate, considering her banged-up condition.

I would hold on to her with everything I had and I would make sure she stayed just the way she was. I would never take the little things for granted, and just as tightly as I planned on holding on to her, I was going to hold on to this dark and dangerous place that was my home. They were both mine, and I would give up anything and everything to keep them.

"It's not a place anyone really wants to call home, but if you give me some time, let me figure some things out, I can make you the queen of my broken kingdom. I can make this a place that isn't so terrible to be." It was a bold claim, one I would battle through hell and move the very earth the Point sat on to live up to. Bax was willing to watch the city burn and eat itself alive for Dovie. I wanted the opposite. I wanted to build it up, give it legs, make it a place that could stand tall and proud.

"There is good on those streets. I know that's what you're fighting for, even if you have to do it in a nontraditional way."

"How can you see that through all the messed-up stuff that has happened to you since getting involved with me? Why aren't you running the other way?" It would have been the smart thing for her to do the second after I kissed her. Her fate was sealed from that very instant.

"That bad stuff didn't come from you. Like Karsen said—

bad things happen and we just have to deal with them, and I can see it because I've been looking at you for a long time, Race—all of you. I know exactly who you have to be and who you want to be."

If I could rip my heart out of my chest and physically hand it to her for safekeeping, I would. For a long time I had avoided collecting *things,* avoided feeling attached to much of anything because of the fear that it would get taken away from me. I could tell by the look in Brysen's eyes and the slant of her mouth that nothing was going to take this girl away from me, and that made risking everything I had for her a no-brainer.

"I'm not going to tell you that I'll take care of you anymore. But I am going to make it my mission from here on out to see to it that you can take care of yourself. You already have the fight in you; we just need to give you a little oomph and some street smarts to go with it."

She lifted a blond eyebrow at me and the conversation was cut short as the doctor finally made an appearance. He poked and probed at her until she growled at him, and he told her he did indeed want another CT scan of her head. That knot on her temple seemed to be a concern, but as long as she was awake and looking at me, I wasn't going to freak out.

Before a couple nurses showed up to wheel her off to radiology, she flashed me a grin that looked an awful lot like the one Dovie had given to Bax and asked me, "Do I get a crown if I get to be your queen?"

That made me burst out laughing, which had the nurses giving me a scolding look.

"I'll give you whatever you want." And I would until both the parts of the man I was ran out of things to give.

We weren't really a good bet on making this work, but I was a guy who liked the long shot, and I always put my money on the long shot. I was hoping the fact that we were undeniably in love with one another put the odds on our side.

THEY WANTED TO KEEP Brysen in the hospital overnight. Her CT scan came back all clear, but that knot on the side of her head was some cause for concern, so they just wanted to keep her under observation. Since there was only room for one of us to stay with her in the room they moved her to, I let Karsen curl up in the chair for the night and wandered off to find out what happened to Booker.

Karsen had informed me that he had taken two bullets in the chest. One went right through his shoulder and the other had lodged somewhere in a rib near his lung. Apparently, since the shots had been fired through the door, the momentum had been slowed enough to prevent the bullets from doing irreparable damage. The hulking giant was going to make it just as soon as he came out of surgery to dig the bullet out of his rib cage. He was still in post-op when I located the wing of the hospital he was in, and since I wasn't family and he was still unconscious, no one would agree to let me in to see him. I was annoyed by that, but could understand it, and I think I shocked the hell out of the stone-faced nurse I was agreeing with when I told her I needed all his medical bills and expenses forwarded to me.

Ex-cons who offered themselves out to be hired muscle for other criminals weren't the type of guys that had medical insurance, and even if his actions had been self-serving, Booker had still taken a bullet for my girl when I wasn't there. There was no way I wasn't going to repay the guy in the only way I could. Plus

I liked him; he reminded me of Bax and I understood his motivations, the things that made him tick. He was the kind of guy I wanted to have on hand moving forward.

I spent the night in the waiting room. I wasn't ready to leave Brysen alone just yet, even though I knew the direct threat to her was gone. I must have drifted off while I was sitting there, because when my hand that was braced under my chin got nudged, my head fell to the side and I jerked away to find Titus looming over me with two cups of coffee. I blinked my eyes and yawned and took the proffered cup as he frowned down at me.

"Did you sleep sitting like that?"

I yawned again and shook my head a little bit to shake out the sleepy fog that was gathered between my ears.

"Yeah. They only allowed one of us in the room with her and I let her sister stay. What are you doing here so early?"

He took a sip out of his own Styrofoam cup and looked at me over the rim. "Had to get the girls' statements, and now that Booker is awake, I need to talk to him as well. Seems like a pretty cut-and-dried case of attempted kidnapping and attempted murder. I don't see any issues shutting it down pretty quick as a self-defense shooting."

I rolled my neck around on my shoulders until there was a pop loud enough that people on the other side of the hospital could hear it.

"Good. He was fixated on her. He blamed Brysen for her mom crashing into his parents while she was drinking and driving. His rage was totally misplaced and misguided. She didn't have anything do with the reason he was so infuriated."

Titus snorted and reached up to adjust his tie.

"Someone is always having to pay for the sins of their parents." I didn't know all of Titus's history, but I knew his and Bax's mom had a major drinking problem and had a history of going to bed with really dangerous men. Bax's dad was a murderous, cold-blooded mobster, and Titus's old man was doing life in prison for a killing spree that included three cops as his victims. My own father had left a legacy of deceit and dishonesty that I never wanted to be associated with, so I understood the point he was trying to make.

"It never seems to get any easier, does it?" He sounded gruff and I couldn't imagine how much harder it was for him, constantly trying to fight the good fight and hold the moral high ground in a place that was steadily sinking into the rot and mire. He had already had to compromise his morals in terms of pretending he didn't know exactly what Bax and I were up to, and I wasn't really sure how much more tension could be added to that tightrope he was walking before it snapped under his feet.

Just then, Karsen appeared at the edge of the room pushing a disgruntled-looking Brysen in a wheelchair. She looked disheveled and messy, but her eyes lit up from the inside when she saw me. I got to my feet and clapped a hand on Titus's beefy shoulder.

"No, it never gets easier, but there are some things and some people that make the fight worthwhile."

I made my way over to the girls and first kissed Karsen on the cheek then bent down to drop a kiss on top of Brysen's head.

"Are you ready to blow this place?"

She nodded and looked up at her sister. "We were just talking about that. Where exactly are we going to go? The condo is a mess, I don't know if the bank took the house from Dad yet, and there isn't enough room at the loft for all of us."

I rubbed a hand across the back of my neck and thought about it for a second.

"You guys can crash at Bax and Dovie's. They have a guest room big enough for both of you until I can get the condo back in order."

Brysen immediately started to shake her head at me. "No. Where are you going to go?"

"Back to the garage for a week or so. I just have to get the blood and stuff out of the condo."

Titus made a noise behind me and I gave him a look over my shoulder. He shrugged at me and gave me a smirk. "That sounds like it's becoming your full-time job—cleaning up the blood."

I definitely had to do it far more often than I wanted to admit to. Not that I was in any kind of rush to tell him he was right.

"Why don't you take Karsen to your brother's and I'll keep Brysen with me in the city until I get things straightened out in a more permanent way." I glanced at the girls. "Does that work for you?"

Brysen just stared at me for a minute and then looked at Karsen. "Bax and Dovie's place is closer to the high school, so I guess it's fine for now unless you want to see if Dad's still at the house." Her tone indicated that she didn't have much faith in her dad still hanging around after the curtain had been pulled back on his selfish actions.

Once again, Karsen proved that she was too wise and too aware for someone of her young age. "No, I'll go to Dovie's for a while. I think I've had enough of both Mom and Dad for right now."

Once that was settled, we all filed out of the hospital and

went in opposite directions once we hit the parking lot. I helped Brysen into the Stingray and fielded her rapid-fire questions about Booker's condition and about how Dovie was doing. She seemed far more concerned about everyone else's well-being than her own, but she was alert and totally on point and claimed that even though she had a nasty shiner and an enormous bruise on her temple, she felt fine. She wasn't shaky, didn't seem to be stewing or gloomy over the fact that she had been attacked or seen a man murdered right at her feet. In fact, she asked me to take her somewhere to get her hair fixed and just seemed ready to keep on rolling like nothing major had just happened to her.

I didn't buy it for a second. Dovie had done the same thing initially after being snatched and scarred by Novak. It only took a few days for the nightmares to set in and then the moment of silence when it became obvious that she was lost in her head and reliving her moments of terror over and over again. I was just going to have to brace myself for when the storm hit with my pretty blonde.

Only I took her to fix her hair, which turned out even edgier and more like a twenties flapper than it already was, took her to get something to eat, took her back to the loft so she could shower and take a nap, and she still seemed rock solid. The next day she wanted me to take her shopping for some essentials, she wanted to go by the restaurant to explain why she was missing so much work and make sure she still had a job, and she wanted to go by the university to square up with her teachers. That night she cuddled into my side and fell asleep like there was nothing in her world to keep her up. The day after that, she wanted me to take her to Dovie's so she could say thank you and see her sister. I dropped her off with a kiss, fully expecting her to be an emotional mess considering Dovie was still all banged up and had killed a man for her, but when I went back to pick her up after touching base with Nassir and Bax about business stuff, she was her typical cool and collected self and surprised the crap out of me by practically jumping me as soon as we got back to the loft.

I would never turn Brysen down when she wanted to have sex, but I was stunned, trying to treat her with care and delicacy considering her ordeal, but she was having none of it. She pushed, pulled, kissed, sucked, scratched, and writhed against me until it was too much to take and I ended up losing control and fucked her like I normally did. When it was over, I was left breathing heavy with her curled naked and satisfied against my chest. She had a sexy little half smile on her face and her eyes were heavy-lidded and sultry as she stroked a lazy hand up and down my chest. I wanted to question her about it, ask her how she was doing and make her tell me how she was really feeling, but before I could form the words, she was breathing evenly and had dozed off on me again, sleeping like a damn baby while I pondered what her actions, or rather nonactions, meant.

When she stirred an hour or so later, she rolled over onto me so that she was straddling my waist and looking down at me with her hands braced on my chest. Her blue eyes always reminded me of the prettiest summer day, and even with her bruised face she was still the most beautiful girl I had ever seen. The way she was handling herself, her resilience, made her even more amazing in my eyes and I kind of envied her. After Novak's goons had kicked my ass and left me broken, I had holed away in this fortress for months and months, afraid of what else I might lose in the game I was playing with the Point. She was far braver and stronger than I was.

"Tomorrow I want to start getting things moving on the condo. We should have someone pull all the carpet out of there and put in hardwood." One of her pale eyebrows arched sexily and she gave me a sardonic grin. "It's easier to get blood off of hardwood than it is to get it out of carpet."

I just stared at her until she grabbed my hands and put them purposefully over her bare breasts.

"Stop acting like I'm going to fall apart, Race. At first it was sweet, but now it's starting to annoy me."

I gave the full globes a squeeze and rubbed my thumbs over the velvet-soft tip of each. Her nipples puckered fast and hard at the sweeping touch and I told her, "I don't necessarily think you're going to fall apart, but you went through a pretty major trauma and that had to have affected you. I just want to be here for you if you need me."

She lowered her face to mine and kissed me hard then rubbed the end of her nose against mine.

"I don't feel bad. It sucks Dovie had to shoot someone, it sucks Booker got hurt, it sucks Karsen had to witness all of it, and it really sucks that my mom got drunk and set all of this in motion, but Drew was out of his mind and I don't have any guilt over the fact that he's gone and all of us are still here."

She sat up and reached behind to wrap a hand around my dick, which was way smarter than the rest of me and already jumping to do whatever she wanted it to do.

"Race, if we're going to do this—make this work—if I get to be the queen to your golden king, then you have to trust that I can handle this stuff. I barely survived a deranged stalker who spent a year pretending to be my friend. My mom is in rehab. My dad is a gambling addict and more than likely on the run from my boyfriend, my best friend is Annie Oakley and lives with a car thief, and my little sister has a full-blown crush on an ex-con that looks like he kicks babies for fun. I can handle all of that and I will handle whatever else comes our way. Okay?"

"Okay . . ." It came out strangled and more like a groan because she started moving her hand up and down and rubbing her thumb over the head that was already pearling up with excitement. If she could handle it, then I could handle it, and if this was the end result, she wouldn't hear me complain ever again.

She scooted over so that she was kneeling at my side and hovering over my very excited dick while she worked it over and gave me a look that had my heart racing and libido howling in anticipation.

"But the fact that you want to be there for me, that you are overly concerned about how I'm holding up, really turns me on and makes me want to do really naughty things to you."

That made me laugh, a laugh I almost choked on when her warm lips took the place of her hands and she sucked all my hard and throbbing flesh into her mouth. I started out wanting to get her dirty, to ruffle her feathers and thaw some of that chill that seemed to be around her. Now, as she worked me over, drove me crazy with every dip and flick of her tongue, I understood she was perfect, so damn perfect just the way she was, and she didn't need to get dirty or mussed up. She just needed me to bring it out in her. I made her bold. And all I could do was thank whoever it was that had been looking out for us all this time for that, because as she moved over me, played with me, tormented me to the edge of my control, she never looked away from me and

I knew this was the girl that was not just my balance, my compass, but she was also my match in every way. Not only would she take what I gave her, she would turn around and give it right back to me.

She added her hands to the mix, moved them between my legs, and wrapped one around the base of my cock as just the hint of her teeth scraped along the sensitive underside of my shaft and I stopped thinking about it all and just appreciated her and us as I let go and she caught me.

Chapter 19

Brysen

I T TOOK A FEW weeks to get the condo back in a condition that didn't resemble a crime scene. While we were in the process of changing the floors out, Race decided he wanted to get rid of all the furniture and replace everything so that there were no reminders of what the place used to be. He was still watching me with careful eyes and still handling me like I might break, but each time he took me to bed, and each day that passed where I didn't fall apart, he settled down more and more. I was determined to show him and myself that I could do this—live this life and not let it grind me down. It was what had to happen if I was going to be with Race and we both knew it. In all honesty, I really was okay. Drew had stalked me, very nearly destroyed my life from the inside out, and if I thought about it hard enough, I could still feel his fingers around my neck as he tried to take my life with his bare hands. He wasn't a good person. Even if he had a lot to be furious at my family for it didn't justify the way he went about things.

Before moving back into the condo, I asked Race to see if we could get into my parent's house so Karsen and I could get the rest of our personal stuff we had left behind. I also wanted to grab my mom's things, because even though she wasn't going to be out of treatment for a long time, she still needed to have something familiar and tangible to come back to. Race and Bax went by the house and came back and told me that there was a FOR SALE sign in the front yard and it looked like the place had been vacant for a while. There were those locks Realtors use to keep people out on all the doors, but they were no match for a professional car thief, and a few days later, my sister and I were going room to room trying to find as much of our old life as we could in a rush. I only wanted things that had good memories attached, but I didn't stop Karsen from grabbing several family photos and other things from the house that I personally would've left behind.

When I stuck my head in my dad's office, I wasn't at all surprised to find it cleaned out. He had left not only us, but all his other responsibilities high and dry. I didn't miss the way Race's eyes got dark and his jaw clenched when he looked over my shoulder into the empty room. I knew my dad owed him and Nassir a lot of money, but that anger was on my behalf, not because of the debt. I wasn't going to ask Race to let it go, to just let my dad disappear and forget about the debt. Not because I knew deep down he couldn't do that and still expect the rest of the people who owed him money to pay up, but because I was starting to really believe people needed to suffer the consequences of their actions. Maybe if my mom had gone to jail after the accident, she would have been forced to be medicated and wouldn't have ended up such a wreck. And maybe, just maybe, Drew would have felt like his father and brother's deaths hadn't been in vain and that justice was served and none of this nightmare would have had to happen. In the end, it landed me in Race's lap, and as long as that was the end result, I wouldn't complain about the rough ride it had been so far.

I had a minor attack of nerves the first time I had to enter the condo. I thought I was going to forever see Booker's bleeding body and Dovie standing in the doorway with a gun pointed at Drew, but with the shining new floors and all the modern, brightly colored furniture Race had let me and Karsen pick out, it was like going into an entirely new space, a space that felt more like home, even with its ugly past and bloody recent history, than any other place had in a long time.

Race and I settled into a pretty easy pattern really quickly. I still went to school, still went to work at the restaurant, and he still ran around town, still came home with blood on his hands and clothes, and there were nights he called and told me he was just staying at the loft because it was close to dawn and he was burned out. I could read between the lines and tell that meant he had to do something really bad, something he hadn't shaken off just yet and wasn't ready to bring it into this place that was his safe haven. I wasn't like Dovie. I didn't just let him go without knowing what he was doing, who he was going to be with, and I wanted him home even when he was raw and still covered in the city. If I was in, then I was all the way in, and he never tried to give me pat answers or brush me off. Even if it made me cringe and my tummy hurt to know what he was up to after dark, he always told me flat out and I tried my best not to stay up all night worrying about him until I heard him come up the stairs.

It took a few more weeks for me to realize that Karsen wasn't nearly as settled into the new routine and life as I was. I started to notice that she was really quiet, that she seemed kind of listless and uninterested in what was going on around her. I asked Race what he thought about it, considering he had taken Dovie under his wing and practically raised her when she was only sixteen. He suggested just talking to her instead of trying to guess because the teenage-girl mind was like a labyrinth, so I pulled my sister aside one afternoon and asked her what was going on.

At first she tried to tell me that she was just adjusting to a new place, that she missed Mom, but the more I pressed the more I could tell something else was going on with her. I let it go for a few days until I came home from work one night and noticed that she not only had a fat lip, but was also missing a huge chuck of hair. Her hair looked as jagged as mine had after leaving the hospital. Since there was no hiding the damage, she broke down and told me that things at school had only gotten worse since the house had gone into foreclosure. The rich kids were picking on her, the boys were harassing her, and when one of the girls had gotten in her face about Mom being in rehab, Karsen had lost it and smacked her in the face, which had led to a catfight in the hall. She told me she was probably going to be suspended and that she didn't want to go back to the Hill ever again. She felt strongly enough about it that she had already looked into alternative schooling, because she knew there was no way I was going to let her drop out, and there was no way either Race or I was going to be comfortable sending her into the war zone that was the public high school in the Point. She had taken it upon herself to find a charter school that was really close to where Dovie and Bax lived. It was a school that was just a step down from a private school, and even though she would have to wear a uniform, she was convinced it was the best option and wanted me to go with her to enroll. I was never going to get used to how mature she seemed, how she seemed to be taking to this new life and our new set of circumstances like a duck to water.

I told her I wanted to check the school out before I agreed, but I think she knew it was a done deal. I couldn't find anything wrong with it after I toured it and talked to the principal and teachers. Karsen seemed to think it would be a good fit, so I filled out all the paperwork and her transfer only took a few days to be approved.

I was just getting back from taking her to get her hair fixed and buying the khaki and black she was going to have to wear for her uniform when my phone rang. I was getting ready to kick my shoes off and toss my keys on the counter but paused because I didn't recognize the number. That wasn't unusual, considering my boyfriend had about five different phones on hand at any given time and that my best friend was always using a different prepaid cell.

"Hello?"

There was a lot of noise in the background, I heard someone yelling and someone else shouting, and then there was the sound of a door slamming shut and a deep voice asked, "Is this Brysen?"

I frowned. "Who's asking?"

"This is Detective King, Bax's brother."

"Oh, yeah, this is Brysen. What can I do for you?"

I figured he was just following up on everything that had happened with Drew, but my heart started to thunder when he sighed and told me very matter-of-factly, "I just called Race and Dovie down to the station. I have some news for both of them and I think it would be smart if you and Bax made your way in as well. I already called him because he would kick my ass if I didn't."

My hands curled around the keys I was still clutching until the metal dug sharply into my skin.

"What happened?"

"I can't tell you until I talk to Race and Dovie. Just trust me, you want to get here as soon as possible."

I hung up and bolted for the door with Karsen hollering after me, asking what was wrong. I made it to the police station in record time and didn't have to search too hard to find Bax prowling around in front of the main intake desk like a dangerous, dark predator. His midnight-colored eyes flared a little when they saw me and he stopped midpace to stalk over to me.

"Titus called you down here too?"

I nodded and craned my neck around to see if I could see my guy or Dovie anywhere. There were people all over the place. Some in uniform, some in business dress; most were in street clothes and there were far too many in handcuffs who looked like they had just been picked up off any corner in the Point for my comfort.

"Do you have any idea what is going on?"

Bax grunted and rubbed his hand roughly over his head. It was obvious that he was as agitated as I was, but his concern came across as barely leashed violence.

"No. But if I don't see Dovie in the next five minutes, I'm finding my brother's office and getting some goddamn answers."

Well, that was fine by me. He could storm the castle and I would just follow along behind him. I was going to tell him that I was all for that plan when his spine snapped straight and all of his impressive bulk went stone hard. His teeth snapped together with enough force that I heard it and the star tattooed on his face started to throb as red heat moved up his neck and into his face.

I turned to see what had him reacting so violently and could only frown in confusion as a beautiful young woman with endless amounts of jet-black hair and a body that would stop traffic faltered as she saw him and then made a move to walk past both of us.

Bax suddenly moved around me, practically knocking me over as he loomed unmoving in front of the woman, forcing her to a stop and look up at him. She had really amazing eyes that were almost navy blue in color and I could see the way she shook when Bax got right in her face and literally growled at her like a wild animal.

"Hey . . ." I tried to interject because we were in the lobby of a police station after all.

Bax ignored me and barked out in short, clipped tones, "What. In. The. Fuck."

"Hello, Shane." Her voice was surprisingly calm in the face of all that dark rage sweeping off of him. It was strange to hear anyone use Bax's real name besides Dovie, and it was obvious he didn't like it.

"You bitch. I should put your head through that wall after what you did to Dovie. She thought you were her friend." His eyes blazed like the very pits of hell at her and I could almost see the rage rolling off of him in thick, suffocating waves.

The woman blinked slowly and she went really pale but she refused to look away from him. She had some serious balls. Bax was scary and the way he was looking at her was like he already had a shallow grave dug somewhere in the city for her body.

"No one has friends in the Point, at least that's what I thought. I'm trying to make it right." Now her voice cracked a little and I noticed that her bottom lip started to quiver slightly. She was far more frightened than she was letting on. Whatever else Bax had been ready to lay into her about was cut off when Titus suddenly appeared and smacked Bax across the back of the head, startling him enough to move away from the young woman as he reached up to rub the sting.

"Leave her alone, asshole. She's trying to help." Titus sounded annoyed and frustrated in equal measure.

The woman looked between the two men then at me, and was smart enough to bolt while she had an opening. She left without saying anything to either brother.

"Who on earth was that?"

Bax retaliated by ramming his elbow hard into Titus's very flat belly, which had the older brother sucking in a breath and glaring as his sibling. Bax turned his dark eyes on me and bit out, "Reeve Black. She's the person who told Novak Dovie was on her own the night he had his guys grab her off the street. She got into bed with him over a blood debt and he called it in and used it to hurt Race and Dovie. She should be in jail for capital murder, but she cut a major deal with the feds and went into witness protection. She's supposed to be as far away from here as they could put her. I told this idiot"—he pointed at his glowering brother—"if I ever saw her again I wasn't going to be responsible for my actions."

"And I told you to stop saying shit like that to me. Remember, I'm a cop."

"Why are we here, *Detective*?"

Titus scowled at Bax and flicked a narrow-eyed look at me as well. He crooked his finger and motioned for us to move closer to him.

"I got a call from one of the federal marshals handling all the witnesses in the Novak case." I saw his Adam's apple bounce up and down as he met Bax's hard stare. "Race and Dovie's old man was murdered last night in the secure location WITSEC found for him. Hartman was willing to give the names of major arms dealers, drug suppliers south of the border, and all kinds of other information the RICO unit was chomping at the bit to get their hands on in this case. He had a full security detail, was located out in the middle of goddamn nowhere, and someone still managed to get to him."

I bit down on my lip and shared a worried look with Bax. "How are they handling the news?"

"Dovie is a sweetheart, so I think she's mostly worried about Race since he hasn't said a single word. The asshole tried to have Novak kill her, so I think she's just relieved that that's one threat she'll never have to worry about again. Race just kind of zoned out; I've never seen him like that before. That's not all, though." He rocked back on his heels and put a hand on the butt end of the pistol attached to his belt. "With Hartman being so insulated, we know the hit had to come from the inside. It had to be someone handling his move and relocation."

Bax swore. "A fed?"

Titus nodded. "Probably."

Bax dropped about every dirty word I had ever heard and clenched his hands into fists. "Not enough we have to worry about the bad guys, now we gotta worry about the good guys too?"

"That's about the shape of it."

"Why was Reeve here, Titus?" It was a sharp change in subject and obviously Bax wasn't happy that the stunning woman was anywhere near his city.

"Because she has information I'm going to need if I have any chance of flushing out our dirty fed."

That had Bax swearing again. "What kind of info?"

Titus shook his head and scrubbed his hands over his short hair. "That's the line where brother and cop cross, Shane. Leave her alone, I need her to do my job and I will be seriously pissed if you get in my way."

I was tired of the masculine posturing when I needed to take care of my man. This was a lot to process and I just wanted to get to Race. "Where is Race?"

"In my office with Dovie." Titus stopped Bax with a hand on the center of his chest as he went to maneuver around him. "Look, I need this girl to stop what is happening in the Point. She is absolutely necessary. I told Dovie all of this and she gets it, so you need to use your head and not go off half-cocked because I will shut you down so fast it'll make your head spin. You got me, Bax?"

Bax didn't say anything, just pushed forcibly around Titus and stomped his way across the precinct toward a glass door that had DETECTIVE KING stenciled on it in black letters. I went to follow him, my head spinning and stuffed with the excess of information it had just been handed out, when Titus reached out to stop me.

"Race is a good man. He's in a tough spot right now and making some really difficult choices, but he's always been a lot softer at his center than Bax. His dad was a piece of shit, a murderer and a goddamn oily son of a bitch, but when it hits him, when it really settles, he's gonna need a hand working through his old man being gone."

I tilted my chin up a little defiantly. "I'm not going anywhere."

"Good."

I went to go get my golden god when he suddenly came out of the office, Bax and Dovie following behind. Bax had Dovie folded into his side, and even though her eyes were dry, she was way paler than normal and she was clutching Bax like he was what was keeping her tied to the here and now. Race looked like he always looked. That beautiful dimple flashed at me, his blond hair glimmered like gold, and when he reached me he put both hands on my cheeks and gave me a sweet kiss. If I didn't know him as well as I did, I would have thought he really was okay, but there were fine lines of tension bracketing those evergreen eyes, and even with the dimple flashing, I could see the way his teeth were clenched together behind the smile. He grasped my hand in his and started to pull me toward the front door before I could even ask Dovie if she was okay or offer her up a hug.

Race didn't look directly at me, he just said softly, "I have some stuff to take care of. I'll meet you back at the house later, okay?"

I looked at his face, saw all that darkness and moodiness moving behind the green, and wrapped him in a tight hug. "As long as you promise to come home tonight."

His eyes shifted away from me and I could see he wanted to argue that point.

"Seriously, Race. Come home."

After a minute he nodded his agreement, dropped a hard, stinging kiss on my mouth, and walked away toward the Stingray. I watched him until he got in the car and raced out of the parking lot. I muttered a few choice words under my breath and was going to head in the opposite direction where the BMW was when I was stopped by Bax's heavy hand on my arm. Dovie gave me a lopsided grin and rubbed her cheek on Bax's side.

"He'll be all right. He just has to work through it." His tone was gruff. "I'm glad it was someone else, because I would have killed the guy if I ever got the chance."

I shuddered at that and watched as Dovie looked up at him under her rust-colored eyelashes. She huffed a little and shifted her gaze to me.

"Don't let him try and turn this into his fault, because he will."

I nodded and told her, "Call me if you need anything."

She nodded. "I'm fine. I have what I need." She curled farther into Bax as he guided her down the steps and off to that wicked chrome-and-black monster of a car he drove. I swore when he started it up the engine sounded like a million demons roaring for release from their prison underground.

I wasn't in the mood to go to class, but I had no excuse to skip when I had already missed so many, so I went, and found myself checking my phone every five minutes. Each time it came up blank it made my heart hurt. I didn't have to work that night, so I went back to the condo, helped Karsen with her homework, made a simple dinner, and texted Race no less than five times to see where he was and to find out how he was doing. All went unanswered. I was worried, but I was also starting to get pissed. I watched some stupid reality dating show with Karsen, gave myself a pedicure, and paced back and forth until midnight came and went. I stared at my phone and at the zero calls and zero messages and decided enough was enough. I had no doubt Race was at the garage, he was suffering alone, and I wasn't going to stand for it.

I knocked on Karsen's door and told her I was leaving for the night. She just gave me a knowing look and then went back to whatever she was doing on her phone. I think the poor thing had had enough of everyone else's drama to last her well into her own adulthood.

I got to the garage and punched in the code on those steel security gates, relieved to see the Stingray in the spot where the Mustang used to sit. I opened the side door and practically ran up the metal steps into the loft. When I entered the big, open space I almost tripped over Race, who was sitting in the center of the floor, a half-empty bottle of Scotch in his hand, and his green eyes hot and glassy. I sank down to my knees next to him and took the bottle out of his hand.

"You promised to come home."

His chest rose and fell and his tongue darted out to run along his lower lip. Even drunk and moody, he was the prettiest man I had ever seen. I reached out to cup his cheek in my palm and his eyes drifted shut and he turned to nuzzle into the touch.

"That 'being there' thing works both ways, handsome."

"I feel like shit because I feel like shit." His breath was high octane, but he wasn't slurring, making me wonder how long he had been hitting the bottle. Maybe it had been an all-day event and he wasn't really as inebriated as he seemed.

"What are you talking about?" I pulled the bottle out of his hand and ran my fingers through his hair. It always felt like gold silk.

"He wanted to kill Dovie. He was in Novak's pocket. He cheated on my mom all the time and he cut me off without a thought. He was manipulative and so fucking heartless. He deserved to die, I was going to let Bax kill him if it came to that . . . but now . . ." His head fell forward on his neck and I saw his shoulder hitch up and then drop. "I feel terrible."

I rubbed the back of his neck and tried to get some of the

tension out. "He was your dad. Of course you feel terrible. It doesn't matter how awful he was, he was still your father. You're allowed to be sad about it, but what you aren't allowed to do is try and take responsibility for it."

His head shot up and he looked at me as I scooted over him so that I was sitting on his lap. He put his hands on my waist and lifted both of his eyebrows up at me.

"What do you mean?"

"It isn't your fault your dad turned on Novak's guys to make a deal to save his own skin and it so isn't your fault that Novak has more poison to spread around even though he's long gone. Your dad ended up where he did because of his choices, not because of anything you did."

He grunted and climbed to his feet, still holding me. Considering he didn't stumble or stagger at all, I really doubted he was as drunk as I first thought.

"I know that, I just needed a minute and maybe you saying it out loud for it to sink in." He headed to the foldout bed and tossed me in the center of it with far less finesse than he had been showing me since Drew's attack. "And I was going to come home, I just had to sober up first and get my head back on straight. This is the kind of stuff that has no place there."

Since he was standing at the edge of the bed looming over me, I reached up under his long-sleeved T-shirt and started to work it up over his always impressive torso. I would never get tired of seeing his abs flex and contract when I trailed my fingertips all along the dips and ridges.

"You're wrong. I told you all along I want all of you; that includes this part of you. I get it, Race, you do what you have to do, not always what you want to do, but with me, that can't be the case. I *always* have to be what you want to do, not what you *have* to do. You bring it home with you and we'll battle through it together just like you told me."

Since I had the top half of him naked, I decided I needed to get the rest of him that way as well. I reached for the button on his jeans and worked the zipper down, happy to see that even if he was feeling conflicted and melancholy, his always active sex drive wasn't similarly affected. I worked my hands into the back of the fabric and gave his firm backside a squeeze while leering up at him.

He gave his head a rueful little toss and his dimple appeared and called to me. This time it was a real smile and that made my blood sing.

"You've been what I wanted to do since the beginning, Bry. How could you even question it?"

I wiggled a little closer so I could kiss him right over his heart and pushed his pants the rest of the way off of his hips. "Then come home so we can actually have sex in a bed and I can take care of you like you always take care of me . . . remember?"

He kicked his jeans off and stood before me in all his perfect gilded glory and lowered his head to give me the sweetest, most poignant kiss I had ever experienced. Any doubt I had lingering about how we were going to survive being together disappeared as our breath mingled together and I literally tasted his devotion on his smoky, Scotch-flavored tongue.

"All right, I'll bring it home and we can wrestle around it together."

I squeezed his biceps and squealed a little in surprise when he lifted me up and started to yank my pants down my legs. "I'm not scared." I was breathless and my heart rate had kicked into overdrive.

His eyes shifted from moss to midnight and black velvet and the dimple got even more defined. I wanted to kiss it.

"Good."

Impatient hands that were rough got the rest of my clothes off and finally, finally the Race I was used to going to bed with was back. His touch burned, his mouth was everywhere and left marks in its wake, and he used dirty words and pulled my hair. It was awesome and oh so welcome. He made me whimper, he made me gasp, and he made me scream his name over and over when he put his mouth between my legs and wouldn't let up until I was breaking all apart over his thrusting tongue and stroking fingers. I thought I was spent, thought he would crawl up over me and sink inside to ride us both to a soft and mutually satisfying end, but Race was keyed up, on fire, and had other plans in mind for me. I told him I wasn't scared and he was going to make me prove it.

His fingers dug into my hips as he turned me over on a soft gasp and pulled me to the edge of the bed. He situated me where he wanted me on my hands and knees while he stood behind me and bent to drop a kiss on the bowed curve of my spine. One of his hands twisted in the short cap of my hair at the back of my head and the other skipped across my hip and dipped back between my legs where I was still tender and sensitized from his earlier ministrations.

It made me whisper his name and then choke on it when he suddenly thrust inside of me without any kind of preamble. In this position I could feel every inch of him ripple and flex as he moved inside of me. He felt huge, felt powerful and unhinged, as he moved behind me. That, combined with the stroking, gliding motion of his fingers, and there was no way I was going to last very long.

"Race!"

He grunted, pulled my hair a little tighter, and I really tried not to get lost in the sound of skin smacking skin and the way his heady motion was making my arms shake. I felt pleasure start to uncoil at the base of my spine, heard him swear and say my name on repeat. Just as my arms gave out because my orgasm was just that strong—just that consuming—Race grunted and then groaned and let go of his caveman hold on my hair as he folded over my collapsed form. I felt his lips brush back and forth along the back of my neck and his hands run up and down my sides as they fluttered while I tried to find my breath.

"Thanks for coming after me."

I thought back to me begging him not to leave me when they were taking me to the hospital and told him the opposite of what he had told me, even though it meant the same thing. "Always."

He rolled off of me and pulled me onto his chest and rubbed his chin across the top of my head.

"I thought we weren't a good bet, but now I would go double or nothing on us any day."

I pinched his taut skin right above his ass and told him, "How about you don't bet on us at all because you know we're just going to be a sure thing?"

He chuckled, which made his chest rumble under my cheek.

"I love you, Brysen. You keep me *me*."

"I love you, Race, whoever you have to be and who you are."

There was no more probably about it, and there was no doubt we were going to survive it, even if the Point was going to continually test us along the way. I was ready to give that bitch a run for her money if she thought she was going to take my man from me.

Chapter 20

Race

T HIS CITY WAS WHAT the Point would be if it was clad in stripper shoes, whore-red lipstick, and then coated in glitter and sequins. The neon lights and ringing bells were annoying and alluring, and the aimless tourists, so willing to hand over their money, that flooded every sidewalk and spilled out of casino doorways made my skin crawl. To me gambling, risk taking, wagering good money, wasn't a joke, and this place had turned what I did in back alleys and on the streets into a family activity that people were taking entirely too lightly for my peace of mind. I couldn't wait to get back home, which surprised me. Who would've ever thought there would come a time in my life when I wanted to rush back to the Point?

I cut a look at Brysen, who was taking in the entire setting of the ghastly strip club we were standing outside of with a puckered mouth and a frown. I don't know if it was the location or what we were here to do that had such a sour look stamped on her pretty face. Hell, maybe it was both. When I told her where I was going and what the plan was, I had expected her to get upset and ask me not to leave. She had surprised me by asking to come along and telling me she wanted to be the one to lay it all out on the table for my latest target. At first I had refused, but when she explained it was the last step in closing all the doors to the past, I relented. I made her promise no less than a hundred times that she wouldn't leave me, wouldn't hate me if things went south and I had to get physical. She just looked at me like I was stupid and told me that she was always going to be on Team Race and that I needed to get over myself. So we packed Karsen off to Bax and Dovie's for a long weekend and hit the road.

Booker offered to keep an eye on the younger Carter, but she was still giving him puppy-dog eyes and fawning over him in a way that was going to be trouble as soon as she was old enough for him to forget that she was just a kid.

"You ready for this?"

Brysen's baby blues flickered to me, then to the door, and she nodded stiffly. "Let's just finish it."

I kissed her on the center of the forehead and then put my hand on her lower back as we walked inside. It was miles away from the District. This was like the Disneyland of strip clubs and it almost made me want to laugh. It was all for show and it was obvious the dancers were here for a quick buck and a cheap thrill, not for survival like the girls in the Point.

The man we were here to see wasn't at one of the tables by the stage or in one of the velour booths off to the side. Nope, he was sitting at the bar with his head bent over a rocks glass. He didn't look up when Brysen sat on the bar stool next him as I hovered off to the side over his shoulder, ready to step in if she needed me.

Brysen turned in the seat and shook her head when the bartender asked her if she wanted anything. Finally the man looked up at her and I saw shoulders tense and then fall in rapid succession. "Brysen."

"Dad."

Brysen's dad visibly started at the sound of her soft voice.

"I'm here to give you an out, Dad. Race brought me here to offer you one shot, one chance, and if you don't take it . . . well, then whatever happens next is all on you." She made a disgusted noise low in her throat and met my gaze as I watched her over the top of his head. "I'm fine, by the way, and so is Karsen. Mom will be getting out of her program soon, and I'll be encouraging her to file for divorce just in case you were wondering what's going on with your family."

He looked like the weight of her words hit him like a physical blow and he slumped even farther over his drink.

"I don't have the money. I just don't." He sounded dejected and pathetic. I saw Brysen roll her eyes.

Interesting he mentioned money since this fancy strip club wasn't cheap, but I wasn't going to point that out unless I had to.

"You're pathetic. You poisoned Mom, you lost everything we had. You used me, and when it came time to pay for your mistakes, instead of facing them like a man, you ran. What kind of moron thinks they can hide from a bookie? Jeez, Dad, don't you think everyone who can't pay up runs? Race wouldn't be very good at his job if he just let them go, now, would he?"

Brysen sighed heavily and told him in a tone that held no room for negotiation, "I want you to understand that this offer has nothing to do with me or Karsen. Frankly, I would like nothing more than to see you suffer just a fraction of the way you made the rest of us suffer the last year."

He just gazed at his drink almost like he couldn't hear her

speaking. I leaned my elbow on the bar on the other side of him and lifted an eyebrow at him when he glanced at me out of the corner of his eye. "Better listen to her or this conversation moves outside with me."

He gulped and looked back at his daughter.

Brysen understood that he owed well over three hundred thousand dollars, and by now, the interest on that had to be up over 75K. There was only one way to make it back and that was the same way that he had lost it—gambling.

"Nassir and Race are looking into setting up an offshore site. Online gaming that can't be traced back to us and that can't be shut down like a physical location. I'm talking high-stakes, no-holds-barred online gambling. The buy-in is gonna start high at a hundred K per seat. Race has a guy working on the security aspect of it, making it untraceable and making sure the funds are invisible, but he doesn't want him to waste time with the actual programming of the site. That's where you come in. Build it, run it, and the guys are willing to give you a cut after your debt is clear. Be mindful that it's your neck that'll be on the line if the feds hack into it, Dad. This is your one shot to get out from under your own stupidity."

Her dad turned his head and looked between us with consideration. "What kind of cut would I get?"

Maybe I would crush his ball sack just for fun. I gritted my back teeth and narrowed my eyes at him. I answered because Brysen just looked disappointed and disgusted. "Ninety–ten."

He made a choking sound in his throat. "Sixty–forty."

I pushed off the bar and inclined my head toward the door. "Let's go, Bry. This was a wasted trip."

She swung her long legs off the stool and rose to come over to my side. She shook her dad's hand off when he reached out for her. He scrambled to say, "Eighty–twenty is fair after the debt is paid."

We had a stare-down for a long minute until I begrudgingly agreed. "Fine."

I started for the door with Brysen in front of me and told him, "You will stay away from Brysen and Karsen, and you will grant your wife a divorce with zero headache or I will be back. You don't need to come back to the Point to set the site up, but if you choose to, remember those conditions, and keep in mind if you decide to run again how easy it was to find you."

That was the end of it as far as I was concerned. From here on out it would be Booker's job to make sure the man was doing what he was supposed to be doing, and if he slipped up in the slightest, I was going to give the go-ahead to make him bleed—a lot.

I wheeled out of the parking lot and headed back toward the hotel where we were crashing for the weekend. It wasn't a terrible drive, just a little over six hours, but I hadn't been sure which way things were going to go with her father, so we had made arrangements at one of the casinos that was off the Strip to stay for a couple days.

Brysen reached out and curled her hand over mine where it was resting on the gearshift.

"You didn't have to let him off so easily. Not for me."

She might think that way now, but after how sideways it turned me to hear about my own dad's death, deserved or not, at the hands of another, I knew there was no way I could do that to her.

"If he follows through, it's a win-win. If not, then he can deal with the repercussions and we'll just move forward like we always do. We'll focus on your mom, making sure she stays on her meds, gets into therapy, and tries to stay on the path to recovery so you and Karsen have a shot at having at least one redeemable parent."

I was doing the same thing with my own mother. We weren't reconciled by a long shot, but with my dad gone and all the money tied up by the government, she had nothing and no one and I couldn't justify keeping her frozen out. It was what my dad had done to me, and if I had learned anything the last few months, it was that I was going to be many different things, but being like my father was not one of them. I set her up in a condo in the same building the girls and I lived in, and told her that as long as she made an effort, tried to adjust to life in the Point, I would help her out. So far it was hit-or-miss. She was asking for money left and right, but she had also gone out and gotten a job in an office as a secretary to help support herself.

Seeing the conflict it created within me when I was forced to say no to my mom when she was being frivolous, Brysen took it upon herself to be the gatekeeper. She flatly informed my mom that any money she was asking for had to be approved by her first before I would hand it over. My girl had a way easier time shutting Lady Hartman down than I did, and the requests were coming fewer and farther between, and when they did come, it was for actual things she couldn't afford.

I got to the hotel and reluctantly handed over the keys to the Stingray. I didn't like to let my car out of my sight after the untimely demise of my Stang. I followed Brysen up to the room and grunted in surprise when she jumped me as soon as the door shut behind us. I put a hand under her ass and she climbed up into my arms and started to kiss me all over my face.

"You're so hot."

I laughed and walked with her to the bed. I tugged her hands out of my hair and kissed the center of each of her palms. I was happy that doing right by her made her so happy.

"You still want to be the queen of a kingdom that's a long shot?"

She giggled and narrowed her eyes at me when I shifted my weight so I could dig into my front pocket. I pulled out the cheap little ring I had found in the gift shop when I had been wandering around talking to Nassir about my plan this morning. It was a little gold crown, tacky and completely ridiculous, but she went silent when I slid it onto her ring finger and told her: "One day I'll buy you a real crown and you'll wear it forever."

She looked at the ring, and then at me, and I saw her eyes get glassy and shiny.

"That's your boldest move yet, handsome."

It didn't feel bold, it just felt right. She felt right—the perfect match to both sides of me—the bored, rich kid from the Hill and the bookie making the city run with blood and illegal money.

"I'm at my best when I'm being bold." I kissed her pulse where it was thundering under the delicate skin of her wrist, and she settled more fully onto my lap, which had things in my pants getting their own ideas about how we should spend the rest of the weekend.

"That is most definitely true. You know that as long as the kingdom is where you're at, whatever that looks like is where I want to be, Race. I don't think it's a long shot; I think it's pretty even odds with you, Bax, Titus, and even Nassir there to fight for it."

I wasn't sure about that. The outside threat was still an

unknown. Bax and I both had plenty to lose now, Titus would always let the lines and regulations of the law confine what he was willing to do, and Nassir was a survivor, so I wasn't sure that if things started to turn, how committed he was to fighting the good fight. Only time would tell who came out on top, but for now, Brysen was working my shirt up over my head and looking at that little plastic ring like I really had given her a piece of Midas's treasure. This was where I wanted to be, who I wanted to be, and the Point would just have to wait her turn to take any more of my soul.

The End
Titus's story coming soon . . .

ACKNOWLEDGMENTS

I'M GOING TO START out with my professional team, which makes me so much better than I really am. It takes a lot of work to get a good book out into the world and I'm very lucky that the peeps that have my back are all so wonderful and fun to work with. I adore all my ladies at HarperCollins. My editor, Amanda Bergeron, is a doll and we didn't even have to have our first fight over the ending of this book. I adore working with her and really she makes all these stories I tell so much better. She is damn good at her job and that makes working with her a treat . . . until I get my first rewrites back and then I want to murder all the things!

Jessie Edwards works endlessly to make sure these books end up in the right places and the right hands and I am full of confidence that if I ever created a major scandal, she would be all over it and making sure I came out looking better than when I went in. She's also the one who gets me out to Middle America to see you guys in the wild, so she totally gets a high five for that.

Alaina Waagner is who you all have to thank for the cool treats and contests that get thrown out there in the world. All those posters everyone loves so much and all the book give-aways are all her. She's a sweetheart and handles the marketing not only of my books but of me and all my crazy, and she does so with smoothness and calmness that I envy. I would choke me if I had to deal with me for reals!

I love all of the people at my publishing house who put in such hard work on my behalf to make these books a success, and I know I wouldn't be on a bookshelf or an internationally published author without them. I owe them more than just simple words of gratitude, but that's all I got ☺.

My agent, Stacey Donaghy, is wonderful and I couldn't do any of what I do without her. Sometimes I think we might share a brain, and I love that when I tell her I'm supersmart, she goes, "Of course you are. You never fooled me." I love that she thinks I'm talented and doesn't try and change the way I do things. I never thought I would be at this level of success in life just by being who I am and doing things I'm passionate about, but Stacey helped me make that possible. I adore that she tells me she is a fan first and my agent second. It really makes me feel like she supports me in standing by every single creative choice I have made to date.

Oh, I'm pretty sure there is no way I can ever put how much I love and value KP Simmon into words. I never thought I needed a publicist . . . WRONG. Holy KP makes Jay's life so much easier . . . She is a mentor . . . seriously, I want to be her when I grow up. She is a friend. She is a confidante. She is a book lover. She is a media genius and she is the most business-savvy woman I have ever met. She wasn't scared of me or any of my boys. I love that she dived in headfirst with the Point series and has just kept moving full steam ahead ever since: www.inkslingerpr.com is amazing and I am so honored to have them representing me.

My right-hand lady, Melissa Shank, is a Texas angel. I don't know how I would get anything done without her. She runs my fan page. She helps me out at events. She handles my giveaways. She plans my parties. She listens to me bitch about stupid stuff all the time. She's just wonderful and irreplaceable and there are not enough adjectives to describe how glad I am to have her on my team. If you want to hang out with me and Mel on a regular basis, feel free to join Crownover's Crowd. *https://www.facebook. com/groups/crownoverscrowd/* We try and keep it fun and informative, and by "we" I totally mean Mel ☺.

In my personal life I always have to shout out to my parents and my bestie. Really I am blessed to have such a strong and supportive unit as my inner circle. I love that I get to share my success and my journey with them, and I know even if it all goes away tomorrow they will still love me and support me in whatever it is I choose to do . . . but good Lord, please don't let it be gone tomorrow!

My friend Carolyn Pinard proofread Race's book for me before I sent it off to Amanda. She brings in all the commas and fixes all my run-on sentences. She's a lovely lady and I'm glad to have her not only as the grammar police but also as my friend. We totally got evacuated at Book Bash at two in the morning and didn't even want to kill each other when we had to hike up and down twelve flights of stairs. That's when you know you have a real pal . . . if you want to hit her up for some commas . . . carolynpinardconsults@gmail.com.

As always, I have to sneakily thank Mike Maley for watching my furry family while I'm on the road. He's such a good guy and I really couldn't come out and hang with all my readers as often as I do without him.

Okay, book people, there are just so many of you I have no idea how to throw my arms around all of you at once and squeeze.

The authors, the bloggers, the readers, the event planners . . . the book friends. There is just so much love for words, books, stories, and this passion we all share out there that it fills me up with happiness. Nothing is better to me than books, so how can I not love the people who love books as much as I do? And for those of you who don't love this book . . . or that book . . . or any of my books, I still love you just as much because at least you are reading and that's all that really matters to me. At least you gave it a shot, and if it didn't work for you, fair enough. On to the next one.

I don't ever name-drop blogs because I think all bloggers big and small deserve mad props for doing what they do . . . but there a few bloggers out there who really have a special place in my heart, and I am so honored to share not only a book relationship with them but an honest-to-God friendship that means the world to me. I hope you know who you are, and if you don't . . . well, then I'm doing something wrong on my end!!

As always, I enjoy hearing from my readers and always make it a Point (ha, see what I did there?) to try and respond to all correspondence I receive.

You can find me at any of these places on the Interwebs:

jaycrownover@gmail.com
https://www.facebook.com/jay.crownover
https://www.facebook.com/AuthorJayCrownover?ref=hl
@jaycrownover on Twitter
www.jaycrownover.com
http://jaycrownover.blogspot.com/
https://www.goodreads.com/Crownover
http://www.donaghyliterary.com/jay-crownover.html
http://www.avonromance.com/author/jay-crownover

WELCOME (BACK) TO THE POINT IN THE THIRD

INSTALLMENT OF THIS EXCITING SERIES

Better When He's Brave

Titus King has always seen his world in black and white. There is a firm right and wrong in his mind, which is why as a teenager he left behind the only family he'd ever known to make a better life for himself. Now a police detective in one of the worst cities in the country, there is no way he can deny his life has turned into a million different shades of gray.

The new criminal element in the Point has brought vengeance and destruction right to Titus's front door, and walking the straight and narrow seems far less important. The difference between right and wrong is nothing compared to keeping those he loves alive.

Reeve knows all about the new threat trying to destroy the Point. She knows how ruthless, how vicious, and how cruel this new danger can be . . . and instead of running away, she wants to help. Reeve has a lot to repent for and saving the city, plus the hot cop that she hasn't been able to forget, might just be the only way she can finally find some inner peace.

It will take two brave souls to fight for love when the entire city is poised on the brink of war . . . and they are standing right in the crossfire.

Summer 2015

LOVING THE MEN OF THE POINT?

KEEP READING TO SEE WHERE IT ALL STARTED

Better When He's Bad

Sexy, dark, and dangerous, Bax isn't just from the wrong side of the tracks, he is the wrong side of the tracks. A criminal, a thug, and a brawler, he's the master of bad choices, until one such choice landed him in prison for five years. Now Bax is out and looking for answers, and he doesn't care what he has to do or who he has to hurt to get them. But there's a new player in the game, and she's much too innocent, much too soft . . . and standing directly in his way.

Dovie Pryce knows all about living a hard life and the tough choices that come with it. She's always tried to be good, tried to help others, and tried not to let the darkness pull her down. But the streets are fighting back, things have gone from bad to worse, and the only person who can help her is the scariest, sexiest, most complicated ex-con the Point has ever produced.

Bax terrifies her, awakening feelings she never thought she'd have for a guy like him. But it doesn't take Dovie long to realize . . . some boys are just better when they're bad.

AVAILABLE NOW

CHAPTER 1

Bax

THERE ARE VERY FEW things that can kill the buzz of post-sex mellowness. Getting coldcocked in the side of the head by a pair of knuckles that felt like they were encased in steel ranks right at the top of the list. My ears rang from the blow as my head snapped around from the force. I would've reacted, but an uppercut had my chin flying back and my skull ringing solidly against the brick wall behind me. Now I was seeing stars and swallowing blood. Not like these guys cared about a fair fight, but eventually I was going to get my wits back, and there was going to be hell to pay. I spit out a mouthful of blood and took the cigarette the guy who had inflicted the blows offered me.

"Long time no see, Bax."

I lifted a hand and worked my jaw back and forth to see if it was broken. Nothing ruined a mellow, postorgasm mood like dealing with a bunch of clueless idiots and the thought of losing some teeth.

"How did you find me?" I blew out a stream of smoke and leaned back against the wall of the apartment building I had

just exited. The copper taste of blood was tangy on my tongue.
I made sure it landed on my assailant's wing tips when I spit out
another mouthful.

"Five years is a long time for a man to go without." He lifted
his eyebrows and flexed those hands I knew from experience
were capable of far worse than a little smackdown. "No pussy,
no booze, no blow, no fast cars, and no one who gives a shit who
you are. I know you, kid; I knew the first thing you would want
when you got out was tail. I gave Roxie a heads-up to call me
when you came knocking."

He was wrong. The first thing I went for was the fast car.
Granted, I used it to haul ass to a sure thing I knew wouldn't say
no, but still, pussy came after a quality ride.

"So you took it upon yourself to make sure my welcome
home sucked as much as possible?"

"If I know Roxie, and I do, you don't have anything to complain about." His merry band of thugs all chuckled and I just
rolled my eyes. There was a reason Roxie was a sure thing, and
not just a sure thing for me, even though I had been out of com-
mission for the last five years.

"I'm not here for me. Novak wants to see you."

Novak. The name made normal men shake in fear. It usually only came up when people were talking about murder,
mayhem, and general discord on the streets. He was ruthless. He was cold-blooded. He was untouchable and a legend
in the Point and beyond it. In the shadows and back alley-
ways he was king. Nobody crossed him. No one walked away
from him. No one dared defy him . . . no one except for me.
I wanted to see Novak as well, but I wanted to do it on my
terms.

I finished the cigarette and put it out under the sole of the heavy black boots I had on. I was a lot bigger now than when I had gotten locked up. I wondered if these guys had bothered to notice. Living a life full of booze, drugs, and easy girls, no matter how young and active you were, isn't a recipe for healthy living. Getting all that unceremoniously yanked away changes not only how a man lives mentally, but also what he becomes physically, be it by choice or not.

"I don't want to see Novak." At least not right now. My ears had finished ringing and all I had now was a splitting headache. These guys didn't have the element of surprise anymore, and if they wanted to push the issue, it was going to get bloody and ugly really fast. I didn't care even if I knew the goons were more than likely packing.

The guy who had delivered the blows just stared at me while I stared back. I wasn't some scared kid anymore who wanted to belong . . . who wanted these guys to be impressed. Sacrificing five years of your life for a bunch of bullshit has a way of leaving a mark on a guy. Novak should've known that.

"Race is missing."

Now, that had the desired effect. My eyes narrowed and my shoulders tensed. I pushed off the apartment building and ran rough hands over my shorn hair. Having hair in the joint was a bad plan, and even with the wicked scar that curved across the side of my scalp, I had no intention of growing the jet-black locks back. Low maintenance was necessary in my line of work—well, my former line of work—but that was a problem I didn't want to think about now, or ever.

"What do you mean he's missing? Like he went on a trip, or like Novak made him disappear?" It wouldn't be the first time

Novak took it upon himself to make a problem go away with a bullet between the eyes.

The guy shifted on his feet and my patience vanished. I lunged forward and grabbed him by the collar of his fancy button-up shirt. I wasn't eighteen and scrawny anymore, so I saw the fear flash in his eyes as I literally pulled him to the tips of his toes so we were now eye-to-eye. I heard the slide of a gun get pulled back, but I didn't take my gaze from his as he clawed at my wrists for purchase.

"Answer me, Benny. What do you mean Race is missing?"

Race Hartman was a good dude for the most part. Too good and too smart for this life. He should have never gotten caught up with Novak, should have never been out on the streets with me the night everything went to hell. Doing a nickel to keep a guy like Race out of the clutches of a piece of shit like Novak was a sacrifice I had no trouble making, but if the idiot hadn't heeded my warning and walked away like he was supposed to when they slapped the cuffs on me, I was going to level the entire city.

Benny tried to kick me in the shin with his sissy wing tip and I tossed him away from me. I shot a dirty look at thug number one, who was holding a gun on me, and flipped him off.

"Bax . . ." Benny sighed and moved to smooth out his shirt where I had wrinkled it up by manhandling him. "Race went to ground the second you got busted. No one heard anything from him; he wasn't around. None of the girls even saw him. Novak kept an eye out for him in case all that mess the two of you created came back to bite us in the ass, but nothing. Then last week, when the word was out you were getting out, he popped back up. He came around making threats, telling Novak it was bullshit you went down for what happened. I thought he had a death wish, but then . . . poof, he was just gone after stirring up the hornet's nest. Now, you tell me why a smart guy like Race would do something like that?"

I didn't know, but I didn't like it. I didn't have any friends in this world, anyone I trusted, aside from Race Hartman.

"Tell Novak to back off. I'll see what I can do to get a pulse on him, but if Novak had something to do with Race going AWOL, he will regret it."

"Pretty brave making threats when you haven't even been out of lockup for a full twenty-four hours."

I snorted and stepped around Benny like he wasn't worth my time, which he wasn't.

"Five years is a long time to go without; it's also a long time to work on a grudge and grow the fuck up. You don't know me, Benny. Novak doesn't know me, and I don't care what kind of muscle or firepower he wants to throw at me, if he had anything to do with Race going missing, I'll make him pay. Tell Roxie thanks for ratting me out."

"You get what you pay for." I wasn't sure if that was a dig at me or at her.

"I don't know about you and your ugly mug, but I've never had to pay for it in my life."

I saw him scowl and took advantage of his distraction to lunge forward and slam the hardest part of my forehead right into the bridge of his nose. I heard a satisfying *crunch,* and then his scream of pain as his cronies hurried forward to keep him from folding to his knees in the dirty alley. I gave my head a shake to clear my vision, because the move hadn't done a thing for my headache. I stepped around my now howling and blood-gushing adversary, tossing over my shoulder as I made my way to the mouth of the alley:

"You might not want to underestimate me, Benny. That was always your downfall."

My name is Shane Baxter, Bax to most people, and I'm a thief.

Asa

Starting over in Denver with a whole new circle of friends and family, Asa Cross struggles with being the man he knows everyone wants him to be and the man he knows he really is. A leopard doesn't change its spots and Asa has always been a predator. He doesn't want to hurt those who love and rely on him, especially one luscious arresting cop who suddenly seems to be interested in him for far more than his penchant for breaking the law. But letting go of old habits is hard, and it's easy to hit bottom when it's the place you know best.

Royal Hastings is quickly learning what the bottom looks like after a tragic situation at work threatens not only her career but her partner's life. As a woman who has only ever had a few real friends she's trying to muddle through her confusion and devastation all alone. Except she can't stop thinking about the sexy southern bartender she locked up. Crushing on Asa is the last thing she needs, but his allure is too strong to resist. His long criminal record can only hurt her already shaky career, and chasing after a guy who has no respect for the law or himself can only end in heartbreak.

A longtime criminal and a cop together just seems so wrong . . . but for Asa and Royal, being wrong together is the only right choice to make.

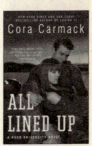

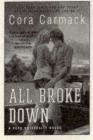

Available in eBook

Available in eBook

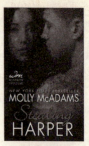

Available in eBook

Available in Paperback and eBook

Available in Paperback and eBook

Available in Paperback and eBook

Available in Paperback and eBook

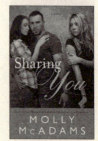

Available in Paperback and eBook

Available in Paperback and eBook

Available in eBook

Available in eBook

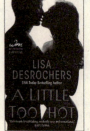

Available in eBook

Available in eBook

Available in Paperback and eBook

Available in Paperback and eBook

Available in Paperback and eBook

Available in Paperback and eBook

Available in Paperback and eBook

Available in Paperback and eBook

Available in Paperback and eBook

Available in Paperback and eBook

Available in Paperback and eBook

Available in Paperback and eBook

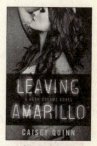

Available in Paperback and eBook